Diamond Dreams

Sandra Heath

A SIGNET BOOK

SIGNET
Published by New American Library, a division of
Penguin Group (USA) Inc., 375 Hudson Street,
New York, New York 10014, USA
Penguin Group (Canada), 10 Alcorn Avenue, Toronto,
Ontario M4V 3B2, Canada (a division of Pearson Penguin Canada Inc.)
Penguin Books Ltd., 80 Strand, London WC2R 0RL, England
Penguin Ireland, 25 St. Stephen's Green, Dublin 2,
Ireland (a division of Penguin Books Ltd.)
Penguin Group (Australia), 250 Camberwell Road, Camberwell, Victoria 3124,
Australia (a division of Pearson Australia Group Pty. Ltd.)
Penguin Books India Pvt. Ltd., 11 Community Centre, Panchsheel Park,
New Delhi - 110 017, India
Penguin Group (NZ), cnr Airborne and Rosedale Roads, Albany,
Auckland 1310, New Zealand (a division of Pearson New Zealand Ltd.)
Penguin Books (South Africa) (Pty.) Ltd., 24 Sturdee Avenue,
Rosebank, Johannesburg 2196, South Africa

Penguin Books Ltd., Registered Offices:
80 Strand, London WC2R 0RL, England

First published by Signet, an imprint of New American Library,
a division of Penguin Group (USA) Inc.

First Printing, March 2005
10 9 8 7 6 5 4 3 2 1

Copyright © Sandra Heath, 2005
All rights reserved

 REGISTERED TRADEMARK—MARCA REGISTRADA

Printed in the United States of America

Without limiting the rights under copyright reserved above, no part of this publication may be reproduced, stored in or introduced into a retrieval system, or transmitted, in any form, or by any means (electronic, mechanical, photocopying, recording, or otherwise), without the prior written permission of both the copyright owner and the above publisher of this book.

PUBLISHER'S NOTE
This is a work of fiction. Names, characters, places, and incidents either are the product of the author's imagination or are used fictitiously, and any resemblance to actual persons, living or dead, business establishments, events, or locales is entirely coincidental.

If you purchased this book without a cover you should be aware that this book is stolen property. It was reported as "unsold and destroyed" to the publisher and neither the author nor the publisher has received any payment for this "stripped book."

The scanning, uploading, and distribution of this book via the Internet or via any other means without the permission of the publisher is illegal and punishable by law. Please purchase only authorized electronic editions, and do not participate in or encourage electronic piracy of copyrighted materials. Your support of the author's rights is appreciated.

One

*I*f anyone had told Ellie Rutherford that having a dish of deviled kidneys spilled into the lap of her mourning gown would lead to a passionate kiss with a complete stranger, she'd have thought them utterly moonstruck. But that was exactly what happened at the Crown Inn, Hounslow, on a bright morning at the beginning of October 1804.

The year was proving a terrible one for Ellie and her father, Josiah, who were on their way to London from Rutherford Park, their pleasant home on the Isle of Wight. Not only had Ellie's mother passed away early that summer after a long illness, but now a shocking letter from the Unicorn Bank of Ludgate had advised Josiah that there were no funds left in his account. He was penniless.

Already stricken by the loss of his beloved wife, Josiah found this new catastrophe almost too much to bear. He'd believed his financial situation to be secure, only to learn it was the very opposite. It was therefore hardly surprising that as he picked at his breakfast in the crowded dining room of the Crown Inn, he looked very frail and older than his fifty-five years. He'd been a handsome man in his youth, tall and straight, with dark coloring and a roguish smile, but now his hair was white and his features marked with grief and despair.

He and Ellie were both clad in black, and barely aware of the Crown Inn's racket going on around them. Neither was hungry, in their present mood finding even toast and marmalade beyond them, let alone the gargantuan meals so many other travelers demanded. Hounslow was the first stage out of London and the last stage in, and its hostelries were busy night and day. Although the Crown prided itself particularly on its clean and comfortable beds, Josiah hadn't slept at all the night before. His anxiety about the future so oppressed him that he hardly knew how he was going to cope with that afternoon's important appointment at the Unicorn Bank.

Ellie—short for Eleanor—was twenty-six years old, unmarried, and content to remain that way. She had always been allowed the liberty of waiting until she found true love before venturing into wedlock, and now she was determined to remain single in order to take care of her father. Beneath the swathes of mourning she was slender and attractive, with a gently feminine face and a quiet disposition. Fate had not chosen to grant her beauty, but her eyes were the color of bluebells, and her light brown hair, at present completely concealed from the world by a black bonnet and veil, was long and curling, with honey glints that always shone in the sunlight.

She was at pains to bolster Josiah's spirits if she could. "I'm sure this business with the bank will prove to be a terrible mistake, Father," she said, but her voice expressed more hope than she felt.

"Ellie, my dear, I fear we must face it that my funds have all been wickedly embezzled."

"But the Unicorn is a *trusted* bank."

Josiah gave a mirthless laugh. "Caesar trusted Brutus."

"Even so—"

"Don't pin your hopes upon a happy outcome, Ellie, for I have been in this world long enough to know when I have been rooked. Someone at the bank has been very clever, and I am his victim. Mark my words, there will be nothing whatsoever I can do to extricate myself from this. Nothing at all."

Ellie fell silent. *There must be another Mr. Rutherford,* she thought. What else could explain it? Her father had never gone against the bank's advice, as was being suggested now, nor had he withdrawn vast sums, thus emptying his accounts. As for mortgaging Rutherford Park to the very hilt . . . It was totally monstrous, and went against everything in which he believed.

He looked sadly at her. "My dear, I do so hate to see you in black, so you must promise me something. When my time comes, you are not to wear mourning for more than a few weeks. Promise me."

"Father—"

"Promise me," he insisted.

"Very well, but God willing, that time is a long way off yet."

"God willing indeed," he murmured.

She lowered her eyes to the folded newspaper on the table. Her father had bought it from the boy in the courtyard, but had yet to even look at it. There were headlines concerning the self-crowned Emperor Napoleon's warlike intentions in Europe, and the British government's need for allies, but it was another column entirely that caught her eye:

> *It has been announced that prior to its inclusion next summer into the hilt of the new Sword of Concord that has been commissioned for the royal regalia, the famous red diamond of India will be put on display with the Crown Jewels in the Tower of London. This will be the first time it has been seen in public since it was presented to King George I in the year 1721.*

Just as it crossed Ellie's mind that she had never heard of diamonds being red, the deviled kidneys cascaded into her lap. An overworked maid, hailed from several directions at the same moment, had been trying to squeeze past Ellie's chair in order to take the fateful dish to a large and disagreeable Somerset squire at the next table. The squire had a rather snappy dog, which chose that very moment to get in the maid's way. She tottered, and screamed in dismay as the deviled kidneys splattered hotly over Ellie's mourning clothes. Ellie leapt up with a cry, the farmer roared that his breakfast had been ruined, and his disagreeable dog began to snap at the maid, who, fearing dismissal for such a calamity, dissolved into tears.

Ellie could have burst into tears as well, because the chenille-trimmed black silk gown was the only one she had that was suitable for the all-important visit to the bank. She tried to mop the mess away with her napkin, but the Crown

Inn's cook did not believe in skimping with hot spiced sauce.

The innkeeper, drawn by the commotion, appeared from nowhere and immediately ushered Ellie and the maid away from the dining room. Josiah followed as they were taken to the kitchens, where a number of maids flocked to do what they could to clean the gown. Josiah was placated by the genial innkeeper who led him into an adjoining parlor, ushered him into a particularly comfortable old armchair by the fire, and pressed upon him a glass of the hot ale flip that many travelers thought beneficial in the colder weather. The parlor was warm; the innkeeper lingered to talk; and the combination of his droning voice and the ale flip upon an empty stomach gradually sent Josiah into a deep doze.

Ellie, in the meantime, had been told that the inn maids were certain they would be able to return the gown to its former perfection. It would only take an hour, they vowed. She was loath to unpack another gown from the luggage, which had already been loaded onto the carriage for the remainder of the journey into London. Not only would another garment have to be pressed, but by the time that was done, the black gown would probably be ready anyway; so, when it was suggested that for the brief interlude she might wear one of the maid's dresses and remain in the kitchens, she accepted. The suggestion was made tentatively, because such a dress was hardly suitable for a lady, especially one in mourning, but it was, after all, a very temporary measure, and full propriety would soon be restored. So the spoiled black silk with its fashionable train was replaced by a faded blue linen that barely covered her ankles, even though it had been let down several times. Her black bonnet and veil were superseded by a starched mobcap that looked brittle enough to crumble into fragments if she did not take good care.

She could have joined her father in the parlor, but on learning that he was asleep, she decided not to disturb him. Instead, she sat on a bench, just outside the back door of the inn, to enjoy the October sunshine and look at the kitchen garden. It was a beautiful early-autumn morning, still almost as warm as summer, but with that subtle change of light that told of winter's approach. Two men were digging up the last of the potatoes and carrots; another was planting spring lettuce under glass; and two boys were up ladders, gathering rosy apples from a rather old tree by the gate into the adjacent inn yard. All was noise and clatter beyond the gate as stagecoaches came and went, but the garden was tranquil. A robin sang on an outhouse roof, and at the far end of the garden, secluded among tall straggling clumps of goldenrod and Michaelmas daisies, was a small pond where ducks chuntered contentedly.

Ellie adored ducks. There was something about them that always made her smile; so when a plump kitchen maid came out with a bowl of scraps for them, Ellie was on her feet in a moment. "Oh, please, may I feed them?"

"Why, yes, madam, of course," the maid answered, looking at her as if she had taken leave of her senses.

Ellie gladly accepted the battered enamel bowl of scraps and went to the pond. She scattered some of the scraps, then, laughing as the ducks' bills pattered against her skin, crouched with some crusts of bread in her palm. The October sunlight shimmered like diamonds through strands of cobweb among the Michaelmas daisies, and lay in bright shafts across the dew-soaked goldenrod. For these few moments she was carefree again, and the feeling was good—almost intoxicating, in fact.

She did not see the tall gentleman come to lean on the gate from the inn yard while his carriage team was changed; nor did she see how swiftly he straightened again on seeing her. She knew nothing of his startled expression, as if confronted by a ghost, or of how he hurriedly opened the gate to approach her. But she did hear his step at last, and rose to her feet in some embarrassment, forgetting that he could not possibly know she wasn't really a maid. She was horribly conscious that instead of being in deep mourning, she wore a really dreadful dress that displayed her ankles to the world, and her hair was topped by a flimsy mobcap that had been laundered and starched so many times it resembled paper.

She guessed the gentleman was about thirty, maybe a little older. He was dark-haired, muscular, and dressed so superbly that his tailor had to be one of the very best in Bond Street, for his dark blue tailcoat fitted him to perfection, and his cream cord breeches might almost have been sewn onto his form. An intricate neckcloth burgeoned at his throat, a wine red silk waistcoat was visible beneath his coat, and the simple frills of an exquisitely starched shirt peeped from his cuffs. All this she saw in a glance, but what transfixed her most was his face, which was handsome in a way that cut through her defenses like a knife. Perhaps it was his eyes, clear and gray, with a directness that was almost commanding; or maybe it was his lips, so firm and finely formed, so ready to smile . . . or to kiss. . . .

Shocked by the intensity of her reaction to this complete stranger, she emptied the last of the scraps onto the grass, then looked awkwardly at him. "Sir?"

"Who are you?" he asked, unable to tear his gaze from her.

"I . . ." She didn't know what to say, for the inquiry was rather blunt. Was this what maids were to expect from gentlemen? She felt the urge to put him in his place by making him aware he was speaking to a lady, but knew it would do her reputation no good to divulge her real identity. "My name is Ellie," she said at last, opting to continue being a maid.

A faint smile played upon his lips. "Just Ellie?"

"I see no need to tell you more, sir."

"Then I will simply say that my name is Athan."

"Sir." She bobbed a curtsy, thinking that Athan was a very unusual name, and that it suited him well.

He continued to gaze at her, and she became self-conscious. "I . . . I had better go back inside," she said, and began to walk past him, but he barred her way.

"Please don't go."

"Sir—"

"A few moments of your time is all I ask."

"Why?" Let him see what it felt like to be asked something in a blunt manner.

He was taken slightly by surprise, and gave a quick laugh. "Because I implore you?"

She had no idea which way to take him. Was he flirting with her? Or merely amusing himself by teasing an inn maid? "Is it your custom to go about bothering maidservants?" she asked then.

Her well-spoken voice brought a shadow of puzzlement to his gray eyes. "No, it isn't, and if that is what I appear to be doing, I apologize." He regarded her closely. "Are you *really* a maid?" he asked then.

"Yes, of course. Why else would I be dressed like this?" she answered.

"It's just that you do not sound like a maid, and now that I look at your hands, they seem rather smooth and ladylike to be accustomed to hard work."

The situation was running away with her, and she didn't know how to stop it. "Must a maid look or sound a certain way, sir? Must she be ill-educated in order to fit her position? Perhaps I am a great heiress fallen on hard times." *Oh, how true, how true!*

He hesitated. "Or an actress?" he ventured.

She was insulted, knowing that gentlemen were usually interested in actresses for the basest of reasons. "If you have set out to offend me, sir, I assure you that you've been successful."

He hastened to right the wrong. "Forgive me, it's just. . . ."

"Yes?"

"It's just that I could think of no other explanation for . . ." Again he didn't finish.

Whatever was on his mind now seemed too awkward to say, and Ellie would dearly have liked to know what it was, except that it was hardly likely to be flattering to her. She wanted to be thoroughly incensed with him, but was somehow unable to be so. There was something about him, something so gentle and appealing that she wanted to forgive him everything.

He smiled a little sheepishly. "Believe me, my intentions are not base."

She knew she should leave him and go back to the inn, but somewhere deep inside her there lurked a little of the coquette, for she made no move. Her pulse had quickened, and she was aware of a flush on her cheeks that had nothing to do with the heat of the sun. There was something in the air, a wild magic that would make her remember these moments for the rest of her life.

"It's just that I feel I know you," he said then.

"We have never met before, sir."

"I realize that," he said softly, so softly, almost like a sigh.

They gazed at each other, and she had to look away. What was happening? She ought to bring the encounter to an end, but simply could not bring herself to do it.

He reached out suddenly, putting his gloved fingers to her chin and making her look at him again. "Do you really and truly work here?"

"No," she admitted reluctantly.

"Ah, I thought not. You aren't a maid at all, are you?"

She hesitated. "No," she whispered.

"And you will not tell me who you really are?"

"I cannot."

He searched her eyes. "Do you know Lawrence, the royal artist?" he asked suddenly.

She drew back slightly. "I am acquainted with him, yes. He painted my portrait a few years ago."

Ellie had found Mr. Thomas Lawrence, fashionable genius or not, a trifle too amorous for comfort. For the princely sum of one hundred sixty guineas he'd agreed to paint her full-length portrait, and although it was more usual for the sitter to go to the thirty-two-year-old artist's London studio, in this case Lawrence made an exception because he wished to visit the Isle of Wight. He had come to Rutherford Park in 1801, after completing a portrait of Lady Mary Templeton and her small son. There had been whispers about his attachment to Lord Templeton's sister, and it was said that his lordship had been most relieved when the artist departed for the Isle of Wight. Ellie had been equally relieved when Lawrence's carriage drove away from Rutherford Park.

After completing her portrait, he'd returned to London to paint Mrs. Wolff, the beautiful wife of the Danish Consul, another lady with whom he was subsequently rumored to have had an affair. Gossip also connected him with the Princess of Wales, and the actress, Mrs. Siddons, as well as the latter's two daughters. When it came to the fair sex, the royal artist's name was always improperly prominent. Nothing about him would have surprised Ellie, who knew how he'd striven to add her name to his list of conquests. Nevertheless, the portrait he'd painted of her had been a wonderful likeness and exquisitely finished. Say what she would of him as a man, she could not fault his artistic brilliance.

While this was going through her head, the gentleman's

eyes had sharpened. "He painted your portrait? May I ask what sort of composition it was?"

"What sort of—?" Perceiving a possible unwelcome implication, she gave him a cool look. "What, exactly, do you mean, sir?"

"Please answer."

"It was just a portrait, sir, very formal, with a pedestal, ivy, and heavy dark red curtains. Nothing untoward, I assure you."

"And that was the only likeness Lawrence painted of you?"

"Yes." She was bewildered by his persistence. "What is this, sir?"

"Humor me, Ellie, and tell me if you can be categorically certain that he painted just one portrait of you, a formal pose, with your name to identify the canvas?"

"Absolutely."

"There is no chance whatsoever that it is marked simply as a portrait of a lady?"

"Certainly not. Mr. Lawrence would not have received a single guinea if he had been so thoughtless and remiss as to cast doubt upon my virtue." Well, now she understood his inquiry if she was an actress, for such persons were seldom named on portraits. "Sir, if you think you have seen another likeness of me, which I imagine is what prompts your interest in me now, then the sitter is someone else, and if she is identified merely as 'a lady,' then your suspicion about her being an actress is probably also correct. However, if I am right in my guess that this other portrait is less than proper, then I find it offensive that—"

He broke in again, clearly desperate to find answers to something of great importance to him. "Perhaps you have a sister? A cousin even?"

"No! And if I did, I assure you they would *not* be actresses!"

"Ah." On that sad note he was at last prepared to abandon the subject, but not to entirely abandon his interest in Ellie. "I may have mistaken you for another, and aroused your justified indignation in the process, but I would still like to know more of you."

"I, on the other hand, do not wish to divulge anything," she reminded him.

He smiled. "Will you at least tell me if there is someone else in your life?"

"There isn't anyone, sir, but even so—"

"Then agree to meet me again."

"No." But oh, she wanted to. She wanted to so much that her heart seemed to be spinning within her.

"Meet me again," he repeated.

"No." The single word was final. Her father needed her too much for her to even think of embarking upon . . . upon what? She had no idea what was really in this gentleman's mind, and only had his word that his intentions were not base.

His fingers slid to her cheek, and he caressed her with his thumb. "Then there should at least be a memory for us to savor, a reminder of what might have been, what *should* have been."

"Please let me go," she begged, but the words meant nothing, for she was his willing captive.

"First . . . a kiss," he whispered, and drew her toward him. She succumbed to the dream, stepping into a fantasy that all the rules forbade. Her body was alive, stirring with feelings never before encountered, and the touch of his lips was exquisite joy. An incredible yearning, warm and beguiling, spread through her, and the need for fulfillment swept irresistibly into her veins.

Their lips moved together, and their bodies were so close they might almost have been one entity. Suppressed emotions tumbled through her, finding expression in this shameless moment that was teaching her so very much about herself. She could feel the outline of his body, and how hers seemed to fit so perfectly to him. Oh, she wanted to surrender everything, to lie down on the grass and give in to the spellbinding desire that had ignited from the moment they looked at each other, but it was all wrong. *Wrong!*

With a gasp she pulled away from him. "No! Please!"

"Ellie—"

"I want you to forget this ever happened," she said breathlessly, her senses still so scattered that she found it difficult to collect herself.

"I will never forget," he answered.

She wanted to explain her situation and why she had apparently masqueraded as a maid, but she was suddenly craven. No matter how drawn she was to him, she shouldn't have permitted his advances; nor, if he were truly a gentleman, should he have so presumed upon her honor. It was best to end matters here and now, and to do it completely. "Please leave, sir."

"My name is Athan."

"Please leave . . . Athan."

He turned to go, but then caught her hand and raised the palm to his lips. "Goodbye, Ellie."

"Goodbye, Athan," she whispered.

But as she watched him walk away, she did not know how very much she would regret spurning him, because before the next dawn she would be all alone in the world.

Two

Ludgate Hill was filled with people, traffic, and even a phalanx of smartly uniformed soldiers as Josiah Rutherford handed Ellie from the carriage outside the Unicorn Bank. An idle breeze played with her veil and the weepers on his sleeves and top hat as she put a gentle hand on his arm. "I'm sure all will be well," she said in as reassuring a tone as she could manage.

"You are too trusting of your fellow man, my dear," her father observed. "I fear the embezzling rats will have left no smell."

If he was right, it was unicorns, not rats, she thought, glancing up at the sign above the bank's doors. Surely a bank as reputable as this could not be guilty of such a despicable crime?

Josiah patted her hand. "When we go inside, I wish you to adjourn to the corner by the windows. Few people care to sit there because they are so visible from the street. And when I leave afterward, I merely wish you to follow me out. There must be no scenes inside. The bad news will be imparted out here. Do you understand?"

"Yes, Father."

He drew himself up. "Right. Let's face the music, my dear."

The bank vestibule was opulent, with Ionic columns, dark oak walls, and a marble floor of quite exquisite design. Groups of gentlemen, many of them accompanied by ladies, stood around or lounged on the elegant chairs and sofas provided. There was a low murmur of voices, and drifts of tobacco smoke hung in the warm, motionless air. There were marks of mourning everywhere, not for the late Mrs.

Rutherford, of course, but because—as Ellie was to learn later—only the previous day one of the bank's senior partners, a Mr. Albert Forrester-Phipps, had died after falling from a cliff near his home outside Dover. All employees were in black, and so were many of the clients, so that few paid particular attention when Josiah and Ellie entered. Some male glances lingered on Ellie, trying to gauge if she was young or old, beautiful or ugly, but she was so enveloped in black that it was impossible to tell.

She moved to the corner her father had mentioned, and sure enough it was deserted. She sat down, clasped her black-gloved hands over her reticule in her lap, and watched her father approach a gleaming desk presided over by a haughty young man who sported a black satin neckcloth of dandyish proportions. On hearing Mr. Rutherford's name, the bank clerk—for in spite of his airs and graces, that was all he amounted to—rose from his chair and beckoned to Josiah to follow him.

As they disappeared through a door at the rear of the vestibule, Ellie lowered her eyes uneasily. It *had* to be an error, she told herself again. Her father simply hadn't done the things the bank claimed. She blinked back tears.

"I know I presume by asking this, but may I be of some assistance?"

Her thoughts were interrupted by a courteous male voice that she recognized with a jolt as belonging to Athan. She was covered with confusion, and relieved to be able to hide behind her veil. "I . . . I'm quite all right, thank you."

"Are you related to the late Mr. Forrester-Phipps?" he asked, the depth of her mourning suggesting this must be so. He wore the clothes he'd had on that morning, but with a black weeper tied around his upper sleeve.

"No, I'm not, sir. I wear black for my late mother."

"Forgive me, I just assumed. . . ." He hesitated then, realizing that her voice seemed familiar. "Have we met before?" he inquired.

"No, sir, we haven't met before." She gave in to the instinct to disguise her tone a little, while at the same time thinking that whoever he was, he felt it necessary to observe at least a little mourning for the late Mr. Forrester-Phipps.

He smiled. "Well, no matter, for I merely wished to be

sure all was well. Seeing you seated alone and in such mourning, and knowing how hot it is today, I feared you might be a little unwell."

"I . . . I'm perfectly well, thank you." She gazed at him, her heart pumping, her lips burning as if he had just kissed her again. Willfully wayward emotions tingled through her, beckoning, seductive, and alluring.

"Are you sure?"

"You are very kind, sir, but there really is no need for concern."

He inclined his head, but as he walked away, another gentleman of about his age hailed him. "I say, Athan, it *is* you, isn't it?"

Athan turned, and when he saw who'd spoken, Ellie thought his smile became a little fixed. The new gentleman was a Corinthian of the highest order, perfectly turned out in a slate gray coat and dove gray pantaloons that were so tight and well fitting that they might almost have been poured over his person. His dark blond hair was precisely curled, and everything about him was well groomed and stylish, even his smile, which seemed to Ellie to be a little too groomed to be genuine. He had pale eyes, blue, she thought, although she could not be sure. The fact that they were so pale gave him a cold look that would have verged on the reptilian had his expression not been so generally amiable and winning.

"Well, if it isn't my old school torment, Freddie Forrester-Phipps," Athan murmured, sketching a bow of sorts, "and suitably turned out for his own father's demise," he added dryly, for suitably turned out in that respect the newcomer most certainly was not. Even the bank's employees were dressed in black, yet the deceased's son went only so far as gray and a black silk rosette fixed to his lapel.

Ellie was able to hear what they said to each other because she was only a few feet away, and that part of the vestibule was relatively quiet.

"You know there was little love lost between the old pater and me," Freddie responded. *Or between you and me,* he might as well have added.

"You're making it plain enough now," Athan replied.

"Look, I don't give a damn about my father, nor did he about me. I couldn't give two figs whether he fell over that cliff, jumped over it, or was pushed, because all I'm interested in is my inheritance, and since your presence here has a bearing upon that important matter, I intend to stick to you like glue."

"Once a bounder, always a bounder, eh, Freddie?" Athan responded. "Well, you are wrong about my presence being of consequence, because I assure you it isn't."

Ellie wondered why Athan was at the bank, for it seemed increasingly likely he wasn't simply a customer.

Freddie smiled at Athan. "Tell me, how is your delectable auburn-haired ward?"

Athan was surprised. "I didn't know you and she were . . . ?"

"Acquainted? Oh, yes, we met last summer. The same social round, you know. While you remained in the wilds."

"I see. As it happens she is very well, but she is *not* my ward, as I think you know."

"Maybe not within the small clauses of the law, but she may as well be, for she resides beneath your roof and has your protection. Oh, her dear Mama is there too, of course, to make everything proper. Anyway, ward or not, please give her my felicitations when next you see her." Freddie smiled again, then took out a snuffbox and opened it with a flourish. "Would you care for a pinch?"

"No, thank you."

"As you wish." Freddie regarded Athan. "As I recall, the lady in question was on the Marriage Mart last year, but, of course, you were not free then. Now that you're a widower, do you have designs upon her?" he asked bluntly.

"That would be between her and me," Athan replied with equal bluntness.

Freddie smiled. "Well, there she is, living beneath your roof, a beauty with a great fortune. With Mama to make things proper, of course. I tell you, the young lady would have been in my marriage bed before now."

"It would seem the offensive schoolboy has become an offensive adult," Athan answered crushingly.

Not without a touch of jealousy, Ellie wondered who the unnamed but exceedingly fortunate young lady was, but then all such thought was banished from her mind as there came the sound of raised voices from the area beyond the vestibule. An awkward hush descended as the contretemps continued, and after a few moments Athan left Freddie to stride purposefully to the desk where the supercilious young man in the spotted neckcloth was once again in command. A few sharp words had the latter on his toes in a second to find out what was going on. The argument was momentarily louder as the door opened and closed, and Athan's left hand drummed on a pile of documents on the desk. She could see his profile now, flawless and strong, yet with an odd hint of vulnerability that even at such a moment as this seemed to reach out to her.

The unseen fracas continued, and Ellie, suddenly realizing that one voice belonged to her father, rose anxiously to her feet. At last Athan could stand it no more, and with Freddie once again at his heels, he strode to deal with the disturbance himself; a few seconds later there was abrupt silence. Everyone in the vestibule stirred uncomfortably, for such goings-on were hardly the thing.

Ellie moved forward hesitantly, worried about her father, who so seldom raised his voice that she knew this incident denoted grave tidings. Worst fears realized? *Oh, please, no. . . .*

The door opened again, and her father emerged, his figure somehow more frail, bowed, and careworn than ever, crushed by the baleful relentlessness of fate. His dismayed daughter did not need to see his face to know that there was no hope. She glanced through the door before it closed behind him, and saw Athan confronting a number of bank employees, none of whom seemed able to meet his gaze. Freddie stood nearby, his pale eyes sharp and darting, missing nothing.

Ellie followed her father outside, where he paused by the waiting carriage. "All is lost, Ellie, all is lost," he whispered, leaning on her arm as if without the prop he would sink to his knees. "Barely a penny remains. What have they done to me? What have they done? We have lost everything, even the house. Oh, dear God, dear God. . . ."

"We will engage a lawyer, Father, and he will soon have it properly sorted out," she declared firmly as she assisted him up into the vehicle, but she knew her voice sounded hollow.

"A lawyer will avail us of nothing, my dear, nothing at all," he whispered, sinking weakly back against the upholstered seat. "The bank is doing all it can to protect its own."

"Its own? What do you mean?"

"Simply that I am up against the memory of a dead man. It would seem that the hand of the late Albert Forrester-Phipps may—only may—be involved, and if that is indeed the case, no one in authority at the bank will put profits at risk by admitting to such chicanery. I am ruined, Ellie, and there is nothing I can do about it."

Ellie stared up at him from the pavement. "But you're innocent, Father, so the law *must* be on your side," she said, "and if Mr. Forrester-Phipps was indeed involved, then—"

"Then nothing, Ellie. Nothing at all. Ranks have been closed, and not to protect me, of that you may be sure."

The moment was too much for her, and before getting into the carriage she flung back her veil, just to feel the air move against her skin. She closed her eyes and lifted her face toward the sky. This horrible year wasn't happening, she told herself, it just wasn't happening. In a while she would awaken in her bedroom at home at Rutherford Park, it would be spring again, and she'd hear her mother's gentle laughter in the topiary garden outside.

But when she opened her eyes, the nightmare was still there. She was looking up at a classically proportioned window on the bank's second floor. Suddenly Athan stepped to the glass to look out, and she glimpsed Freddie Forrester-Phipps in the room behind him—Freddie, whose father might be the cause of Josiah Rutherford's continuing nightmare. At first Athan gazed at the buildings across the street and was clearly speaking angrily, presumably to Freddie, but then something drew his eyes down to her. Time seemed to stand still, and his lips moved to her name. "Ellie?" He turned quickly away, and she knew he was coming down to her.

She longed to wait for him, to rush into his arms where she knew it would be safe, but such a thing was totally out of the question. So for the second time that day she turned her back upon him, this time climbing hastily into the carriage, which drew away and had vanished into the incessant traffic of Ludgate by the time Athan emerged from the bank.

From the window he had only seen Ellie, so did not realize that she was with Josiah Rutherford. His face was pale as he gazed in the direction her carriage had gone. "Ellie?" he breathed, unable to quite believe that in spite of the evidence of his own eyes, he had really just seen the woman he'd kissed so passionately that morning in the garden of the Crown Inn. After a final glance up and down the street, he went back inside, deciding to put the matter behind him. Before coming to the bank he'd been to Thomas Lawrence's house in Greek Street, Soho, but the artist was away for the next couple of months, so interrogating him was out of the question.

"Perhaps it's for the best anyway," he murmured to himself, "for you're only chasing dreams, and besides, my lad, you've already committed yourself to another."

In the meantime he would be absent in St. Petersburg, where he would enjoy a long stay with his married sister, Louise, whom he had not seen in far too long. He had already applied for a special license. His lawyer would deal with everything during his absence and would have the license waiting when he returned. The marriage could then take place as soon as possible. Time alone would tell if he'd chosen the right bride, but at least he'd have done what honor and duty demanded, and with luck would be able to forget the delectable and mysterious Ellie.

Josiah was in no fit state to face the long journey home to the Isle of Wight, not even the first stage as far as Hounslow, so instead he and Ellie took rooms at a modest city hostelry. The Golden Lion was neither fashionable nor disreputable, but somewhere in between, and its prices were more suited to their severely reduced circumstances. From the third-floor window of her plainly furnished bedroom Ellie could look between gables opposite at the great dome of St. Paul's Cathedral.

Before retiring that night she almost went to her father's room. Almost, but not quite. On reaching his door she paused. All was quiet within, and thinking he'd managed to go to sleep, she returned to her own room. She lay awake for a long time, watching the moonlight move slowly across the bedroom floor. The sounds of London were just beyond the window, as was the first chill of autumn in the air.

Sleep came at last, and with it tortured dreams. It seemed her mother was trying to awaken her, but that her slumber was far too deep to be disturbed. Yet she was restless, tossing and turning, afraid of some unspeakable thing that would be there if she opened her eyes. Then came the pistol report. It shattered the quiet of the night, and wasn't a dream, for the entire inn was awakened. Doors opened, and sleepy voices could be heard. Ellie lay there in the darkness of her bed, gazing up at the ceiling. Somehow, even before the innkeeper tapped reluctantly at her door, she knew what had happened. Her father was dead. Her mother had tried to arouse her so that she would go to his room and prevent the terrible thing he was about to do, but sleep had remained supreme. Now it was too late.

The innkeeper was at the door. "Miss Rutherford? Are you awake?"

Slowly, as if still asleep, she slipped from the bed and pulled on her rose muslin wrap. Her light brown curls were in too much of a tangle to waste time by brushing them now, and she could not see her little slippers. She was cold and trembling, riven with guilt. If only she'd gone into her father's room, maybe she would have sensed his intentions and been able to prevent his suicide. If only. Maybe. But the deed was done now, and she had to face the world alone.

With a trembling hand she opened the door. Candlelight flickered in the passage, and she saw a number of other guests, as well as inn servants, all pale and shocked. The innkeeper's eyes were gentle and sympathetic. "I have some terrible news to impart, Miss Rutherford."

"My father?" she whispered.

"I fear so."

She closed her eyes and leaned weakly against the door jamb. From nowhere came the echo of Athan's voice. *"I know I presume by asking this, but may I be of some assistance?"*

Assistance? She longed for him to be with her now, but at the same time was filled with doubts about him. What exactly was his connection with the Unicorn Bank and the

Forrester-Phipps family? If it was the last thing she did, she would see that everyone concerned in her father's ruin was brought to justice, and if Athan was included in that number, then so be it.

Three

*F*ar away in St. Petersburg that same night, the Winter Palace was in darkness as Prince Paul Dalmatsky, an elegant, cultured, and manipulative courtier with a predatory liking for handsome young men, conducted his twenty-three-year-old nephew, Prince Valentin Andreyov, across the great throne room of the Romanov czars. Paul had just returned to Russia after a year's absence abroad. No one knew where he had been, not even Valentin, his only relative.

Valentin's preferences lay solely with the fair sex, so that the only thing uniting him with his uncle was the tie of blood. They were both determined at all costs to protect and advance their family, and it was in this connection that Paul was conducting his sole kinsman to the nearby Diamond Salon to view the imperial jewels and regalia. There were only servants to witness the men's progress through the palace, and the few words Paul and Valentin uttered were in French, the language of the court; indeed, so little did either of them know of their native tongue that they could barely speak it.

Paul was seventeen years older than Valentin, but still surprisingly boyish and slender-waisted. He wasn't afraid to show his sensuous, almost feline face to the world, but no one could see the identity of the man at his side. Valentin was careful to remain enveloped in a hooded cloak that completely concealed the splendid blue and gold uniform of a lifeguard officer in the Semeonovsky Regiment of the Imperial Guard. He had been banished from court and his estates confiscated, and if this madness were to reach the ears of the czar, whose close friend and favorite aide-de-camp he had once been, the punishment would be severe. To be in the Imperial Guard at all was a great honor, but to be so close to the czar was the greatest prize of all; yet he had forfeited the latter privileges, and was in very real danger of being dishonorably discharged from his proud regiment, all because he had been idiot enough to try to seduce the czar's beautiful Polish mistress, Maria Naryshkina. Valentin therefore glanced around continually, fearful that at any moment someone would apprehend them.

They had come by boat from Paul's splendid palace on Dalmatsky Island, one of forty-two such islands that formed the delta of the River Neva, upon which the Russian capital was built. Snow was falling outside, the first of an unexpectedly early winter, and a thin cloak of white already lay over St. Petersburg. Czar Alexander and the court had been delayed at Tsarskoe Selo, sixteen miles south of the capital, but would return the following day. Tonight, which also happened to be the feast of the Holy Guardian Angels, was therefore the last opportunity to show Valentin the diamond.

Paul's candelabrum cast little glow over the vast throne room. Columns of Russian marble stood in ranks; vases, jars, tables, and consoles, made of porphyry, jasper, and malachite, loomed ghostly in the shadows. High overhead was an exquisitely painted ceiling, with magnificent lusters. The edges of the floor were decked with climbing plants and great arrangements of hothouse flowers that made it seem as if summer still lingered. The effect was enhanced by air as warm as July, heated by stoves concealed among draperies and banners.

There were sentries from Valentin's regiment on duty outside the jewel salon, but at a word from Paul they moved away to a respectful distance. Once in the room, Paul placed the candlestick on an inlaid table. The swaying light caught upon countless gems in specially strengthened armoires that would surely require blowing up before they would surrender their priceless contents. Such was the twinkling radiance from thousands of facets that the room might have been filled with fireflies. The grand imperial crown of Catherine the Great, which was encrusted with nearly five thousand diamonds, was the greatest item by far, and close to it lay the imperial scepter and orb. Coronets, tiaras, diadems, necklaces, brooches, rings, belts, and livery collars were everywhere, together with an astounding array of precious stones accumulated through centuries of Romanov rule.

The jeweled lights were reflected in Paul's soft brown eyes as he looked at his nephew. "Today is the feast of the Holy Guardian Angels, my boy, and I am your guardian angel. Oh, yes, believe me, for I watch over your interests as best I can, and it was for you that I was absent from St. Petersburg for such a long time." He beckoned Valentin over to one cabinet in particular, and then pointed. "What do you see?"

"See?" Valentin followed the angle of his uncle's finger. "Well, a ruby the size of a walnut, I suppose." He had a cultivated air of boredom, which it was his habit to emphasize by occasionally studying his long, highly polished fingernails, but his civilized veneer did not run very deep. He had never been known for his patience, charm, or sweet nature, and he was a hothead with a streak of cruelty that made him feared by his serfs.

Paul let the insolence pass for the moment. "No, boy, you see the diamond that was presented to Peter the Great in the year 1721."

"Diamond? But it's red!"

"Red diamonds are the most rare of all, and therefore the most precious, and this one is actually one of a pair of perfectly matched stones. They were stolen from a Hindu idol in southern India, but the thief, a loyal subject of Czar Peter, was himself robbed by the British, and only managed to hold on to one to present to Czar Peter. The other is now in the Tower of London, and will soon be incorporated into a new sword for the British royal regalia."

Valentin could not have cared less about either diamond. There was a pretty dancer from the Imperial Ballet School waiting for him at his lodgings, and he'd much rather be enjoying her charms than inspecting the czar's jewels. Finding the room warm and claustrophobic, he took off his cloak and let it fall to the floor. He wore his thick dark hair in a queue at the back, and in two side-plaits, a dashing style that he carried off with considerable verve, and that went well with the swaggering walk that no amount of misfortune seemed to check.

His uniform was a brave sight in the costly light around him, from his tight white breeches and gleaming Hessian boots, to his gaudily gilded blue dolman jacket and the fur-trimmed pelisse fixed over his left shoulder. Under his right arm he carried his white-plumed black shako, festooned with silver ropes and tassels. Such was the abundance of gold braiding on his dolman and pelisse that he shone almost as much as the imperial jewels. But what glittered most was the miniature icon of his patron saint, St. Valentine, set with pearls and sapphires, and worn on a gold chain around his throat.

He would have flung himself into a nearby chair while his elder remained standing, had not Paul reached out and given one of his side-plaits a painful tug. "Mind your manners, you boor! Does your generation know *nothing* of how to go on?"

Valentin was equally incensed. "Lay hands upon me again, and I'll—"

"You'll what?" Paul breathed, suddenly producing a tiny jeweled dagger and pressing the blade to his nephew's cheek. "I don't think you'll be doing anything, will you, my boy? Mm? I heard the other day of an officer who was thrown out of the Guards for loosening the top button of his uniform at dinner after a ball. Even the lowest peasant, had he a button to loosen, would not have sinned so greatly. You, however, seem capable of every sin there is. Why? Because your brain is in your breeches. You have so earned the czar's displeasure, that if you aren't careful you'll be cashiered and banished forever to the furthest northern waste of Siberia! There you'll be able to cool your rampant manhood in ice for twelve months of the year for the rest of your worthless life!"

Valentin's brown eyes cooled. "I do not need reminding of my situation."

"But I think you do, you charmless puppy! By all the saints in heaven, I cannot believe that you sprang forth from my dear sister! If someone told me you were a changeling, I would believe it! Not only have you attempted to bed Maria Naryshkina, but you've continued to promote the French cause, even when it's become perfectly clear to all and sundry that Napoleon is Russia's enemy, and that it is to Britain that we must now turn for an ally."

"Napoleon is the greatest man alive!" Valentin cried passionately. "And with God's will the czar will realize this again soon."

"Perchance when the Corsican commandeers the imperial apartments here in the Winter Palace?" Paul suggested acidly, returning the dagger to its hiding place. "Oh, Alexander may once have tolerated your childish hero worship of a foreign tyrant. He may even have jested with you and called you Monsieur Valentin, but should you express such French views again now, believe me, you'd be speaking treason."

Valentin looked away angrily. In his opinion Napoleon was and would remain the greatest leader the world had ever known; as for the British, they were only to be despised for the unremarkable creatures they were. Feeling the continuance of his uncle's contemptuous gaze, he looked at him again. "Will you come to the point of all this? I have no business being in this place."

"Then pay attention now, and take good note of the red diamond."

"It's just a diamond that happens to be red!"

"Show me respect, boy!"

"Respect?" Valentin cried. "You've been absent for well over a year, during which time I've had to exist as best I can, and now you're back you expect me to be at your beck and call?"

"Yes, that is exactly what I expect, Valentin, and if you fail me in the slightest way, I'll wash my hands of you. Is that what you want?"

Valentin would have liked to strike his uncle, but instead shook his head meekly.

"Very well. Look again at the diamond, for that precious red stone—or rather its twin—can be your salvation. Are you prepared to give my proposition intelligent consideration?"

"As God is my witness," Valentin murmured, and crossed himself.

The older man looked at the diamond again. "You are my only living kinsman, Valentin, and before I die I wish to see you restored to what is rightfully yours. You alone can make certain that our proud family not only continues to a new generation, but does so in possession of all that belongs to it. In order to regain the czar's favor, you must do something that pleases him, something that captures his delight and makes him regard you as his beloved friend again." Paul paused for dramatic effect. "I happen to know that Alexander fervently believes the two diamonds belong together in Russia, and that the British should return what they stole." Then he gave a quiet laugh. "Alexander also desires a commemorative soup tureen made of the finest British porcelain."

"A *soup tureen*?" Valentin gaped at him, for what had tureens to do with diamonds?

"You know how fond the czar was of his grandmother, and how fond *she* was of British porcelain? I have told him of someone who makes the most exquisite soft-paste porcelain in the whole of Britain, possibly in all Europe, and now nothing will do but that the czar possesses an example of this magnificent ware. He would especially like it if such ware were placed in his imperial hands in July on the feast day of Saints Peter and Paul, our great city's patron saints, at a grand supper that is to be arranged at my palace."

A clock chimed in the passage outside, and Paul automatically inspected his jewel-studded fob watch to check the time. A frown immediately darkened his brow, and he shook the costly timepiece. "By the bones of Saint Joseph, I wish I knew what was wrong with this cursed watch," he muttered. "It has given me nothing but trouble ever since I went to that place, yet my watchmaker tells me there is nothing wrong!"

"Went to what place?" Valentin asked.

"Oh, it doesn't matter." Paul closed the watch and returned it to its place. Then he smiled coolly at his nephew. "Go to England, my boy, and solve your problems by bringing the soup tureen and the second diamond to Russia. Make Alexander's dream of uniting the jewels come true. That is the way to regain everything that is at present lost to you."

Valentin's jaw dropped. "How in the name of all holy icons am I supposed to bring the second diamond here? It's in the Tower of London, which is surely one of the most secure fortresses in the entire world! I may despise the British, but I think they know full well how to lock away precious jewels!"

"It should come as no surprise to you now to learn that my absence from here was spent in Britain. I believe not only that the other diamond can be easily removed from the Tower, but that it can also be smuggled here to St. Petersburg without anyone even knowing it has gone."

"How?"

"Why, in the very fabric of the soup tureen, of course."

Valentin stared, his imagination captured at last. "You *really* think it can be done?"

"Oh, yes, but it must be understood that my name is to be kept out of it."

"Why?" Suspicion crept in.

"Don't fear that I am preparing a trap for you, or that my motives are in any way unfriendly, for that is not the case."

"Then what *is* your motive?" Valentin demanded. "I refuse to believe that it is simply to do with family honor."

"My reason is between me and my Maker. All I will say is that in London I was able to engineer several encounters with a vain, overconfident young woman whose ambitions reach much farther than her undoubted charms. She was able to confirm the whereabouts and new identity of an Englishman I've been desperately seeking for the past four years."

Valentin shivered, even though the room was hot. "Who are these people? The girl and the Englishman?"

"They are to do with a matter of the heart . . . of *my* heart. Have you never heard the saying 'as jealous as a Dalmatian'? Now then, do you wish to continue with this?"

Valentin's tongue passed nervously over his lower lip; then he nodded.

Paul again put his hand into his coat, this time drawing out something wrapped in a soft cloth. Gently he folded the cloth back, and in the candlelight Valentin saw what appeared to be the second red diamond.

Seeing his nephew's startled expression, the older man gave a low laugh. "No, boy, seeing is not believing. This is merely glass, a carefully cut bauble that will fool the British for long enough." He wrapped the stone again and pressed it into Valentin's hand, then looked at the younger man's face in the twinkling light of the surrounding jewels. "Now we will return to the island and I will explain everything in minute detail. Come the dawn, it will be as if you conceived the plan yourself."

But as they retraced their steps through the palace, Paul's voice rang ominously through Valentin's head: *All I will say is that it is a matter of the heart. Have you never heard the saying "as jealous as a Dalmatian"?*

Common sense urged Valentin to draw back from the brink, because anything that involved his uncle's sexual tastes was bound to be dangerous in the extreme. But Valentin was always ambitious, seldom sensible, so the warning rang ever more faintly through his head. By the time he and his uncle were being rowed back to Dalmatsky Island through the heavily falling snow, the final faint echo had disappeared.

Four

Josiah Rutherford was laid to rest on a bright autumn morning a week and a day after his death, at the burial ground of St. George's, Hanover Square. For Ellie's sake, the innkeeper at the Golden Lion had conspired with the amenable doctor summoned at the time of the tragedy, and Josiah's death was registered as an accident caused by a faulty firearm. Thus he could be laid to rest alongside his beloved wife, who had chosen to be buried at the church where she and Josiah had been married all those years before.

The graveyard was nowhere near the fashionable Mayfair church, but lay on the Oxford road, directly opposite the northern boundary of Hyde Park. It had been summer, warm, green, and breathless, when Ellie's mother died; now the air was fresh and cool, and the plane tree overhanging the Rutherford graves was bright with autumn foliage. High overhead, seagulls soared white against the heavens, and a light breeze sent wisps of smoke threading between gravestones and mausoleums as a gardener burned leaves he'd raked.

The clergyman and gravediggers had departed, leaving Ellie alone, clutching the posy of pink, purple, and red asters that she had purchased from the flower woman at the entrance to the burial ground. There were always asters at Rutherford Park at this time of the year, so it seemed the perfect flower to leave. She was conscious of squabbling sparrows on the roof of a nearby mausoleum, and the scraping of another gardener's wooden rake as he collected more leaves for the fire. Beyond the wrought iron perimeter fence the capital went about its business, unconcerned by her private sorrow, uninterested in what was to become of her now.

Behind the veil she would now be obliged to wear for another six months, her eyes were red from weeping. She now had nothing, and no one. The lawyer she'd engaged to deal with the bank had presented her with a bill after concluding—rather too swiftly for her liking—that the books were entirely in order. Whatever had happened to the Rutherford fortune had been her father's doing, not that of the Unicorn Bank. Ellie could not believe this, and strongly suspected her lawyer of taking payment from both her *and* someone at the bank, but for the moment there was nothing she could do to fight the situation.

Her father had left a scribbled note telling her that there would be sufficient funds from the selling of Rutherford Park to support her, but it soon transpired that his hope in this respect was in vain. The same lawyer informed her there would be no residue whatsoever, and advised that severe retrenchment was her only option. Retrenchment? She had already been forced into that by the iniquitous bank, and could retrench no further. Rutherford Park was about to be seized because of the mortgage of which the Rutherford family had known nothing, and by further ill luck, all Ellie's mother's jewelry had been kept at the Unicorn, which had promptly seized it. What was left with which to retrench? The nightmare seemed never ending, and Ellie had no idea what to do next.

How could her father have left her alone like this? No matter how desperate the situation, they would have been able to face it together. As it was . . . she had no one. Her only remaining relative was an estranged maternal uncle she hadn't seen in fourteen years, and whose whereabouts were completely unknown. And even if she knew, there was no guarantee he would be prepared to give her a roof over her head.

What alternatives were there? She closed her eyes. Seeking employment was essential. But in what capacity? She wasn't fluent in languages, music, or art, which rather precluded any thought of becoming a governess. Her skill with needle and thread was adequate, and she wasn't even good-looking enough—or forward enough—to consider the world of theater, even supposing it would consider her. In fact, she was useless for everything. As far as she could see, there was only one respectable course open, and that was to seek a position as companion.

Tears wended down her cheeks, and she cursed a society that left gentlewomen so ill-equipped to cope with hardship. When this odious year had commenced she had been so happy, residing in luxury at Rutherford Park, lacking for nothing, and adored by her doting parents. Then her mother had fallen ill and died three agonizing months later. Next had been the Unicorn's shocking letter and her father's suicide. Now it was up to her how the future unfolded.

She bent to place the asters on the freshly dug earth, and the petals fluttered prettily in the breeze. Determined not to start crying again, she began to walk back toward the entrance, but then halted as one of the gardeners called after her.

"Madam? A word if you please . . . ?"

She turned. The man, elderly, bearded, and dressed in shabby brown, had snatched off his floppy felt hat as he walked quickly after her. "Begging your pardon, madam, but I've just found something among the leaves that I seem to recall was always on the lady's grave next to the new one of this morning."

"My mother's grave? Elizabeth Mary Rutherford?"

He nodded. "That's the one, madam, and if she was your mother, then you have my condolences."

"Thank you."

"This is what I found. It just appeared on the grave one day about a month after the lady was laid to rest." The gardener held out a little ceramic disk, exquisitely painted with her mother's first names in gold and a wreath of flowers of such delicate colors that they seemed almost ghostly. Ellie did not need to be told who had made it, for the only person capable of such beautiful work was her mother's estranged brother, John Arbuthnot Billersley. "Did you see anyone leave it?" she asked

The gardener shook his head. "No, madam, and I'd forgotten all about it until it turned up among the leaves a moment or so ago. Then I remembered which grave it had been on, and so called you quickly before you left. I thought that as you were the only mourner today, you might wish to either keep the disk, or replace it on the grave."

"I'll put it back on the grave," Ellie said, then searched in her reticule for a coin to give him for his trouble, even though she could ill afford such a gesture.

"Thank you kindly, madam," he replied, and went back to his work.

Ellie returned to the grave and laid the disk against her mother's headstone. Then she looked down at it. How had Uncle John known about his sister's demise? He hadn't been in touch with the family in at least fourteen years, and they certainly had not known how to contact him. Yet somehow he had found out, not only about her death, but exactly where she had been buried. It was a mystery. Except . . .

From nowhere she suddenly remembered Toby Richardson, her uncle's old friend from Oxford University. As young men they had stayed at Rutherford Park one summer, and as far as she knew they had remained friends ever after. Maybe Toby would know where her uncle was now? As she recalled, Toby had intended to become a barrister, so maybe her good-for-nothing lawyer would at least be of assistance in tracing him.

With new resolve she again began to walk toward the entrance of the burial ground, but then she halted once more because another funeral procession was just arriving. And what a funeral. There was a great line of carriages, and countless mourners. Someone important was about to be laid to rest.

Rather than push her way through, Ellie decided to wait discreetly at the side of the path until the cortege had passed, but as she did so she recognized Freddie Forrester-Phipps among the family mourners. This time he was in full black. This was the funeral of Freddie's father, lately senior partner of the Unicorn Bank.

Ellie's feelings were very mixed as the coffin was carried past. How grand a farewell for Albert Forrester-Phipps; how small and private a parting for Josiah Rutherford. It was as if fate wished to punish her still more by rubbing salt in the wounds of grief. She observed the great phalanx of mourners from behind the anonymity of her veil, and to

DIAMOND DREAMS

her shock suddenly found herself looking at Athan. He was among a group of gentlemen immediately behind the family, a position so prominent that once again she wondered exactly what connection he had with the Unicorn Bank.

The breeze played with her veil, and for a moment her face was revealed. As luck would have it, Athan happened to glance toward her at that very moment. His lips formed her name. "Ellie?" His steps faltered, and then he hastily withdrew from the procession, standing on the other side of the path until the last mourner had passed. Her heart had almost stopped within her, and she thought of pushing out through the gate to the hackney coach, but then thought again. What was to be gained by such a flight? Besides, now that she knew he very definitely had something to do with the Unicorn Bank, perhaps there were things she ought to say to him. So she remained where she was, steeling herself inside for the coming encounter.

Removing his top hat fully, he came toward her. "We meet again, Ellie," he said, sketching a bow and then trying to see her face, which was once again hidden by her veil.

"It would seem so, sir." His closeness reached out to her like a magnet, and she felt her heartbeats quicken. She had to watch how the breeze ruffled its invisible fingers through his dark hair, and how his lashes cast shade upon his eyes in the autumn sunlight. The attraction she felt was almost unbearable, making her want to fling caution to the winds and slide her arms around his waist and kiss his lips. Oh, to be held by him, to be pressed close, cherished, needed, desired. . . . Wild emotions swung so bewilderingly through that she could barely assemble rational thought, let alone confront him with candid questions about the bank.

"Why so formal, Ellie? I believe that at our first meeting you called me Athan."

"Our first meeting is best forgotten, sir."

"I don't wish to forget it."

"Then perhaps your redheaded ward-who-is-not-a-ward would prefer you to forget it," she replied, taking a stab in the dark about his relationship with the lady of whom he and Freddie Forrester-Phipps had spoken.

He regarded her. "I had no idea you could overhear so much at the bank."

"You and Mr. Forrester-Phipps were not exactly whispering, sir." She turned back her veil and revealed her face to him again.

"That is true." He took in every detail of her face, the contours of her cheeks and lips, the sorrow in her lovely blue eyes, and the shadows that told of nights weeping into her pillow. She was a living dream, a mirror image that had haunted him from the moment he looked down from the window of the bank and saw her there as she was now, her veil raised, her sweet features revealed for all to see . . . for *him* to see. . . . He pulled himself together. "Perhaps it is time we introduced ourselves properly. I'm—"

"No! Don't tell me, for I do not wish to know." The perverse reaction was instant and undeniable. Learning his name would somehow confirm the attraction she felt toward him, an attraction to which she was sure she had no right.

"Then at least let me know who you are," he said, not understanding her at all, but wishing he did.

She hesitated. "My name is Rutherford," she said then, "and I am the daughter of the late Mr. Josiah Rutherford."

He didn't respond, but it was clear he was shaken.

"I see the name is not lost upon you, sir."

"I . . . know that his circumstances were very unfortunate," he said carefully.

"My father's circumstances were more than just unfortunate, sir!" Her anger surged. "Although, no doubt that is how the Unicorn Bank prefers to describe what happened."

"Do I detect a note of accusation?"

"Yes, sir, you do. The Unicorn Bank should be denounced throughout the land."

"May I ask why?"

There seemed no cunning in his voice, no hint of an attempt to fob her off, just a genuine puzzlement. She drew back slightly, beginning to hope that he didn't deserve castigation after all. "What is your connection with the bank, Athan?" she asked.

"I am a partner."

Her heart hardened again. "Indeed? Then you know exactly why I feel as I do."

"No, Ellie, I do not. If there has been some regrettable misunderstanding . . ."

"Is that what you'd call it? Oh, well, I suppose the deliberate ruination of an honest man is regrettable, but it was certainly *not* a misunderstanding! Your bank embezzles its customers' money, sir."

"So the single use of my first name was an unfortunate slip of the tongue, was it?"

"Yes."

He drew a long breath. "I trust you can substantiate the charge you make concerning the bank?"

"You know I can't."

"With all due respect, Ellie, I don't *know* anything."

She gazed at him. "I would like to believe you, sir; indeed, I would like it more than you can know, but the fact is that you must be lying. You *have* to know all about it because you are a partner in the bank, and were there that day, when it was plain you held some sway with my father's accusers. My family's fortune remains in the bank's clutches, and my father's good name has been besmirched. He's innocent, sir. It's the bank that was—and still is—guilty!"

"Ellie, I think we should discuss this properly, and more calmly. Perhaps this is not at all the wisest place."

"Even if we were to discuss it over tea with the Archbishop of Canterbury, it would make no difference. While this vile stigma attaches to my father's memory, you and I can never indulge in polite conversation," she replied. She caught up her heavy black skirts to walk past him, but he so far ignored the rules as to catch her arm and make her stop again.

"Forgive me, Ellie, but I still think you owe me an explanation."

"*I* owe *you* an explanation?" she cried incredulously. "Sir, the facts are that your bank cheated my father out of his fortune, and then foreclosed upon him. It secretly raised a heavy mortgage that he did not take out, confiscated my mother's jewels, and is even now seizing my home. It not only robbed my father of everything he possessed, but of his will to live as well." She pointed an accusing finger back at the fresh grave. "Your bank did that, sir, and I will find a way of exposing you and your fellow partners for the scoundrels you are. I hope you never sleep easily in your bed again."

"And I hope that I do, Ellie," he countered, still holding her arm. "I fear I cannot promise immediate action on your complaints as I am about to leave the country for a while, but on my return you have my word that I will look into the matter."

"The word of a partner in the Unicorn Bank is worthless, sir." With that she wrenched herself free and ran from the burial ground. She was sobbing so much that when she reached her waiting hackney coach she could barely instruct the driver to take her back to her lodgings.

But as the shabby vehicle lurched away in the direction of Tyburn, she knew that her attraction toward Athan was as strong as ever. She wanted to despise him; instead, she yearned for him. He had awakened senses that ran through her blood like wildfire. No longer an innocent miss whose unfulfilled existence had seemed too set to continue blandly to the grave, she had become a woman, newly conscious of passion and her need for love.

It was as if Athan had entered a dark room and lighted a candle, and she could only burn upon the flame he'd created.

If she had remained at the burial ground for just five minutes more, she would have witnessed an extraordinary display of unfilial fury from Freddie Forrester-Phipps. Ever since his father's death, Freddie had been dogging the family lawyer, pestering him to know the exact terms of the will. At last, provoked beyond endurance that this pestering should continue even at the graveside, the harassed man of the law blurted that Freddie, even though the only child, would get nothing at all. The entire fortune had been left to his first cousin, who had behaved more like a son to the dead man than Freddie ever had.

The revelation led to an unseemly tussle at the graveside between Freddie and his cousin, which only ended when they were pulled apart. Freddie insisted that the lawyer repeat what he had said, and in this the gentleman obliged him. There was no doubt, he said, that Freddie was now reaping a harvest of his own sowing. With his dissolute, reckless, careless existence, he had so alienated his own father that he'd been entirely disinherited. And there was nothing he could do about it.

Five

Just over two months later, on the late evening of New Year's Day, 1805, a pony and trap halted by the lodge at the turnpike gate at Nantgarth in the Welsh county of Glamorgan. The main road from Cardiff to Merthyr, some seventeen miles away to the north, passed along the lower slopes of the valley. So filled with ruts, potholes, and rivulets, the road was a grim prospect even in daylight, let alone at night. It was cold and dark, and the weather was wet and windy. Collieries, iron works, and other industries scarred the otherwise picturesque valley of the River Taff, and the looming mountains were scattered with isolated farms and countless sheep, but the drenching first-of-January murk obliterated everything.

The brightly lit Griffin Inn stood just beyond the gate, its creaking sign depicting the mythical beast, half eagle, half lion, that was the badge of the local landowner, Lord Griffin. There was merriment within, laughter and singing so raucous that it could be heard above the racket of the weather. Bedraggled curls clung to Ellie's forehead as she huddled on the trap beside her uncle, John Billersley, whom she had managed to trace through his old friend Toby Richardson, now a successful London barrister. It had been Toby who'd informed him of her mother's death, and who'd written urgently to John on learning of Ellie's circumstances. She'd been aware of something odd about her uncle's whereabouts, for Toby had declined to tell her anything about him until he'd had a response to the letter. Only then, when clearly given permission, had he divulged the address.

As soon as she'd met John Billersley on alighting from

the stagecoach in Cardiff, she'd realized he was no longer a wealthy man. She also soon realized that it was no coincidence that he'd left a beautifully decorated ceramic disk on her mother's grave, for he now depended upon the making of porcelain for his livelihood. He had always been a talented artist, and Ellie remembered how her parents had teased him about his eccentric hobby of decorating plates. The last few hours had taught her that the uncle of the present did not in the least resemble that uncle of the past. What on earth had happened during the intervening years? She knew it must have been something calamitous. He had no wife or children, having always been a bachelor, and his china works were, he said, very small, new, and barely productive, but he nevertheless welcomed her into his life, and for that she would be eternally grateful. So she clung unashamedly to his arm, so glad to have him that it was all she could do not to keep crying.

Her hooded traveling cloak was soaked, and she was colder than she ever remembered before. She was weary after three days of winter traveling from the Isle of Wight, and relieved that her new life had begun. Turning to look back along the turnpike, she couldn't even see the cliff-enclosed pass where the Taff, a fine salmon river, roared south through rocks toward Cardiff and the sea, some eight miles distant. Lord Griffin's splendid castle home was perched like an aerie on the east cliff, but she had not seen so much as a single light to betray its presence. All she knew was that it was there, and that Lord Griffin, who had lost his wife fairly recently, was her uncle's landlord, and famous for his stud of milk white horses. Ellie somehow pictured his lordship as a middle-aged, possibly even elderly, widower who smelled of stables and seldom removed his boots.

John Billersley was tall and thin, with slender, artistic fingers, but his sad, rather kindly face put his niece oddly in mind of a benevolent Great Dane dog. He wore his graying hair long enough to be tied back with a stiff navy blue ribbon, although at the moment his dripping hat was tugged down so low that not a lock could be seen. Like her, he was muffled in overclothes to stave off the worst of the weather, and also like her, he was signally cold and desirous of reaching the warmth of his hearth. He therefore impatiently eyed the gatekeeper's door.

"Oh, come on, Huw Jenkin, come on!" he breathed.

A hand lantern shone suddenly in the doorway of the lodge, and a man emerged, accompanied by a black-and-white collie. The gatekeeper was slight and dark, and by the unsteady light of the lantern Ellie saw that he had the delicately formed features of the Welsh. He was swathed in a heavy cloak and had an ancient blunderbuss over his arm, for he took no chances with possible robbers.

"Hurry up, man!" John grumbled.

"*Nos da*, Mr. Bailey," Huw called back, relaxing as he realized who the travelers were. He nodded at Ellie and spoke to her as well, but as he used only Welsh she did not understand him. However, she did understand that he had addressed John Billersley as Mr. Bailey without being corrected.

"What did he say to me, Uncle?" she asked, holding the hood of her cloak as a vagrant gust of wind threatened to sweep it back from her head.

"He just welcomed you to Nantgarth, my dear."

"He knows about me?"

"Everyone hereabouts knows my niece is coming to live with me."

"Why did he call you Mr. Bailey?"

Her uncle hesitated. "All in good time, my dear, all in good time."

Huw addressed John Billersley again and, laughing, pointed toward the inn.

"What's he saying now?" Ellie asked, frustrated at not being able to understand.

"He's reminding me that the Mari Llwyd goes around the area tonight, and that it is at the inn right now."

"The Marie what?"

"The Mari Llwyd, the Gray Mare," her uncle explained as Huw struggled to open the gate, which seemed to have jammed somehow. "It's a sort of pagan hobbyhorse and is accompanied by a noisy company of mummers and dancers. The ancient custom is for it to visit local houses on this day to mark the passing of the darkest of winter."

"Someone should have reminded Mother Nature," Ellie

murmured, for this had surely been the darkest day since the Creation.

Her uncle laughed. "Maybe this is her way of showing grave disapproval for such an irreligious custom. Anyway, Huw merely warned me that the procession is about to leave the Griffin, so I must either drive on quickly, or be prepared to endure the Gray Mare's attentions."

At last Huw succeeded in opening the gate, but as Ellie's uncle prepared to flick the reins to move the tired pony on, the door of the inn burst open, and a riotous crowd erupted into the dismal night. Torches fluttered and smoked as white-sheeted mummers, one beating a steady rhythm on a drum, capered around a man, also in white, who carried a horse's skull that was fixed to a pole and decorated with colored ribbons. Adults of both sexes followed, their faces blackened, holly and ivy in their hats, and ribbons pinned to their clothes. Children dressed in animal costumes—bears, foxes, squirrels, and rabbits—ran shrieking and laughing into the rainswept darkness, and suddenly the deserted turnpike was swarming with people. Atrocious weather or not, everyone for miles around seemed to have come to join in festivities that turned time backward by hundreds of years.

Ellie shrank against her uncle as the weird procession passed by, but then became aware of one figure limping behind the others and then standing motionless near the inn. It was a youthful man, or so she thought from his lean and rangy build, and he was dressed as a spotted dog, black on white. At least . . . Her eyes blinked, and in that split second he'd gone. No one with such a limp could have run off that quickly, or even slipped back into the inn! A little unnerved, she clung still closer to her uncle.

As soon as the trap was free again, John urged the pony forward. The sounds of merrymaking were soon lost in the noise of the night, and at a signpost that indicated the way to Castle Griffin, the trap turned to the right into a little upward-sloping side valley. At first the way was flanked by the cottages of Nantgarth, which was little more than a hamlet that had sprung up at the conjunction of the two valleys. There was a small school, attended by children from miles around, and a shop that provided essentials, including a twice-weekly wagon service to and from Cardiff.

The rain suddenly stopped as the last cottage was passed, but the wind continued to bluster and moan. A hundred yards farther on, at the edge of a dense mixed woodland, was a humpbacked stone bridge over the new Glamorgan Canal, the cutting of which had been demanded by local industry because the Taff was too dangerous and the roads too often impassable. On the far side of the waterway, hidden among tall evergreens, was the small china works upon which her uncle, once so well-off, now depended for his existence. The silhouettes of two bottle-necked kilns rose against the background of woodland, and as the trap crossed the bridge, Ellie saw a cobbled way leading down a little wharf, where a barge was visible in the swinging light of a lantern on the corner of an outbuilding. There were other lights too, those of Nantgarth House, John Billersley's modest double-fronted dwelling attached to the china works. Ellie would soon learn that the road continued past the house to a fork about a quarter of a mile farther on. One branch crossed the valley and ascended the opposite side to Castle Griffin; the other was little more than a bridle way that led up to the inconveniently isolated parish church, high on the bleak mountainside a mile or more from its nearest parishioners.

The trap drew to a halt by Nantgarth House's garden gate, and Ellie saw her new home for the first time. Whitewashed and neat, it faced south toward the road, along a clinker path that was flanked by tiny square lawns and bare flower beds. In daylight it would obviously have splendid views across the valley, but right now everything was so dark it was impossible to see anything. And all the time the wind howled through the nearby trees like the wild hunt itself, arousing images of the Mari Llwyd, and the young man dressed as a spotted dog.

"Here we are, my dear," her uncle said as he alighted to make the reins fast to a holly tree overhanging the garden wall. The gusting air rustled through the wet leaves, making them glint in the darkness, and now and then Ellie caught the exhilarating smell of the surrounding mountains, a mixture of springy turf, heather, and sheep. The wind was a living entity, whispering to her through the eaves of the house and among the swaying branches of the trees, and filling her with the certainty that at last she was close to her proper place in the scheme of things. Somehow she had never truly belonged at Rutherford Park; however, she belonged here, maybe not at Nantgarth House itself, but certainly among these mountains.

The door of the house opened, and a plump middle-aged woman in a dark blue gown, floppy mobcap, and crocheted shawl looked out anxiously. Ellie guessed she must be the housekeeper, Mrs. Lewis. The guess was confirmed a moment later when Ellie's uncle raised a reassuring hand.

"We're here safe and sound, Mrs. Lewis. I hope you've already suffered a visit from the Mari Llwyd?"

"Oh, yes, sir. Some hours ago."

The woman's lilting English came as a huge relief to Ellie, who'd heard little but Welsh since leaving England behind.

"Thank heavens for that," John replied. "Did you keep your promise to be about making *dowset* and *cacen gri* to welcome my niece?"

"Of course, Mr. Bailey. You didn't think I'd forget, did you?"

"I've never known it yet, but I'm so damned cold and hungry tonight that if you'd let me down, I think I'd eat *you* instead!"

Mrs. Lewis threw up her hands and laughed. "I'd be too tough by far for your soft English teeth," she replied, then disappeared into the house, calling in Welsh for her son, Gwilym.

Ellie shivered as her uncle assisted her down from the trap. "What's *dowset* and *cacen gri*, Uncle?" she asked.

"Bacon pie and sweet griddle cake, my dear," he answered, "and very nourishing and tasty both are too." He paused. "I know what you're thinking."

"You do?"

"Yes, my dear. That such fare is a world away from the grand dishes I enjoyed in times gone by."

She smiled. "Actually, I was about to express surprise that I am not to eat toasted cheese every day from now on, as I have been given to understand that the Welsh eat nothing else."

"A rare bit of toasted cheese is a favorite, I grant you, but don't believe for a moment that the Welsh have nothing else, for I vow you'll eat better from now on than you ever did before. Good, healthy food—none of your fancy French twiddles." He'd spoken amusingly, but then became more serious and spoke of something rather different. "Eleanor, are you quite, quite certain no one at Rutherford Park knows you have come here?"

"Absolutely certain, Uncle. I was very careful to observe your wishes. When I left the Isle of Wight, there wasn't a soul alive who knew I was coming here. Except you, of course."

He drew her gloved fingers to his lips. "And now that you are here, you are to forget the name Billersley, do you understand? To everyone here, including Lord Griffin himself, I am John Bailey." He spoke quietly and urgently, and was obviously very anxious for her cooperation.

"I . . . yes, of course, Uncle."

Seeing her anxiety, he squeezed her gloved fingers. "I will explain directly, my dear, when we are in the dry and can talk in comfort." He was about to usher her along the path when something on the mountainside behind her caught his attention.

Ellie turned and looked in the same direction, but saw nothing. "What is it, Uncle? What have you seen?"

"I thought I saw a lantern, but probably imagined it. Only a madman would be up there on a night like this," John replied, and ushered her through the gate and along the clinker path.

At last they stepped into the welcome warmth of Nantgarth House's narrow entrance passage, where a mixture of fire and candlelight flickered from a room on the right. A staircase with a door at the bottom led up from the far end of the passage, and there were other doors into the dining room and kitchens. A longcase clock stood against the wall, just inside the entrance. Ellie noticed it particularly because its face was an unusual diamond shape. The pendulum swung slowly, tick, tock, tick, tock—a sound that somehow seemed to be part of the building.

She threw back her hood at last and took off her wet bonnet, and her hair immediately tumbled in rats' tails down about her shoulders. Just then, Mrs. Lewis hurried from the kitchens at the back of the house, driving her lanky, redheaded son before her. The youth had a limp. Ellie was immediately riveted to the spot, for she knew, just knew, that she had seen him earlier in the spotted dog costume. Limp or not, he must have run like the wind itself to be here before the trap.

"Attend to the pony, Gwilym," Mrs. Lewis said to him in English, then saw Ellie and halted as if confronted by a ghost. Her son stared as well, his lips apart on a silent gasp.

Ellie was embarrassed. Was it *so* shocking here in Wales if a lady's hair fell from its pins? "Forgive me, I . . ." She caught her damp locks and tried to pin them up again, but Mrs. Lewis recovered quickly and hastened to reassure her.

"Oh, it's not your hair, Miss Rutherford. It's just that you remind us of someone."

John was curious. "And who might that be, Mrs. Lewis?"

"Oh, just my cousin, sir. She passed away just over two years ago, immediately before you came to Nantgarth."

"I've never heard you mention her before," he replied, turning for the housekeeper to take his soaking outdoor clothes. What he wore beneath was plain and unremarkable, a nondescript gray coat and fawn breeches that once would never have found their way into his possession. As for his sturdy, well-worn top boots, well, they were certainly not the work of Hoby's of St. James's.

Mrs. Lewis nodded at her son again. "Attend the pony, there's a good boy."

"Yes, Mam," he replied dutifully, then stole another glance at Ellie before turning to take his coat down from the row of hooks on the wall.

"What's this, Gwilym?" Ellie's uncle asked. "Time off from the castle stables?"

"Yes, Mr. Bailey."

John could read between unspoken lines. "Never mind, lad, for it won't be long before Lord Griffin returns, and then all will be well again."

"Oh, I hope so, Mr. Bailey, truly I do."

Before the youth could leave the house, Ellie suddenly spoke. "You must be one of the fastest runners in Nantgarth, Gwilym."

"Runners, miss?" He turned, his face puzzled, but his eyes saying something else.

"You were down on the turnpike, dressed as a dog, a white dog with black spots."

Mrs. Lewis laughed. "Oh, dear me, no, Miss Rutherford. Gwilym has been here with me all evening."

Ellie looked at her, then back at Gwilym. "I'm sorry, I'm clearly mistaken," she said, knowing full well that she wasn't. She watched his rather ungainly progress toward the door, which to her astonishment suddenly flew open before him. He went out, and it slammed behind him, again apparently of its own accord, for he had not touched it once.

Then the longcase clock stopped ticking too, and a great shiver ran down Ellie's back.

Six

A door that opened and closed on its own? Ellie was so shaken that she took an involuntary step backward. No, it was impossible. She had imagined it. She was at the end of an arduous journey, and in need of food and a rest. But when she glanced at the clock, she saw it had indeed stopped. That, at least, had nothing to do with tiredness and imagination.

Mrs. Lewis hurried to take her cloak. The housekeeper was a very tidy person, pink-cheeked and bright-eyed, with dimples. "How dreadful a welcome the Glamorgan weather has given you, Miss Rutherford," she said kindly. "What must you think of us?"

"I'm more than glad to be here," Ellie replied, shaking out the crumpled, rather damp folds of the rust-colored woolen gown she wore beneath the cloak. She had been true to her word to her father, and had discarded mourning before leaving Rutherford Park for the last time.

The housekeeper took a crocheted cream woolen shawl from a hook on the wall and placed it around Ellie's shoulders. "It's not much of a shawl, Miss Rutherford, but I thought that after traveling on such a night you'd be in need of something warm around your shoulders."

Ellie was grateful. "It's very kind of you, Mrs. Lewis."

"Not at all, Miss Rutherford." The housekeeper dimpled with pleasure, then herded the two weary travelers through the firelit doorway and into a charming parlor, where a very welcome coal fire danced in the hearth of a surprisingly large fireplace. Pink-and-gold lights danced over whitewashed walls, shutters were closed at square uncurtained windows, and the stone floor undulated quaintly, displaying a definite rise toward the fire. Polished brass candlesticks and ornaments shone on the sturdy oak mantel, where stood a surprisingly elegant and costly mahogany bracket clock that Ellie remembered from a childhood visit to her uncle's then residence in the grandeur of Bruton Street, Mayfair. It was the only evidence she'd seen so far of his much more sumptuous previous life.

The parlor furniture was rustic, and included a bureau cabinet made of oak and inlaid with checker patterns. A cupboard-backed settle was at right angles to the fireplace; two upright oak armchairs had been placed opposite; and directly in front of the fire, to gain the very best advantage from the heat, was a wooden rocking chair that Ellie guessed was her uncle's favorite seat. There were various shelves on the wall, some holding books, others examples of the exquisite soft-paste china made at the works and decorated by her uncle. On the chimney breast above the mantel, occupying pride of place over all else in the room, was a watercolor head-and-shoulders portrait of a young man with long black curls that reached down to his shoulders. He had long-lashed spaniel brown eyes, a slightly olive complexion, and sensuous lips upturned in the merest ghost of a smile, and was wearing strange clothes, perhaps from somewhere in the Orient. Behind him were a wide river, grand buildings, and a tall needle-thin church spire that was unlike any she had seen before.

She went to hold her hands out to the fire. "Whose is the portrait, Uncle?"

"Mm? Oh, I have no idea," John answered. "I purchased it years ago from a gallery in London."

Then she noticed that the bracket clock had also stopped. It must have just happened, for like the longcase clock in the entrance passage, its hands pointed to the correct time. She turned to her uncle. "Doesn't anyone attend to the clocks?" she asked.

John had turned to make sure the parlor door was closed. "What was that? The clocks? Oh, it's Gwilym's fault. There are three clocks he seems to affect, this one, the longcase in the hall, and one in the kitchen. They only work when he is actually beneath this roof. The moment he steps outside they all stop. They'll come on again when he returns from attending to the pony. Mrs. Lewis usually puts them all to the right time again."

Ellie stared at him. "You pull my leg, surely?"

"Not at all, my dear. I've long since learned that Gwilym Lewis is an extraordinary young man; in fact, I'd say he was fey."

"Fey?" Ellie could see again the motionless figure in the spotted dog costume.

John nodded. "Yes, and his mother too, come to that. Gwilym certainly has a strange way with him. He can sometimes move things simply by willing it. I've seen him look at a glass marble and make it roll up and down a table. And he's a horse charmer too, of course. He only has to whisper to them and breathe into their nostrils, and they become his obedient and adoring slaves. That's why Lord Griffin wants him up at the stud. There's nothing that boy cannot persuade a horse to do." He indicated the rocking chair. "I trust you will not mind if I sit in your presence, my dear, but I'm exhausted."

She smiled. "Of course I don't mind, Uncle. So, Gwilym really does have some strange power? I'm almost relieved to hear it, because when the front door opened and closed without him so much as raising a finger, I thought I was seeing things."

"Seeing things? No. You'll get used to it, and thankfully Gwilym is up at the castle most of the time." John eased himself down with a sigh. "Ah, that's better. Driving a pony and trap in such weather soon reminds me of aches and pains I'd rather forget." Settled at last, he smiled at her. "Mrs. Lewis is a tea thrower."

"A what?"

"She upends people's teacups after they've finished drinking, and then reads things from the pattern of the leaves. Something of the sort, anyway. I've heard from one or two acquaintances that the resultant predictions can be discomforting, so I've declined her offers to read mine. However, if you feel so disposed, I'm sure she'd be only too delighted."

"Maybe." Ellie smiled, then changed the subject. "You said you wished to tell me something important when we were alone?"

"Yes. It would not have been fair to regale you with it all while we were on the road, for the weather was alarming enough on its own, without my troubles to add to it."

Ellie was dismayed. *Alarming? Troubles?* Just what was she about to learn?

He bade her sit down on the settle, then looked sadly at her pale, tired face. "Forgive me, my dear, for you've suffered enough of late, losing your parents and your home under such tragic circumstances, but there is no way I can shield you from things here. Ellie, for the last fourteen years I have been forced to seek refuge and anonymity."

Ellie's blue eyes widened. "Forced? By whom?"

"Well, originally, certain rather pressing debts that I was unable to pay. I gambled too deep by far at White's, and lost so heavily to certain gentlemen that I could not hope to meet my debts. Rather than face jail, I decided to vanish. That was why I estranged myself from your mother. I could not bear the thought of her knowing the duns might descend upon me at any moment."

Agitated by having to talk about things that cut through to his innermost secrets, he rose from the rocking chair and began to pace restlessly up and down the room. "The only course I saw open to me was to turn my beloved hobby of china decoration into a living. So I took myself to the Crown Derby works to see if I could be taken on as an artist. Much to my relief they were glad to have me. Six years later I at last persuaded them to experiment with my own formula for what the French call *pâte tendre*, but we know as soft-paste porcelain. I *know* British china can match Sèvres and the others, if only the basic white china can be fine enough and translucent enough. Unfortunately for me, my formula is too delicate to be profitable, so Derby decided against any more experimentation. I moved on to the Royal Worcester works, to try my luck there instead. At first Derby didn't know my whereabouts, but about eighteen months ago, when I'd been at Worcester for three years, they heard a whisper, and immediately wrote to Worcester, threatening legal action, saying I had no right to take my formula elsewhere because it belonged to them. I already had the duns to avoid; now I had my former employers on my back as well. Worcester had been experimenting with my recipe, but were fast coming to the same conclusion as Derby, that it was far too impractical. Some exquisitely delicate pieces had been produced, but the wastage was so heavy that they too chose not to proceed, so I upped sticks in the middle of the night and disappeared from there too."

"To come here to Wales?"

His glance slid away. "Yes."

Ellie had never been all that good at sums, but even she knew there were years unaccounted for. Her uncle claimed that fourteen years ago he severed contact with the rest of the family because of the gambling debts that ruined him. Then he'd been six years at Crown Derby and three at Royal Worcester. He'd been here at Nantgarth for two years, which left three years unaccounted for. "What were you doing for the rest of the time?" she asked.

"Rest of the time?"

She explained her reasoning.

He stopped pacing. "Ah. Oh, nothing in particular. This and that, you know how it is," he answered, glancing at the portrait over the fireplace. "Anyway, no sooner had I departed from Worcester, than I met Lord Griffin, whom good fortune had seen fit to keep from crossing my path while I was enjoying my former high life in London. We were both snowbound at the same inn high on the Pennines, and thus thrust together for company. I found myself telling him all about my formula, although not, of course, about my debts. I must have convinced him of something, for he not only offered to advance me sufficient money to start up on my own, but suggested this site at a very reasonable ground rent. No man could have been more generous and understanding, but I fear that even his patience will be exhausted if I do not succeed soon."

"But what is wrong with your china?" she asked.

"Wastage," he answered promptly. "My formula is so delicate, you see, and with so much sand it always runs the danger of almost turning to glass. But when it works, oh, my dear, you will never have seen more exquisite china." He went to one of the shelves, and brought her a plate. "Hold it up to the fire, Eleanor. There, you see? The flames are visible through it. Not even Sèvres is so fine."

She gazed at the plate, which was beautifully gilded and

painted with wreaths of roses. "Oh, Uncle, it's magnificent," she breathed.

He nodded, pleased. "If only I could produce work of this quality every time, I would be made. But whatever I do, the formula is too delicate. Some say too faulty, of course, but I *know* it is right. All I need is to discover that final tweak that will work the magic." He returned the plate to the shelf, then positioned himself in front of the fire and clasped his hands behind his back.

"I'm sure that Lord Griffin will keep faith with you, Uncle."

"I hope so, Eleanor. Actually, I have reason to think he keeps my best interests at heart, for there has been excellent news from St. Petersburg."

"St. Petersburg?" She looked blankly at him, wondering what the Russian capital had to do with it.

"Lord Griffin is there at the moment," John explained. "He is visiting his sister, Mrs. Brasier, who resides there with her English fur trader husband, a man of great wealth, from all accounts. Anyway, it seems pleasure has been mixed with business, so to speak, because a hasty postscript to Lord Griffin's last letter to his agent stated that Czar Alexander has expressed an interest in the Griffin stud. It is not known yet what will come of this, but Lord Griffin obviously hopes for a great deal as he issued instructions that no horse is to be sold from the stud until his return. This might not be before the spring, as I understand he has been badly struck with the grippe."

Ellie's picture of his lordship promptly extended to him being a sickly invalid as well.

"St. Petersburg is a poor place for the lungs," John continued, "but then what can one expect when it is so far north and built upon a marsh? One might as well expect Venice to boast dry foundations." He shook his head sadly at the folly of man, then added, "However, it cannot be coincidence that my good news from that capital coincides with Lord Griffin's presence there."

"What good news is that, Uncle?" Ellie asked.

"Suffice it that if all goes well, you may see St. Petersburg yourself in the not too distant future."

"Really?" Her eyes lit up.

"I trust so." John's face became more serious. "Now to a rather awkward point. You asked me earlier why people here call me Mr. Bailey, not Mr. Billersley. Well, the truth of it is that when I found myself with Derby, Worcester, *and* the duns in pursuit, I knew it was time to properly cover my tracks. So when I reached that inn on the Pennines, I assumed a new identity, becoming John Bailey. That is why I must beg you to forget the name Billersley. It's important, my dear, for a slip of the tongue might see me in jail after all."

She got up to fling her arms reassuringly around his neck. "I won't let you down, Uncle," she whispered.

He held her. "You're a good girl, Eleanor, and you've suffered much. Your darling mother's demise was a terrible thing, but at least she had been ill. Your father, on the other hand . . . Such an unnecessary accident. It must have been a terrible ordeal for you."

"It wasn't an accident, Uncle," she said quietly, and drew from his arms to tell him the truth about her father's death. "The Unicorn Bank behaved monstrously throughout," she finished, "not only stealing his money, but somehow getting away with it within the law. I don't profess to understand the minutiae of such matters, but I do know that my father was innocent of wrongdoing."

"Retribution will strike the guilty, you mark my words," John assured her.

"I pray so." She seemed to see Athan's face, and had to make herself speak of something else. "Uncle, I would not have come here if I'd realized how much of a burden I would be," she said awkwardly.

"Burden? You? No, never. Please, my dear, it will grieve me to think you feel that way. Promise now?"

"You definitely want me here?"

"You belong with me, Eleanor. We are kin and must help each other."

At that moment the clock on the mantel commenced to tick again, a loud intrusion on the brief silence that had fallen between uncle and niece. Ellie smiled. "Gwilym?"

Her uncle nodded, and at that moment Mrs. Lewis tapped at the door. "Your meal is waiting, Mr. Bailey, Miss Rutherford."

"Thank you, Mrs. Lewis," he replied, then offered Ellie his

arm. "Come, Eleanor, it may not be to a grand dining room that we go, but we may as well keep up appearances."

She smiled. "There's just one thing, Uncle."

"Yes?"

"I loathe being called Eleanor. Will you *please* call me Ellie?"

"One change of name deserves another," he said, raising her hand to his lips. "Come, Ellie, let's to our banquet."

Later that night, when Ellie and her uncle were asleep in their beds, Mrs. Lewis and her son sat facing each other at the kitchen table, a single candle burning low between them.

"It cannot be coincidence, Gwilym," the housekeeper said in Welsh. "She is the living image, the very living image, and she has been sent in time, Gwilym. It is up to us, to you and me, to see that she triumphs."

"And if she doesn't want him?"

"Not want him?" Mrs. Lewis gave a low laugh. "My dear boy, of *course* she'll want him. And he will want her. They already want each other."

Gwilym frowned. "That cannot be."

His mother spread her hands in puzzlement. "I know, Gwilym, and yet my heart tells me it is so. All we have to do is make certain that such things as honor and duty do not override true love."

Gwilym put out a slender finger to press the soft wax at the lip of the candle. "What if you are wrong, Mam? What if it is the other one who should after all be at his side?"

"Should? How can that be so? Everyone else may be deceived, but you and I know how bad she really is, and her mother. We know what is right, and what must be done. We must interfere as best we can."

Gwilym nodded, but then his face turned suddenly pale. "There are others. . . ."

"What do you mean?"

"From the ice. A spotted hound."

"Spotted hound?" Mrs. Lewis's brows drew together. "*Were* you with the Mari Lwyd after all, Gwilym?" she asked.

He shrugged. "Maybe. I do not always know. I can be two."

His mother nodded. "That is true. So it was your fetch she saw?"

"I cannot be sure."

The candle flickered, the flame leapt, and for a moment it seemed that a freshly gathered posy of snowdrops lay on the table between them. But it was only for a moment.

Mrs. Lewis smiled again. "A good sign, Gwilym, a very good sign. He will choose the right bride."

Seven

The following morning Ellie awakened and looked up at the beamed ceiling above her simple bed. Winter sunshine pierced the plain shutters of her south-facing bedroom window, and the chirruping of sparrows in the holly tree had taken the place of the overnight storm. Mrs. Lewis, silent as a mouse, had crept in earlier to tend the tiny fireplace, where flames now flickered warmly, taking the edge off the cold. The walls were roughly plastered, and very white, and the furniture was as rustic as that in the rest of Nantgarth House. She could hear voices by the canal, and the clatter of hooves as a horse and cart was driven down toward Nantgarth and the turnpike.

The bedsheets smelled of lavender and were so crisp and white that they must have been boiled before being starched. A patchwork quilt topped the woolen blankets that had kept Ellie cozy from the moment her head touched the crochet-trimmed pillow.

Mrs. Lewis spoke outside the door. "Are you awake, Miss Rutherford?"

"Yes, Mrs. Lewis, please come in." Ellie struggled to sit up, sweeping her hair back from her face and then stretching her arms above her head. She had slept like a log, and heaven alone knew what time it was now.

The housekeeper came in with a cup of tea, placed it carefully by the bed, and gazed at Ellie as if hoping the uncanny resemblance she had seen the night before would not be there in the cold light of day. But it was, and the woman drew back, whispering something beneath her breath.

Ellie smiled at her. "I really am your cousin's double, am I?"

Mrs. Lewis became self-conscious. "Oh, pay no attention to me, miss. I do rattle on sometimes. I trust you slept well?"

"Indeed I did. The bed is very comfortable, and the linen so fresh that I know I will sleep like a top even when I've recovered from my journey."

Mrs. Lewis was pleased, and as her eyes met Ellie's, they both knew they would get on splendidly. It was a good moment, confirming first impressions of the night before.

"Mrs. Lewis, you'll never know how glad I am that you speak such excellent English," Ellie said then. "I mean to learn Welsh as much as I can, but right now it is quite unintelligible to me."

The housekeeper laughed. "You will soon sort it out, I'm sure. I speak English, and so does Gwilym, because I worked and lived at Castle Griffin for a long time, and Lord Griffin always insists upon English being spoken."

"But you left to come here?"

The woman smoothed her hands down her starched apron. "I was dismissed," she said frankly.

"Whatever for?"

"Because I fell foul of Mrs. Tudor and her daughter."

"Who are they?" Ellie inquired.

"Lord Griffin's permanent guests, Miss Rutherford. Miss Tudor is soon to be officially betrothed to him."

"Really? How old is she?"

"She might be a year or two your senior, Miss Rutherford."

Ellie's impression of Lord Griffin made her appalled to think of such a young woman becoming his wife. She would have liked to ask more, but there was such a wealth of loathing in the housekeeper's voice that she decided not to. Instead she smiled. "Please call me Miss Ellie, for I would much prefer it."

"Thank you, Miss Ellie, that is most kind of you. Now then, shall I open the shutters?"

"If you please."

The woman went to the window, and a moment later the bright light of morning flooded the bedroom as it flooded the valley outside. There, rising above the thick trees on the heights above the pass and the conjunction of the two valleys, were the towers and battlements of Castle Griffin. The great Norman fortress was at once intimidating and beautiful, its grim martial aspect softened by glazed windows that shone in the sunlight, and gardens that spilled down through clearings.

Mrs. Lewis watched how she gazed at the castle. "Would you like to see into your tea leaves, Miss Ellie?" she offered.

Ellie was intrigued. "Yes, if you please."

"Drink up then, and we will see what is there. All that is required is the cup, saucer, and your tea leaves. Just leave a mouthful of tea in the bottom, that's all."

Ellie drank the tea, all the while chiding herself for being a gullible goose; then she handed the cup and saucer to the waiting housekeeper.

"Mind now, miss, I will not see anything, but you will see your secret dreams."

Ellie was puzzled. "But—"

"That is how it happens, miss. The tea leaves are turned, and by looking at them a person sees what he or she really dreams will happen. It is a window into the innermost soul."

"I'll see a . . . a vision, you mean?" Ellie's eyes grew large.

Mrs. Lewis nodded. "Yes, you and only you, my dear. I am but the means through which things are revealed. Do you still wish to proceed?"

"I . . . I think so."

"Very well."

The housekeeper sat on the edge of the bed, then swirled the dregs in the teacup before suddenly turning it upside down in the saucer and looking at the pattern left in the cup. The leaves seemed to have mostly congregated near the lip. Her eyes began to close, and she sat there without moving.

Ellie regarded her uneasily, for the woman was suddenly as stiff and motionless as a statue. The sun must have gone behind a cloud outside, for the room had become darker— dark enough for a candle to have been lit. Someone else was present. Who was it? Ellie's hand crept to her throat, and she was conscious of her heart thumping wildly in her breast. Where was her nightgown? She seemed to be naked! And where was she?

She looked around as the uncertain light fell on fine furniture, rich rugs, gilded plasterwork, and other costly things she knew were not in her room. There was a wonderful soup tureen on the mantel, its gilding and painted decoration clearly her uncle's work. A soup tureen? Why? Surely a vase or an urn would be more appropriate? Above the tureen, just beyond the arc of candlelight, there was a portrait of a young woman, but she could not make out who it was, except that there was something familiar about it. Then she again became aware of the candlelight as someone approached the bedside.

"No, you mustn't light candles during the day, for it's unlucky!" she gasped. She didn't know why she said it, for it wasn't a superstition she had ever known before, but for some reason the words came immediately to her lips.

"But it's night, my darling bride, so there is no need to fear," said a soft male voice.

She looked up. Athan was there, wearing a long silky maroon dressing gown that was so loosely tied at the waist that she could clearly see that he wore nothing else beneath. His nakedness seemed the most natural thing in the world . . . and the most beautiful. Everything about him was beautiful, from the lazily loving light in his gray eyes, the sensuous smile on his lips, and the way his hair was boyishly tousled, to the paleness of his skin and the lean perfection of his body. In a few moments now she would surrender her chastity and her very soul. She remembered she was without clothes, her light brown hair brushed loose, her breasts peeping above the coverlet, but she had no will to hide herself from him.

The anticipation of his lovemaking was so wonderful that excitement threatened to engulf her completely. This was her wedding night, and soon their bodies would be joined in her first act of love. She wasn't afraid, she loved him too much for that, but she was eager . . . so eager. She longed for him, desired him above all else, and was impatient for the gratification she knew only he would ever give her.

Was that wrong of her? Was it lacking in demureness? Oughtn't she to be fearful, an innocent upon the altar of marriage? No, she could never be that. Not with him. She was too honest, too in love, too passionate. He had kindled emotions in her that ought to be shocking, but were not.

He came to the bedside, and set the silver-gilt candlestick on the nearby table, where a crystal bowl of sweet-smelling roses filled the room with fragrance. "You are my bride and I love you, Ellie," he whispered.

"Do you? Do you really?" Her sudden insecurity was almost unbearable.

"My ring is on your finger, my darling, so how can you doubt? You are my life from now on, Ellie."

"Do you swear it?" she whispered.

"Upon my very soul," he breathed. "I am going to make sweet love to you, Ellie. Before dawn I will have proved my adoration over and over, and will have shown you ecstasies and delights that you have not dreamed existed."

"Are there truly such delights?" she asked.

He smiled, and slipped into the bed with her. The candle flames swayed seductively, sending warm shadows over her skin. He leaned over, kissed her on the lips, and drew her down from the pillows so their bodies touched.

The delicious sensation of his skin against hers sent her pulse racing. Her entire being yearned for all of him, wanted to rush toward satisfaction, but she was afraid her utter innocence would disappoint him. "I may fail you, Athan. I'm so green, so ignorant of—"

"I will teach you." He kissed her mouth again, and her lips softened and parted. Oh, such a kiss, slow, luxurious, enticing, and filled with such promise that she thought she would die of anticipation. Kiss followed kiss, and caress followed caress as they explored each other for the first time. Her need for him made her feel as if she would ignite, but at last they were one, her virginity stormed and then vanquished. "Look at me, Ellie," he whispered. "Look at me for this one moment."

She obeyed, her eyes dark with such fierce desire that she would have done anything he wished of her. He smiled, and began to move inside her. "This is love, Ellie. This is true love."

She gazed into his eyes, loving him so much that she thought she would die of ecstasy. Joy tumbled wildly through her veins, and her soul seemed to melt into such a wild storm of gratification that she felt she would drown in its fiery waves. It was too much, too much. . . . Her eyes closed, and she floated away on a sea of pleasure that seemed to stretch to every horizon. This truly was love, the most beautiful love, and it was theirs to share forever, *forever, forever. . . .*

"Are you all right, Miss Rutherford?" Mrs. Lewis's concerned inquiry intruded upon Ellie's blissful reverie.

"I beg your pardon?" Ellie's eyes flew open. Athan had gone, and the room was filled with bright daylight. There was no marriage bed, no gilded plasterwork, and no fragrance of roses.

"Are you all right? I spoke to you several times but you didn't answer."

Ellie managed to smile, for her senses were still whirling in all directions. She could feel the flush on her cheeks and knew that her eyes were bright. The exquisite pleasure of lovemaking was still with her, sparkling through her skin and shimmering through her blood like sunlight through a canopy of summer leaves. "Yes, I . . . I'm quite all right, thank you," she answered a little weakly.

The housekeeper looked at her face and then smiled. "Dreams are very private, are they not?"

Ellie returned the smile as best she could, but didn't say anything. There had to be a logical explanation for what had just happened, and she guessed that it was simply and solely the manifestation of wishful thinking. Whether or not Athan was a director of the hated Unicorn Bank, she remained so fiercely attracted to him that her mind's eye had conjured an impossibly idyllic scene in which there were pleasure and happiness without adversity. It was a fairy tale, brought to life by the fact that in spite of a good night's sleep she was still very tired, not only from traveling, but from everything else that had happened to her during the last year.

Mrs. Lewis got up. "Dreams are what one makes of them, Miss Ellie."

Ellie held her gaze, a trace of superstition still lurking in the shadow of her logical explanation. "Do you *promise* you didn't see anything just now?"

"I promise. All I know is that it has brought a glow to your cheeks and a sparkle to your eyes. What you saw was good, and I am glad."

When the housekeeper had gone, Ellie leaned her head back against the pillows. Oh, how wonderful such a future would be. She closed her eyes, cast her mind back a few minutes, and relived every wonderful moment.

"This is love, Ellie. This is true love. . . ."

Eight

A little later, dressed in an old green fustian gown that had survived the journey from the Isle of Wight with remarkable fortitude, Ellie went down to the kitchens for breakfast. She was still unsettled by what had happened with the tea leaves, but satisfied that Mrs. Lewis had told her the truth about not having seen anything. It would have been too embarrassing for words if the housekeeper had been a silent witness.

Ellie expected to find her uncle taking breakfast, but there was no sign of him. Mrs. Lewis ushered her to the scrubbed table where supper had been served the night before. White geraniums bloomed in pots on the window sills, the red-raddled floor was bright and clean, and four cats sprawled by the hearth, luxuriating in the heat. Fruit bread had just been taken from the wall oven and was cooling on a rack on the table. Blue-and-white crockery—not the work of John Bailey—adorned a great dresser against one wall, and the clock on the mantel had stopped at four, which was when Gwilym had left to commence his daily duties at the Castle Griffin stables.

"Where is my uncle?" Ellie asked as Mrs. Lewis set about cooking her breakfast.

"Oh, he's been hard at work these past two hours," the housekeeper replied, looking around from the pan on the hearth and pointing to a door at the other end of the kitchen.

Ellie had been told the night before that beyond the door there were stone steps leading down to the cellars, from where access could be had to the canal and wharf. Her uncle's few employees worked in the adjacent outbuildings, but he remained mostly in his workroom, which no one else dared to enter because it was where he decorated and gilded the successful porcelain, and mixed together the secret ingredients of his soft-paste formula.

Mrs. Lewis brought Ellie's breakfast of scrambled eggs and fried bacon. "There; that will set you up for the day," she declared.

"It certainly will," Ellie replied, thinking that such a mound would probably set her up for tomorrow as well.

"Mr. Bailey said that as soon as you finish, he would like you to go down to see him in his workshop."

"In his workshop?" Ellie was startled.

The housekeeper raised her eyebrows and nodded. "That's what he said, miss."

"I'm being honored, aren't I?"

"Well, you are family."

After eating rather more of the breakfast than she'd expected, Ellie left the table, but as she approached the door to the cellar, Mrs. Lewis hurried after her with a candle she'd lit hastily from the fire. "Take this, Miss Ellie. It's terribly dark down there when the doors to the wharf are closed, and the stone steps are a very steep spiral. They're well worn too, so please be careful."

Ellie accepted the candle. "Thank you, Mrs. Lewis."

The housekeeper opened the door for her, and a waft of freezing air swept up into the warm kitchen. Or was it that the warm air swept down and left a chill behind? Shielding the flame with her hand, Ellie began to descend. At the bottom there was a large windowless room, deserted except for careful stacks of unglazed, unpainted porcelain that she would soon learn was termed biscuit ware. At the far end were double doors around which she could see daylight. Beyond them lay the busy canal. Clogs clattered on rounded cobbles, people talked in Welsh, and now and then a horse whinnied, presumably a tow horse belonging to one of the barges.

Ellie crossed the dark cellar room with care, for it too was cobbled and therefore very uncomfortable to walk on without clogs. She didn't open the doors, but peeped out through a knothole. She saw the tow horse beside the sixty-foot-long barge that had been waiting overnight, and leaning against the trunk of one of the nearby evergreen trees, the man and boy that crewed the barge. They watched as a cargo of finished chinaware was carefully loaded. Another barge had arrived an hour earlier, to discharge its cargo of what Ellie was to learn included bone ash, Lynn sand, potash, borax, whiting, niter, lead oxide, alum, gypsum, salt, and glass. The wharf was piled with barrels, and men with wheelbarrows took things in and out of a nearby storage shed. The kilns had been fired, and smoke drifted on the air as her uncle's workers—the oddly named turners, lathemen, throwers, squeezers, and saggermen—went about their business. There was a great air of industry, as if Nantgarth porcelain was selling like the proverbial hotcakes, but Ellie knew that there was only such activity when barges came and went; in between it was too quiet to tell of profit.

The tow horse whinnied again, and she heard hooves in the alley that led down beside the canal bridge. By straining a little she was able to see that it was Gwilym on one of the white Castle Griffin horses. People shouted greetings to him, and he grinned back as he slipped lightly from his mount. Hardly had his boots touched the cobbles than there was a cry of dismay from a worker who was just lifting some finished porcelain into the barge. The man's clogs slipped on the cobbles, and he began to lose his balance. Gwilym turned in a moment, and looked intently at the unfortunate man, who seemed to hover in midair, then, impossibly, regained his equilibrium. There were shouts of approval from the workers, who were all clearly accustomed to Gwilym's powers.

Ellie was shaken, for by all the laws of physics and gravity, the man and his load of porcelain should have fallen from the wharf into the barge, but somehow he had avoided calamity. Mrs. Lewis's strange son had used sheer willpower to prevent the accident. Fey was indeed the word to describe him.

She drew back from the knothole, and turned to the darkened cellar behind her. For the first time she noticed there were several doors into adjacent rooms, but nothing to indicate her uncle's whereabouts. "Uncle John?"

"Here, Ellie!"

His muffled voice emanated from the door to her right, so she opened it and went inside. To her relief, the small room inside was warmed by a fireplace, and was quite cozy after the chill and drafts of the stairs and outer cellar, but as she entered, her uncle almost leapt from his tall stool to seize her candle and extinguish it. "Never light candles during daylight, Ellie! Never! For it is very bad luck and an omen of death." There was a frightened note in his voice, an edge that told of total belief in what he was saying.

Shaken to hear words she herself had uttered during the reading of her tea leaves, Ellie stared at him. "Uncle?"

"Nikolai did that too, you see, and within a week—" John broke off, biting back the rest of what he'd almost said.

"Who is Nikolai, Uncle? And what happened within a week?" Ellie was a little frightened by the intensity of his emotion.

He took a deep breath to steady himself, then forced an apologetic smile. "No one, my dear, no one at all. Forgive me, I fear you caught me in a superstitious moment."

"I've never heard of it being unlucky to light candles during the day."

"No? Oh, it's the same as never walking under a ladder. You know the sort of thing."

Yes, she knew the sort of thing; she also knew that he had meant every word of his instinctive warning.

Placing the candlestick on one of the cluttered trestle tables that lined two walls, he wiped his hands thoroughly on a clean cloth, then kissed her on the cheek. "I trust you've slept and eaten well?"

"Yes to both."

He beamed, then waved an arm to encompass the little room. "Welcome to my lair."

Ellie looked around. Samples of soft-paste porcelain were everywhere, stacked on the floor, lining shelves, and even higgledy-piggledy in a wooden crate in a corner. One of the trestles was taken up with his painting and gilding equipment, the other with brushes, oils, cloths, dishes, knives, turntables, and sundry other things necessary for his specialized work. This included metal oxides for all hues, copper to give green, cobalt for blue, manganese for purple, and antimony for yellow.

Her gaze rested on the item her uncle had been working on before she interrupted him. It was a glazed but as yet undecorated soup tureen, twelve inches high, wide, and deep, of the same size and shape she had seen on the unknown mantel when Mrs. Lewis turned the tea leaves. To one side of it, also awaiting painting, lay an elaborate stand, and a high-domed cover with a pinecone knob. She noticed two more tureens set on another trestle, both in the same untouched state, the delicate waxy hue of soft-paste porcelain so fine and fragile that it was only a few steps away from glass. But she had not long since seen one of these beautiful things in its finished state.

Somehow she managed to hide her shock. "Good heavens, Uncle, how many gallons of soup do such tureens hold?"

"Enough to fill Cardiff Bay," he replied dryly, then answered more seriously. "Actually, it's two gallons. Look kindly upon these elegant receptacles, my dear, for my hopes for the future rest upon one of them. I know not yet which," he said quietly.

"Really?"

He went to the table, sorted through a pile of papers, then drew one out. "This arrived just before Christmas. Read it." He thrust it into her hand. "It's from a Prince Valentin Andreyov in St. Petersburg."

"Who is he?"

"I have no idea, except that he appears to be aide-de-camp to Czar Alexander, but I do know his communication pleases me immensely. It's in French, but I'm sure you will have no trouble with that. Read on, read on." John waved a hand at her.

She began to read, then looked quickly at her uncle. "A commemorative tureen for the czar?"

"Yes, my dear, an order for royalty, to be given to the czar early in July, on the Russian day for celebrating the feast of Saints Peter and Paul. We celebrate it on June twenty-ninth. Be that as it may, I have to have a fully completed tureen ready to leave here some time in May, to allow for the voyage to Russia. Have you any idea how important such orders as this are to china manufacturers? Just think how Wedgwood benefited from Catherine the Great's commission for a huge dinner service. They have not looked back since. Whichever of these tureens is eventually selected for decoration, it could be as beneficial as that to Nantgarth. And furthermore, somewhere in Prince Valentin's letter he states that I am to bring the tureen to

St. Petersburg myself, so that the czar can meet me." He paused then, as if in this he perceived a hidden drawback.

"Uncle?"

"Well, I vowed never to go there again."

"Again? So you've been there before?"

"Yes, my dear, I've been there, and it is a place that holds only sad memories, I fear."

Ellie wanted to ask more, but something in his demeanor prevented her.

"Anyway," he went on briskly, "this order from the czar is what I meant yesterday about you seeing the Russian capital, for if I go there, then you, my dear, will most certainly have to come with me."

"Really?" Ellie's eyes shone and her lips parted in a delighted smile. "But how on earth has the czar heard about this little china works?"

For a second she again thought she saw something odd in her uncle's eyes; then his smile returned. "I believe I have Lord Griffin to thank."

She was happy for him. "Oh, I'm so pleased to hear this, Uncle."

"I am too, believe me. And I'm relieved that I have actually managed to produce three perfect tureens. I made twenty-five before I succeeded."

"Twenty-five?" Her eyes widened.

He drew a heavy breath. "They all failed, turning almost to glass, crumbling, distorting, shivering. Oh, anything that could go wrong *did* go wrong. But here are three bites at the cherry, eh?"

"How are they to be decorated?"

He shrugged. "Well, believe it or not, that is being left up to me. The only stipulation is that it must be lavish with gold."

"As befits the emperor of Russia," she said with a smile. "Do you have a particular design in mind?"

"Flowers, I think, for that is what I do best. Prince Valentin intends to visit here when he comes to Britain in a few weeks' time, and he will choose which tureen will go to St. Petersburg."

"Nantgarth is to be graced by a Russian prince? How very grand we will be."

"Indeed." He drew a rather trembling breath. "So much

hangs upon this, Ellie. When I have finished the decoration and gilding, there will be no other pieces to compare with their rare beauty. The czar's soup will be served from a veritable Holy Grail!"

She smiled. "If anyone can do it, Uncle, you can. No one has a more delicate brush, or more artistic ability."

"And no one else has my secret formula." He winked and tapped the side of his nose, but then became serious again. "Would that this new connection with St. Petersburg could put the past entirely to rights, but that can never be."

"I don't understand, Uncle."

"Nor is there any reason why you should, my dear. Take no notice of my ramblings."

She wasn't entirely reassured. "Is there something it's better I should know about, Uncle?"

"Nothing at all, my dear, nothing at all. Oh, don't look so worried, and just be thankful, as I am, for the stroke of unutterable good fortune that crossed my snowy path with Lord Griffin's on the Pennines. If it were not for his generosity in setting me up here, his tolerance concerning the ground rents, and his undoubted hand at work on my behalf in Russia, I would not be in this hopeful position now. I owe him a great deal."

Ellie was reluctant to accept the change of subject, but had no real option, for it was clear her uncle had no intention of elaborating on anything else about his past in St. Petersburg. "What is Lord Griffin like?"

"You ask that in a way that suggests some preconceived opinions."

She colored a little. "Well, I do rather have a picture of him in mind."

"And what picture might that be?"

She told him, and he roared with laughter. "My dearest Ellie, you could not be more wrong. A widower he may indeed be, and rightly keen on the Griffin stud, but certainly not to the point of stinking of horses and wearing his boots in bed! He is young, fashionable, exceedingly good-looking, charming, and amusing, and I have the honor to be able to address him by his first name, Athan."

Nine

Ellie's heart lurched. "His name is Athan?" she repeated faintly.

"Indeed so," her uncle confirmed.

"It's such an unusual name. . . ." She felt quite numb with shock that fate could be so arbitrary as to bring her here. It was just too cruel after everything else that had befallen her.

"Well, the name is not common, I grant you, but I've come across it twice since being here. It seems there was a Celtic saint called Athan, and he has a village named after him."

She wanted to be reassured, but had to probe further. "Does . . . does Lord Griffin have dark hair and gray eyes?" She described in detail the man she had encountered on those three memorable occasions in London, to say nothing of an even more memorable—if completely fantastical—occasion that morning!

"Well, it certainly sounds like him," John replied, and looked curiously at her. "Am I to understand that you and he are acquainted, Ellie?"

"I . . . I may have met him," she said lamely. Then she thought of something that to her mind would confirm it beyond doubt. "Is Lord Griffin a director of the Unicorn Bank?"

John was a little offended. "My dear, if he were I would have told you before now, and I would certainly have promised to approach him about it the moment he returned from St. Petersburg."

"Forgive me, I . . . I didn't mean to . . ." She was too relieved to finish.

"As it happens, Lord Griffin and I have often discussed business matters, and he has mentioned his various connections. The name of the Unicorn Bank definitely did not come up." John observed the expressions crossing her face, then frowned a little. "Have I understood properly, Ellie? You *may* have met Lord Griffin, but did not realize it until I informed you of his first name? How might that be?"

Please don't let her cheeks be as on fire as they felt right now! She had to think of a convincing explanation. "You jump to conclusions, Uncle," she said brightly. "There was a gentleman of that name in a party that called at Rutherford Park two years ago. I noticed the name because it was so unusual, and because of that I also noticed that he came from Wales and was a director of the bank. That's all." May God forgive her such glib untruths. She smiled again. "So . . . you like Lord Griffin a great deal?"

She must have sounded dismissive enough, for he didn't question her further. "Most definitely I like him, and I sincerely hope that his forthcoming marriage to Miss Tudor will prove to be infinitely more happy than his first."

"Oh?" Her unease began to return as she recalled Athan's conversation with Freddie Forrester-Phipps at the bank, including the references to Athan's so-called ward. Miss Tudor and her mother resided at Castle Griffin, so might that mean that Miss Tudor could be referred to as Athan's ward? It was a freshly discomforting possibility.

"Lord Griffin met his first wife, Caroline, in Naples, I believe, and loved her dearly, but she deserted him within months of the marriage in order to run off with a lover. At least, that is my understanding from Lord Griffin himself. Certainly his bride never came to Castle Griffin. But I'm sure Miss Tudor—her first name is Fleur, by the way—will make up for all that sorrow."

"So you do not share Mrs. Lewis's poor opinion of her?"

He leaned against the table, folded his arms, and smiled. "Well, I fear Mrs. Lewis has only herself to blame for falling foul of the Tudors, because she took a dislike to them and allowed them to know. Had she dissembled more, and Gwilym too for that matter, she would still be up at the castle, and he would be having an easier time of it during Lord Griffin's absence. The Tudors are as good as Lord

Griffin's family now, and one cannot blame them if they are not prepared to put up with surly servants."

Ellie raised her eyebrows. "Surly? Mrs. Lewis and Gwilym? Oh, surely not. . . ."

"However you describe it, the fact remains that Miss Tudor and her mother were displeased, and as there haven't been upsets with any other servants at the castle, I can only assume that Mrs. Lewis and her boy were indeed guilty of letting unwelcome feelings show. However, Gwilym's position at the castle is assured, for there isn't anyone else in the whole of Glamorgan who has such a fine touch with horses. As for Mrs. Lewis, well, I am more than happy to have her here. Lord Griffin didn't want to lose her, but he had to back Miss Tudor. It was a very unfortunate business all around."

"Who are the Tudors, exactly?"

"The widow and only child of his lordship's old friend and commanding officer, General Tudor of Ty Newydd, Bridgend. The general, a wealthy man, was not only Lord Griffin's mentor, but once saved his life at considerable risk to his own, so as you can imagine, his lordship felt the death most keenly. Mrs. Tudor feared her daughter would be pursued by the unwelcome sort of fortune hunter, so she asked Lord Griffin for his protection. He felt it was his duty to take care of both ladies, and they have been at the castle ever since."

"Does that mean that Miss Tudor is actually his ward?" Ellie ventured.

"Not in the legal sense of the word. He has simply behaved most honorably, and his kindness has been rewarded by the discovery of new love. Or so it is romantic to think." John pursed his lips thoughtfully. "I only hope the two ladies are being honorable too," he murmured.

Ellie was puzzled by the remark. "Why do you say that?"

"Oh, something and nothing. Apparently there are one or two whispers circulating Cardiff drawing rooms about Miss Tudor's conduct in London during last Season. Lord Griffin had to return to the castle because there was so much needing his attention, and while the Griffin cat was away . . ."

". . . the Tudor mouse played?"

"Maybe. It's suggested, erroneously, I hope, that Miss Tudor spent time in the company of unsuitable gentlemen."

If it were true, Ellie thought uneasily, one of those gentlemen might well have been Freddie Forrester-Phipps, who certainly seemed all that was lecherously unsuitable. It began to seem that her Athan might be Lord Griffin after all. Maybe her uncle simply did not know that his lordship was a director of the bank.

Her uncle spoke again. "But I must emphasize that there is no proof about Miss Tudor's misconduct, just a lot of speculation. I hope it's wrong, truly I do, for I'd hate to think the second Lady Griffin was going to be as unworthy as the first."

"What is Miss Tudor like?" Ellie asked.

"A very striking redhead. I suppose it would not be amiss to say she is beautiful. I've heard her described as a fiery piece, if you'll forgive the expression, but my experience is that she is quiet and charming. Anyway, you'll be able to judge her for yourself, for I do not doubt we will soon be invited to the castle. It will not have escaped Lord Griffin's attention that you will be an ideal acquaintance for Miss Tudor."

An ideal acquaintance? That was open to discussion, Ellie thought unhappily, because if her fears were well founded, the moment Athan, Lord Griffin, saw John Bailey's niece, his most likely reaction would be to keep her away from Miss Fleur Tudor at all costs!

At that moment there were sounds from the stone steps from the kitchen; then came Mrs. Lewis's rather urgent voice. "Mr. Bailey? Miss Ellie? Miss Tudor has called."

Ellie and her uncle glanced at each other; then he answered the housekeeper. "We'll come directly, Mrs. Lewis. I trust you've shown our visitor into the parlor?"

"Oh, yes, sir. Not that it's good enough for Miss High-and-Mighty."

"That's enough, Mrs. Lewis, for whatever your quarrel with the ladies at the castle, I will not have it spill over here."

"No, sir. Of course not, sir."

The housekeeper's steps retreated to the kitchen again, and Ellie's uncle reached for his coat from the hook behind the door.

"Does she call here often?" Ellie asked, smoothing suddenly trembling hands on her skirts. She wasn't prepared for a meeting with Athan's bride-to-be, but then she doubted if she ever would be.

"She's never called here before," he replied, ushering her through the door, then locking it and putting the key in his pocket.

Soon they were up in the kitchen again, where Ellie saw that Gwilym was now visiting his mother, who had given him a still-warm slice of the traditional Welsh currant bread called *bara brith*. Needless to say, the clock on the mantel was now ticking merrily. The youth scrambled to his feet as the two emerged from the cellar.

"Good morning, Mr. Bailey, Miss Rutherford."

"Good morning, Gwilym," Ellie's uncle replied.

Ellie smiled, then turned unhappily to her uncle. "I cannot possibly meet Miss Tudor in this old green dress. I'll have to change."

"Hurry then, for it doesn't do to keep visitors waiting," he replied.

Ellie fled into the passage and then upstairs, pausing at the top as she heard her uncle enter the parlor below. "Why, Miss Tudor, what an honor this is," he declared, then the door closed behind him.

Ellie hastily took a cream woolen gown from the wardrobe. She had only hung it there that morning, and it was still a little creased, but it was good quality and decoratively woven, and she felt it would enable her to better confront Fleur Tudor.

Putting her blue-and-gray cashmere shawl over her arms, she went nervously downstairs again. The longcase clock in the hall ticked slowly, and the murmur of voices from the parlor was interjected now and then by a tinkle of feminine laughter, suggesting the visit was going well. Ellie took a deep breath before entering the room.

Fleur was seated looking away from the door, and all Ellie saw at first was a graceful, narrow-backed young woman in a bright red velvet riding habit that was surely the very last word in modishness. Her profile was beautiful, and her eyes strikingly large; she had a slightly retroussé nose, and an alabaster complexion unmarred by freckles. A single heavy ringlet of rich auburn hair had been permitted to fall past the nape of her neck, the rest of her curls being tucked beneath a black beaver top hat.

She was exquisite, poised, beautiful, and clearly everything a man could desire in a wife, but there was something about the tilt of her head and her pretty laughter that seemed as studied as if she had practiced in front of a mirror. It was a first impression that placed Ellie very firmly on Mrs. Lewis's side of the discussion about the ladies at the castle. The future Lady Griffin was not what she seemed on the surface, and Ellie was reminded of an old verse:

> *I do not love thee, Dr. Fell,*
> *The reason why I cannot tell;*
> *But this I know, and know full well,*
> *I do not love thee, Dr. Fell.*

John rose immediately when his niece entered. "Ellie, my dear, do come in and allow me to introduce Miss Tudor."

Fleur gazed at Ellie with eyes as green as emeralds, and her radiant smile became fixed, as if she had been confronted by a horned devil. The reaction was so reminiscent of Mrs. Lewis's the night before that it seemed Fleur must also have been acquainted with the housekeeper's late lamented cousin.

Ellie's uncle did not notice anything untoward. "Miss Tudor, may I present my niece, Miss Rutherford? Ellie, this is Miss Tudor."

Ellie inclined her head. "Miss Tudor," she murmured, giving the polite bobbed curtsy convention demanded.

Fleur stared at her. "Miss Rutherford," she said then, and returned the nod.

Now even John noticed the atmosphere, and cleared his throat. "Er, do sit down, Ellie," he prompted.

She smiled and obeyed, all the time wondering what on earth there had been about Mrs. Lewis's cousin that produced such a response to someone who resembled her? Given the strange talents of the housekeeper and her son, maybe the cousin had been a witch! Perhaps she had flown around the mountains on a broomstick every full moon. Or dried up the canal, or. . . . She remembered meeting Athan in the garden at the Crown Inn. He too had mistaken her for someone in what might have been a rather shocking portrait. Surely Mrs. Lewis's late cousin couldn't have afforded an artist as fashionable and expensive as Thomas Lawrence?

Fleur drew herself together. "Forgive me if I stare, Miss Rutherford, it's just . . ."

". . . that I remind you of someone?"

"Yes." Fleur gave an awkward little laugh. "But I suppose you know already." The green eyes were sharp and penetrating, like those of a hawk.

"Know? Well, I understand I am the very image of Mrs. Lewis's late cousin," Ellie explained. "That's Mrs. Lewis, the housekeeper here," she added a little awkwardly.

"I know to which Mrs. Lewis you refer, Miss Rutherford," Fleur replied, her manner changing yet again, relaxing slightly, as if Ellie's answer had removed some anxiety.

Ellie's uncle was puzzled. "Just who was this cousin of Mrs. Lewis's?" he asked Fleur. "I was under the impression that Mrs. Lewis had no family at all, except Gwilym."

But Fleur ignored the question and spoke of something else. "Do you expect to be in Nantgarth long, Miss Rutherford?" The tone of the question suggested strongly that a negative response was hoped for.

Ellie felt awkward. "This is now my home, Miss Tudor."

"Indeed? That *is* good news."

Clearly it was very bad news indeed, Ellie thought, beginning to read the other woman like a printed page. Fleur had come here today to play the gracious lady of the castle, to bestow favor upon the china maker's niece, and perhaps take her in hand during the coming summer. Such thoughts had flown up the chimney as soon as Ellie entered the room. Ellie did not know whether to be pleased or not, for although she did not care for Fleur, it wasn't very pleasant to keep finding that one's face had such an effect upon people.

"I trust Mrs. Tudor is keeping well?" Ellie's uncle said courteously.

"My mother is very well indeed, sir."

Ellie's uncle cleared his throat. "Is there any news of

when Lord Griffin will return from St. Petersburg?" he inquired, and glanced fleetingly at the portrait of the young man above the mantel.

"We have not heard from him in some time, Mr. Bailey," Fleur replied. "I fear the need for recuperation after the grippe will keep him in Russia for some time yet."

"Let us hope not."

"Indeed so."

The clock on the mantel suddenly ceased to tick, causing a noticeable silence because there happened to be a lull in the conversation at the same time. *Gwilym Lewis must have left the house,* Ellie thought.

Fleur rose to her feet suddenly. "I really must go now, for it won't do for my mount to become too cool."

Ellie's uncle got up hastily. "It was most thoughtful of you to call, Miss Tudor."

"Not at all, Mr. Bailey, for it is my duty."

Ellie looked at her. Duty? The creature wasn't Lady Griffin yet, merely a guest at the castle, so it wasn't incumbent upon *her* to bestow social largesse upon the latest addition to the peasant population. But as Ellie got up from her chair, her smile was as false as Fleur's. "You are too kind, Miss Tudor."

Fleur inclined her head graciously. "It was nothing, believe me, for I was passing by on my way up to the mountain. I like to ride up there. Perhaps you would walk me to my horse, Miss Rutherford?"

"Yes, of course." Surprised at the request, Ellie conducted the visitor out into the hallway, where Mrs. Lewis, stiff, eyes coldly averted, handed Fleur her gloves and riding crop.

Ellie drew her shawl more tightly around her shoulders as they stepped out into the January sunshine, which shone brightly on the berries of the holly bush over the wall. The only flowers in the garden were snowdrops and the white and pinkish blooms of the Christmas rose. The smell of kiln smoke drifted now and then as the breeze played around the eaves of the house, and she could hear the voices of the china workers and the canal boatmen.

Ellie felt as if Castle Griffin were watching them from above the trees on the mountain opposite. The sun seemed to catch on the arched windows of the towers, making them

DIAMOND DREAMS

seem like prying eyes, intent upon seeing all there was to see at Nantgarth House. Fleur was conscious of the castle too, for Ellie noticed her green eyes flicker toward it, then saw how her lips pursed slightly and how her expression became one of . . . anticipation? Yes, that seemed to be it.

One of the men from the works was looking after Fleur's mount, a superb white mare that was clearly from Lord Griffin's stud. As Fleur went through the gate, she took the reins and waved the man away. He lingered, hoping for a coin for his trouble, but she ignored him, and after a moment he walked off, his expression dark. Ellie happened to be looking at him when suddenly his face changed into a broad grin. He was looking toward the evergreen-shaded alley that led down to the works and canal. She followed his gaze to see Gwilym lurking by one of the buildings. *Lurking* was the only word to use, for the housekeeper's son was clearly trying to keep out of Fleur's sight.

Ellie's attention was torn away when Fleur suddenly spoke coldly to her. "Stay away from Castle Griffin, Miss Rutherford."

Ellie was too startled to respond.

"Stay well away, for believe me, I will make your life impossible if you dare to defy me in this."

Ten

Ellie struggled to recover from the almost hissed warning. Guilt tied her tongue, it being impossible not to conclude that her Athan and Lord Griffin were the same man after all, and that somehow Fleur was aware of the meetings in London. But how? It was impossible. The only other person who knew was Athan himself, and he wasn't yet aware that Ellie Rutherford was here in Nantgarth House. Was he? Could he have discovered where she was, and confessed all to Fleur? But no, why on earth would he do that?

Fleur regarded her coldly. "My, my, how very flustered you are, to be sure," she said softly. "It is plain you are plagued with conscience, my dear."

Ellie really didn't know how to handle the situation and was on the point of confessing everything when common sense gave her a stern prod. Confess when she might be misreading this entire conversation? Better to make sure of the facts first. "Miss Tudor, will you at least do me the courtesy of telling me *why* you wish me to stay away from the castle?"

"You know perfectly well."

"On the contrary, I—"

"Don't play the innocent!" Fleur snapped. "I know an adventuress when I see one, and you, Miss Rutherford, have it written all over you. Who are you? Her sister? Her cousin?"

Mrs. Lewis's relative was becoming a liability, Ellie thought, irritation mixing with the guilt. "I really do not know what you are talking about, Miss Tudor, unless it be Mrs. Lewis's cousin, of whom I know nothing whatsoever beyond the fact that she is deceased and apparently resembled me."

"Don't try to gull me, for we both know the truth. Well, I'm not about to play into your hands. Lord Griffin is mine, my dear, and the sooner you accept that, the better."

The awful creature *must* know about the meetings in London, Ellie decided in dismay, but confession was now the very last thing on her mind. "Miss Tudor, I do not know that I have ever *met* Lord Griffin, let alone decided to take him from you." The words were ambiguous, and not entirely untrue; after all, without seeing Lord Griffin for herself, she couldn't be absolutely certain he was the Athan she knew.

"Oh, you're clever, I'll grant you that, but in me you've met your match. So stay away from the castle, and stay away from him. Be warned, if I hear so much as a whisper about you, I'll make certain that your uncle is turned out of this place. Believe me, I have the influence to carry out my threat, because Lord Griffin will do anything to please me."

Ellie found the future Lady Griffin quite repellent. "Would he be pleased to know you are capable of such obnoxious behavior as this?"

"Take me on at your peril, Miss Rutherford, for I'm not a prissy little miss who fears saying boo to a goose."

Ellie met her gaze without flinching. "No, I realize that, for gossip has you as many things, Miss Tudor, but certainly not a prissy little miss."

"What is that supposed to mean?"

"Tongues are wagging about how much you enjoyed your London Season."

Fleur gazed at her. "You shouldn't pay attention to idle gossip, Miss Rutherford, because invariably it's wrong."

"But not always."

Fleur turned away, stepped onto the mounting block beside the gate, and got on the horse with sufficient grace for Rotten Row. Then she gathered the reins, and looked down at Ellie. "Leave Nantgarth House as quickly as you can, because if you're still here when Lord Griffin returns, I will see to it that not only is your dear uncle turned out on his well-bred ear, but that his debts are called in as well. So think carefully, and put him before your little schemes."

Ellie gave no outward sign of the dismay she felt inside. She dared not take such a threat lightly, especially not when her uncle was already in fear of duns from his past. The last thing he could contemplate was more such trouble because of his niece, so Fleur Tudor's warning would have to be heeded. Ellie Rutherford would have to turn her back on her new home, and somehow make her own way in life after all.

But sad resignation to her fate was suddenly wiped from Ellie's thoughts by a few seconds of pure farce, all at Fleur's expense. From the corner of the nearby alley, Gwilym Lewis decided to don his horse charmer's hat and have a little fun with the woman who'd been responsible for his mother's dismissal, and who was making his own life difficult too. Ellie was aware of the youth standing with his hands in his pockets, eyes closed, lips pursed as if whistling, except that not a sound seemed to come out—at least, not a sound that a human could hear. Fleur's mount, however, certainly seemed aware of something, for it tossed its head and capered around, refusing to come to command. Fleur's face rapidly went the color of her riding habit as the horse danced around as if in time to music. Around went Fleur as well, for all the world like a performer at Astley's Amphitheatre.

Ellie enjoyed her foe's predicament, but Gwilym dared not go too far, so stopped what he was doing and slipped back down the alley. The horse immediately came to order, but Fleur looked anything but composed. Her face remained the same hot hue as her riding habit, her hat had been slightly dislodged, and the coils of her long ringlet were no longer as shiningly even as they had been. She knew she looked a fool, but not that she had been made a fool of, as with a rather ungainly kick of her heels she urged the horse away up the lane toward the fork. Ellie watched as she took the track to the left and began the long climb up the mountainside toward the squat-towered parish church, now clearly visible in the morning sunshine.

Turning, Ellie retraced her steps toward the house, and as she entered she heard Mrs. Lewis working in the kitchens. Ellie went toward the sound and saw the housekeeper kneading dough, banging it so heartily upon the floured table that it was Ellie's informed guess it represented the head of Miss Fleur Tudor. "May I ask you something, Mrs. Lewis?" she asked from the doorway.

Mrs. Lewis stopped kneading and wiped her hand slowly on a damp cloth. "Yes, of course, Miss Ellie."

"Who, exactly, was your late cousin?"

"Why do you ask, Miss Ellie?"

"Because Miss Tudor took one look at me a few minutes ago and behaved exactly as you did last night. It is quite obvious that I am the living image of your cousin, and—"

"Not of my cousin, Miss Ellie," the housekeeper interrupted quietly. "I don't have a cousin. It was just something I felt I ought to say. On the spur of the moment, you understand." She moved to the window, and made much of removing some dead flowers from the white geraniums; then she turned, her tongue passing uneasily over her lips. "Miss Ellie, the person you resemble so greatly is the late Lady Griffin."

Ellie stared.

"Yes. Her name was Caroline, and it is only from a portrait up at the castle that anyone knows her. It might almost be you gazing from that canvas."

And that was the only likeness Lawrence painted of you? Athan seemed to speak in Ellie's ear, and she knew there could no longer be any doubt at all. Connection with the Unicorn Bank or not, her Athan and Lord Griffin were definitely the same man.

Mrs. Lewis looked anxiously at her. "Please sit down, Miss Ellie. I will make a cup of tea and tell you all I can."

Ellie obeyed, and the housekeeper set about placing a kettle on the hook over the fire. "The portrait is, well, a little shocking."

"Shocking?"

Mrs. Lewis cleared her throat in embarrassment. "She seems to be wearing little more than a carefully draped shawl."

"I see." Portrait of a lady? Or an actress? Ellie's thoughts were still in the garden of the Crown Inn, Hounslow.

The housekeeper put tea into a teapot, then brought blue-and-white cups and saucers. "Before his sudden marriage, Lord Griffin had been shamelessly pursued by every single lady in Glamorgan, and half the ladies of London too. Then, just when he found happiness, his new bride left him and never returned. It was very sad. He bore it well, but I often saw him gazing at her portrait with such a look of longing in his eyes that I know he loved her very much." Mrs. Lewis sighed and shook her head sadly. "I know it is not my place to speak of such things, Miss Ellie, but it is the truth."

"And now he loves Miss Tudor instead?"

"Maybe. All I know is that he discouraged her advances for a long time and refused to countenance ending his first marriage in order to take another wife. Then, quite suddenly, there came news that he was a widower, and he promptly proposed to Miss Tudor. Until then it had not seemed he would have considered such a match even had he never married. I still cannot believe he loves Miss Tudor, but feel certain he has decided he must marry again in order to secure an heir to his title and estates. Begging your pardon, Miss Ellie, for now I really am speaking out of turn."

"Mrs. Lewis, when you worked at the castle, did you ever hear anything about Lord Griffin being connected with the Unicorn Bank in London?"

"No, I didn't, Miss Ellie."

"You're quite sure?"

"I'm positive, Miss Ellie." The kettle was boiling, so the housekeeper got up to pour water into the waiting teapot.

Ellie was puzzled. She was now convinced that her Athan was also Lord Griffin, yet there seemed to be a mystery where the bank was concerned. Unless, of course, such a connection were really quite recent, so recent that it must have taken place not long before he set out for St. Petersburg—perhaps even the day she met him. Was *that* why he'd been there?

Mrs. Lewis joined her at the table and spoke again of Fleur. "Now that you've come here, looking so like the lady in the portrait, Miss Tudor probably views you as a great threat. After all, if he loved his first wife as I think he did, then he might think he has found her again in you."

Ellie could almost feel the early-autumn sunshine in the Crown Inn's garden. Yes, he *had* thought he'd found his wife again . . . or at least, that he'd found her sister or cousin. Certainly someone who seemed to be Caroline's living image. If that was what had prompted him to kiss her as he did, then Fleur was wise to be afraid of such a rival.

Mrs. Lewis poured the tea, then looked at her. "I will be honest, Miss Ellie. Gwilym and I hope and pray that you *do* become her rival. There is nothing we would like more than to see you supplant her at the castle."

Ellie blushed. "You oughtn't to say such things, Mrs. Lewis."

"I know, but I also know what a shock he will have when first he sees you." Ellie looked away, for that moment had already happened, and yes, he'd certainly had a shock. And given what had ensued by secluded duck pond, so had she! Still, it was all in the past now, and a further encounter with Athan could not be permitted. "Mrs. Lewis, I share your dislike of Miss Tudor, who does indeed think my looks will interfere with her plans. So much does she fear it that unless I leave Nantgarth House, she intends to have my uncle ejected. There is even a suggestion of prompting Lord Griffin to call in outstanding debts, and you and I both know how parlous my uncle's finances are."

The housekeeper's nostrils flared with fury. "Oh, the iniquitous creature, the diabolical vixen!"

"Quite so, but I dare not ignore her. I will have to seek a position somewhere well away from the castle, so if you should happen to hear of anything. . . ."

Mrs. Lewis leaned across the table to put a gentle hand over hers. "You are safe here, Miss Ellie, and so is Mr. Bailey. Lord Griffin may be intending to marry her, but he will not listen to her on such a matter. When he shakes hands on an arrangement with another gentleman, his word is binding. So defy her, my dear, stay on as you intended, and refuse to be driven from Nantgarth."

"But—"

"I'm right about this, Miss Ellie. Lord Griffin is nothing if not a man of complete honor." Mrs. Lewis placed a cup of tea in front of Ellie.

A man of complete honor who also happened to be associated with the thoroughly disreputable and villainous Unicorn Bank, Ellie thought unhappily, but as she had nowhere else to go at the moment, she would *have* to stay. No doubt, word of Lord Griffin's return would precede him, in which case she would have to do something more positive. In the meantime she would keep her eyes and ears open for any likely situation that presented itself.

Eleven

At Castle Griffin that evening, when all was quiet and the servants no longer in evidence, Fleur took a lighted silver-gilt candelabrum from the stone mantel in the oak-paneled drawing room, which had once been the Norman castle solar. Then she instructed her mother to accompany her to Athan's private apartments.

Mrs. Tudor looked up from her letter writing. "Go to his private rooms? Are you mad?" she gasped, putting her pen down. She was plump, and inclined to rouge her cheeks, which made her look hot as well as overweight, but it was still clear that she had once been very beautiful. Her hair, now pepper-and-salt and thus fully powdered to make it white, had been a rich golden color, and her hazel eyes were still large and eloquent. She was wearing pearls and an indigo satin dinner gown, for she and her daughter would not have dreamed of being less than formal in the evenings. "Fleur, you have been in a very odd mood since you returned from your ride today. What on earth is the matter?"

"I am about to show you, Mama," Fleur replied, sweeping toward the arched doorway in a rustle of peach taffeta. "Come on, for I wish you to see something."

With a sigh her mother rose from the writing desk. "If we're discovered prying into Lord Griffin's private apartments . . ." she began.

"We won't be. At this time the servants are too busy dining in style in the kitchens," Fleur observed dryly, leading the way along the wainscotted passage into the great Norman hall. "Besides, they wouldn't dare to tell tales about us, not when I am so certain to be the next Lady Griffin."

Fleur shielded the candles with her hand, and their satin slippers were silent in the vast hall, where the hammerbeam roof was still blackened by the smoke of long-gone central fires. Two huge chimneypieces at either end provided present-day warmth, and the fires had been banked for the night so they only glowed very faintly. There were no other lights, and the only sounds were caused by the wind moaning around the turrets and battlements.

"Do not count chickens before they are hatched, Fleur," warned Mrs. Tudor. "I know only too well how easy it is to imagine a deed is as good as done."

"Just because things went wrong for you, it doesn't follow that I will be equally as foolish," Fleur responded, gathering her skirts to ascend the ancient oak staircase that rose from the far end of the great hall.

"You're quite mad if you think you can already do as you please," her mother observed. "In fact, you'll be mad if you do as you please even *after* you're wed, for he isn't the sort of man who—"

"Don't presume to offer me advice, Mama!" Fleur halted and whirled about on the stairs, making the candles smoke and gutter, and setting shadows leaping all around.

Mrs. Tudor recoiled a little, but wasn't cowed. "But you *need* advice, Fleur! I still cannot believe you behaved as you did in London last summer. You didn't only encourage one man, but two, and without any thought at all for your reputation."

"That isn't true, Mama. Well, I admit there were two gentlemen, but it's wrong to say I was indiscreet. On the contrary, I was the soul of discretion, and no one knows about it, no one at all."

"There are whispers in Cardiff, as you know full well, and if Lord Griffin hears them. . . ."

"May I remind you that last summer he was still well and truly married to his first wife? I was obliged to look where I could for a prospective husband, and that was what I was doing. How was I to know he would suddenly be free?" Fleur's hand shook with anger, and some droplets of hot wax splashed from the candelabrum.

"If men marry whores, my dear, those whores must have

money," her mother responded. "Silly flibbertigibbets who only pretend they are great heiresses are used and discarded." She looked at Fleur. "You pretended to have a fortune, didn't you? Oh, don't try to deny it, for I know you too well, my girl. General Tudor left us both in penury, and it's Lord Griffin who really supplies the allowances that supposedly come from the general's estate."

Fleur's cheeks were scarlet. "It's not solely my fault that we live a lie here amid Athan's conscience and loyalty."

"Shh!" Mrs. Tudor looked around in alarm. "Guard your tongue, Fleur, for such things shouldn't even be *thought*, let alone said aloud!"

"Well, it's the truth," Fleur answered, but dropped her voice to a much more discreet level. "No matter what Athan and everyone else around here think to the contrary, you were never married to the general, and I certainly am not his daughter! Why, my name isn't even Fleur!"

"All of which makes your wanton behavior in London even more impossible to understand! We have much to hide, Fleur, all of it now guaranteed to destroy your chance of becoming Lady Griffin."

"But nothing will be discovered, Mama." Fleur gave the glimmer of a smile.

"I pray you're right," her mother breathed with infinite feeling.

"And before you think of another sermon, let me remind you again that *you* were the one who went sobbing to Athan, claiming to be the general's widow and begging to be taken care of. Apart from all that, even you must admit that I'd have been an idiot to discourage a Russian prince."

"My instinct was to avoid him at all costs," her mother replied. She'd thought there was something sly and unpleasant about Prince Paul Dalmatsky. He'd been too knowingly tactile, too steeped in vice, too filled with guile. He was like a sated cat, prepared to wait for as long as necessary in order to catch a particular mouse.

Fleur privately agreed. She'd been attracted to the prince by word of his amazing wealth, his palace in St. Petersburg, and his estates across Russia, but it hadn't passed her notice that his glance, wandering and lascivious, had more frequently followed the nearest handsome young man rather than the female of the species. Still, handsome young men could not give him heirs; for that he needed a princess, and for a time she had commended herself for the role, but he had seemed to find her only interesting to talk to, nothing more.

"Which cannot be said to apply to the other gentleman with whom you were far too forthcoming in London," Mrs. Tudor declared.

"I will not have you speak ill of him."

"I thought you had more sense than to fall prey to such an obvious fortune hunter."

Fleur's chin rose haughtily. "Well, that is where you are wrong about him, Mama dear, for he has money of his own."

"If you believe that, then you will believe anything," Mrs. Tudor replied.

"Just as you believed the general when he said he'd marry you?" Fleur retorted.

"He *would* have married me had he not fallen suddenly so ill."

"No, he wouldn't, for he was a sly old dog who knew that you'd continue to warm his bed if you thought he'd make an honest woman of you. And he made sure of your diligence in that respect by pretending he still had all his wealth. So he was a sly *impoverished* old dog!"

Mrs. Tudor looked away. "I know what you say is true, Fleur, but hope that my shining example will serve to show you what a gem you have in Lord Griffin."

"A gem? Yes, that's true, but he doesn't shine. I'm excited by risks, and stolen kisses are so much more rewarding than those that are allowed. I ceased to be innocent a number of years ago now, and my lovers have been many and varied. I *need* lovers, and I always will."

Mrs. Tudor was shocked. "I knew you were wanton, Fleur, but not that you were quite so promiscuous."

"I thrive on carnal pleasure, Mama dear, just as you once did. I may not be the general's daughter, but I'm certainly yours."

"I was never as abandoned as you."

"Only because opportunity didn't pass your way."

Her mother shook her head. "No, even if it had, I would have been too cautious to do as you do. Such wild irresponsibility is dangerous, Fleur, and invites calamity. Please promise to give it all up, and be the woman Lord Griffin believes you to be."

"He will continue to believe in me, Mama, for I am too clever to be found out. Besides, it is not as if he and I are in love, or that we will ever be passionate in bed. He is still in his dead wife's thrall, and I find him handsome but dull. Say what you will of Freddie; at least he knows how to pleasure me. Oh, how he knows." Fleur's green eyes shone, and there was a glow on her cheeks as she remembered.

"Presumably Freddie is the name of the wretched fortune hunter?" her mother ventured.

"He isn't the fortune hunter, Mama dear, *I* am," Fleur pointed out.

Mrs. Tudor shook her head. "Believe me, my dear, bitter experience tells me that he is penniless. I learned a very harsh lesson with the general, and am far wiser now. Your precious Freddie is interested in you simply and solely because you've led him to believe you are an heiress. Take that away, and you won't see hide or hair of him again."

Fleur shrugged. "Maybe, but in the meantime . . ."

Her mother seized her arm. "Promise that your foolishness with him began and ended in London, and that you have been the very soul of chastity since returning here."

Fleur gave a slight laugh. "If it makes you feel better, I promise I've been all that is virginal."

"Which means you haven't! Oh, Fleur, Fleur, you will be the cause of your own downfall."

"And yours too. That's what's really worrying you, isn't it?" Fleur gazed at her in the candlelight. "Well, you can stop worrying, because I will become Lady Griffin as soon as the wanderer returns from Russia, and all will then be well. That is, unless . . ."

"Unless what?" Mrs. Tudor held her breath in dread.

"Come with me now, and I'll show you." Fleur continued up the staircase. Mrs. Tudor gazed unhappily after her, then followed. On reaching the next floor, they proceeded along the gallery, where portraits of Athan's ancestors watched them pass. Suits of armor glinted in the candlelight, and the night wind droned dismally around the line of windows overlooking the castle courtyard.

At last they reached the arched double doors of Athan's

rooms. Mrs. Tudor looked anxiously back along the dark gallery, then gasped. "There's someone there!" she breathed fearfully.

"Where?" Fleur raised the candelabra and looked intently, but saw nothing.

"I—I thought I saw something. . . ."

Fleur was irritated. "There's no one, Mama! Do be sensible; we're safe from discovery. Now then, let's go in, for I need to see something again, and I need you to see it too." Pushing the door open, Fleur virtually bundled her mother inside. The apartments were sumptuously furnished, the paneled walls hung with tapestries, the Tudor furniture beautifully carved and provided with embroidered upholstery, but Fleur hardly looked at anything, for she was intent upon the wall above the carved stone fireplace and mantel. There, glowing softly and almost seductively in the light from the candles, was a portrait that was so much the image of Ellie Rutherford that Fleur could hardly believe it.

Mrs. Tudor followed her daughter's gaze. "What is it, my dear?"

"Do you know whose likeness this is?"

"Yes, of course I do. It's Caroline, Lady Griffin, and very improper she is too. Why, her modesty is saved by little more than a shawl! But then, she proved herself to be no better than she should be."

Fleur drew a long breath. "Be that as it may, would it surprise you to learn that it could also be a portrait of John Bailey's niece?"

"Bailey the china maker?"

Fleur felt a spurt of annoyance. "Yes, of course Bailey the china maker! For heaven's sake, Mama, how many Baileys are there in Nantgarth?"

"Don't raise your voice, dear," her mother replied, glancing over her shoulder again.

"Did you hear what I said?" Fleur asked exasperatedly. "The woman in this painting is the very twin of Bailey's niece."

Mrs. Tudor looked unwillingly at the canvas. "I fail to see why you are so concerned."

"Really? Then you are too complacent by far, and it's no wonder the general ran rings around you. Look at the painting! A woman who is the living image of this portrait now resides at Nantgarth House, and what's more, I believe she plans to usurp me. She *knows* who she looks like, and means to use the knowledge to her own personal advantage."

"Oh, come now, Fleur . . ." her mother began.

Fleur stamped her foot. "She does, I tell you!"

"But he intends to marry *you*, my dear," her mother said soothingly.

"I hope you're right, Mama, because I am very uneasy." Fleur studied the painted face that was so eerily like Ellie.

Mrs. Tudor shuddered. "Then we must make absolutely certain that Mr. Bailey's niece does not achieve her aim. For the moment, however, it's cold here, my dear. Shall we return to the drawing room?"

Twelve

*I*n Russia, Epiphany was a very important occasion in the church calendar, and by eleven o'clock in the morning most of the population of snow-covered St. Petersburg had gathered along the banks of the frozen River Neva, by the baroque splendor of the Winter Palace. Bells rang and seagulls screamed, disturbed by the great congregation that spilled onto the thick ice.

The Neva was just over forty miles long from its birth in Lake Ladoga to its mouth in the Gulf of Finland. It had no tidal ebb and flow, and by the Winter Palace was divided into two by the long spit of Vasilievsky Island, the largest of forty-two islands that formed the delta upon which the beautiful Russian capital was built. In every direction there were handsome waterfronts, with fine wharves and docks, mansions with gardens and trees, and government buildings, of which even the most minor seemed grand enough for royalty.

Vehicles of all sorts cluttered the river, from open four-wheeled droshkies and covered sledges called kibitkas, to troikas, carriages fixed on square sledges that resembled tabletops, and rough carts known as telegas. Ladies and gentlemen stood on the boxes of their carriages in order to see, but the peasants tried to get really close, and had to be driven back by the troops. Bright sunshine glanced on the surrounding snow, and incense drifted as choirs dressed in scarlet sang hymns. There was an air of deep devotion and reverence, except in the palace, from the windows of which the privileged gazed down in more worldly comfort.

In the middle of the river stood an open pavilion surmounted by a golden cross and embellished with icons. It marked and protected the hole that for the past two hours or more had been cut painstakingly through the ice. The pavilion was carpeted with scarlet cloth, as was the processional causeway that had been built out from the embankment steps in front of the palace. Soon the primate of St. Petersburg would immerse a crucifix through the hole into the water and thus bestow a blessing upon it.

Earlier a glittering procession, headed by bishops and archimandrites dressed in cloth-of-gold, had proceeded out of the Winter Palace. The Imperial Family followed, and on nearing the pavilion, found that the clergy had formed an avenue for the twenty-seven-year-old czar and his czarina to pass. Alexander was tall and golden blond, with noble features, a dimpled chin, and gentle blue eyes. Clad in the splendid uniform of a Cossack hetman, he now stood beneath the pavilion. Crimson orders and a number of glittering stars adorned his breast; he was bareheaded and without a cloak, but gave no sign of being so exposed to the intense cold. His tall, beautiful czarina stood just behind him in state robes, her fair curls hidden beneath the traditional Russian headdress known as a *kokoshnik*.

Athan was among the huge gathering. He'd lost weight since Ellie had seen him. There were dark shadows beneath his gray eyes. He was thoroughly enveloped in heavy coats, scarves, and shawls, and had wisely discarded his London top hat for furry Russian headwear that ensured his ears were kept warm. It had been necessary to slip out of the elegant house on English Quay behind the back of his watchful sister, Louise, who had appointed herself his nurse, and had been keeping a very close eye on him, as had her British husband, the fur merchant, Charles Brasier. Neither of them considered Athan to be well enough to go walking in the Russian winter, but the patient was bored and restless.

His only diversion in recent weeks had been a meeting with the czar at the Winter Palace. The fame of the Griffin stud had reached royal ears, and Alexander was impressed enough to want a colt and a mare for the Imperial Stables, which stood beside the Moika Canal in St. Petersburg. With this in mind, he'd summoned Athan to the Winter Palace, sending his own private carriage, and had granted a lengthy audience to discuss the matter. An orchestra had played throughout the meeting, and there was much of the slightly deaf czar's rather garbled French that Athan found hard to understand. However, they'd still managed to get on well enough for Alexander to desire him to accompany the horses to St. Petersburg in the summer, so they could speak again. Since that momentous day Athan's restlessness had become intolerable. He was so tired of sitting by fires at English Quay, drinking possets, and being read to from dull volumes, that today he'd sneaked out like a felon to observe this famous Epiphany ceremony.

At last the hole through the ice was complete, and after many prayers, the primate dipped the golden crucifix three times into the hole; then, with uplifted hands he blessed the water three times. Artillery fired salutes from the Peter and Paul Fortress on the northern riverbank, where the four-hundred-foot spire of the cathedral of the same name rose like a golden needle from within the military ramparts. Not long afterward the procession began to move slowly back along the causeway toward the palace, and then the people swarmed forward like ants. Children were dipped into the river, which was now considered holy, while others scrambled to draw the water, in the belief that it would remain consecrated for years and retain the power to cure the sick.

Athan adjusted his fur hat and pushed some of his wayward black hair away from his forehead. Even wrapped up as he was, his feet no longer seemed to belong to the rest of him, and in spite of thick sheepskin gloves, his fingers were so cold they ached painfully. Never again would he complain about Welsh rain! What he could do with right now was a huge fried breakfast as cooked by the sainted Mrs. Lewis. It was a pity she had upset Fleur and her mother to such an extent that he'd been left with little choice but to let her go. Still, his loss was John Bailey's undoubted gain.

He pressed his lips together and, feeling very homesick for Wales, shuffled his cold feet. Damn Russia and its vile winters. He couldn't stay here until spring, which was what Louise and Charles wanted. He *had* to get home and attend to the important business of selecting and preparing the colt and mare for the czar. He also had to get home and begin preparations to marry Fleur. His lips twisted thoughtfully, for there was also the Unicorn Bank and the accusations laid against it by the mysterious Ellie. Mysterious indeed, for according to the last letter he'd received from his agent, she had declined to divulge where she would go after the sale of Rutherford Park. Well, she was entitled to do as she pleased, of course, but her disappearance would make the inquiries he'd promised to conduct at the bank all the more difficult. It would also make it all the more difficult to see her again. This last thought slid in almost slyly, as indeed it might, for he had no business yearning for Ellie Rutherford when Fleur was the one he'd asked to marry him. He gazed at the scene on the frozen river, but all he saw was Ellie's face.

He lingered a little longer, but was becoming so cold now that he decided it was time to make his way back to English Quay, which lay downstream on the same side of the river as the Winter Palace. His route would take him past the Admiralty and Palace Square, where the impressive prancing Bronze Horseman statue of Peter the Great faced the river, then past the Senate building before he would eventually come in sight of English Quay. He walked carefully, having no desire to slip and add bruises or a broken bone to his health woes, but as the noise of the crowds began to be lost in the jangle of the bells, he became aware of a six-horse, sledge-mounted carriage about fifty yards behind him. Trotting alongside it were half a dozen Dalmatian carriage dogs, such as might be seen with the finest equipages in fashionable Hyde Park. He walked on, and suddenly the dogs milled around him, tails wagging as the carriage drew to a halt alongside him.

The Tatar coachman clambered down from the box and opened the door to reveal two aristocratic Russian men seated side by side. The older of the two was supple and slender for his age and had something of the courtesan about his eyes. The younger was an arrogant officer in the Imperial Guard, with pampered, sulky looks that suggested too much privilege and too little intellect to cope with it. Athan might have wondered about them, had he not felt certain that the young man would commit murder rather than be another man's bedfellow.

The older man addressed Athan in French. "Lord Griffin? I trust you do not mean to walk all the way to English

Quay so soon after your recent illness? After all, apart from your interview with the czar, this is your first venture outside since becoming so unwell."

Athan had no idea who the man was, or indeed how he knew so much. "You have the advantage over me, sir, for we have not been introduced," he replied, also in French.

The first man gave a faintly sardonic smile. "I am Prince Paul Dalmatsky, and this is my nephew, Prince Valentin Andreyov."

Valentin inclined his head.

Athan had never heard of Valentin before, but knew Paul was the owner of the house in which his sister and brother-in-law resided on English Quay. "I am honored to meet you, sirs," he murmured, sketching a bow worthy of St. James's Palace, but when he straightened he looked Paul directly in the eyes. "I'm curious that you should know who I am, sir, after all, wrapped up like this, I'm hardly recognizable."

Paul ignored the question. "My carriage is at your disposal, Lord Griffin. Please allow me to convey you the rest of the way to English Quay."

Athan did not want to accept the offer, for by now he was convinced that this uncle and nephew had been watching him outside the Winter Palace.

Seeing his reluctance, Paul addressed him again. "Please, my lord, for our Russian weather will not do you any good when you are still unwell, and the czar would be very displeased with me if he discovered I had failed to offer the owner of the Griffin stud the comfort and shelter of my carriage."

"You seem to know a great deal about me, sir," Athan replied.

"It is my business to know things." Paul nodded peremptorily at the Tatar, who stepped swiftly forward, and before Athan knew what was happening, he was being bundled into the carriage.

"There, my lord, we have saved you from the cold," Paul murmured as the carriage drove on again.

"There was no need, sir, for I am of the opinion that exercise is beneficial." Athan had no option but to make himself as comfortable as possible on the empty seat opposite.

"Exercise when one is ill? How very British," Paul answered with a slight laugh. "You know what is said in Russia? That the baths are the people's first doctor, vodka their second, and raw garlic their third."

"Indeed?"

Valentin said nothing, but his eyes continued to glitter in a way that made Athan wonder what was going through his head. Not anything wise or humane, that was certain.

"It is good that relations between our two countries are amiable again," Prince Paul observed.

"Indeed, sir, for there is much need of unity against the French." Athan felt rather than saw the cold twitch of Valentin's sensuous lips, and guessed that he disagreed entirely.

Paul continued smoothly, "The czar strongly desires an alliance. He was appalled by the execution of the Duc d'Enghien last year, and by Bonaparte's coronation as Emperor Napoleon. Both are an affront to the royal houses of Europe. You know, I suppose, that the czar has sent a special emissary to London to discuss a treaty?"

Athan cleared his throat. "Well, there are rumors, of course, but I believe the matter is supposed to be secret."

"As it happens, my nephew is soon to go to Britain as well," Paul supplied.

"Really?"

Valentin spoke at last. "I do not look forward to it, for the British have no idea how to heat their houses. They have never heard of stoves, but light foolish fires that heat only the vastness of the heavens."

"We have a quaint attachment to the open hearth, Prince Valentin," Athan answered.

Valentin's dark eyes returned his gaze for a moment, then flickered away, leaving Athan fully aware of his animosity.

Paul's smile was a study in cultivated charm. "Lord Griffin, I will be honest with you. It is no accident that we have accosted you in this way."

"I didn't for a moment think it was," Athan replied.

"I am given to understand that you own a china works?"

Athan blinked. "I beg your pardon?"

"A china works, for the making of fine porcelain. *Pâte tendre*, I believe it is called."

"Well, I own the land upon which such a china works stands," Athan corrected, wondering where on earth this could be leading. It was one thing for the czar to have heard about the Griffin stud, for when it came to horse breeding the world was actually rather small, but he couldn't even begin to guess how word of John Bailey's small venture had reached the ears of someone like Prince Paul Dalmatsky.

"Mr. John Bailey is the proprietor?" Paul inquired.

"He is."

Paul smiled coolly. "Mr. Bailey's skills are renowned, Lord Griffin."

"They are?"

"Oh, yes. Valentin has been making inquiries and feels that Mr. Bailey is the very best for the task of creating a commemorative soup tureen for the czar."

Athan tried not to show the utter astonishment he felt. He did not doubt that John could—if exceedingly fortunate—produce one of the finest soup tureens in the world, but with levels of wastage being so very high, it might be some time before he managed to fire one sufficiently well for decorating. On the other hand, of course, the success of such an imperial order, even for a single tureen, would mean immeasurable fame for the Nantgarth china works. "I . . . I'm sure Mr. Bailey will be most interested to hear of it," he said at last, knowing the words were a masterly understatement. John would dance a joyful jig when he heard the news.

"It is on account of this tureen that Valentin is going to Britain," Paul went on, "and in this he is hopeful of enlisting your assistance, my lord."

"Mine?"

"Yes. It occurred to me that perhaps you might offer him the hospitality of your Berkeley Square town house in London, and of Castle Griffin itself?"

Athan's expression became a little fixed, for he was astonished at the audacity of the request. He was even more astonished when Paul went on, "Our families are connected, after all. Your sister and brother-in-law reside at a very reasonable rent in one of my properties. Mr. Brasier's fur business flourishes at the moment, so let us hope that it continues to do so."

There was no open threat in the words, but it was there all the same, and Athan was forced to tread very carefully for Louise and Charles's sakes. "Then of course Prince Valentin may reside temporarily in my properties."

"You are too kind, my lord," Prince Paul murmured, "and as you now feel well enough to leave the house, I can only imagine you will wish to return to Britain as soon as possible in order to oversee the matter of the czar's horses."

Athan was beginning to feel that his thoughts had somehow been read.

Paul smiled. "Perhaps you would find it convenient to make the journey with Valentin?"

Athan managed another bland smile. "You are too kind, Prince Paul."

"Not at all. Ah, here were are, at your sister's door."

The carriage swayed to a halt on a waterfront that was lined with trees and fine gray and gold mansions, many occupied by the British. Equally as many were occupied by the Russian nobility, including two grand dukes, for this was one of the most coveted addresses in St. Petersburg. The property rented by Louise and Charles was particularly imposing, with a balustraded roof adorned with statues, finely proportioned windows on four floors, a handsome colonnaded porch, and a blue door with a bronze lion knocker. Like all houses throughout Russia on this important day of Epiphany, it was being cleaned throughout, with furniture brought outside and many windows opened so they could be polished. It was a custom with which nothing was allowed to interfere.

The Tatar climbed down from the box again and opened the carriage door, and Athan climbed gladly out, trusting that in spite of all that had been agreed, he would somehow manage to evade all future contact with Prince Valentin Andreyov. But as he turned to bow to the occupants of the vehicle, Paul leaned forward a last time.

"My name is not to be mentioned in connection with this business, Lord Griffin, for it is entirely Valentin's affair, and I do not wish to take any of the credit. I trust you will humor me in this?"

"Of course."

"You will not bring my name into it at all?"

"If that is your wish."

Paul gave another thin smile. "The commission for a tureen from Mr. Bailey is a matter of some urgency, because it is required here in St. Petersburg by the day of Saints Peter and Paul—that's by our calendar, not yours—and I know the delicate and painstaking completion of porcelain will take months. Leaving for Britain is a problem, however, because the Neva is in the full grip of winter and therefore icebound, but the Gulf of Finland is open farther west at Riga, where my private yacht is always in readiness. My nephew leaves for that destination in the morning. My *voiturier* will call for you at eight."

Tomorrow? Athan was appalled. "Sir, I don't think that's possible. My passport must be—" he began, but Prince Paul interrupted quietly.

"I have already attended to your passport, Lord Griffin. Everything is signed and settled."

"You seem to be damned sure of me," Athan replied, more than a little annoyed by this entire encounter.

"I did not doubt that when it comes to family, you would be a man of reason, Lord Griffin." Paul smiled again. "The post horses have all been arranged, and the traveling carriage prepared. There is nothing to hamper your departure."

"Even so—"

Again the polite but firm interruption. "Be sure to bring a firearm with you, for it is wild forested country, and hungry bears and wolves are a danger at this time of the year. *A bientôt,* milord."

The Tatar had already returned to the box, and the carriage pulled smartly off, the sledge runners whining over the packed snow. The Dalmatian dogs fell into a loping gait beside it, and the whole striking equipage sped away.

For Louise's sake Athan would go along with the Russians' wishes, but he wasn't a fool, and knew that there was far more to Prince Valentin Andreyov's visit to Britain than the mere acquisition of a soup tureen from John Bailey's china works.

Thirteen

A few days later, in the kinder climate of a Welsh winter, Ellie set off on horseback just after midday to explore the mountainside above Nantgarth. A sidesaddle had been found for her at Castle Griffin as soon as it was known John Bailey's niece would be coming to live at Nantgarth House. It was a rather old-fashioned saddle, once owned by Athan's grandmother, but it was more than adequate.

It was January twenty-fifth, which was, so Mrs. Lewis informed her, St. Dwynwen's Day. Dwynwen—pronounced Dwinn-wen—was a fifth-century princess whose well was to be found on the mountain by the gate of the church that was dedicated to her. She was the patron saint of Welsh lovers, St. Valentine being of little importance to people hereabouts.

Ellie was dressed in a mustard yellow woolen riding habit and brown beaver hat, and mounted on her uncle's sturdy bay cob, Tomos, whose appearance in Hyde Park would surely have sent the beau monde into a universal attack of the vapors. He was rather old, decidedly shaggy, and of a stubborn turn of mind, but he was generally very comfortable; she was informed that the ascent of Nantgarth mountain would be nothing to him. She had also been assured that the rain that had fallen so heavily overnight would not return until the evening, enabling her to enjoy a dry ride; however, looking back at the new clouds burgeoning to the southwest over Cardiff Bay, she wasn't confident that this would be entirely so. But she was prepared to take the chance.

Men were shooting woodcock in the woods as she rode

along the valley road to the fork, where she glanced right toward Castle Griffin before turning Tomos up the track the parishioners of Nantgarth had to climb in order to attend worship. Her purpose was to investigate something rather curious about her enemy, Fleur, who rode up to the church almost every day, although never at the time of any service. She left her horse by St. Dwynwen's well at the churchyard gate and went into the church, where she remained for sometimes as long as two hours. Ellie had never seen anyone else, just Fleur, whose bright red riding habit and white horse were clearly discernible from Nantgarth House. What on earth did the future Lady Griffin do up there? Ellie couldn't envisage Fleur diligently reading the Bible, or doing anything else remotely religious, so the mystery had to be investigated.

The track led up through a shallow draw, where a little stream cascaded between clumps of heather and whortleberry. Windblown silver birch trees, naked and slender, hung over the water, their branches rubbing together in the light breeze, as if willing spring to hasten. Oak trees grew there too, but they were as cold and barren in January as the rest of the draw, which in warmer months would be filled with bluebells and foxgloves. There would be forget-me-nots and ferns along the fringes of the stream, and smooth green sheep paths would wend between islands of cool green bracken. The mountain air was bracing yet sweet, and overhead, white clouds raced across the blue sky, chasing the most recent shower and bringing the next one hard upon their heels.

The clouds were advancing more swiftly than anticipated, but by now Ellie was halfway between Nantgarth House and the church, and too intrigued by Fleur's odd activities to want to turn back. She ought to be able to reach the church before any rain began to fall, and with luck would be able to wait safely inside and then return between downpours. Well, that was the theory of it; the practice would no doubt be far less convenient. Reaching the top of the draw, she managed to persuade Tomos into a grudging canter as the track traversed the undulating breast of the mountain.

From up there the view was magnificent, allowing her to see the market town of Pontypridd, four miles to the north, and as far as Cardiff to the south. She was also able to see how coal mining and other industries were beginning to change the landscape. The Taff followed its rocky course through the valley, while the smooth silver ribbon of the canal snaked along the eastern flank. Far below, looking almost snug amid the evergreen trees, were Nantgarth House and the china works.

The elevation also permitted a much better view of Castle Griffin. Now she could see that the gardens were a succession of terraces and lawns that seemed to tumble down clearings on the thickly wooded slopes. She saw fountains and flower beds, summerhouses and dovecotes, symbols of the gracious living the centuries had imposed upon the once grim feudal stronghold. Beyond the castle, on the slopes overlooking the Taff valley, she could just make out the stables and pastures of the Griffin stud. It was easy to see why the Normans had chosen such a spot for a castle, because it completely commanded the narrow pass below. No one could go by undetected, and certainly an enemy army would be completely at the castle's mercy.

Ellie rode on. She hadn't met anyone since leaving the house, so it came as a shock to ride over a small brow and be confronted by not only the church and churchyard, but also by someone with two white horses, a mare and a colt, at the well by the gate. For an awful moment she feared an encounter with Fleur, but was then relieved to realize it was only Gwilym. He was trying to coax his charges toward the little square, stone-edged pool that was St. Dwynwen's well, and where, oddly, Ellie noticed a white handkerchief had been spread on the water. An ancient thorn bush grew nearby, its crooked branches covered with little knots of cloth that suggested something more pagan than Christian.

Gwilym turned quickly the moment he heard Tomos's hooves. "Good afternoon to you, Miss Ellie."

"Good afternoon, Gwilym. What are you doing?" she asked, maneuvering Tomos closer.

"The mare is barren, Miss Ellie, and the colt needs to be as strong and healthy as it is possible to be, so I have come to ask St. Dwynwen for her help."

"But isn't she the patron saint of Welsh lovers?"

Gwilym smiled. "And of friendship and animals. That is her symbol." He pointed at an exposed rock that had been incorporated into the churchyard wall, and upon which was carved what seemed to be a crescent moon.

"Will you mind if I watch?" Ellie asked.

He shook his head. "Watch if you wish, Miss Ellie, for it will make no difference to me, but first I must wait to see if St. Dwynwen will grant my request." He turned toward the spring, where the handkerchief floated motionless.

The mountain air seemed suddenly still, and Ellie held her breath. She could hear her own heartbeats, and—she thought—those of the horses too. Suddenly the handkerchief moved, as if something in the water had twitched it. Ellie gasped. "What was that?"

"Don't be afraid, Miss Ellie, for it is an eel."

Her eyes became larger. "An *eel*? All the way up here? But—"

"It is no ordinary eel, but a sacred fish, and it has given me a sign that St. Dwynwen has heard me. The eel appears when she is lending her help. Today she shows me that she is giving her blessing to the mare."

Ellie's gaze was still upon the handkerchief, which twitched again. Then she heard the splash of water, and the handkerchief heaved as the eel—if that indeed was what it was—surged up in order to plunge down again. Then the spring became still once more. "Has . . . has it gone?" she asked.

Gwilym nodded. "Back into the heart of the mountain." He bent to retrieve the handkerchief, with which he then wiped the mare's belly. Then he squeezed the water out and limped over to the thorn tree to tie the handkerchief among the other cloths. Coming back, he paused to look at her for a moment. "There is something in the church for you to find," he said suddenly.

"Find? What do you mean?"

He spread his hands. "I don't know. The knowledge comes to me, but I do not always understand it. In the church, hidden, is something your eyes should see." Then he seemed to forget all about that and returned to the horses, taking their bridles and drawing their heads toward his. There was a faraway look in his eyes, and he seemed to rock slightly as he began to make soft sounds to them, sometimes whispering, sometimes clicking his tongue; then he breathed into their nostrils, as if imparting his own spirit.

Ellie was transfixed. The magic of ages seemed to swirl around the mountainside, bringing echoes from ancient times, when druids and wizards had walked this land. Gwilym Lewis was part of that Wales of long ago, the Wales of St. Dwynwen, the Mari Llwyd, and Merlin. The mare nuzzled his face and brushed against him, so willing to do his bidding that when he stepped aside and pointed at the well, she went to the water and drank.

Ellie was so rapt in what was happening that Gwilym's sudden light laugh gave her a start. "There now, they will be fine and healthy from now on. The colt will become a fine stallion and sire many foals, and the mare will be a dam many times over."

"You can be so sure of that?"

The question surprised him. "But of course, Miss Ellie, there is no doubt. They will be all that is required when they start their new life in the emperor of Russia's stables."

"They are going to the czar?" Ellie remembered what her uncle had said.

"Oh, yes, and I will accompany them, because they will not be afraid if I am with them."

"From all of which I take it there has been further word from Lord Griffin?"

"No, miss," Gwilym replied, "nothing in weeks now, not since the letter with the bit at the end about the Russian emperor inviting his lordship to his palace." He smiled. "I just know what is to be, Miss Ellie. The czar will want a mare and a colt, and I have decided that it will be these two."

"When you say you know, you mean . . . ?"

He tapped his head. "I know in here, miss."

"No one has told you?"

He shook his head. "No, miss."

"Oh." Ellie didn't doubt that he was telling the truth; after all, he had power over horses, clocks, and doors, and he certainly managed to prevent the accident at the wharf. So why shouldn't he know what was going on in St. Petersburg as well?

Gwilym looked intently at her. "But there are things that

are hidden from me, miss, important things with which I cannot help you."

She returned his gaze, finding him almost hypnotic. Sound became deadened, and it was as if the breeze checked, remained still, and then flowed again. Unsettled, she shifted a little on the sidesaddle. "I . . . I think I may be going to Russia soon too."

"You will, Miss Ellie?"

She nodded. "Nothing is certain, of course, but I am hoping that when my uncle goes there, he will take me too."

Gwilym looked at her, as if reading words written across her face. "You will go, Miss Ellie," he said quietly.

"You can see my future?"

"I can see that you will cross seas, and . . ."

"Yes?"

"That you will hold a diamond in your hand, a diamond as red as blood."

She stared at him. "But diamonds aren't red—" she began, then broke off as she remembered what she'd read in the newspaper at the Crown Inn, just before those fateful deviled kidneys had plummeted into her lap. What was it now? Something about a famous red diamond going on display at the Tower before being incorporated into a new Sword of Concord for the royal regalia?

Gwilym glanced up at the lowering skies. "You'd best go into the church, Miss Ellie, for the first raindrops are about to leave the clouds. Take Tomos around to the shelter at the back, for he is old and his fetlocks give him pain if he gets too wet." Then, almost as if he had waved a wand, it did indeed begin to rain again. Ellie didn't question what he said about Tomos, but led the cob through the gate. Gwilym's voice followed her. "Be on your guard, Miss Ellie. Be on your guard."

She took Tomos behind the ancient weather-beaten stone church, with its squat tower. It seemed to hug the mountain, determined to not only stand the test of time, but defy the worst of the fierce winds that often shrieked over the mountains from the sea, eight miles away. Snug between the church wall and the rise of the mountain was a sheltered spot where gnarled holly trees and overgrown ivy provided a little retreat. After making sure Tomos was secure and comfortable, she hurried around to the front of the church again. She glanced toward the gate before entering the porch, but of Gwilym and the horses there was now no sign.

It was unexpectedly light in the church, because the rough walls were mostly whitewashed, although there were some exposed facings. A single bell was all that was to be found in the belfry, and its rope was dangled beyond an arch at the foot of the tower. The stone-flagged aisle was lined with dark oak pews, a low arched doorway gave into the tiny vestry, and there was a beautiful barrel-shaped wooden ceiling in the sanctuary, where a beautifully worked altar cloth of exquisite colors set off a handsome display of simple but very old plate. Slender white candles stood sentinel, and a board on the wall announced the numbers of the hymns sung at the last service. Or perhaps it was the hymns for the next service. Ellie could not really have said.

Rain now drummed heavily on the slate roof, which was exposed above aged oak rafters, and gusts of wind buffeted the church as a sudden squall swept across the mountain. Ellie glanced all around, but saw nothing she would not have expected to find in a church, certainly nothing to indicate Fleur's purpose in coming here so often and staying so long. Nor was there anything to suggest what it was that Gwilym said was to be found here.

Amid the racket of the squall it suddenly seemed to her that she could hear coughing and the shuffling of feet, as if a congregation were present. And there was the scent of flowers. She looked toward the altar again, and seemed to see the misty figures of a bridal couple. Then the groom's voice—Athan's voice: ... *to be my lawful wedded wife, to have and to hold from this day forward, for better for worse, for richer for poorer, in sickness and in health, to love and to cherish, till death us do part* ...

Tears pricked Ellie's eyes, so distracting her that she didn't hear another horse outside by the gate. It wasn't until hurrying footsteps echoed beneath the porch that she knew she was no longer alone. Dismay followed swiftly as a figure in a red riding habit ran into the church. Fleur was the last person she'd expected to see, because the almost daily visit to the church had taken place that morning. It seemed a second visit was required today.

Fleur was caught unawares. Seeing a movement near the altar, she turned, her eyes bright, an eager smile leaping to her lips, but her expression froze like ice when she realized it was only Ellie. She took a moment or so to recover, then gave a short laugh. "Well, well, if it isn't the china maker's niece."

"I'm sorry to disappoint you," Ellie replied.

"Disappoint me?"

"Well, it's clear you expected to find someone else here." Ellie was pleased to note that her foe's clothes were rather wet, her riding boots mud-spattered from dismounting by the well, and that her beautiful red ringlet had so lost its gloss and curl as to resemble a horse's tail.

A light passed through Fleur's lovely green eyes. "Someone else? Indeed not, for who on earth would I hope to find here? St. Dwynwen herself?"

"Well, certainly not the ghost of the first Lady Griffin," Ellie ventured, surprised at her own boldness, not having realized the taunt was on the tip of her tongue.

"Well, at least you are no longer playing the innocent." Fleur looked past Ellie toward the sanctuary, at least, that was what Ellie thought. The feeling was so strong that Ellie even turned, half expecting to see someone else there, but there was no one.

She looked at Fleur again. "I honestly didn't know of my resemblance to Lady Griffin when last I spoke to you."

"My dear Miss Rutherford, I imagine that you and honesty are strangers."

Ellie laughed in disbelief. "Oh, come now, Miss Tudor, for it is to *you* that honesty is unknown. Lord Griffin is far away in Russia, yet here you are, quite clearly engaged upon a tryst of some sort. Oh, don't try to deny it, for I've seen you coming up here almost every day. Now, if I were asked to guess your purpose, I'd have to say I thought you were involved in a clandestine liaison of some sort."

Fleur's face had now gone very pale. "And you would be wrong, Miss Rutherford."

"Would I?"

Time hung, and the squall raged across the mountainside

outside, howling around the church tower, and blustering in through the porch, scattering a few leaves that had survived from the autumn. Ellie quelled a shiver, determined not to display any sign of weakness as Fleur advanced a step or two.

"Yes, Miss Rutherford, you would be wrong. Oh, dear, did you think you had discovered a weapon to use against me? Well, think again. Whatever my purpose in coming here, you cannot prove anything. It's your word against mine, and no matter how like his beloved Caroline you may be, he will stand by me. Why? Because he has asked me to be his wife, and he is the sort of man who will stand by his word, no matter what. You will need proof of my wrongdoing, my dear, and that is something you cannot possibly have, because I am innocent."

"I notice that you do not mention love," Ellie said then.

"Love is for fools, for it blights common sense and drains ambition. But do not make the mistake of imagining that because I do not love him, he does not love me. He did not propose to me simply out of duty and honor, but because he loves and desires me too. Oh, yes, it's true, and I can see in your eyes that the news sorely disappoints you."

Ellie thought back to the garden of the Crown Inn. How could he love Fleur if he was so strongly diverted by a face that reminded him of the wife he'd lost? The kiss she, Ellie Rutherford, had shared with him that momentous day had been something utterly wonderful, something so fine and rare that Fleur's claims of possessing his love seemed empty.

Ellie's silence made Fleur less sure of herself, and she tried a different tack. "Why are you here?"

"I'm sheltering from the rain."

Fleur met her gaze, then glanced toward the sanctuary again, before giving another of her supercilious smiles. "How are the family pots coming along?"

Ellie was stung by the disparaging comment, but dissembled with a screen of bland civility. "They are coming along very well indeed," she replied.

"So Mr. Bailey now has . . . two sound plates to daub successfully in lieu of rent to Lord Griffin?"

"I did not realize it was for you to worry over his lordship's accounts, Miss Tudor."

"Oh, it's for me to worry about everything, my dear. Certainly I worry about your welfare."

"I'm honored."

Fleur's responding smile was the thinnest imaginable. "Don't be, for your gratitude is ill placed. Unless, of course, you wish to thank me for discovering a way in which you may spare your uncle."

"And what way might that be?" Ellie asked, sensing the other's eagerness to impart unwelcome news.

"Why, your departure for pastures new, of course."

"If Lord Griffin wishes me to go, then I will, but I will not move an inch simply because *you* wish me to, Miss Tudor. You may indeed be on the point of becoming mistress of Castle Griffin, but you have yet to wear a wedding ring. I prefer to wait and see what happens."

"Are you threatening me?" Fleur breathed.

"You do not appear to have much confidence in your hold upon his lordship," Ellie murmured.

"Oh, I have confidence, Miss Rutherford, certainly enough to know that your uncle *will* be turned out of Nantgarth House the moment Lord Griffin returns. I was going to call upon you on my way back to the castle, but this chance meeting saves me the bother. You see, I have already spoken to his agent, voicing my considerable doubts about John Bailey's character and the nature of his relationship with his so-called niece."

Ellie gave a shocked intake of breath. "That's a monstrous suggestion, absolutely monstrous!" she cried, her hands clenching into fists as she struggled against the urge to fly at her foe.

"Monstrous? I thought it was rather convincing. Anyway, a letter will be dispatched to St. Petersburg today, requesting immediate permission to commence proceedings. Of course," Fleur went on, strolling down the aisle and passing black-gloved fingers from pew to pew, "the letter need not be sent at all if you give me your word you will leave."

"And where do you suggest I go? Apart from perdition, that is."

"It has come to my notice that the Lady Brecon is seeking a governess for her sons, who are at present residing on the family estate in North Wales. You are more than suitable for the post, Miss Rutherford, and I wish you to apply for it forthwith."

"I'm sure you do."

"You have until seven o'clock this evening to decide. If I have not heard from you by then, a courier will take the letter to Cardiff to be sent immediately to St. Petersburg. It will take six weeks at the very least to arrive in Russia, and the same for his lordship's answer to return, but you may be sure that your uncle's days at Nantgarth are numbered."

The rain stopped, and the squall died away at the same time, leaving the church quiet except for a light breeze that was sufficient to swirl the dry leaves a last time over the church floor. A shaft of watery sunlight filtered through the thick medieval glass of the lead-latticed windows.

Fleur held Ellie's gaze. "I suggest you go back to Nantgarth House now, Miss Rutherford."

"I'm not in any hurry," Ellie replied, sensing the other wanted her out of the way in order to do something, and seeing how yet again Fleur's eyes went in the direction of the sanctuary.

"Go!" Fleur ordered imperiously.

Ellie folded her arms and held her ground. "No," she replied. She had nothing to lose by antagonizing this odious creature, who intended to do her worst no matter what.

Fleur wasn't accustomed to being defied and didn't quite know what to do because she'd expected the despicable threats to cow Ellie into helpless tears. Instead, there were anger and barefaced defiance, with the added suggestion that the china maker's niece had spirit enough to physically strike her enemy. Discretion therefore had the better part of Fleur's valor. "Very well, I will leave, for I do not wish to remain in your company for any longer than is necessary. Just be sure to send word to me before seven," she said, and turned on her heel to march out.

Ellie waited a few moments, then went to the porch to watch as the figure in red rode angrily away along the track to Nantgarth. Seeming to touch the ground where Fleur rode, a washy, indistinct rainbow arched the mountain. Fleur's figure shimmered, then disappeared beyond the haze of color. How good it would be if the awful creature really did vanish like that, Ellie thought as she made her way back down the aisle to the low-roofed sanctuary.

Gwilym had said there was something to be found in the church, and Fleur's manner suggested the sanctuary was the wisest place to start looking. But what for? Ellie began to look as thoroughly as she could, while at the same time showing due respect, for it was hardly proper to scavenge around an altar. She had all but given up when she saw a tip of folded paper protruding behind the lower edge of the curved wooden ceiling, which came low enough to be within reach of her fingertips if she stood on tiptoe. Originally it must have been tucked well out of sight, and had slipped slightly, but as she stretched up to try to pull it free, she heard fresh steps approaching outside. Too heavy to be Fleur's, they must belong to a man. Alarmed that it might be the person Fleur had hoped to meet, Ellie abandoned the attempt to take the paper and instead cast swiftly around for somewhere to hide. The only place she had time to reach was the altar itself, and she flung herself on the floor behind it just as the steps entered the church. She heard spurs on the stone floor, then the slither of a waterproofed cloak being flung back over shoulders.

"Fleur?" he called, but only an echo answered, and to Ellie's unutterable dismay he began to walk down the aisle. She pressed so low to the floor that if she could have melted into the stone she would. Please don't let him see her! *Please!* He reached the sanctuary, and the sound of his steps changed as he trod on the square of dark blue carpet that had been laid there. As Ellie held her breath and lay motionless, from the corner of her eye she saw his spurred boots as he paused and looked up at the wooden ceiling exactly where the paper was hidden.

His back was toward her as he reached up, his height making it a simple matter to pull it from its place of concealment. Ellie dared to turn her head to try to see him properly. His back was toward her, but she could see that he was not old, and that he had dark blond hair, cut very short and worn in tight curls against his head. There was something familiar about him, and as he turned, at last she saw why: It was Freddie Forrester-Phipps!

She didn't know whether to be shocked or not to gaze

again upon the pale profile and light blue eyes of Athan's "school torment." After all, on hearing of the rumors about Fleur's Season, Freddie's was the first name that had leapt to mind. She watched as he unfolded the note and read whatever it said, then refolded it and placed it very carefully in his breast pocket, making certain that nothing unsightly spoiled the lie of the costly material. His Corinthian attire had been well protected by the heavy waterproof cloak that he'd flung back on entering. The only blot on his appearance was a little muddy rain upon his gleaming boots, but even that seemed loath to be there.

He wasn't smiling today, and she noted that, as she'd thought at the bank, he really was rather reptilian. If Fleur really was seeing him behind Athan's back, and there seemed every reason to suspect she was, then Ellie thought her completely and utterly mad. How could any woman be so taken in by this man's false smiles and sly eyes that she was prepared to risk losing everything?

Freddie didn't delay, but strode out of the church again, and Ellie got slowly to her feet as she heard him loudly urging his horse away from the churchyard gate in the direction of Pontypridd. Gwilym had promised her there was something to discover here in St. Dwynwen's church, and oh, how right he had been, but what could she do with her new knowledge? Fleur was right; she had no proof of anything. If only Freddie's arrival had been delayed a few more minutes, perhaps she would have at least had the note, whatever it was, but she hadn't had time. She was left with strong suspicions, and that was all.

In such circumstances, did she dare to pit herself against Fleur? Or did her situation remain completely unchanged, leaving her with the stark choice of applying for the position of governess with Lady Brecon, or being embroiled in a horrible, shameful scandal that would ruin her uncle?

Fourteen

Prince Paul's yacht, the *Troitskoe,* a sleek schooner with a slender blue-and-gold hull and a figurehead of a Dalmatian dog, had been becalmed for days off the island of Bornholm. Nights were long in these northern latitudes, so that the moon and stars shone far more than the sun, and tonight the aurora borealis was in full color, as if a monstrous show of fireworks were taking place just beyond the horizon. It was St. Valentine's Night by the British calendar, if not by the Russian. The weather was very cold and clear, the sea as still as a millpond, and the water was so cold that floats of ice were visible here and there. There was ice on the schooner's rigging too, and upon the rail where Athan leaned to watch the glories in the sky. He'd seen the northern lights before, but never quite like this. Every color of the rainbow seemed to be pulsing overhead, and everything was so quiet that he could even hear the display rustling and swishing, as if the gods were whispering.

He was loathing the voyage because he didn't like Valentin, whose name day this was, but who did not even begin to understand the meaning of love. Paul's odious nephew knew how to paw a woman and how to bed her with almost military precision, but he certainly knew nothing of the lovers over whom his patron saint kept watch. Valentin liked to pass the time in idle debauchery and had brought two women along for this purpose. One was a curvaceous, sloe-eyed girl from a village by the Black Sea; the other was a willowy creature with flaxen hair worn in a single braid curled on top of her head. Both dressed in flowing robes of such transparency that their nakedness beneath was plain to see, so it was as well for them that Valentin liked the stove in the state cabin to be kept as hot as possible. Tonight things had become particularly embarrassing, and Athan had taken the first opportunity to come up here on deck.

He'd been alone for quite some time, just enjoying the night sky, when he heard a familiar step. His heart sank as Valentin spoke. "You must have whistled, Lord Griffin."

"Whistled? What do you mean?" Athan turned reluctantly.

"Simply that it is said you must whistle to bring the lights to you, and clap your hands to drive them away again."

Athan looked up again at the fluttering draperies of color, and Valentin came to rest his elbows on the rail. He was still dressed in his Semeonovsky Regiment uniform, which he didn't remove even between the sheets. "It is also said," he continued, "that if blood red appears among the colors, there will be war."

"There is always war," Athan pointed out, "and there always will be while Bonaparte lives and breathes." He spoke deliberately, by now having more than gathered that the Russian was a fervent Francophile.

Valentin looked at him with dislike, then dissembled behind a smile. "The Finns call such a sky as this *fox fire*," he said on a new note, "because they believe the arctic fox starts it by brushing the snow into the air with its tail. What do you call it in Britain?"

"Apart from the aurora borealis?" Athan shrugged. "The northern lights or the Merry Dancers."

"The Merry Dancers? That is a good name. I like it. Now then, you told me earlier today that if we were in England now, it would be my saint's day. Is that right?"

"Yes."

"If you see the Merry Dancers in the heavens on St. Valentine's Day, does it augur well for affairs of the heart?"

Athan gave a short laugh. "I really have no idea."

"You are not in love, Lord Griffin?"

The sweet face of Ellie Rutherford seemed to appear before Athan.

Valentin straightened from the rail to look at him. "You do not answer, and yet I believe there is a future Lady Griffin. A lady named Fleur?"

"Maybe." Athan knew he was being less than fair to

Fleur, to whom he had proposed, and who had accepted him. So Valentin was right, there was indeed a future Lady Griffin, but all Lord Griffin could think about was Ellie Rutherford! Then something struck Athan and he turned curiously. "How did you know I was betrothed?"

"You told me, of course." Valentin laughed.

"No, I didn't."

Valentin shrugged. "You must have done, for how else would I know?"

How else indeed, because Athan *knew* he hadn't mentioned Fleur. A feeling of unease had beset him ever since his first meeting with Prince Paul Dalmatsky and his nephew, and now it surfaced strongly again. Something was very wrong about this whole business, and the more he thought about it, the more convinced he became that there was much more to it than a damned soup tureen.

Valentin cleared his throat. "I think I have had enough fresh air. Come back to my private apartments, and we will drink a little more vodka and toast the health of St. Valentine."

"Er, no, thank you, I rather think I've had enough vodka tonight." Go back into that decadent hothouse? Athan would rather freeze!

"The British have no stomach, Lord Griffin, for you have but sipped at it."

"Nevertheless, I'll stay out here a little longer."

"As you wish." Valentin's eyes met his for a moment, and the moving light from the heavens was sufficient to reveal rather more in their expression than he might have wished, for Athan saw . . . hatred. Yes, that was it, hatred of all things British.

Athan waited on deck until the sound of rather kittenish female laughter once again drifted from the direction of the state cabin, signifying Valentin's resumption of carnal pleasures. The fellow was insatiable, Athan thought as he returned to his own cabin, which was very comfortably fitted, with a canopied bed, an array of cupboards, a table and chair, and a washstand. There was a stove that made it as warm as July, except that on the other side of the window there hung icicles as white as snow. But it was to the washstand that Athan's startled eyes were drawn, for there, on the polished wooden surface in front of the oval mirror, was a posy of fresh snowdrops.

Astonished, he went a little closer, for it was as if someone had left him a valentine. The flowers had clearly just been plucked, yet no one had left the yacht in days, and even if they had, he did not somehow think snowdrops such as these would be in bloom yet on Bornholm. So where had they come from? Who had put them there? But as he reached out to the crisp white flowers, they slowly faded from view, and his fingers touched only the gleaming wood. Yet he felt sure he could smell the gentle, fresh, rather poignant fragrance of one of spring's daintiest, most fragile flowers.

A beguiling atmosphere moved around him as he raised his eyes to look into the mirror. It was an atmosphere that brought echoes of Wales, echoes as old as the mountains and as magical as the ancient myths. The image of his face in the glass seemed to be transparent, and through it he could see another face, gentle and feminine, framed with light brown curls, and with wistful bluebell eyes that seemed to penetrate his heart like one of Cupid's arrows. Her lips moved as she said his name, although he did not hear her voice. *"Athan?"*

He replied as if it was the most natural thing in the world, but his voice too was mute. *"Ellie?"* Once again he reached out, this time toward the glass itself, and his fingers sank through as if into water. . . .

When Athan had gone up on to the deck a little earlier, far away in Nantgarth everyone had sat down to a rather convivial supper of Welsh cider, oaten cakes, and slices of good ham that had been cured by Mrs. Lewis herself. The kitchen was firelit, and there were no northern lights outside, but the sky was brilliant with stars and the moon was red, promising a hard frost before morning. An owl hooted in the holly tree, and somewhere in the woods a vixen screamed.

The reason for the little celebration was that John had satisfactorily completed the first stage of decorating the tureens and was so pleased with his progress that he'd insisted the housekeeper and her son join Ellie and him at the table. Not that anyone had been permitted to view the tureens' progress, for he had a rather superstitious fear of letting anyone see his work once the painting had commenced. It was therefore a matter of some concern to him that he would probably *have* to show them in their unfinished state when the czar's representative called at Nantgarth.

By the time Athan finished speaking with Valentin on the *Troitskoe,* Mrs. Lewis had cleared away the tablecloth, poured the last measures of cider, and then joined in the general conversation, which had begun to turn upon whether or not there was really such a thing as magic.

"Come now, Mrs. Lewis," John declared challengingly, "you don't *really* expect me to believe in magic, do you? Oh, I know that Gwilym has some power or other over horses—"

"—and doors and clocks," Ellie added.

"And doors and clocks," he conceded, "but—"

"—and eels," she interrupted again. Sherry before the meal, followed by cider during it, had a great deal to answer for.

"Eels?" Her uncle looked blankly at her.

Mrs. Lewis and her son exchanged glances, but said nothing.

"Oh, take no notice of me," Ellie said quickly, her already flushed cheeks going a little more pink. She wore a deep golden velvet gown that probably looked ridiculously formal for such a friendly little supper, but she had not been able to resist the temptation to dress as she would have done had she still been at Rutherford Park. In a way, the gown was also another gesture of defiance at Fleur, whose threats and warnings she had elected to ignore. Well, which she seemed outwardly to ignore, but which inwardly worried her so much that she often felt quite sick. The letter to Athan, if it existed, was by now well on its way to St. Petersburg, and she could only wait to see what transpired. She hadn't been able to bring herself to tell her uncle what might happen, and didn't know whether her silence was due to cowardice or her desire not to worry him. Perhaps it was a little of both. Whatever the truth of it, her continuing state of apprehension was the reason for this evening's little overindulgence in sherry and cider.

DIAMOND DREAMS

The housekeeper looked at John. "Tea leaves can show one's dreams, Mr. Bailey, but there are other things that can close the miles, things that only Gwilym can do."

"What things?" John inquired, looking from mother to son.

"Gwilym will show you, but you must promise not to speak. Not a single word must you utter, or it will be ruined."

"As you wish," John replied.

Mrs. Lewis nodded at Gwilym. "Show them, there's a good boy."

"I can only show one of them, Mam," he reminded her.

She smiled again. "Then you know which one it must be."

His chair scraped and he limped outside. The door opened and closed for him, and the clock stopped and then restarted. Ellie was surprised at how swiftly such strange occurrences had begun to seem almost normal. Nothing seemed impossible in this place. On his return, Gwilym put a little posy of snowdrops on the table in front of her, then brought a small looking glass that he arranged so Ellie's face and the flowers were both reflected. Then Gwilym resumed his seat at the table, closed his eyes, and began to rock very slightly.

As Athan entered his cabin on the *Troitskoe* and observed the snowdrops on the washstand, Mrs. Lewis looked intently at Ellie. "No one else, not even Gwilym, will see what you see, Miss Ellie. Look deep into the glass, and forget everything else."

Ellie felt lightheaded. She was floating away; drifting up into the icy night sky, where the moon was so red, and the stars were like diamonds upon moving veils of colored gauze. There was light everywhere, swirling and swaying, crackling softly, as if a thunderstorm were imminent. Somehow the looking glass was still before her, and the posy of snowdrops. The perfume of the flowers seemed to be part of her, and she could see through her reflection in the glass, to another face beyond. It was Athan, her love. *"Athan?"* Her lips said his name, but her voice was silent as she reached out toward him.

"Ellie?" He reached toward her at the same time. The glass resembled warm water and was drenched in moving

lights of every color of the rainbow. Their fingers touched, then linked together, and she felt him pulling her into the glass. It was impossible, yet she slipped through as easily as if it were a door. It was a phantasm, she told herself, because she was actually seated in the kitchen at Nantgarth; yet it *felt* so real.

His fingers grew more firm, clasping hers, flesh to flesh. She was no longer in the kitchen, but in a room built of wood, with a glazed window that faced over . . . an almost frozen sea. Oh, such a sea, so many colors turning to ice beneath a sky that blazed like a fiery rainbow. Her lips met his, and she heard his breath escape on the softest groan as he held her tightly to him. For these uncanny moments they were free to do as they wished. Nothing else mattered. Fleur might never have existed, or his first wife Caroline, or indeed the Unicorn Bank; there wasn't anything to stand between Ellie Rutherford and this man whom she loved as much as life itself. They were a single entity—one heart, one soul—forged together in a kiss that did not bow to reason or propriety.

And when the kiss ended, as end it had to, there was so much they wished to say, but they were both too spellbound. They spoke with their eyes, their bodies, and their emotions. They knew they were meant to be together, but that in the true world to which they must both return there were things that could only keep them apart. She leaned back in his arms with a sigh as he bent his head to kiss her naked shoulder. Erotic sensations tingled over her skin, then gathered voluptuously inside her. She ached with desire, and all thought of resistance was banished to the dazzling skies outside.

He drew her toward the canopied bed, and she went willingly, eagerly . . . wantonly. There was no ring on her finger, but she did not care; besides, she had only to remind herself that none of this was real, but remained a wonderful, beguiling chimera through which she was granted the man she craved. There was no restraint upon her senses, no thought that this was wrong, just the sheer joy of being intimate with the man who'd dominated her thoughts and life since that day at the Crown Inn. She sank onto the bed, her light brown hair catching on the pillow, her cheeks flushed, her blue eyes dark with emotion.

Athan lay with her. There was no obstacle now, nothing

to prevent them from consummating their fierce desires. Arousal pounded through him as he undid his breeches before leaning over her to draw up the folds of her golden velvet skirts and rest his hand gently upon her naked thigh. Her breath caught with anticipation. *Now, please, take me now....*

"Damn it all, Mrs. Lewis, when is something going to happen?" exclaimed her uncle's impatient voice.

The phantasm was shattered. Everything began to slip away—the cabin, the radiant northern sky, the desire . . . Athan. . . . Ellie tried to cling to him, tried to defy the inexorable force that suddenly dragged her back through the looking glass. She was falling through the night sky, between the stars, and past the red moon. Someone was screaming, and she realized it was she herself. Suddenly she was in the firelit kitchen again, not on her chair, but on the floor, where she lay sobbing and distraught.

The other chairs scraped. She heard her uncle's appalled cry, "Dear God, what's happened, what's happened?"

Then Mrs. Lewis was kneeling beside her, gentle hands on her shoulders. "It's all right, Miss Ellie. You're safe now."

The housekeeper's voice was soothing amid the utter chaos that still seemed to be revolving around Ellie. Nothing was steady, the kitchen floor seemed to be swaying, and her senses were torn and scattered. "Athan?" she whispered.

"Hush now, no names," Mrs. Lewis breathed quickly, mindful of John coming to look anxiously down at his niece.

"Ellie? Are you all right, my dear?" he inquired, his face pale with shock. "One moment you were sitting there, the next you fainted."

Gwilym looked reproachfully at him. "Because you spoke, Mr. Bailey."

"Well, nothing was happening," John answered defensively. "She just sat there in complete silence, staring at the looking glass."

Mrs. Lewis helped Ellie to sit up, and managed to whisper warningly to her without John hearing. "Sh, not a word out of place, Miss Ellie, for his lordship is betrothed to another."

Ellie looked swiftly at her. "You know? You saw?"

The housekeeper shook her head. "You said his name," she explained, then turned brightly to John. "There, she's beginning to be herself again. I fear our Welsh cider is a little more potent than was realized."

"Cider?" John looked at her. "I thought we were supposed to be experimenting with magic."

"Well, it doesn't always work."

"Are you sure you're all right now, my dear?" John asked Ellie as she was helped to her feet.

Ellie managed to smile at him. "I just fainted, that's all. Mrs. Lewis is right, I've had a little too much cider, especially after the sherry I had before supper."

Mrs. Lewis tried to make her sit at the table again. "Come, my dear, I will heat some milk for you. That will do you more good than cider."

"I . . . I think it's best if I go to bed," Ellie answered.

"Oh, but—"

"No, truly," Ellie insisted, then went to kiss her uncle on the cheek. "I'll be perfectly well again by the morning, and must remember in future to avoid cider."

She made good her exit, but once in the entrance passage, where the longcase clock ticked relentlessly, closed her eyes and paused. "Oh, Athan," she whispered, "Athan, I do love you so. . . ."

On the *Troitskoe,* Athan had struggled to keep Ellie with him. His fingers had gripped so tightly that he knew he was hurting her, but even so she slipped from him. She became more indistinct, seeming to blend with the looking glass; then suddenly it was all over. There was just the cabin, the Merry Dancers . . . and the faint scent of snowdrops.

He was so shaken that he could only stand there, gazing at the mirror as if at a ghost. Was he losing his sanity? But no, his lips were still bruised from shared kisses, his body was still responding, and he knew that he really had been with her. He also knew that she loved him, as he loved her.

Fifteen

The events of St. Valentine's Night seemed very far behind when the *Troitskoe* entered the Norfolk port of Lowestoft, and Athan traveled reluctantly on to London with Valentin. Once in the capital, he saw to it that Valentin was installed at his Berkeley Square house, while he himself took up temporary residence at his club. If Valentin thought this odd or discourteous, he did not say, and Athan had the feeling that the arrangement more than suited him. If only the Russian intended to remain in London to conduct some unspecified business or other, but unfortunately he still meant to travel on to Castle Griffin in order to consult with John Bailey. When this visitation could be expected was not quite clear, but as far as Athan was concerned, it was bound to be too soon.

It was intriguing to ponder the nature of Valentin's business here in London. Athan felt certain it would be shady and underhanded, possibly even sinister, given that Prince Paul Dalmatsky had a hand in it along the way. Conversations with Valentin during the voyage from Riga had convinced Athan that he was simply his uncle's cat's-paw. Whatever was going on, it proceeded entirely at Paul's bidding, and for some reason or other that slippery nobleman wished his involvement to remain secret. Valentin had been duped into thinking it was all about the soup tureen for the czar, but there was something else as well, something his uncle was at very great pains to keep to himself.

With Valentin intent upon his own affairs and not in any need of shepherding, Athan was able to devote a few days to the Unicorn Bank before thinking of traveling on to Castle Griffin to attend to the selection and preparation of a mare and colt for the czar. At the bank he had made a thorough nuisance of himself, questioning all concerned, and raising points that quite clearly made some people uncomfortable. But no matter how many times he and his accountant examined the books, it appeared clear that Josiah Rutherford had indeed been the architect of his own destruction. Ellie's father appeared to have become involved with someone named John Arbuthnot Billersley, with whom he had made very unwise investments and transactions, and had lost everything. That was all that could be discovered. Who Billersley was, or where he might be found, remained a mystery.

Another thing that seemed uncomfortably clear was that the hand of the late Albert Forrester-Phipps, Freddie's father, was faintly but definitely detectable in it all, but as that gentleman was now very much deceased, there did not seem much likelihood of ever getting to the bottom of it. However, Athan also unearthed the rather shocking fact that Forrester-Phipps Senior's fall from the Dover cliff had not been an accident or indeed the malicious act of a third party. It had been kept very quiet indeed that he had actually committed suicide, choosing to depart this world before his nefarious activities at the bank were exposed. The bank, of course, had an eye upon its reputation and its profits, and so was more than eager to keep the secret.

Most of Athan's information was obtained from a junior clerk, who had also seen a letter Josiah Rutherford had handed to the bank on the last day of his life. In it were instructions that all funds remaining after the sale of Rutherford Park were to be used to provide for his daughter. Rutherford had included his painstaking figures for everything, and the precise sum, he believed, would be available for Ellie. Athan's informant may have been young and inexperienced, but he had a sensible head on his shoulders and knew that the computations were accurate. Yet the bank's figures differed radically, and all to Josiah Rutherford's detriment. The shadows of John Arbuthnot Billersley and Albert Forrester-Phipps loomed too large for any sunlight to fall upon Ellie, and the letter, of course, had since disappeared.

Being a director of the bank did not make Athan wish to be part of the conspiracy that seemed to have infiltrated everything at the premises in Ludgate. For Ellie's sake he intended to get to the heart of it, and to this end had secretly installed a very trustworthy spy to look into the matter. He was sure this would soon pay dividends, but knew that even if things were turned around to Ellie's benefit, there remained the small matter of where on earth she might be.

It was this latter problem that led to him paying an unannounced call upon the painter Thomas Lawrence, who had now returned to his house and studio in Greek Street, Soho. The March weather was brisk and windy as he alighted outside the front door with its Doric pilasters and handsome frieze, composed himself for what was bound to be a disagreeable interview, and then rapped his cane upon the gleaming dark green paintwork.

On being admitted, he was requested to wait in the small entrance hall. The house was rather modest for one who'd already risen to becoming the royal artist. Lawrence was still only about thirty-six, and had been fashionable for many years, commanding vast sums for his work. Although only the son of a Bristol innkeeper, he was talented, poised, charming, and witty, and there were few great names in the land that had not sat for him. Nevertheless, he was frequently in financial straits, a fact that often led him to sell paintings, and it was the disposal of one painting in particular that was of interest to Athan.

It was some time before Lawrence's latest client, a long-faced naval officer, departed, and Athan was conducted up to the artist's studio. Lawrence, chestnut-haired and of an amiable visage, was cleaning his brushes as his caller entered. "Good day to you, Lord Griffin. How may I be of service?"

"You can tell me why you painted two portraits of Miss Rutherford of Rutherford Park," Athan replied without beating around the bush.

The artist became rather still. "I . . . I beg your pardon?" he replied carefully.

"You heard me, I fancy, sir. You were commissioned to paint Miss Rutherford's portrait, a conventional affair with curtains, a pedestal, and so on, yet you painted another as well, did you not?"

Lawrence feigned puzzlement. "No, sir, I did not paint

two. I remember the commission well, for it was most agreeable on the Isle of Wight, but I vow I did not paint more than one likeness of the young lady."

"If you wish me to call you a liar, then I will, sir," Athan replied shortly.

The artist put down the brushes, then wiped his hands on an oily cloth. "I do not know your purpose, sir, or indeed your problem, but it is hardly acceptable for you to enter my house and abuse me in such a way."

"I'll abuse you further by bloodying your nose unless you tell the truth!" Athan snapped. "At least do me the courtesy of admitting that, unknown to Miss Rutherford, you presumed to paint her in a pose that was improper to say the very least."

Lawrence's tongue passed over his lower lip. "And if I did such a thing, what business would it be of yours?" he inquired.

"I now own the second portrait." Athan looked away for a moment. He'd bought the picture because he'd been so attracted to the then anonymous sitter. Being thoroughly tired of pursuit by all and sundry in the Marriage Stakes, he'd invented a wife. Enter Caroline, Lady Griffin, the adored but ungrateful bride who'd bolted with a lover, but whose existence kept the clamor of would-be Lady Griffins at bay. How very dramatic then to have come face-to-face with Ellie Rutherford and to know he was looking at Caroline.

Lawrence looked curiously at him. "Sir, if you have purchased the portrait, is it not a little late to throw your hands up in shock?"

"I met her after I had purchased it and knew she *had* to be the sitter. I also knew she wasn't the sort of young woman who would pose for you in a shawl and nothing else!"

Lawrence took the precaution of positioning himself strategically behind a table that was laden with his painting implements, and then nodded. "Very well, I admit to painting the second portrait, but I swear I did not do it out of any disrespect for Miss Rutherford. I loved her, you see."

This last was said in such a matter-of-fact tone that had it not been for Lawrence's reputation having gone before him, Athan might have thought him glib. But the fellow was known to be sentimental to the point of foolishness, and was always in love with someone—in love with being in love, in fact. "You loved her, sir? That still did not give you the right to paint her in such a manner."

"I know," Lawrence admitted, "but I did not identify her on the work."

"I'm aware of that, but the likeness is unmistakable, and therefore a threat to the lady's reputation. That's one reason I am here, to find out if there are any more such daubs of her."

"None, sir."

"Do you swear it?"

Lawrence held up his hands in submission. "Oh, most certainly, sir. I painted the original portrait and the one you have now. That is all."

"How well acquainted with her were you?" Athan asked then, unable to stifle a pang of jealousy that this talented but undeserving fellow had known Ellie before he did.

"I painted her portrait, that is all," Lawrence replied. "Oh, I importuned her, and promised my eternal love, but she was indifferent to me, so I nursed my broken heart for a while, then fell in love elsewhere."

"Have you any idea where she is now?"

The artist looked blankly at her. "Well, she's at Rutherford Park, isn't she?"

"No. Her parents are both deceased, Rutherford Park has been sold, and I do not know where to find her." He'd pretended to have Caroline, and not to know where she was; now he really did have her, but still did not know where she was.

Lawrence was dumbfounded. "Her parents are deceased?" The thought of Ellie all on her own was romantic and appealing, and he gave a faint smile. "Why, I'm of a mind to love her all over again," he sighed.

It was too much. Athan strode around the table and dealt him a thudding blow to the chin. With a grunt, Lawrence sagged at the knees, and then clutched at the table to support himself, but his senses were reeling, and he only succeeded in hauling the table over as he fell. Jars, paints, brushes, and cloths went in all directions, and to make matters complete, the palette he'd been using upon the naval officer's portrait was knocked over as well. It landed upside down on the artist's head, then slid slowly to the floor over his right ear, leaving lurid blue, yellow, pink, and green oil paint over his chestnut hair.

Athan stood over him. "I warn you, Lawrence, that if you ever do such a disreputable painting again, of any lady, you will have me to reckon with. Is that clear?"

Lawrence tried to speak but couldn't, so confined himself to nodding instead.

"And if I ever hear an unwelcome whisper about Miss Rutherford in particular, I will tear your tongue out. Is that also clear?"

Lawrence's eyes widened, but he nodded quickly.

There the mystery would have to rest, Athan thought as he quit the house in Greek Street and drove off to an appointment with his lawyer to collect the special license that had been applied for before the visit to St. Petersburg. Athan didn't want the license, didn't want Fleur, but honor and principle made it certain he would take both.

Tomorrow he was leaving for Castle Griffin, where Fleur Tudor waited in anticipation of a betrothal, not an imminent wedding. But his mind was made up. He had to stop his nonsensical yearnings for a woman who was only part fact and mostly dream, and apply himself to the bride who was entirely fact, and who had every right to expect to wear his ring. He tried to tell himself it was for the best that he couldn't find Ellie, but he knew it wasn't for the best at all. If there were an honorable way out of wedding Fleur, he would take it, because he knew that she wasn't the bride for him. The events of St. Valentine's Night had sealed his fate. No other woman but Ellie could have turned his blood to fire in his veins or aroused him to such a pitch of unstoppable need that the frustration of interrupted passion remained with him even now. He was restless, unfulfilled, and unhappy, and could only be saved by Josiah Rutherford's elusive daughter. Did she feel the same way? Did she feel the exquisite pain of thwarted desire? Did he haunt her dreams as she haunted his? Did her body crave the physical joy that had so nearly been theirs on St. Valentine's Night?

He gave an ironic laugh as he looked out of his carriage window at the London street. How could he let his thoughts wander like this? How could he let them so ransack common sense that he could no longer distinguish fact from fantasy? No matter what he had convinced himself at the time, he knew now that Ellie couldn't possibly have been with him on the *Troitskoe*. His reprehensible love had led him to imagine—or dream—that he'd lain on a bed with Ellie Rutherford. It had led him to believe he'd have made sweet, passionate, erotic love to her if the dream had not ended as it did, cruelly, shockingly, hurtfully. . . .

Sixteen

Athan's traveling carriage drove the final miles home to Castle Griffin in bright sunshine, with daffodils nodding in the verges, catkins and pussywillows brightening the hedgerows, and the first fresh greens of spring coloring the surrounding landscape. Cottagers were busy in their gardens, sowing in readiness for the summer, and the Merthyr turnpike was busy because it was market day in Pontypridd. The air was still cool, but even so he'd lowered the window glass in order to inhale the sweetness of the mountains. The welcome sounds of his homeland were gentle upon his ears: two men greeting each other in Welsh, a flock of sheep calling on the slope above the road, and in the distance the muted roar of the Taff as it squeezed between rocks on the valley floor.

The sky was a translucent blue, just blue, with no otherworld colors to raise visions and deceive the senses. It looked . . . well, as it should. He needed the normality of everything being in its allotted place and time, but after the erotic mysteries of St. Valentine's Night he knew that nothing would ever be quite the same again. How easy it was, in this ancient Celtic land of legends, myths, and magic, to believe in the fantastic and supernatural . . . to therefore believe in *all* his encounters with Ellie Rutherford. He'd tried to think only of Fleur, but Ellie was both around him and in him. She flowed through his veins, filled his mind, and dwelt in his heart. She was in the sky, the trees, and the very mountains, and he couldn't drive her away because she was part of everything now. This was no caprice, but the deepest and most consequential form of love. He'd loved her from the moment he'd gazed upon her unnamed portrait and called her Caroline. There was no escape from the fact that no matter how many times he lay with Fleur, it would be meaningless, whereas to lie only once with Ellie would mean fulfillment in the truest sense of the word. To have Ellie as his wife, to go to sleep beside her every night and awaken beside her every morning, would be a joy forever.

Sometimes he heard her voice so clearly that he expected her to be there, but she never was. To daydream of her was to seek the impossible. She had disappeared from Rutherford Park on purpose, deliberately cutting off all ties with the past, and in so doing she had closed the door upon him as well. If the exquisite romance of St. Valentine's Night had any basis in fact—which he prayed it did—then at least he could be sure she had not gone lightly from him. She'd struggled to stay as much as he'd struggled to keep her. The beauty of those shared moments on the *Troitskoe* had proved their love for each other, but she'd been torn from his arms by something, he knew not what. Now he only had her portrait and knew that when he set foot at Castle Griffin again, his first thought would be to look at her likeness. Yet his future *had* to be with Fleur, to whom he'd proposed, and who deserved a better husband than one as reluctant as he. A gentleman's word was his bond, or so they said. It was an honorable maxim; indeed, it was the guiding principle of his class, yet his conscience told him there was a world of difference between his bond and doing what was actually the right thing. Nevertheless, he would stand by his bond, and the special license was ready and waiting in his luggage.

He looked out at the wild scenery of the gorge. A young woman with light brown curls was walking down a steep path, a basket of bread over her arm. His heart quickened and he sat forward, but it was only a stranger. His sadness returned, and he leaned his head back against the carriage upholstery to try to think of other things: preparing the two horses for the czar, perhaps, or calling upon John Bailey to tell him what he knew of the order for the soup tureen. Not that the tureen would be news to the china maker, because Valentin had sent a letter to Nantgarth House some time before Christmas, but there was another reason for calling at Nantgarth House: to make the acquaintance of John Bailey's niece, who, if suitable, would be invited to Castle Griffin to be a friend for Fleur.

The carriage halted at the turnpike gate, and Huw Jenkin hurried to open it with his collie at his heels. "Welcome home, my lord! Oh, it's good to see you back!" the gatekeeper cried, snatching off his hat and bowing respectfully.

"Thank you, Huw. It's good to be back," Athan called back, and the carriage swept through. Soon it turned off the turnpike to climb up through Nantgarth, but it wasn't until the bridge over the canal that Athan glanced out and saw Gwilym Lewis riding one of the Griffin horses out of the evergreen shadows of the works alley. Gwilym's eyes met his, and suddenly Athan felt compelled to call upon John Bailey there and then. Why wait? Besides, it would postpone for a little longer the moment when he had to confront Fleur and behave as her future husband.

Leaning out, he instructed the coachman to halt at the gate of Nantgarth House. The whitewashed property was dazzling in the sunlight, its windows fresh and sparkling, its front door newly painted blue. The south-facing garden was filled with daffodils, crocuses, and the last of the snowdrops, but its real glory was a bright pink camellia that bloomed in a sheltered corner. Athan climbed quickly down, intending to hail Gwilym and ask a few brief questions about the stud, but to his astonishment there was no sign of the housekeeper's son or his horse. Puzzled, Athan glanced back over the bridge toward Nantgarth, and then ahead toward the fork, but the youth on the white colt might as well have never been.

The door of the house opened, and Mrs. Lewis hurried out in a green-and-white gingham dress. "Oh, my lord, my lord, how wonderful it is to see you again!" she cried, her mobcap wobbling as she came to open the garden gate for him.

Athan returned her smile. "It is good to see you again too, Mrs. Lewis." He glanced around again. "It was my intention to speak to Gwilym, but he seems to have gone."

"Gwilym is up at the castle, my lord."

"He was here a moment since. I saw him."

"Really?" The housekeeper looked up and down the lane. "Well, he didn't come to see me, and for that will be told off, you may be sure." She stood aside on the path. "Do come in, do come in, my lord."

Athan did as he was bade. "Mrs. Lewis, you'd be flattered indeed if you knew how often I spent my time in St. Petersburg dreaming about your cooking."

She blushed with pleasure. "I will cook for you right now, my lord," she declared, making fast and loose with the contents of John Bailey's larder. "You do not look at all well and clearly were not looked after properly in that foreign place. Some good Welsh air, Welsh cooking, and Welsh company will soon put you right."

"Most likely, but I hardly think it proper for me to be fed at Mr. Bailey's expense."

"At least allow me to cut you some of my *bara brith*."

"Ah, now you've persuaded me," he laughed.

She beamed, and ushered him into the house.

"Has Miss Bailey arrived yet?" he asked, as they stepped into the entrance hall.

"Miss Who, sir?"

"Miss Bailey. Mr. Bailey's niece."

The housekeeper turned. "Yes, Mr. Bailey's niece is here, sir, but Miss Ellie's surname is Rutherford."

Suddenly the very air around him seemed to become muffled, and all he could hear was his own heart beginning to race.

Mrs. Lewis watched his face, and then smiled a secret sort of smile as she took his hat, overcoat, and gloves. "Mr. Bailey is down in the cellar, and I will tell him you have called, my lord, but Miss Ellie is in the parlor. Please go right in."

Before Athan could recover from his shock, the housekeeper had hung his coat on a wall hook, placed his hat and gloves on a rush-seated chair, and hurried away. He expected her to announce him to Ellie, but she walked past the parlor door and disappeared into the kitchen. The longcase clock ticked slowly and steadily, unlike his heart, which now thundered in his breast.

A name whispered through the house. *Ellie* . . . He gazed toward the closed door, rooted, unable to move. The latch lifted slowly, and the door opened. He couldn't breathe. Timeless things brushed his face and seemed to trifle with his hair. Whispers were all around him, audible, yet just beyond hearing. He heard sweet music, a snatch of melody from a distant harp, then a draft stirred strongly along the passage, bringing with it the scent of snowdrops.

"Ellie?" He found his voice, and her name escaped the confines of the otherworld and became fact.

"Is that you, Uncle John? Did you call me?" At last her shadow fell across the parlor doorway. She wore a yellow-sprigged muslin gown, and her light brown curls were piled up so loosely that they seemed about to fall down again at any moment. She had a book in her hand, and her forefinger was between the pages to mark the place. There was no light of precognition in her bright blue eyes, nothing to show anticipation of his presence, just the natural interest of a niece who'd heard a man say her name and believed it could only be her uncle. But then she saw him. Her breath snatched, the book slipped from her hand, and she had to reach out to the doorjamb to steady herself.

"Ellie?" he said again, unable to quite believe this was real. Would she disappear if he touched her?

She did not know what to say or do. A score of emotions formed a maelstrom inside her, but love and desire broke free of the wild swirl that rendered her so helpless. This was real. He was here, in Nantgarth House, and she could see in his eyes that everything she had experienced, he'd experienced too. They were intimate strangers, willful partners in stolen passions, and had shared impossible kisses and caresses even though they'd been hundreds of miles apart. Seeing him now, the unbelievable was somehow no longer beyond reason.

The longcase clock whirred and began to strike, breaking a moment so spellbinding it was almost opiate. Athan tried to pull himself together, to appear at least a little in command of himself. "Perhaps we should talk?" he suggested, thinking how woefully inadequate the words were; but then wasn't he woefully inadequate in the face of such moments as these?

She nodded and drew back into the room, but went only a few steps before turning. He was close behind her, close enough to reach out and touch the softness of her hair. She closed her eyes. Remembered fantasies were too real to resist or deny, even had she wanted to. But her senses were out of control, her willpower was nonexistent, and her wits had been beguiled. His arm moved around her waist, and she was pliant and willing as she let him pull her to him. They were each other's tender jailer, and there was no thought of anyone else, not of Fleur, or of the possibility that John might enter at any moment.

As they kissed, echoes of a distant past seemed to sound softly within them both. She could smell the mountains on his clothes, taste the wild heather on his lips, and feel eternity in his embrace. This was so right, so right. . . . Their lips moved luxuriously together, their hearts beat in unison, and their souls became one. Nothing could be more right and true than this, nothing at all. . . .

But even such a kiss had to end, and they drew apart, their faces flushed, their eyes darkened with love. He brushed a stray curl from her forehead. "I can't believe I've found you again, right here in Nantgarth. I feared you were lost to me forever. . . ."

She pulled from his arms. "I knew we were bound to meet, because I knew who you were," she said quietly.

"You came here because of me?" He was startled.

She shook her head. "No, I didn't know then. It's something I've realized since. It was something my uncle said, and I put two and two together. I'd been wondering how it would be when we met." *But there hasn't been time for you to have received the letter Fleur says she prompted your agent to write. . . .*

"How could you doubt it would be like this?" he asked. "Surely, after the things that have passed between us—"

"—even though we both know we've been so far apart?" she finished for him.

He gazed at her. "Do you doubt that it all happened?"

"No," she whispered.

"Nor do I."

He tried to take her hands, but she had to step backward. "There is too much that really does separate us, Athan," she said.

"If you mean that wretched business of the bank, I *swear* that I knew nothing. I only became a director that day we met. All that had gone before was—"

"I was thinking of Miss Tudor," she interrupted, for somehow the Unicorn Bank was inconsequential right now.

He had to look away. Fleur was someone of whom he didn't wish to speak, of whom he didn't want to even think.

"You do not deny that you are to marry her?"

"No," he admitted.

"Then you know that you and I must—"

"You and I are all that matters!" he cried, seizing her arms and pulling her toward him again. "I know I've asked Fleur to be my bride, but . . ." His voice died away, for he knew there could be no buts.

She longed to tell him what she'd seen up at the church and damage Fleur Tudor all she could before Fleur's lies ruined her uncle's reputation and livelihood beyond redemption, but the fact remained that there was no proof of anything. Whatever she said, even if she mentioned Fleur's threats, Cardiff tittle-tattle, or Freddie Forrester-Phipps's presence here in Glamorgan, she couldn't substantiate anything. Fleur was bound to deny it all, and would probably burst into helpless little tears about Ellie Rutherford's lies.

Yet there was no doubt in Ellie's mind that the moment Athan returned to the castle, Fleur would almost certainly regale him with the so-called shocking rumors she'd heard about the uncle and niece living at Nantgarth House.

But as Ellie stood there in miserable indecision, feeling damned whichever decision she made, the door opened and her uncle came in with a beaming smile.

"Athan! My dear friend, how truly *delighted* I am that you've returned at last!"

Seventeen

John hastened to take Athan's hand in both his, but then looked at him in concern. "You're too pale and thin, sir, so it would seem that Russia didn't agree with you any more than it once did with me."

"The St. Petersburg winters are notorious for afflictions of the chest, and I fear I fell victim. I had no idea you'd been there too." Athan struggled to appear relaxed, for the truth was that he, rather unfairly, resented the interruption to his meeting with Ellie. He tried to mask his discomposure by glancing up at the portrait of the young man over the fireplace, and in so doing was startled to suddenly recognize the spire of the Peter and Paul Cathedral in St. Petersburg in the background. He'd seen the portrait before without realizing where it had been painted, but was now struck by the coincidence of it being the Russian capital. The subject of the painting had never surprised him, however, for he'd long since guessed why there would never be a Mrs. John Bailey. Now it would seem that John's memories of St. Petersburg were concerned not only with the vagaries of the climate.

John ushered Ellie to sit down on the settle, then made Athan sit there too. "A glass of sherry?" he offered, going to the decanter on a table in the corner.

"That would be agreeable," Athan replied.

"Yes, I had the misfortune to visit the Russian capital and am afraid that the good memories I have of the place are by far outweighed by the bad. But enough of that, for you're home in Wales again now, and all is well. Mrs. Lewis is going to bring us some tea and *bara brith* in a little while, which will do your constitution the power of good." John finished pouring three glasses, then brought two to the settle. "Well, Ellie, *is* Lord Griffin the young gentleman you spoke of from the Isle of Wight?" he asked.

"Yes, he is," she answered, catching Athan's inquiring eye and deciding to do what she could to put him in the picture. "Lord Griffin, I told my uncle that I thought that you were among a party of gentlemen that called at Rutherford Park one afternoon a year or so ago. . . ."

"Yes, I recall," he replied.

To their relief John didn't inquire further, but took his seat on his rocking chair, and raised his glass. "To our health and happiness," he declared.

They raised their glasses and shared the toast.

John cleared his throat. "When it comes to health, nothing good ever came out of St. Petersburg, but when it comes to business, it is a different matter, eh, Athan? I gather we both have reason to celebrate in the latter respect, you with your horses, me with my tureens."

Athan was taken aback. "You know about the horses? But—"

"I'd be willing to wager that Gwilym Lewis knew at practically the same moment as you," John interrupted with a wry smile. "Don't ask me how, but he's been certain enough to have already selected a mare and a colt, *and* to have been up to St. Dwynwen's well with them to seek her blessing. Ellie saw him up there with them, didn't you, Ellie?"

"Yes, indeed." *And Gwilym Lewis wasn't the only person I saw up there,* Ellie thought.

Athan was philosophical about Gwilym. "I suppose I should no longer be surprised by anything about Nantgarth's very own Merlin, but somehow it comes as a shock every time. The supernatural is around us more than we even begin to know." He glanced at Ellie, and she at him.

John chuckled. "And am I to blame the supernatural for your lack of surprise when I mentioned tureens?"

Athan returned his smile. "No, sir, you are not. I merely confess to having traveled back from Russia in company with Prince Valentin Andreyov."

"So he's safely here in England?" John sat forward.

"Yes, and will shortly be coming to Castle Griffin. He means to consult with you then about the minutiae of the czar's order. It was because of my acquaintance with him that I decided to call here before going on to the castle. I thought you would appreciate knowing he'd arrived in the country."

"That's most considerate of you," John replied warmly. "Well, I have no fewer than three tureens from which Prince Valentin may choose, although as you may guess, I had to throw away many more than that before I had even one that was good enough."

Athan was sympathetic. "You still haven't quite established the formula?"

"On the contrary, in recent weeks I feel certain that I have at last, but now it seems there may be a fault of some sort with the smaller of my two kilns. I've made every inspection and correction imaginable, but can't find out what it is, yet I know there must be something, because if the formula itself were still at fault, I'm sure I wouldn't get any decent porcelain at all." He gave a broad grin. "But tureens are all I need to be going on with, and they are all almost completely decorated. Oh, they're rare items, I can tell you, and I'm as pleased as punch. Whichever one goes to St. Petersburg will be a splendid advertisement not only for this little works, but also for British ceramic ware in general. We'll show the French, eh? The supremacy of Sèvres and its likes will soon be at an end. Now, let us talk of something else that is pleasing. I refer to your betrothal to Miss Tudor. Are we soon to have a date for the wedding itself?" he asked then.

"Nothing is fixed." Athan looked uneasily at Ellie, who kept her eyes upon the fire.

John laughed. "It soon will be, you mark my words. You know what ladies are when it comes to such things. I imagine Miss Tudor has decided upon her wedding gown ten times over."

There was a tap at the door, and Mrs. Lewis came in with the promised tray of tea and a plate of warm buttered *bara brith*. When the housekeeper had withdrawn again, and Ellie had attended to the duties of hostess, Athan diverted the conversation to the matter of his progress at the bank, which was something he was anxious for her to know. "Forgive me for mentioning this, Miss Rutherford, but with regard to the inquiry you made just before your uncle joined us, concerning the proceedings at the Unicorn Bank. As a partner, I—"

John was dumbfounded. "You are a partner of the Unicorn?"

"Indeed so, but I assure you I wasn't at the time of Mr. Rutherford's unfortunate experiences. When a senior partner, Albert Forrester-Phipps, died quite suddenly, I was approached to take his place, and I decided it would be a wise investment. That was why I was present the day Mr. Rutherford last went to the premises in Ludgate Hill, and in view of the tragic events that followed, the matter naturally preyed upon my mind." Athan worded it all as carefully as he could, bearing in mind that he and Ellie were supposed to have met only briefly on the Isle of Wight, so he was ambiguous about the whys and wherefores of his interest in what befell Josiah Rutherford. "I thought of it a great deal while I was in St. Petersburg," he went on, "and immediately on my return to London I investigated the entire case."

"What have you discovered?" John asked.

"That something certainly went on at the bank that ought not to have done, although I have yet to uncover evidence that Miss Rutherford could use to prosecute the bank." Athan explained everything he'd learned, and then came to Josiah's supposed associate, John Arbuthnot Billersley.

Ellie was pouring her uncle another cup of tea, and her hand jolted so much on hearing the name that she almost dropped the teapot. John was so appalled that he leapt up from the rocking chair. "But that's impossible!" he cried in utter disbelief.

Athan looked at him and at Ellie's suddenly pale face. "Is this Billersley person known to you?" he asked.

Ellie fixed her gaze low again, and left any response to her uncle, who hesitated, then answered very unwillingly. "In a manner of speaking," he said.

"What does that mean?" Athan asked.

"It means that I knew someone called John Arbuthnot Billersley, but he is now deceased, and has been for some years." John's guilty gaze caught Ellie's, and became imploring. *Don't expose me, Ellie, I beg of you. . . .*

"Deceased?" Athan looked from one to the other again,

and knew he wasn't being told the truth. "Now look, how am I going to be able to help in this matter if you aren't being entirely honest with me? You both know more about this Billersley person that you care to admit, and I expect you to do me the courtesy of including me in the secret."

"Uncle?" Ellie looked inquiringly at John, who sat down again slowly, his shoulders slumping as he decided to own up. "Very well, very well, but Athan, you should know that what I am about to say may result in the termination of my lease here, maybe even in my incarceration in debtor's jail, but I am left with no choice. You see, *I* am John Arbuthnot Billersley."

"You?" Athan was astounded.

John nodded. "Yes, but I swear upon everything I hold dear that I have had nothing whatsoever to do with my late brother-in-law's finances." He looked urgently at Ellie. "You must believe me, my dear. I may be guilty of adopting a false identity here in Nantgarth to escape my duns, but that is *all* I have done."

"I believe you, Uncle."

"What duns?" Athan demanded. "I don't recall your mentioning such circumstances when you and I first met in that inn on the Pennines."

"No gentleman likes to admit to debts." John looked unhappily at him and explained what had happened over the past fourteen years, including his visit to St. Petersburg.

When he'd finished there was a long silence, broken only by the crackling of the fire; then Athan drew a long breath. "I know the truth when I hear it, John, and am prepared to accept your reason for deceiving me. Your secret is safe with me, for it is not my inclination to tell tales to duns."

John was almost sick with relief. "Oh, thank you, *thank you*! And . . . and my lease here?"

"Is secure, although I cannot vouch that will remain the same should the duns actually catch up with you, which they may, of course."

"I pray not," John said with feeling.

"So do I. Duns are an unseemly breed." Athan gave a faint smile, then proceeded. "I also accept that you are unaware of how your name—or that of another man named John Arbuthnot Billersley, which seems highly unlikely— comes to be associated with this business at the Unicorn."

Ellie fumbled with the teapot, and then put it down with a resigned clatter. "I do not think it can possibly be chance that my uncle's full name should turn up in this dreadful matter of my father's finances. I think someone at the bank knew they were brothers-in-law, and chose to use the fact."

"Who?" John demanded. "This deceased Forrester-Phipps person? But I've never heard of him before."

Athan drew a heavy breath. "I think Ellie is right," he said, forgetting to be formal. "Someone deliberately used your name. The late Forrester-Phipps was clearly as much of a slippery rogue as his son, with whom I had the misfortune to go to school."

And the misfortune to share Fleur Tudor, Ellie couldn't help thinking.

John buried his head in his hands suddenly. "Everything is falling in around me," he said brokenly. "I was a fool all those years ago to plunge in over my head and end up pursued by the duns, but running away from them is the only wrong thing I've ever done. Yet I've paid the price over and over. All this time I've tried to make up for that sorry lapse by leading an honest life, devoting everything to creating the finest soft-paste porcelain in Europe, possibly the world, but each tiny step forward results in a blow that sends me reeling again."

Ellie hurried to kneel beside him, and put her arms around his shoulders. "Don't despair, Uncle, for I am sure Athan will expose the villains at the bank, and your name will be kept out of it." She looked beseechingly at Athan, who nodded to signify that he would do all in his power.

Neither of them had yet noticed their slips of the tongue with first names, but John began to do so when he looked up in time to see their exchanged glances. Bachelor he might be, but he was not a stranger to love; nor was he fool enough to believe in a single passing encounter a couple of years ago on the Isle of Wight. They obviously knew each other far better than that, although he couldn't imagine why Ellie hadn't said anything to him before now. For the moment, however, his own personal problems still weighed upon him like millstones. "These baleful influences upon my life cannot all be due to the finger of fate. There *has* to be something—or someone—behind it all."

Athan thought he was still referring to Freddie's father.

"Look, John, if there is anything to be discovered about Forrester-Phipps, my man will worm it out; of that you may be sure. But it may take a little time, and—"

John held up a hand. "No, it's not his name that I fear. Athan, when you were in St. Petersburg, did you by any chance encounter a nobleman named Prince Paul Dalmatsky?"

Athan was surprised. "Why yes, as it happens, for he owns the house in which my sister and brother-in-law live. He also happens to be Prince Valentin Andreyov's uncle."

John, already pale with stress, now became quite ashen. "Dalmatsky is Prince Valentin's uncle?" he repeated.

"Indeed so. Why do you ask about Dalmatsky? Are you acquainted with him?"

"Not really. He and I met once in St. Petersburg." John's gaze, almost anguished, went to the portrait.

Once again Athan was aware of not being told the entire truth. "Come now, John. There is clearly much more to this. What exactly is the situation between you and him?" *Apart from similar sexual preferences* . . . The silent addendum had to be added, if only because of the portrait looking down at them all from the mantel.

John got up, but Ellie continued to kneel by his rocking chair. "Very well, I admit to being less than truthful. There is enough ill feeling and downright loathing between Prince Paul Dalmatsky and me for it to be certain to me now that this so-called order for the czar is no more than a wicked trap to lure me back to St. Petersburg in order to kill me."

"To . . . to *kill* you?" Ellie whispered.

John gave a heavy sigh. "I now believe that Dalmatsky has been searching for me as assiduously as the duns. He is behind this business."

Athan got up from the settle. "Well, he *is* involved, although he was at pains to request me not to mention his name. He said it was because he didn't wish to steal any of his nephew's thunder."

"There you have it then—this is *all* Dalmatsky." John closed his eyes for a moment. "That's why I've been so specifically requested to accompany the finished tureen to St. Petersburg. I fooled myself into hoping it was all due to your good offices."

"I didn't need to mention you to either of them, for they commenced this tureen business before I met them."

"Then I would even hazard a guess that Dalmatsky is behind my real name being raised at the Unicorn Bank. Nothing would surprise me where that monster is concerned, and implicating me in my brother-in-law's tragic case would be typical of him. A little blackmail here, a little bribery there, and he soon gets what he wants. I tell you, he's evil through and through."

Again he looked at the portrait, and Ellie saw how he struggled not to reach up to the painted face. She had not led so sheltered an existence that she couldn't guess about the handsome sitter, and although she'd never viewed her uncle in that light, she realized that such leanings would explain a lot about him.

Athan watched him too. "Why would Dalmatsky go to such lengths?"

"Revenge. I stole the heart of someone he loved, and his cruel pride will never be satisfied until I have breathed my last."

Athan's eyes cleared. So that was it: a bitter quarrel about a beautiful young man. Such a circumstance was just the sort of thing to stir a man like Dalmatsky into devising an intricate reprisal. No wonder the slippery Russian had been so anxious to keep his name out of it. He spoke gently to John. "Are you able to tell us about it?"

John glanced down at Ellie, then at Athan. "Perhaps not," he said.

Ellie smiled. "Please tell us, Uncle, for I'm sure I have guessed much already, and I am not a wilting violet."

John hesitated, then decided to unburden himself of a story that had darkened his days for far too long.

Eighteen

John took a deep steadying breath before speaking. "Well, it was four years or so ago, after I left Royal Worcester in the middle of the night and before I came here. I didn't spend all the intervening time in St. Petersburg, for I was some time in Berlin, and in Vienna, but the months I was in St. Petersburg meant only one thing to me . . . Nikolai Trepov. He was twenty years old, and I loved him at first sight." John's voice was soft, low, and redolent of sweet memories. "He was such a gentle boy, kindly and warmhearted, but I did not know he was someone whom Prince Paul Dalmatsky regarded as his personal property, for the entire Trepov family were his serfs. Dalmatsky and I were acquainted, quite well so, actually, for we had a number of shared interests. We were never . . . er, well, you know, we simply got on. I liked him enough to foolishly confide about my debts, the duns, and my decision to change my identity on returning to Britain. Oh, how bitterly I now regret my lack of caution, for such things would have been far better left unsaid."

"You weren't to know, Uncle," Ellie said.

"Simple common sense should have tied my tongue," he replied wryly. "Anyway, I never saw the darker side of him, and neither of us was aware that we had Nikolai in common, but I was soon to discover that Dalmatsky was not only besotted with Nikolai, but secretly kept him in great splendor at his palace on Dalmatsky Island. It was something Dalmatsky was anxious to keep very quiet, because although a noble may use a serf as he pleases, to actually set him up in luxury was another matter. Dalmatsky would have been treated with scorn." He hesitated. "Am I embarrassing you, Ellie, my dear?"

"No." It was the truth, for even though it was not of a young woman that he spoke so tenderly, she could still understand his feelings. Besides, he was her uncle John, and as deserving of happiness as anyone else. She got up and went to hug him again, and he held her tightly.

"You're a good girl, Ellie, a credit to my dear sister, and a joy to me."

She kissed his cheek, then looked at him. "What happened to Nikolai?" she asked gently.

He paused, then moved from her to go to the shelf on which stood examples of his porcelain. He pretended to study them as he spoke of Nikolai. "He . . . died," he said, the catch in his voice expressing only too eloquently the anguish he still felt. "Dalmatsky found out about us and was so furious that he took a horsewhip to Nikolai. It was winter, and the Neva had just begun to freeze when Nikolai fled from Dalmatsky Island in fear for his life. Dalmatsky set his pack of savage guard dogs after him. They were Dalmatians, naturally, half-starved, maltreated brutes, and Nikolai had almost reached the next island when the ice gave beneath him. There was nothing he could do to save himself; he slipped beneath, and the current of the river carried him away. Dalmatsky blamed me for the tragedy, even though he was the one who'd beaten Nikolai and had him pursued over unstable ice by a murderous pack of dogs." John drew a long, shuddering breath. "Then *I* was the one who had to escape for my life. I left St. Petersburg like a felon, traveling night and day to Riga, where I managed to take passage on a ship bound for London. Even in England it soon became clear that Dalmatsky was still in pursuit, so I began calling myself John Bailey, and did my best to disappear. That was when I happened to be snowbound at that inn on the Pennines, and met you, Athan. The rest you both know."

Ellie had tears in her eyes. "It's a very sad story, Uncle John."

"Indeed so, indeed so," he murmured, then composed himself again. "And now I must forget all about soup tureens for Russia, since the entire order is obviously spurious and has nothing whatever to do with the czar himself."

Athan spoke up quickly. "John, you may indeed be right about Dalmatsky and Andreyov, for I wouldn't trust either of them an inch, but I believe the order for the soup tureen is genuine. Oh, Dalmatsky may have prompted it, there is no way of knowing that or not, but I do think the czar is aware of and approves the order for the tureen."

"You do?"

"Yes, because he himself mentioned it to me during an audience I was privileged enough to be granted. He's a little deaf, you know, and inclined to speak softly and quickly. I didn't understand him sometimes, but looking back, I realize now that he did mention a soup tureen. At the time he seemed to be talking about ordering a British flute and tambourine, which really didn't make sense at all, but there was an orchestra playing during the audience, and we had been discussing music a few minutes earlier. Anyway, that is beside the point, because if you abandon the order, you may be cutting off your nose to spite your face. Don't you owe it to yourself—and your china—to complete the tureen and reap the benefit? I think you should proceed."

Ellie was horrified. "And be murdered when he reaches Russia? Oh, no, that is too much of a risk. Nothing is worth his life!"

John smiled at her. "Your alarm for my old hide is warming but unnecessary, my dear, for I will not go, a fact for which I must apologize to you."

"To me? But—"

"I promised you would see St. Petersburg, and now I renege upon that promise. Forgive me, my dear." He turned to Athan. "Athan, I know you are trying to bolster my flagging courage, and I am indeed reassured by what you say of the czar, but I cannot and will not return to St. Petersburg now that I know Dalmatsky is involved." His tone was flat and uncompromising.

"That is up to you, of course. I have to return myself with my horses, and I'm perfectly willing to deliver the tureen for you. I intend to make the journey some time in May. Will the tureen be ready then?"

"Yes, most certainly, for that was when I would have left. The czar is to have the tureen early in July, when they celebrate the feast of Saints Peter and Paul."

"Then I will deliver it for you," Athan said, "but you will serve your cause far better if you accompany it yourself and see it *personally* into Alexander's hands."

"You do not know Dalmatsky as I do, Athan. If I return to St. Petersburg, I will die there."

Athan gazed down at the floor for a few moments, then looked at John again. "Do you really and honestly believe that this whole thing, all the plotting, expense, trickery, and subterfuge, is done simply and solely to satisfy Dalmatsky's thirst for revenge upon you?"

"What else can I think?" John spread his hands.

"Nothing, I suppose," Athan conceded, "except . . . well, I have a hunch that there is still more to it, something that actually has nothing to do with you at all."

"Such as?"

Athan shrugged. "I really don't know, but no matter how bitter the rancor between you and Dalmatsky, involving Andreyov as well seems unnecessary. Why bother with dragging him into it? Letters alone would have enticed you back to St. Petersburg with the tureen. Am I right?"

John thought for a moment, and then nodded. "Yes, I suppose so."

"So why Andreyov's journey to Britain?" Athan paused. "He didn't continue here to Nantgarth with me because of some business or other he had to conduct in the capital. He declined to confide the nature of this business, but it seemed to have him in a lather, so its importance cannot be doubted."

John looked at him. "The Dalmatsky spider spins a vast and complicated web. Andreyov's purpose here could concern just about anything you care to mention, anything at all."

"Then why not let him get on with it on his own? Why is he involved at all in the order for the tureen? Dalmatsky tried to pretend that the order was all Andreyov's idea, but I could tell that it wasn't. If I'm not mistaken, there are two things happening in this. One is Dalmatsky's plot to be revenged upon you, John; the other is something else entirely. It merely suits Dalmatsky to link the two together through the tureen."

Ellie looked at them both. "Two birds with one stone?" she asked.

What their answer might have been was never known, because suddenly the raised voices of Mrs. Lewis and another woman were heard in the passage outside; then the parlor door burst open and Fleur entered in a flurry of red riding habit. Her lovely green eyes were sparkling, her lips parted in an overjoyed smile, and she totally ignored Ellie and John as she ran to fling her arms around Athan's neck.

Athan hesitated, and then put his hands to her waist, neither holding her close nor pushing her away. "Fleur? I . . ."

Fleur clung to him. "I was just returning from a ride along the bank of the Taff when I saw your carriage! I couldn't believe my eyes! Oh, this is the most wonderful surprise, truly it is. We didn't expect you for weeks yet!"

Athan couldn't speak. His gaze was torn to Ellie, who had to look away from the guilt and torment in his eyes. She longed to accuse Fleur of playing him false with Freddie Forrester-Phipps, but in the absence of proof she did not dare. Proof. Such a small word, but of such immeasurable importance.

Fleur knew she had the initiative and was determined to make the most of it. Ellie's refusal to bow to threats, and her complete disregard of the post with Lady Brecon, had persuaded Fleur she was definitely an adventuress as skilled as herself, so seeing Athan's traveling carriage outside Nantgarth House hadn't been the delight she claimed, but a horrid jolt. Now here he was, as cozy as could be in this poky little parlor, glancing at the china maker's daughter as if at his precious Caroline returned!

The fact that he'd left St. Petersburg far earlier than expected, and so couldn't have received the agent's letter, meant Fleur could now tell him to his face about the incestuous goings-on she'd invented for the residents of Nantgarth House. Not here and now, of course, for she wished him to be alone for such a revelation, and she had to prepare herself to weep copious anguished tears at having to speak so ill of his friends. What she *could* do now, however, was make it abundantly clear who was going to be the next Lady Griffin.

"Oh, Athan, my dearest, most darling love, you're home again at last!" she breathed, and kissed him on the lips, casting propriety to the four winds because they weren't alone. It was a calculated kiss, a declaration of war, and Ellie knew it.

Fleur drew back, managing to look blushing and overcome by her own temerity. "Forgive my forward conduct, but you cannot possibly know how I have longed for this moment. Being apart from you for so long has taught me that I adore you, Athan, and that our marriage cannot come soon enough." The performance was consummate, conveying such an utterly angelic air that she all but sprouted wings and a halo.

John was sharply conscious of the charged atmosphere now Fleur was among them, and belatedly understood why Ellie and Athan had been so secretive about knowing each other. Why hadn't it been the first thing he'd thought of? They were rightly ill at ease on being confronted by the third party they wronged with their clandestine love. He didn't much care for Fleur, and nothing would have delighted him more than a true romance between Ellie and Athan, but Fleur had prior claim upon Athan's wedding ring. That was the heart of the matter, and as soon as Athan departed, John had every intention of instructing Ellie to discontinue whatever it was that was going on. If anyone knew the consequences of having three when there should only be two, it was John Arbuthnot Billersley.

Fleur gazed adoringly at Athan, her lovely eyes sparkling like stars. "Life has been utterly dull in your absence."

"I'm sure you amused yourself, Fleur," he replied lamely, and glanced again at Ellie.

The glance provoked Fleur. "Do you not think Miss Rutherford is like your late wife?" she inquired.

A shocked silence descended over the parlor, and this time Athan couldn't bring himself to look at Ellie, to whom he had yet to confess everything about the portrait. He answered, but very uncomfortably, "Er, yes, I suppose there is a certain likeness."

Fleur realized she'd been a little hasty, and pretended to be overcome with embarrassment and confusion. "Oh, dear, how . . . how dreadful of me. I'm truly sorry, Athan, Miss Rutherford, for I spoke without thinking. . . . Please forgive me."

"Of course," Athan replied, but Ellie remained pointedly silent.

Fleur gave her a look of pure daggers, then smiled at Athan. "Actually, Miss Rutherford and I might have been good friends, I think, but she speaks of taking a position as governess to Lady Brecon's children, so our acquaintance cannot possibly blossom."

Athan's eyes quickened with surprise, and not a little dismay. Was this true? John was no less disconcerted. "What's this, my dear?" he asked Ellie.

"Well, Miss Tudor certainly mentioned such a post to me, but—" Ellie began, but Fleur broke in.

"*I* mentioned it to *you*?" She gave an incredulous laugh. "On the contrary, Miss Rutherford, it was you who told me. How on earth would I know about such a post?"

Again Ellie didn't respond, and the atmosphere tightened a little more. Athan cleared his throat, realizing with a shock how little love was lost between the two women. It simply hadn't occurred to him that this might prove the case. But then, there was so much that he hadn't foreseen, so much he wished he could deal with decisively, so much he wished were different. "I'm sure there is a misunderstanding," he said, and at last extricated himself from Fleur's clinging hold. "And now I think it's time I made my presence felt at the castle. Thank you for your hospitality, John. Rest assured that I will do all I can in the matters of the tureen and the bank. Good day to you."

"Good day, Athan."

Athan turned to Ellie. "And to you, Miss Rutherford."

She inclined her head. "Good day, Lord Griffin."

He hesitated, wanting so much to blurt out the whole truth and shame the very devil, that the words were almost on the tip of his tongue, but then Fleur linked her arm through his again, and gave a trill of pretty laughter.

"I will ride in the carriage with you. My horse can be tethered behind. Oh, I've been *longing* to talk to you."

Ellie remained in the parlor, leaving John to accompany them to the door. Her emotions felt torn in all directions, and she did not see how there could possibly be a happy outcome from such a tangle. She was no match for someone like Fleur, whatever the latter might think to the contrary, and it was clear that no matter how much Athan loved Ellie Rutherford, he would marry Fleur Tudor. Perhaps Lady Brecon would have her governess after all.

John returned, closed the parlor door carefully, then confronted his niece. "Am I right to suspect your dealings with Lord Griffin of going beyond mere casual acquaintance?"

For a moment she considered lying, but could not. "Yes," she admitted.

"Would I also be right to read something into your intimate use of each other's first names?"

She hung her head. "Yes."

"Then it has to stop, is that clear? While any hint of pre-contract exists with Miss Tudor, you are not to have anything to do with him. Do you understand?"

"Yes."

He sat in his rocking chair. "May I ask how you really met? And don't repeat that nonsense about the party of gentlemen on the Isle of Wight, because I know it isn't true."

So she told him everything, excepting the supernatural encounters that she and Athan knew to be true, but which would probably sound a little lunatic to anyone else, even her uncle.

John looked gently at her. "You must have an eye to your reputation, my dear. If you and Athan are meant to be, then fate will do all that is necessary. That is one thing Russia taught me the hard way. Nikolai and I wished to be together, but destiny decreed otherwise, and if it has decreed that Miss Tudor is to be Athan's bride, then there is nothing you—or he—can do about it."

"You cannot order me not to hope," she answered.

He smiled sympathetically. "I know, my dear, I know." His glance moved to Nikolai Trepov's portrait as he remembered how much he had hoped in the past. He looked at the beloved face, and suddenly regretted giving way in the face of Paul Dalmatsky's vengefulness. "I've been craven, have I not?"

"Craven?"

"Yes. By deciding so quickly not to go to St. Petersburg, I have admitted to my fear of Dalmatsky. An English gentleman should show more backbone. I *will* go to Russia after all, and to hell itself with Dalmatsky. If I have to confront him, then I will."

Ellie was alarmed by his tone. "Don't be reckless, Uncle John. There is no need to take risks."

"On the contrary, there is every need. There is a risk in everything, and it is time I faced my particular demon." He went to his writing desk. "I will send word to the castle immediately. You and I will accompany Athan on the voyage, my dear, and that is my final word."

Nineteen

*I*n London at dusk that same day, Valentin waited in the Jolly Roger tavern in Lower Thames Street. The tables were partitioned by old blue velvet curtains that were greatly in need of cleaning, and the seats were rough benches. The uneven stone-flagged floor was seldom brushed, and the smell of tobacco smoke and stale ale was almost noxious. The Jolly Roger was the haunt of villains and whores, but a great many gentlemen were to be found there too, gentlemen of the fancy who came because of a notorious cockpit in the yard behind.

Valentin was seated as far from the street as he could be. He had not come for the cockfighting, or indeed to sample the dubious ale, but to keep an appointment with the man who was so vital to the successful theft of the diamond from the Tower of London, that without his cooperation the whole stratagem would surely fail. A serving girl had earlier brought a lighted candle to the table, but Valentin had extinguished the flame, fearing his face might be glimpsed. Two books lay on the table at his elbow, and his gloves had been neatly placed on top of them.

He had not worn his uniform since disembarking at Lowestoft. His hair was still long, but he'd abandoned the queue and side-plaits, and now wore it tied back simply with a black ribbon. He kept the collar of his greatcoat turned up, and did not remove his top hat, which was pulled well forward over his forehead. There was something about his shadowy figure that kept all and sundry at bay. Whores glanced in his direction, but did not approach him, and if pickpockets and footpads wondered what valuables might be about his person, not one of them contemplated lying in wait for him when he left.

Glancing at his fob watch again, he exhaled irritably. The fellow would rue it if he played games!

"Prince Valentin?" A man halted at the table, his well-spoken voice revealing just a trace of Northern Irish accent. He wore a military cloak over the uniform of a major in the Twenty-seventh Inniskilling Fusiliers, a battalion of which regiment was at present providing the garrison at the Tower.

"Major Carver?" Valentin responded, looking up quickly, but not bothering to get to his feet. He retrieved his gloves and pushed the books aside, for they had now served their purpose of identifying him.

The newcomer slid onto the settle opposite. He was in his thirties, of medium height, slightly built, with receding sandy hair, freckles, and nervous blue eyes. He glanced uneasily around, then looked at Valentin. "Let's get this over with, so I can be out of this flea nest."

"I had begun to think you'd cried off, Major."

"I thought about it, you may be sure of that," the other replied with feeling.

Valentin smiled coldly. "But you decided your career was worth too much to you."

"That's about the truth of it."

"Well, if you were fool enough to dally with your commanding officer's wife. . . ." Valentin shrugged. He had learned the lesson the hard way, so this stupid Irishman could do the same.

Major Carver looked at him in the shadowy light. "You're army too, aren't you?" he said, sensing the experience in Valentin's words.

"No," Valentin lied.

The other shrugged. "But you *are* Dalmatsky's nephew?"

"Yes."

"And I'm supposed to do all I can to assist you in this . . . endeavor?"

"You know you are, Major, and let me warn you not to treat me as if I'm a blockhead from the Neva marshes, for I assure you I'm not. Now then, which night are you on duty?"

"Tomorrow."

Valentin smiled. "So soon? It is good."

"You may think so; I certainly don't," snapped the other, glancing around again for fear of seeing a fellow officer among a party that had just arrived for the cockpit.

"What is the plan?" Valentin asked.

"A fire."

Valentin looked blankly at him. "A fire? At the Tower of London? That's nonsense!"

"The jewels are kept guarded in strong metal cages in the Martin Tower. Without keys, these cages will require crowbars to prize them open, so to think of simply stealing anything swiftly and without detection is out of the question. But if there were a fire, and the jewels were in peril, then they would have to be rescued. My informed guess would be that they would be broken out and removed to the Governor's residence at the other end of Tower Green. If I'm correct, then I will have an opportunity to exchange the fake for the real diamond."

"And if you are wrong?"

Major Carver was exasperated. "Do you have a better notion, sir? Because if you do, I wish you would share it!"

Valentin flushed. "The removal of the diamond is *your* task, Major, not mine."

"From which response I take it that you have nothing sensible to say."

"Be careful, Major Carver, for I am not accustomed to insolence."

"You surprise me," the major replied dryly.

Valentin's hand moved toward the small pistol he always carried against his heart, but then he thought better of it. He could hardly shoot anyone in here and expect to get away with it. Besides, the fellow was necessary to the plan. His hand slid away again, and he quelled his anger in order to give Carver a bland smile. "Tell me about your fire, Major."

"I know where and how to start it without being seen. It will be in an adjacent tower, and by midnight it will have taken sufficient hold for the sentries in Tower Green to spot it. The troops will be mustered and all efforts made to extinguish it. The Tower engines will prove inadequate, and engines will come from all over. Crowds will gather, and there will be general panic. When the flames threaten the Martin Tower, the jewels will be taken to safety."

"To the Governor's house?"

"I would lay odds upon it," Carver replied.

Valentin smiled. "And what, precisely, is my role to be?"

"I plan it all to be at its height at midnight, which is when it also happens to be high tide on the river. You are to be in a boat at Tower Stairs at that time, and I will bring the diamond to you. You *must* be there, however, for I dare not absent myself for more than a few minutes without risk of being missed."

"So all I am to do is be in a boat at Tower Stairs at midnight?"

"Well, by all means be there without a boat if you fancy a swim in the Thames with the diamond between your teeth!" snapped Major Carver.

"At least I would still have teeth with which to perform the feat," Valentin growled, dearly wishing to knock the Irishman's down his throat.

There was an uneasy silence, then Carver exhaled slowly. "Are we agreed about the fire?"

"Yes."

"May I ask a question?"

Valentin spread his hands. "By all means, although I do not guarantee to answer it."

"How, exactly, do you mean to get the stone out of England?"

"In a most novel way that is almost guaranteed to escape detection," Valentin replied.

"And that is all you mean to tell me?"

"I do not know you well enough to share my secrets with you, Major Carver."

"Then a word to the wise, Prince Valentin. The diamond may be small, but if its theft is discovered, you may count upon it that Russian involvement will be the first suspicion. The fact that Czar Alexander possesses the twin jewel will be reason enough for the finger to point. That will mean that anything and everything Russian will be searched and searched again. No ship will be able to leave port until it has been turned inside out, and no traveler will be left unsearched, even a Russian prince."

"Nevertheless, the diamond will reach St. Petersburg safely."

Major Carver studied Valentin in the gloomy light. "You seem very sure of that," he murmured.

"I am. Oh, I am, for the hiding place is ingenious. Anyway, that is not your concern, for you will have discharged your part of the bargain by then. When are you expecting me to hand over the fake diamond? Now, I suppose?"

"Of course."

Valentin laughed and shook his head. "Oh, no, my friend, I am not that big a fool. I will bring the false diamond with me in the boat, and when you hand me the real one, I will hand you the fake. That way I will be certain of seeing both diamonds together. It wouldn't do for me to discover that you had given me back the fake, would it?"

Carver flushed in the dim light. "You question my honor, sir?" he demanded hotly.

Valentin didn't flinch. "What sort of honor is it that permits you to bed your commanding officer's new bride?" he pointed out with monstrous hypocrisy.

"Damn your eyes," breathed the other.

"Let us just concede that we have a healthy suspicion of each other, and my way of doing things will guarantee that there is no sleight of hand on either part."

"I can see your reasoning, and even agree with it, but for me to actually walk out of the Tower with the diamond is taking a grave risk. The fact that it's missing could be noted before I have time to replace it with the fake, but if I take the fake with me now, the exchange can be done on the scene in a second, without anyone the wiser."

"And I may end up with the same piece of pretty glass that I brought from St. Petersburg. Besides, do you really imagine that in the heat and panic of a conflagration, the temporary absence of one small stone is going to be noted? I think not. Be at ease now, Carver, for all will go according to plan. I will be there in the boat at midnight, and I will have the false diamond ready. You bring me the real one, we exchange them, and go our separate ways."

"And that is the last I will hear of you and your damned kinsman?"

"The very last."

"So be it." The major got up again, and strode out of the tavern.

* * *

Athan lay naked in his bed at Castle Griffin. The curtains hadn't been drawn at the windows, and a shaft of moonlight shone across Ellie's portrait in the adjacent room. He gazed toward it, longing for her to be at his side, longing to hold her close, to make love to her as they both needed so very much. Just to think of her aroused his senses . . . and his body.

A woman's shadow moved across the open doorway, and he leaned up on an elbow. "Ellie?" The name slipped so naturally from his lips, for he could only think that it was she; but it was Fleur's red hair that caught the moonlight, Fleur's slender body that was revealed through the diaphanous muslin of a loosely tied robe.

If she'd heard Ellie's name, she gave no sign. She came to the bedside, and he could smell her perfume, as sweet and seductive as lilies. "Don't send me away, Athan," she whispered, pretending to be a trembling virgin swept by a beguiling mixture of love, desire, confusion, and bewilderment.

"Please go, Fleur, for this is—"

"—is right," she said softly, and put a finger to his lips to prevent him from saying more. "Being parted from you has taught me how much I love you, Athan, and now that you're home again, I cannot bear to be beneath the same roof and not be with you. I have never felt like this before, but I know I must follow my heart. I am yours." She slipped the robe back from her shoulders and allowed it to slither to the floor. She played the role of half-martyr, half-siren so well that Athan did not see the real Fleur Tudor at all. He saw a timid creature emboldened by circumstances beyond her control.

"Put the robe on again, Fleur," he said gently, striving to remain on the right side of honor, but battling his own treacherous senses.

"I'm going to be your wife, Athan, so what harm is there in anticipating our vows? You want me. I know you do." She knelt on the bed beside him, and put trembling fingertips to his face. "I'm so afraid you don't want me anymore," she whispered. "When I saw you and Miss Rutherford today—"

"Miss Rutherford?" He hoped his voice did not tell tales on him.

"She really is so like the portrait of your Caroline that I . . . I fear her." Fleur squeezed a pathetic tear or two. "She will steal you from me if she can, I just know she will."

"I have given you my word that you will be my wife, Fleur, and that has not changed."

Her tortured gaze moved to the portrait, shining so clearly through the doorway. "You keep Caroline in your rooms, where I cannot yet come openly. You have her face before you when you go to sleep, and there to gaze upon again when you awaken. I fear her hold upon you, my darling, and now that Miss Rutherford is here. . . ." She hid her face in her hands, and surrendered to well-rehearsed weeping.

"If . . . if the portrait upsets you to that extent, then I will have it removed." He didn't know what else to say. He'd felt unhappy enough about this marriage even before this, but faced with the effect Ellie and the portrait had upon Fleur, he felt worse than ever. He was a man of conscience, and right now his conscience pricked as if it would pierce his heart. He had a duty to this woman, and had no one else but himself to blame for the situation in which he now found himself.

"Remove the portrait?" Fleur whispered. "You'll do that for me?"

"Yes, of course," he answered, hating himself.

Her shoulders shook as she choked back fresh sobs; then before he knew it, she'd pulled the bedclothes aside and flung herself down to curl against him, flesh to flesh. Her little whimpers seemed all that were innocent, but the same could not be said for her roaming hand, which somehow, by accident of course, came to rest against his groin. Her breath caught, and a delicious shiver passed through her. "Oh, Athan, Athan, *please* make me yours," she begged, her lips moving against his shoulder.

He closed his eyes. It was Ellie he wanted, Ellie who'd stirred his body so that desire pulsed fiercely through him; but Fleur was here, yearning for him to take her. . . .

Twenty

Athan believed Fleur was being carried away by erotic feelings unknown to her before now. She pressed to him so that he felt the brush of her nipples, and her fingers, trembling and tentative, moved toward his virility. "Let me show you the sort of wife I will be," she whispered. "Let me prove that you do not need Caroline's likeness to know happiness again."

"Fleur, this really isn't right," he said, beginning to pull away from her, but her perfume was like an opiate to his resistance, and to his shame he allowed her to coil around him like a serpent. She put her lips to his in a kiss that was meant to convey a confused, irresistible yearning, but that actually revealed how very long it had been since she'd known virginity. He was even fooled by her shuddering little gasps as her fingers ventured to enclose his virility, for her actions weren't those of a chaste young woman driven instinctively by overpowering love and desire, but the skills of a calculating woman of the world. Fleur knew that if she could seduce him now, then nothing could halt their marriage. She would be compromised beyond redemption, and he'd *have* to marry her.

But just as temptation had the better of him, and he was about to slake the tormented need he had for Ellie, he glanced again at the portrait in the other room. His arousal faded into shame, and he rolled away to get out of the bed on the other side. The moon was pale upon his lean but muscular body as he went to put on his dressing gown, which lay at the bottom of the bed.

Fleur was shaken. She had been so sure of him, so certain he'd passed beyond the point of no return . . . and now this.

Still doing up the dressing gown, he came to look down at her. "I think it best if we forget all about this, Fleur."

"Forget it? But that's not possible," she replied, pretending to look stricken to the point of heartbreak. She was genuinely shaken by her failure, so it wasn't too difficult to feign.

"Then you must pretend to forget it," he said, beginning to regain his proper wits, "for that is what I intend to do. When we meet at the breakfast table tomorrow, there will not be a word about tonight. Is that clear?"

"How cruel you are," she whispered, and slipped from the bed to don her robe.

"This is for the best," he said again. "The fact that we are to be man and wife doesn't allow us to flout the rules as we choose."

She paused. "We're still to be married?"

"Nothing has changed."

Her green eyes took on a different light. "Then I am content," she said softly. "I do love you, Athan. I know ours is supposed to be a marriage of convenience more than anything else, but I've fallen in love with you."

He hesitated, then took her hand and raised it briefly to his lips. "I'm touched to be so honored, and flattered that you came to me like this, but it would be wrong."

Her fingers closed timorously over his. "I know that now. Do you forgive me?"

He smiled. "There is nothing to forgive."

She bit her lips, blinked back tears, then hurried from the apartment.

Racked with remorse, Athan remained by the bed. Fleur—and her mother—were dependent upon him, and had become his responsibility in every sense of the word. He loved Ellie, and always would, but he owed a debt to General Tudor that had to come before a quest for personal happiness. Even now, just when he'd found Ellie again and knew more than ever just how deeply and truly he loved her, he knew he would have to give her up. He was obligated to Fleur, who plainly needed him far more than he had ever realized.

Athan went through into his dressing room and began to select clothes suitable for a ride to Nantgarth through the cold misty air of a March dawn. His heart felt as if it were breaking, and the sting of salt blurred his eyes. Word of his betrothal to Fleur had spread, which meant that any hint of romance with Ellie, no matter how devoted and true that romance might be, would compromise the latter's reputation, perhaps irreparably. He *had* to consider Ellie in all this, before he sacrificed both her and his own integrity.

As Athan dressed for the painful task of ending things with the woman who meant everything to him, Fleur went to speak to her mother. Mrs. Tudor was pacing nervously up and down in her apartment, waiting for the clock to point to half past the hour. This was the time Fleur had reckoned to be in Athan's bed, his seduction underway or possibly even accomplished, so that her shocked mother could walk in and discover them in flagrante delicto. Fleur's sudden return was therefore quite a shock. "Fleur? But, I . . . I thought . . ." she began.

"So did I, Mama, so did I," Fleur hissed, "but as you can see, I did not achieve what I set out to do."

"Oh, dear. Well, perhaps another night?" Mrs. Tudor ventured.

Fleur flung away exasperatedly. "Not before I'm married to him, that much is for sure!" she snapped. "And do you know what? When he first saw me, he thought it was her, that . . . that *potter's* niece! He actually said her name. Oh, I was right to fear her."

Mrs. Tudor fell wisely silent.

Veils of mist were draped low over the valley, taking on a luminous hue as the sun began its approach to the eastern horizon. The first birds were stirring—a blackbird in the holly bush, pigeons in the woods, and a bird of prey far up on the mountainside—as Athan dismounted in the alley beside Nantgarth House.

He wore a caped greatcoat over a brown coat and fawn breeches, his shirt was undone at the throat, and beneath his top hat his hair was disheveled. During his hectic ride down from the castle he had wondered over and over what he would say to Ellie. What words could possibly convey the utter desolation he felt? Would she understand? Would she think he was callous and unfeeling? Would she accept that this was the hardest decision he had ever had to make? How could she ever forgive him, when as God was his witness he knew he could never forgive himself?

He paused by his sweating horse, then removed his gloves and hat, and rested them on the wall. Then he took off his heavy coat, and tossed it beside them. "Oh, Ellie, Ellie, my love," he whispered, glancing up at the darkened window which he knew from Gwilym belonged to Ellie's room.

His heart was a millstone within him as he went around to the gate and up the path, pausing halfway to gather a handful of earth from a flower bed. He tossed it up at the window, then waited, but the moments passed without anything happening. So he threw another handful, and this time Ellie's face, pale and sleepy, peered cautiously out. She saw him, and her lips parted. He gestured for her to come down to the back of the house, then retraced his steps around to the alley, past his horse, and down to the wharf, where an empty barge was moored. His boots seemed inordinately noisy on the steeply rounded cobbles, but there was no one around, and the canal was as still as a mirror, its surface reflecting the changing light of the predawn sky. He waited outside the double doors of the cellars, listening for the first sounds within that would tell of Ellie's approach.

It was then that he heard the canal water swirling and gurgling, and when he turned he saw that the surface had broken up into something akin to a whirlpool. He took an involuntary step backward as water splashed between the barge and the wharf; then his breath caught as something long, lithe, and silvery leapt out of the whirlpool and twisted in the air above the water, before plunging down out of sight once more. What was it? An eel? A shiver passed through him, for although he knew there were eels to be found in the canal, he couldn't even begin to explain away the whirlpool. No mere eel, no matter how large, could cause such an effect. For a moment he wondered if the canal had somehow sprung a leak, but he knew that couldn't be. A leak was a leak, and wouldn't stop and start as this had done. He went cautiously to the edge of the wharf. The black satin water was without a ripple, and he could see his reflection against the sky.

Then he heard a sound from the cellar doors behind him, and turned swiftly to see candlelight shining beneath them. Then he heard the bolts being pulled back, and at last she was there, her curls in a sleepy tangle, her nightgown white in the shadowy light. There was a warm woolen shawl around her shoulders, and she'd placed the candle on the trestle behind her, so that she was silhouetted against the glowing flame.

"Athan? Why have you come here like this? If my uncle should awaken and discover us—"

He went quickly to her. "Forgive me, I know this is wrong and that I ask much of you, but I simply had to see you."

"What is it? What's wrong?" Her face was in shadow, but the candlelight was bright upon her hair.

"Oh, Ellie, Ellie," he breathed, submitting to temptation one last time by taking her in his arms and seeking her lips. *Kiss me, kiss me, my darling love, for this must be goodbye....* His mouth was tender, yet imperative, and he held her to him, consigning to memory every beloved curve of her body. For these few moments he could set duty and obligation aside and be true to the love that had come into his darkness like a beacon. He worshipped Ellie Rutherford, and were he to marry Fleur ten times over, nothing would change that.

He dragged his lips from hers, and kissed her cheek, her nose, her forehead, and her eyes, before burying his face in her warm hair and sliding his fingers into the soft curls at the nape of her neck. "I love you, Ellie. You do know that, don't you?" he whispered.

She nodded, giving herself to the embrace with an honesty that almost frightened her. She belonged to him, and he to her, but she knew that something was wrong. He would not have come here like this if all were well, and as she held him, she could feel his pain. It was the end. Yes, he had come to tell her they must not continue....

He cupped her face in his hands and turned her so that he could see her eyes, their blue changed to lilac by the candlelight, and her lips, so soft and tender from his kiss. Thomas Lawrence had never seen her like this, yet had somehow caught her very essence in the illicit portrait that had been the start of all this. "Ellie, there is something you don't know, something about Caroline. You see, she never existed."

"Never?" She leaned back in his arms and looked up at him.

"I invented her to fend off the enormous field of runners in the Marriage Stakes. Well, when I say she did not exist . . ."

"Yes?"

"She did, except that she was called Ellie Rutherford, and I fell in love with her when I saw her portrait for sale in a London gallery. The sitter had no name, but I lost my heart to her."

Ellie was startled. "Are . . . are you saying that the portrait you asked me about at Hounslow really was one of me? That Mr. Lawrence painted a *second* likeness?"

"Yes, and I fear it was not as demure as it ought to have been, because the fellow had formed a passion for you. He allowed his imagination free rein, so to speak."

She blushed a little. "I see."

"I don't think you can begin to imagine how I felt that morning in Hounslow, when I leaned over that gate and saw . . . Caroline come to life. Lawrence is no dunce; he captured your face so bewitchingly that I *knew* you were she. Chance is an ethereal thing, Ellie, contriving to take me past that gallery on the very morning they decided to display your likeness in their window. Chance also caused me to lean on that gate while my horses were being changed, and there you were. It then took me to the bank, where I actually spoke to you without realizing it, and it showed your face to me again as you were leaving, and again at St. George's Burial Ground. Now it plays the unkindest trick of all by bringing you to Nantgarth. Chance seems determined to prove we should be together, but fate has other ideas entirely."

Tears filled her eyes. "Something has happened, hasn't it? It must have done for you to ride down here at this hour. You've come here now to tell me we must not see each other again, because you are going to marry Miss Tudor."

Her perception cut through him like a knife, and his throat tightened with emotion. "Forgive me, Ellie," he whispered brokenly. "Forgive me for hurting you, for loving you, for wanting you so much that I have broken rules and made you break them too."

"You did not *make* me so flout propriety that I kissed you within minutes of our having met," she reminded him.

"No, but I knew I was betrothed to Fleur, and so I was very much in the wrong. I stepped willingly and eagerly into a fool's paradise when I saw you and gave in to my heart, but you didn't know how false I was being; how false I've continued to be." He turned away, and ran his hand wretchedly through his hair. "Seeing Fleur again has forced me to confront my perfidy." He faced her again. "Not because I love her, so please do not think that, for it simply isn't so, but she *is* my responsibility. I respected and revered her father, General Tudor, more than any other man, and on his death he charged me to take care of his wife and daughter. I gave him my word, Ellie, and now I have given my word to Fleur that she will be my wife. That has to be the final word."

"I know," she whispered. Yes, she knew it was the final word, and had done from the moment she'd realized he was to marry Fleur, but by trying not to think about his betrothal, she too had been in a fool's paradise. In that she had been as guilty as he.

He caught her close again, crushing her in his arms as if that would keep her with him forever. "In my heart I will be your husband, Ellie. Nothing will ever change that."

Her bitterness was momentarily too raw to be hidden. "She doesn't deserve you, Athan." Little did he know how true that was.

"I know you and she do not like each other, but—"

She wished she'd held her tongue.

He looked intently at her. "There's more to this, isn't there? Tell me."

Her lips parted. The words were there, on the very tip of her tongue, but without evidence she knew she must draw back from the brink. "Whatever I say, Athan, it will be my word against hers, but you may believe me when I say she doesn't deserve you. You may feel obligated to her father, but even so I beg you to think very carefully before you exchange vows with her. If you trust Mrs. Lewis and

Gwilym, as I think you do, then give serious thought to whether you ought to also trust their judgment where Miss Tudor is concerned."

Athan put a hand to Ellie's chin and made her look at him. "If you know something, anything, I think you should tell me."

"Without proof, your honor would still bind you to her."

"Oh, Ellie, can't you see that I am not so honorable that I would not grasp any reed that might save me from a marriage I do not want? Where is honor in that? Nowhere. I am a sorry creature, Ellie, desiring and loving you so much that I actually hope for a way of escape from a match that is of my own doing. And this, even though I now know—" He stopped, and looked away.

"Even though you now know what?" Ellie asked.

"That Fleur loves me," he answered simply.

Ellie stared at him, then moved out of his arms. "You really think that?"

He nodded. "I don't merely think it, Ellie, I *know* it. She came to me tonight, so terrified that your likeness to Caroline would lead me to cast her aside that she actually offered herself to me. She was crying, and it was more than my conscience could bear."

Resentment flared through Ellie, resentment against Fleur, against cruel fate, against *him*. . . . "So you've come straight here to spare your scruples by telling me to forget you? Well, I take my hat off to her, for to be sure, her performance must have been worthy of Drury Lane."

"It wasn't a performance, Ellie."

"Yes, it was, Athan." Ellie turned away and pressed her shaking palms to her nightgown to try to compose herself, but it was impossible. She was angry, distressed, heartbroken, and confused, and in no state to keep to herself things that in a calmer moment she might never have said. She faced him, her eyes bright, her body quivering with barely suppressed feelings. "Maybe what I am about to tell you will make me no better than she is. It will certainly make you think I am a nasty spiteful cat, determined to have you at all costs, but that is a risk I am prepared to take. You see, while your marriage to her remained solely a matter of your honor, I would have found it painful beyond belief, but I would have endured it. But I cannot stand silently by and watch you and your honor being gulled by the lies and mischief of a bride whom I have come to detest. Fleur Tudor doesn't love you; she loves herself, and I suggest that before you allow yourself to be completely taken in by her pretty tears and protestations of love, you ask her about your friend, Freddie Forrester-Phipps." There, it had been said.

Athan stared at her. "Freddie? What are you saying?"

"I don't know exactly what I'm saying, Athan, except that two and two usually add up to four." Emotion swept all before it as Ellie told him what had happened when she was in St. Dwynwen's Church, and when she'd finished, she held his gaze. "I cannot substantiate anything, Athan, but I swear that it is all the truth. Fleur Tudor really isn't the sweet, tremulous creature you seem to think."

He was so thunderstruck by the revelations that he didn't know what to say.

"Which illusion have I shattered, Athan?" she asked dryly. "The one about me, or the one about her?"

"Do you honestly believe I would think you capable of inventing such a tale?"

"Then . . . you believe me?" Hope tried to stir through her, but she forced it away. Victory was not hers yet, not by any means.

"I certainly believe everything you've said, although, like you, without proof . . ."

"At least promise that you will confront her about Freddie Forrester-Phipps."

He nodded. "I will."

Ellie gazed at him. "And what will you do when she denies it all and then dissolves into more virginal sobs, quivering lips, and helplessness?" she asked softly.

He couldn't answer.

Ellie went to pick up the candle. "I think you are quite right, Athan," she said, her voice barely audible because she was so choked with tears, "things must be completely ended between us. Chance tried its best, but Fleur Tudor and your sense of duty have combined to play a winning hand."

"Don't leave like this, Ellie," he begged, taking a step after her.

She turned, and something in her eyes halted him. "Fleur

did tell me about the post with Lady Brecon, you know; indeed, she threatened all manner of things if I didn't take it, including telling you of some particularly disgusting and untrue things about Uncle John and me."

Athan stared. "Surely that cannot be!"

"Oh, it can, Athan, it can. She told me she had spoken to your agent about it and persuaded him to write a letter that would be sent if I did not bow to her wishes about Lady Brecon. Well, I didn't bow to her wishes, so I imagine the letter was sent. You, of course, have returned earlier than anticipated, but believe me, she will tell you about the rumors, although not that she invented them, of course. Oh, yes, poor dear Fleur is quite ruthless when it comes to getting what she wants. And I, fool, had actually been cowed into silence about everything. Well, you have cured me of that. Anger and outrage are sterling remedies for stupidity, and although I realize that I may not have helped Uncle John's situation by parting from you like this, I'm glad I've spoken my mind."

"Nothing you could ever say or do to me would make any difference to my regard for your uncle, who I *know* would not be involved in the things that appear to have been suggested. Heaven knows, if there's one thing John Bailey wouldn't do, it is conduct an affair of any sort with a woman! And even if he were to be so inclined, it wouldn't be with his own niece. As for you, my darling Ellie, I know your qualities as I know my own, and so I would never give such a filthy rumor a hearing. So if Fleur, or anyone, repeats such a thing to me, they will receive short shrift, of that you may be sure. Please, Ellie, what more can I say?"

"Please? Please what, Athan? You came here to end whatever it is that has been between us. Well, you have accomplished your purpose, and from now on we will be as formal toward each other as we should have been all along. There isn't anything more to be said, except, perhaps, that I cannot stay here at Nantgarth."

"Don't say that," he said quickly, knowing he could not bear to lose her.

"You ask too much, Athan. How can I remain here now? I have said things that I should have kept to myself, and now I no longer have the courage or fortitude to exist here in misery while your new life with her unfolds at the castle.

I must leave; surely you can see that? Perhaps the best thing after all would be for me to write to Lady Brecon."

"And become a governess? Oh, Ellie!"

"Why not? It is better than being a scullery maid."

"I love you, Ellie."

She looked at him in the swaying light of the candle. "Please go, Athan," she said softly.

"Ellie . . ."

"Just go, for this achieves nothing. Your decision has been made, and so has mine."

He considered standing his ground, even considered going to her and forcing kisses upon her unwilling lips that would make her change her mind, but her gaze forbade everything. With a heart that was suddenly even heavier than it had been when he arrived, he turned and left.

The candle fluttered as she hurried to push the bolts across the doors, as if by so doing she could end this brief but vital chapter of her life, but she could only fumble with the cold metal. Her fingers seemed incapable of performing such a simple act, and her eyes were blinded with tears. The candle slipped from her fingers and extinguished as it fell with a clatter upon the cobbled floor. She pressed her hot forehead to the door, her eyes tightly closed as she tried to compose herself. It was over, *over,* and she had to get on with the rest of her life.

She closed her eyes and sank slowly to her knees, careless of the chill stone. Wishful thinking could be so cruel. In her secret heart of hearts she had believed what appeared in the teacup, believed that she and Athan would one day share a wedding night, but now she knew it would never be so.

Then, as she knelt there so brokenly on the cobbles, it seemed she could hear Gwilym's voice in the distance. *Call him back, Miss Ellie. Call him back, for all is not yet lost. . . .* Her eyes flew open again, and she scrambled to her feet to open the door. But as she ran out into the misty dawn she could already hear the diminishing sound of Athan's horse along the lane. He had gone back to the castle, back to Fleur.

Gwilym stood by St. Dwynwen's well, his face contorted with concentration. Up here the first rays of the sun were beginning to finger the eastern horizon, but down in the valleys everything was still swathed in mist.

"Call him back, Miss Ellie," he said softly. "Call him back, for all is not yet lost. . . ." But he too could hear the echo of hooves in the hidden lane, and when he looked at the handkerchief that was spread upon the well, it remained very still. A chance of happiness had just been there for the taking at Nantgarth House . . . but had been dashed aside by folly.

Twenty-one

The next night found Athan struggling to appear as if all was well, Fleur exulting that her hold upon him seemed as strong as ever, and Ellie worrying John by retiring early to her bed, from where he could hear her stifled sobs. In London, however, events were in progress at the Tower that were about to have the entire capital in uproar, and that would affect the lives of everyone at Castle Griffin and Nantgarth House.

As promised to Valentin, Major Carver started the fire that was intended to be at its height at midnight, when the Thames tide was at its fullest flow. It was half past ten when a sentry on duty near the Martin Tower, where the jewel house was located, noticed the unusual croaking and flapping of the famous ravens. Then his attention was drawn to a billow of smoke coming from an open window. He raised the alarm by firing his musket, and the entire complement of Inniskilling Fusiliers immediately turned out.

Carver found himself briefly in command, his senior officer having been invited out to dinner, so he himself ordered the nine Tower fire engines to be brought into action. But soon flames began to lick into the night, and engines from all over London were sent for. He requested floating engines on the river, and sent to another barracks for men to control the vast crowds that soon gathered on Tower Hill to watch a conflagration that no one had ever thought to see. There was nothing the brave major did not do to try to save the Tower of London from disaster. He would be highly commended for his strength in the face of adversity, and would even be promoted, and all for a fire he'd started himself because he was being blackmailed.

His commanding officer returned at last, and took over, paying heed to Carver's advice that the jewels and regalia were about to come under threat in the Martin Tower, and should be carried to safety at the Governor's house. An urgent search was made for the keys to the sturdy metal cages containing the jewels, but they could not be found, so crowbars were used. The precious items were carried across the flame-reddened grass of Tower Green, where acrid smoke drifted and the soldiers' hurrying figures loomed like wraiths.

Carver went too, of course, seeing to it that everything was taken into a delegated room. He oversaw everything, and was there to carefully palm the red diamond when it was placed on a table with other small jewels. No one saw the swift movement of his hand, or missed the jewel, because the soldier who'd brought it was already hurrying back to the Martin Tower to see if there was anything else to be rescued.

It was almost midnight when the collapse of a floor in the tower where the fire originated caused such confusion and extra alarm that the good major was able to slip away unnoticed. There was so much smoke that he could barely be seen as he slipped out of the Tower and made his way swiftly down toward the stairs, where Valentin waited in a small rowboat.

The boat swayed as Valentin stood, an anonymous cloaked figure in the darkness. Carver descended the steps to where the high tide lapped, and now and then the rowboat nudged the stonework. After glancing around, to be sure there was no one near enough to see what followed, he took the diamond from his pocket and held it up for Valentin to see.

"The fake, if you please," he said.

Valentin produced the counterfeit gem, and for a few moments both were in full view, glittering, red, and indistinguishable from each other. Then they changed hands and were once again hidden from view.

Carver lingered. "This is definitely the last I will hear of you or your uncle?"

"But of course, Major, for we are men of our word." Valentin smiled, his teeth gleaming in the flame-ridden darkness.

A retort burned Carver's lips, but he thought better of it, and simply inclined his head before turning to make his way back to the Governor's house. But it was already too late. He reckoned without the vigilance of the soldier who'd brought the real diamond from the Martin Tower, and who had taken something else to the place of safety, only to immediately observe the diamond's disappearance. After glancing all around, he mentioned it to the nearest officer, who also searched for any sign of it. Within minutes another alarm had been raised, this time for theft.

Valentin was already rowing away into the middle of the river, the diamond secured against his very heart. He heard the whistles and shouts of the fresh alarm, but didn't realize what they signified.

Carver knew, however, and his dismay was huge. He hesitated, knowing he did not dare be caught with anything on his person. He drew briefly into the shadow of a deserted sentry box and, with one mighty throw, hurled the fake into the Thames. For a second it caught the light of the conflagration in the great fortress, then disappeared forever beneath the tidal waters. Carver hurried back to his duties, blending among his fellow officers and men as if he'd never been away. His involvement in the diamond's disappearance would never be known, although it would haunt him for the rest of his career. Fear of discovery would eat away at him and make him a very bitter man.

Valentin rowed right across the river to the curiously named Pickle Herring Stairs on the opposite shore. Crowds of onlookers had congregated there too, but no one paid him much heed as he made the boat fast and then pushed up through the press to the equally curiously named Pickle Herring Street. There, some way from the stairs, a hackney coach waited for him, the driver having been paid very well for his patience. Soon Prince Valentin Andreyov and the famous red diamond were being conveyed back into London, across London Bridge and through the City toward Mayfair, where he alighted as if from an evening in the stews of Southwark. Feigning inebriation, he wove unsteadily across the pavement to the front door of Athan's Berkeley Square town house, and allowed the servants to take charge of him.

Later, as the London newspapers prepared headlines about the great fire at the Tower, and the audacious stealing of the famous diamond, Valentin lounged comfortably on his bed, still wearing his boots, and drinking vodka from a bottle. He smiled as he brandished the bottle at the air. "Well done, Uncle Paul. Now all we have to do is get the little red bauble out of Britain and into the czar's hands."

The first steps toward accomplishing that would commence tomorrow when he traveled to Wales. All that was to be hoped was that the china maker proved as easy to coerce as Carver, and that he performed his unwanted task with equal ingenuity.

Come the following day, the newspapers would be filled with claim and counterclaim about events at the Tower. Had the fire started accidentally, or was it arson? Had the diamond been stolen, or had it simply rolled away underneath something and was waiting to be found? No one would believe the latter possibility, of course, because everyone knew the diamond was one of a pair, and that the Czar of All the Russias not only possessed the other, but wished to have both.

So vociferous and aggressive would the press become in the coming days, and so heated its accusations against the czar, that the Russian ambassador, Vorontzov, would feel obliged to lodge an official complaint. So too would Novosiltzov, the special envoy Alexander had sent to rally British support against Napoleon. For Prime Minister William Pitt and his cabinet, the whole thing would threaten to become a full-blown diplomatic incident of sufficient magnitude to render cohesion against Napoleon impossible. And all because of the double-dealing machinations of a slippery St. Petersburg courtier who may indeed have wished to see his nephew and heir reinstated to imperial favor, but whose real purpose was to destroy the Englishman who'd once stolen the heart of a handsome young man named Nikolai Trepov.

As the flames and smoke at the Tower lit the skies above the capital, at Castle Griffin a newborn foal, still wet and bewildered by her new life, struggled to her long legs, encouraged all the while by the gentle nudges of her dam. Lantern light slanted across the stable as Athan and Gwilym watched. They grinned at each other, for it had been a long and difficult birth, requiring all Gwilym's skills, but all was now well, the mare was unharmed, and her new daughter was perfect.

"Let's hope this scene is repeated in St. Petersburg," Athan said, knowing that the stud's reputation hung upon such things.

"It will be, my lord, for I have chosen with care, and St. Dwynwen granted her blessing."

"Would that the sainted lady bestowed her favor upon everything," Athan murmured, half to himself, half to the night air beyond the stables. The stars were out, and it was very cold and still—as cold and still as his heart had been since he'd betrayed his love for Ellie. If ever a man was in a cleft stick, it was him. No one should ever have to choose between love and duty, for it was the most cruel choice in the world. He'd made his decision, but could he abide by it? All he knew was how overjoyed he'd been to receive John Bailey's message saying that he—and therefore Ellie—would definitely go to St. Petersburg after all. The voyage was several months away yet, but it would come, and with it the chance to be with Ellie again.

Gwilym looked at him. "St. Dwynwen smiled upon you, my lord, but then withdrew her blessing."

"Mm? What was that?" Athan roused himself from his thoughts.

"She sent her eel, my lord. She helps animals . . . and lovers."

Athan straightened and regarded the housekeeper's son more intently. "You know, don't you, my horse-charming friend? You know about Miss Rutherford and me?"

Gwilym nodded. "Yes, my lord."

"Am I still to marry Miss Tudor?" *Please say I am not. . . .* Such a craven question should not have been asked, not even thought of, yet Athan couldn't help himself. His desire to escape from the now unwanted match had been there since he'd met Ellie, but had become greater now that he knew how Fleur had conducted herself in his absence. He had also spoken to his agent, and knew that

Fleur had indeed claimed to have heard vile rumors about the relationship between Ellie and her uncle. As a result, it was all he could do to be civil to Fleur, let alone gently disposed.

Gwilym's eyes flickered to the stable entrance beyond Athan, as Fleur herself suddenly appeared there. She had put a warm cloak over her green silk dinner gown, and the diamond comb in her hair sparkled in the light from the lantern. Her breath was silvery as she came in. "But of course you are to marry me, Athan," she said in a light, almost kittenish tone that belied the stab of alarm she'd felt on arriving just in time to hear the question. She was aware of an inexplicable cooling in his manner over the past day, and was so troubled about it that she'd simply had to come out here to the stables, even though she loathed the very thought of observing the birth of a foal.

Athan turned to her, masking his dismay with a quick smile. "Forgive me, Fleur. I was just testing Gwilym's power to predict."

"Maybe he can tell us the exact date of our wedding," she murmured, smiling as she came to link her arm through his. The scent of lilies coolly drifted over him, and there was something distinctly chill about the feminine rustle of her clothes.

"This is perhaps not a suitable moment for such a discussion," he answered, knowing there would never be a suitable moment.

She managed to keep smiling and looked instead at the new foal. "How charming. What shall you call it?"

"Would you like her to be named after you?" Athan suggested.

"Well, I . . ." Have that clumsy, gangling creature bear her name? Fleur thought not!

Gwilym glanced at her. "Perhaps Miss Tudor would prefer the foal to be called by the Welsh word for flower."

"And what might that be?" Athan inquired, not being particularly accomplished in the language.

"Blodyn," Gwilym answered. He didn't know why the suggestion had entered his head, just that it had, and that it needed to be uttered. He was agreeably surprised by the effect his words had upon Fleur. Her breath caught, and

her green eyes became visibly alarmed. Gwilym wondered why, but no answer came.

Athan pulled a face. "Fond as I am of all things Welsh, I cannot say that I much admire any of the female names that commence with *Blod*. I find them singularly unbecoming."

Fleur remained ominously silent, and the gaze she darted at Gwilym was both frightened and poisonous. Then she changed the subject in a way so obvious that it was clumsy, and she could not hide the sudden unease in her voice. "How . . . how long will you be out here, Athan?" she asked, clinging to his arm like a helpless kitten.

"Oh, a little while yet. I must be sure mother and daughter are definitely all right."

"Gwilym will stay with them, won't you, Gwilym?" Fleur said firmly, at the same time trying to draw Athan toward the stable door, but to her annoyance he would not come.

"I know Gwilym will remain here, Fleur, but I prefer to stay too. I was away far too long, and need to reacquaint myself with absolutely everything."

"But you were away from me too," she pointed out, finding it all she could do not stamp her foot with frustration. She had been trying to keep him at her side ever since his return, but it was no easy matter. The reassurance he'd given when she'd gone so unsuccessfully to his bed was no longer a comfort, because today he seemed to have cooled so much toward her that he was almost a different man.

He remembered his promise to Ellie. "Yes, I was away, and it so happens I encountered an old friend of yours. Freddie Forrester-Phipps."

Somehow Fleur managed not to react unduly. "Mr. Forrester-Phipps? Well, I'd hardly say he was a friend, exactly . . . more an acquaintance."

"I think he believes himself to be a little more than that."

Color rushed into her cheeks. "Why? What on earth has he been saying?"

Athan saw the flush, and the start of fear that suddenly changed her eyes. Ellie's judgment was right. There *was* indeed something to be discovered here. "He merely asked to be remembered to you. He is obviously enamored."

"Indeed? Well, I am not similarly taken with him."

Athan smiled. "Of course not."

Her glance darted uneasily to his face again, uncertain whether or not he meant anything by the bland answer, but she couldn't read him at all. Again she changed the subject. "Athan, Mr. Forrester-Phipps is of no interest whatsoever, for I am too concerned with being with *you*. You have been away a long time, and you are soon to go away again. Some time in May, as I understand it. Am I never to be with you?"

"I know I will be going away again," he replied, "but nevertheless—"

"You could take Mama and me to St. Petersburg with you," she broke in, wondering why such a thing had not occurred to her before.

"It would hardly be practicable," he replied. Her suggestion did not suit him at all, because the return to St. Petersburg was his chance to be with Ellie again. He knew his motives were ignoble, but he really couldn't help himself.

"But, Athan, if it is considered practicable for Miss Rutherford to go, then surely—"

"Your reputation would be jeopardized, Fleur."

"Why?"

"Because your mother finds the journey from here to London a severe trial, so will be completely unable to countenance a distance as great as from here to St. Petersburg. Your reputation would be worthless if it became known you'd traveled alone with me." That at least was true, and owed nothing to his private reluctance.

"If Mama were not there, Miss Rutherford would be my chaperone," Fleur said then.

"I hardly think so, given the intense dislike you have for each other."

Fleur's green eyes took on a confrontational glint. "Very well, I accept that she and I are not exactly bosom friends, but I really would like to see St. Petersburg. How can you deny me such a chance, Athan? Especially when there is an obvious and happy solution to the problem."

"Solution?"

"We could be married before we leave."

Silence descended. In his mind's eye he could see the special license that had been put away out of sight in his desk—the special license of which Fleur knew nothing because he could not bring himself to take any step at all that would finalize his understanding with her. At last he found his tongue. "There would be too much to arrange," he said.

"Too much? Athan, the journey is *months* away."

"I do not want a hasty marriage. Fleur, this business in St. Petersburg is important to me, and should be out of the way before we contemplate a wedding. Better a bridegroom who is free to put his entire endeavors into such a matter than one whose mind is constantly elsewhere."

Yours is constantly elsewhere anyway, Fleur thought, thinking of Nantgarth House. But still she managed to smile. "I do not need a grand wedding, Athan, just a simple ceremony will do. St. Dwynwen's, not St. George's, Hanover Square, that's all I ask. Please, my darling, for you *know* how much I have come to love you."

"Do not press me in this, Fleur, for the matter is closed. I will not hear of any wedding plans until *after* St. Petersburg."

She pulled petulantly away from him. "You do not care if you hurt me!" she cried.

He was already uncomfortable at the turn the conversation had taken in front of Gwilym; now he became appalled and nodded quickly at the youth. "Leave us for a moment, if you please."

"My lord."

As Gwilym slipped out into the night, Athan faced Fleur. "This is poorly done, Fleur. Such matters should be conducted in private, not in a stable with someone else present, a servant, at that."

"You leave me no choice, for I've found it impossible to spend time with you today."

"I'm just back from a long absence and have many things to do," he replied.

"How am I expected to feel?" she demanded. "You returned yesterday, full of promises that all is well and we will be married come what may; then today you behave as if you despise the very sight of me."

"You are wrong," he answered, but knew she wasn't. If this conversation had been conducted yesterday, he would have repented his treatment of her, but today was very different.

"Then prove it. Let me come to St. Petersburg with you,

and let Miss Rutherford and I be each other's chaperone, whether or not we like it."

"Why should she put herself out for you, who have been no friend to her since she arrived? It would be totally outrageous to request her to enter such an arrangement, especially as her uncle provides her with protection."

"Protection? Is that what you think?" There was a sudden edge in Fleur's voice.

Athan turned to face her fully. "Yes, that's what I think," he said levelly.

"Well, local whispers have it very differently."

"Oh?"

Everything about him should have warned Fleur not to proceed, but she hated Ellie too much to be sensible. "Yes, Athan, they do. It would seem that Mr. Bailey and his niece do not behave as properly as they should. In fact, they behave most *improperly*."

Athan gazed at her, for the first time actually disliking her. It just did not seem possible that she was General Tudor's flesh and blood, for she appeared to lack all nobility of character, kindness, or even amiability. She was self-centered and malignant, and the more he was with her, the more he doubted his ability to ever honor his word to marry her. "That is a monstrous calumny, Fleur," he said after a moment, "and I am saddened you should think fit to repeat it."

"It is only calumny if untrue."

"But it *is* untrue."

This wasn't at all the reaction she'd expected, and her chin rose defensively. "Well, I suppose you would say that, wouldn't you?" she cried. "Anything that touches unfavorably upon Miss Rutherford *has* to be untrue! Heaven forfend that she should have a fault!"

"You've said more than enough, Fleur," he replied quietly. "It is vile to use the names of John Bailey and Miss Rutherford in such a way, and I forbid you to utter another word on the matter. I have already spoken with my agent, who tells me he hasn't heard these rumors except from you, so I wonder greatly about their origin. Do I make my position clear? If you mention such things again, you will not only incur my considerable wrath, but make an utter fool of yourself in the process. Why? Because your abhorrence of Miss Rutherford is written too plain, and because you clearly know nothing whatsoever of John Bailey's character. Now, I think you had better go back inside, before the night cold becomes too much."

Fleur gazed at him, shaken to the very core. Was there nothing, *nothing* she could say or do to loosen Ellie Rutherford's hold upon him?

"Please go, Fleur, before this meeting deteriorates any further."

"Athan—"

"Good night, Fleur."

Twenty-two

The overnight frost still lay in the hollows as Athan dismounted by St. Dwynwen's well, tethered his horse to an iron loop in the churchyard wall, and walked swiftly up the path toward the porch. It was midmorning, the vibrancy of spring was beginning to cloak the mountains, and in the distance to the south he could see the sparkle of the sea.

He didn't know what he expected to find up there, but just knew he had to come. His boots rang on the stone flags as he strode down the aisle toward the sanctuary, where he inspected every inch of the ceiling's edge. There was nothing. It would have been too much to hope that he'd find an incriminating note linking Fleur with Freddie Forrester-Phipps, but that was what had lurked at the back of his mind as he'd set off on a ride before breakfast.

The harsh words he'd exchanged with Fleur had left him feeling far too troubled to face her across the table. The aspect of her character that he'd seen in the stable had repelled him, and he knew that he had to consider very seriously indeed the damned and damnable duty of making her his wife. And so here he was, prying like a spy, hoping to find evidence that would release him from his obligation. But there was nothing.

With a sigh he quit the church again, but just as he'd untethered his horse at the gate, there was a splash in the well. He turned in time to see a shaft of silver. An *eel*? Damn it all, eels might be able to make their way for miles along almost waterless ditches, but they couldn't climb mountains! He went closer to the well. The water was still rippling, but that was all. The eel, if that was what it had been, had disappeared.

Then some sixth sense made him turn to look along the mountain track in the opposite direction from the way he'd come. A rider appeared over a brow, a woman in mustard yellow on a sturdy black cob. *Ellie!* He gathered the reins, mounted, and urged the horse toward her. She realized it was he, reined in, and then began to turn Tomos to ride back the way she'd come, but the cob was no match for his much faster horse. He caught up with her just as she was about to ride down into the draw, and when she ignored his calls, he rode alongside her and leaned over to grab Tomos's reins.

"Let me go, Athan!" she cried, trying to urge the cob on.

"All I want is to talk to you, Ellie," he answered, keeping a tight grip until Tomos had halted completely and there was nothing further Ellie could do.

She looked accusingly at him. "There is no more to be said between us."

"Are you going to ignore me all the way to St. Petersburg?"

She didn't answer.

His gray eyes pleaded. "Just a few minutes of your time, Ellie. Please, I beg of you."

Reluctantly she gave in. "As you wish," she said, hoping he could not hear in her voice how very much she wanted to be with him.

He stretched out a gloved hand to hers, but she pulled away. "No, please, Athan. Your decision has been made, and I know it was the only decision that was possible in the circumstances, so it is unfair of you to waylay me like this."

"Have you written to Lady Brecon?"

She avoided his eyes. "Not yet."

"Then don't write at all. Ellie, hope is not yet lost."

"Are you still betrothed to Miss Tudor?"

He drew a long breath. "Yes, but—"

"How can there be buts, Athan? A betrothal is binding, and that is all that matters. She has a claim upon you; I do not."

"You have every claim in the truest sense of the word," he said softly.

"You do not play by the rules, sir," she replied.

"I love you, Ellie, and I begin to despise the woman to whom I am engaged."

"I may not like Miss Tudor, but it is hardly her fault that you and I have met, so it ill becomes you to—"

"You were right when you said she would tell me about the rumors concerning you and your uncle. She did, last night, and there was something in the way she did it that I found utterly detestable. If I had seen her in that light before, nothing on this earth would have made me ask for her hand. But now I have this betrothal that is utterly abhorrent to me, and I still have a love for you that breaks my heart with its intensity. I *cannot* marry her, Ellie."

"That is between you and she."

He searched her eyes. "Do you still love me, Ellie?"

She looked away. "It makes no difference if I do or not."

"It makes *every* difference. Look at me, Ellie. Look at me and deny you love me." He stretched across to take her chin in his hand and make her meet his eyes. "Deny your love for me, Ellie, and I will accept what you say."

"Please, Athan . . ."

"Deny it, if you can."

Tears shone in her blue eyes. "You know that I love you," she whispered.

"And if I were free . . . would you be my wife?"

An incredulous nuance lit her eyes, and her lips moved, as if she sought words, but then she nodded. "Yes."

His breath escaped on a triumphant note. "Then all is far from lost after all," he said gently, and before she knew it he stood in his stirrups to lean right over and gather her close to kiss her on the lips. It was a moment charged with emotion, and he never wanted it to end, but he tore himself away and turned his horse to ride away.

Ellie gazed after him, her heart bruised by her love, her lips bruised by his. She whispered his name, and it seemed the air took up the sound, breathing it across the mountain and carrying it up to the very sky.

As Ellie and Athan confessed their feelings anew on the slopes high above the valley, a travel-stained post chaise was approaching Nantgarth House from the direction of the turnpike. The slightly built postilion was tired after traveling overnight, and tired too of dealing with his unpleasantly high-handed foreign passenger. He didn't care how important Prince Valentin Andreyov was in his own godforsaken land; here, he was just another fancy cove with too many airs and graces. But the postilion knew how to make such graceless, disagreeable passengers suffer for their arrogance, and there hadn't been a rut or pothole between here and the capital that remained unexplored. With luck Prince High-and-Mighty would have found the journey one of the most uncomfortable he'd ever encountered. Of course, what the disgruntled little Englishman didn't know was that Russian roads were ten times worse, and therefore the loathed passenger hardly noticed a bump.

Valentin was splendid in his uniform again, no longer feeling the need for anonymity. He knew the diamond's theft had been discovered almost straightaway, but was confident that his name hadn't been connected with the crime, except inasmuch as he was Russian, and *anyone* of that nationality was viewed with suspicion by the British populace, who were, in general, suspicious of all foreigners anyway. It felt good to be in military trappings again, he thought as he stretched his long legs, encased in tight white breeches, upon the seat opposite. The gold braid on his blue dolman jacket was by far richer than any he had observed upon a British army officer, and the quality of the fur trimming on his pelisse was superior in every way. His white-plumed shako was on the seat beside him, and the miniature icon of St. Valentine around his neck glittered in the March sunlight. He was conscious of his good looks and virility and hoped that one of Athan's maidservants would be amenable, for he was not a man to spend the night alone if it could be avoided.

Perhaps he could improve upon a mere maidservant, and enjoy the charms and redheaded beauty of the ambitiously obliging Miss Tudor, who had been so eager to become Princess Dalmatsky that she had answered any and every question put to her. She had unknowingly confirmed that John Bailey of Nantgarth House was in fact John Arbuthnot Billersley. The fact that the lady was now betrothed to Athan made no difference to a man like Valentin, who was quite prepared to seduce her under the very roof of her husband-to-be. In fact, Valentin thought it would be amusing to do so, if only because he knew that behind the polite smiles and courtesy, Athan, Lord Griffin, disliked him intensely. Well, Valentin Andreyov cordially despised the entire British nation, so had no scruples about anything he did on British soil.

He glanced at his fob watch, a handsome ruby-studded timepiece of French manufacture, given to him by his uncle. It was eleven o'clock exactly, but he was hungry enough for it to be time for dinner at the very least. He hoped that at Castle Griffin it was the custom to eat well at midday.

The chaise passed over the humpbacked bridge at the canal, and Valentin saw the china works and screen of evergreens. The whereabouts of the manufactory had been ascertained from Huw Jenkin at the turnpike gate, and now a note was to be given to the postilion to deliver into John Bailey's hand. It had been written before Valentin left Berkeley Square, and its content was brief and to the point, the intention being to alarm the recipient into submission from the outset:

> *John Bailey. If you wish to remain free and without blood on your conscience, admit me at midnight tonight. Be alone. Andreyov*

The chaise jolted to a standstill at the gate of Nantgarth House, upon which residence Valentin looked with utter disdain. Why was his uncle concerning himself with a man who lived in such a humble abode? Then something drew his attention to the holly tree that spread over the garden wall. A tall, lanky, redheaded youth was standing beneath the branches, arms folded, lips smiling in a way that made Valentin feel oddly uncomfortable. From nowhere, a savage Dalmatian dog leapt up at the carriage door, barking and growling, and scratching furiously at the handle as if it would get at the horrified passenger.

The horses shifted nervously, and the alarmed postilion vaulted to the ground to try to pacify them. Rooks, startled from the evergreen trees, circled noisily overhead, but their cries were lost in the dog's ferocious din. But then, as swiftly as it had appeared, the dog disappeared again. One moment it was there; the next it had gone. Valentin's mouth was dry and his hand shook as he lowered the window glass to look cautiously out.

Gwilym was still beneath the holly tree, still smiling, and

something about him struck a nerve in Valentin. "Why do you grin?" he cried in halting English. "Is it your dog?"

"I have no dog, sir," Gwilym replied. "Dalmatians can be dangerous," he added, "and should be regarded with caution."

Valentin regarded him uncertainly. "What do you mean?" he demanded.

"Why, nothing, sir." Gwilym spread his hands in innocence, then turned to limp away toward the alley.

Valentin felt a cold finger pass down his spine, and shivered as superstition reached swept over him. He was so intent upon Gwilym that he didn't realize the postilion had come to the chaise door.

"You wanted me to take a message to the house, sir?"

With a start, Valentin looked down at him. "Here," he said, and thrust the note into the man's outstretched hand. "Give it to Mr. Bailey. No one else."

"Yes, sir."

Valentin watched the man go up the garden path to the door, which soon opened to his knock. Valentin saw the housekeeper's gaze move toward him, and then how she shook her head at the postilion. Clearly she was saying that *she,* not a bumptious English groom, would deliver any note to Mr. Bailey. The postilion held his ground, however, and after a second glance at the carriage, the housekeeper withdrew inside.

A few minutes passed, then John Bailey appeared in the doorway. He was wearing a color-streaked leather apron, and the sleeves of his shirt had been rolled up above his elbows. He'd been called from his workroom in the cellar, and wasn't at all pleased, but had come instantly on being told that "a foreign gentleman" was at the gate. He glanced toward Valentin, who inclined his head coolly. John broke the sealed note and read. His face waxed pale, and even across the garden Valentin could see how his tongue passed over suddenly dry lips. There was the briefest of nodded acknowledgments, then John withdrew into the house again. Mrs. Lewis bestowed a final haughty gaze upon the postilion, who turned on his heel and came back to the carriage. A moment later the horses were stirred into action for the final few miles to Castle Griffin.

Valentin looked at his watch again, and to his dismay

the hands still pointed to eleven o'clock exactly. He shook it, then listened. There was no tick. He wondered if he'd forgotten to rewind it, but a quick test soon proved this was not so. For some reason the watch had simply stopped. His thoughts went back to the nighttime visit he and his uncle had paid to the Winter Palace, and something his uncle had said: *By the bones of Saint Joseph, I wish I knew what was wrong with this cursed watch. It has given me nothing but trouble ever since I went to that place, yet my watchmaker tells me there is nothing wrong!*

Had his uncle come here to Nantgarth? Something told Valentin that he had.

A little later, Fleur was just on her way downstairs for a late breakfast. She had lain on in bed in the hope of arousing Athan's conscience about his treatment of her the night before, and it had not been an agreeable surprise to learn that he'd gone out riding some time before. Feeling a little foolish, and more than slightly angered by his obvious indifference—for that was how she viewed it—she made her maid's life a misery for a while, then ordered a bath that required a number of footmen to prepare. She then lingered in the rose-scented water, plotting how she would make Athan sorry once she was his wife.

Now, wearing a buttercup yellow muslin gown and with her gleaming red hair piled on top of her head, she descended the great staircase to the main hall, where ancient stonework and richly carved oak paneling darkened what little light pierced the tall arrow-slit windows. A blue-and-white embroidered shawl trailed on the steps behind her, and there was a battle gleam in her eyes. Athan had behaved abominably toward her during the night, and had slighted her this morning, so on his return she would do all she could to plague his conscience. Soft little sighs, heartfelt glances, maybe the shimmer of unshed tears, all should be guaranteed to make him repent his harshness.

She heard the carriage at the door and paused at a spot on the staircase where a shaft of daylight struck from one of the high windows. A footman hastened to the main doors, which gave off the great hall.

Valentin strode in like a victor marching triumphantly into his vanquished foe's domain. He made a splendid sight in his gaudy uniform, seeming all gold braid and shining icon; there was something of the wild hordes from the steppes about his hussar-styled hair, the little side-plaits swinging to his military gait. If he had wanted to make a devastatingly attractive impression upon Fleur, he could not have done better than this. Aware of her elegant figure highlighted on the staircase, and guessing who such a lovely redhead must be, he strode to the foot of the steps and swept the sort of a lavishly dashing bow that brought echoes of the Winter Palace into Athan's Norman fortress above the Taff.

He straightened again, gazing up at her with melting dark eyes that seemed to strip her of every last garment. "Miss Tudor, I presume?" he said softly.

Fleur's hand crept to her throat, and her heartbeat quickened. "You must be Prince Valentin Andreyov," she replied.

He smiled. "Your servant, mademoiselle," he breathed.

Fleur's cheeks warmed, and her green eyes became lustrous as she returned his smile. "Welcome to Castle Griffin, sir."

"It is the greatest of pleasures to be here." *Oh, what a pleasure,* he thought, sensing the absence of virtue from her character. Here was a woman to warm his bed and then be discarded for the worthless creature she was.

Fleur gazed back at him, thinking how handsome and dashing he was, and once again imaging herself as a princess in St. Petersburg. She already played with fire by keeping Freddie Forrester-Phipps dangling in the hope he might steal General Tudor's wealthy daughter from Athan, so why not burn her fingers a little more with this exciting man . . . ?

Twenty-three

Ellie could not help but know something was wrong. Her uncle had barely spoken since her return from her ride, and even now, at dinner, he was sullen to the point of being morose. She had tried to ask him what was the matter, but he'd insisted all was well. But it wasn't all well, and she knew it. She'd inquired of Mrs. Lewis if anything had happened while she'd been out, and had learned of the mysterious young man in uniform whose carriage had stopped at the house.

The fact that this young man had driven on toward the castle implied that he might be Prince Valentin Andreyov, whose presence was expected there. Ellie was curious about the note that had to be put in her uncle's hand and no one else's, and thought it very odd that not a word had been exchanged with the prince. She would dearly like to know the contents of the note, and could only construe that it was connected with Prince Paul Dalmatsky, who, let it not be forgotten, was Prince Valentin's uncle.

Dinner at Castle Griffin was no less awkward, consisting of fragmented conversation in French, in which Fleur was adequate but no more, and her mother entirely without knowledge. There were many awkward pauses, interspersed with Valentin's insensitive vainglory, Fleur's subtly flirtatious laughter, Athan's almost monosyllabic responses, and Mrs. Tudor's silent disapproval. Fleur's mother, clad in fussy orange lace, knew exactly what was going through her daughter's head, and found it hard to credit that even now Fleur was prepared to play close to the edge of discretion. First there had been the foolishness with this Russian's uncle, then the presumably continuing dalliance with Freddie Forrester-Phipps, and now this. Many a fault Mrs. Tudor had shown over the years, but she'd always had the wit—and cunning—to confine herself to one man at a time.

Fleur was feeling reckless because of Athan's continuing coolness. She was afraid of losing him, but instead of behaving with the utmost decorum, she couldn't help trying to be fascinating. She wanted to make Athan jealous, so he would regret having admonished her so cruelly. At the same time she was so strongly attracted to Valentin that she intended to have him, no matter what. And so she was delightful and beguiling, a sparkling figure in sapphires and midnight taffeta, her red hair haloed in the light of the candelabra on the table.

If Athan's eyes had not been so fully opened about the woman he had engaged to marry, he might not have been so shrewd an observer now. He was superbly turned out in a black velvet evening coat, quilted white waistcoat, and white pantaloons. A simple pearl pin put the finishing touch to his white silk neckcloth, and had he tried, he could not have made a more subtle contrast with his male guest's gaudy uniform.

Watching Fleur with Valentin, Athan knew it was only too possible that she was involved with Freddie in some way. She might be General Tudor's only child, but her character and way of going on were such that he knew she must never become Lady Griffin. The betrothal had to be ended, and Fleur and her mother sent away from the castle. If he had to set them up in a house somewhere, then he would. Anything, provided they were not here, and provided he was no longer engaged to Fleur. But ending a betrothal was no easy matter, and if Ellie were to then become his wife, she would be condemned too as the cause of Fleur's downfall. Ellie had to be shielded, so he would have to deal very delicately with Fleur. Perhaps a solution would come to him overnight. He prayed so, for he did not know how long he could continue to suffer these two women beneath his roof—or Prince Valentin Andreyov, God rot his treacherous Russian soul.

The meal at an end, the quartet prepared to adjourn to the drawing room. Fleur made certain Valentin escorted her, thus leaving Athan to conduct her mother. Fleur and

Valentin swept on ahead, placing a convenient distance between themselves and the others. Fleur immediately came to the point. "When shall you come to me, Prince Valentin?" she inquired in French, her tone brushing close to huskiness.

"You waste no time, mademoiselle," he replied.

"I do not think you are a man to bother with the frills of seduction, sir."

The glimmer of a smile played around his sensuous lips. "And you, it seems, are not a woman to bother about the frills of being betrothed."

Her green eyes met his. "Would you prefer it if I were?"

"That would make me a fool, mademoiselle."

"Athan has an appointment in Merthyr the day after tomorrow. He will be away for two nights."

"How very accommodating of him," Valentin replied softly.

"Yes, but I want you now, sir, tonight. When it is a little more dangerous." Fleur trembled with sexual excitement. She would always thrive on breaking the rules, and right now she could think of no rule better to break than that of monogamy. She wanted to punish Athan by putting fresh horns on him.

"I will take you on the floor here and now, if you wish," Valentin answered. "That will make it certain that your future husband knows you are angry with him."

"How perceptive you, to be sure," Fleur replied with a toss of her head, but then gave him a sideways glance of considerable sensuality. "Will you come to me tonight?" she asked softly, glancing back in case Athan and her mother had come up a little closer than anticipated, but they were still several yards behind.

Valentin nodded. "But it will be late. I have some business to conduct first."

"Business?" She was curious.

"Nothing with which to concern your pretty head," he assured her.

"What time?"

"The small hours, I fear." He smiled. "But I promise to reward your patience."

"I'm sure you will, sir," she breathed, gazing at him and picturing herself as his princess.

"One thing I ask."

"Yes?" Her lovely green eyes caressed him.

"Show a little more prudence from now on. You are a very accomplished flirt and clearly an experienced temptress, but it will not do for Lord Griffin to perceive it too. Be reserved with me, perhaps even a little cool, so any suspicion he may entertain will be completely allayed."

Fleur looked sharply at him. "Are you saying I'm obvious, sir?" she demanded.

"But of course not," he answered smoothly. "I'm just thinking of you, my dear. A rift with him will harm your reputation, and that will not do at all. I think too highly of you to want that."

She softened again. "And I of you, Prince Valentin," she said, the words little more than a wistful sigh.

As they walked on, he thought what a faithless trollop she was and decided to give her no consideration at all between the sheets. He wasn't in the least concerned with her reputation, but he *was* concerned with what he'd heard of Athan's ability with a pistol. A confrontation at dawn with seconds would not be a sensible way to end this visit to Britain.

Behind them, Mrs. Tudor had witnessed the lengthy exchange, and could stand no more. "Forgive me, my lord," she said to Athan, "but I fear I have a terrible headache. Would you please be so good as to excuse me for the rest of the evening?"

"By all means, Mrs. Tudor. I'm sure Fleur will be so occupied being the perfect hostess that Prince Valentin will not take too much note of your absence."

She looked uncertainly at him, then gave an awkward smile. "Thank you, my lord." Catching up her orange lace hem, she hurried away in the direction of the staircase that led up to the private apartments.

Athan was about to walk on after the others when Gwilym stepped out of the nearby shadows. Athan gained the impression he had been there for some time. "A word with you, sir?"

"Gwilym?"

The horse charmer came closer. "I think you should know, sir, that the prince has requested a saddle horse to be ready for him at about half past eleven."

Athan was startled. "He intends to ride at that time of night?"

"Yes, sir."

"What do you know of it?" Athan asked, seeing something in the youth's eyes.

"Just that he is going to Nantgarth House to see Mr. Bailey."

"Is he, be damned. How do you know?"

"I just do, sir." Gwilym hesitated. "I can see that he does not arrive there," he offered.

"Meaning what, exactly? A nasty fall?"

"I can make his horse do anything, sir," Gwilym reminded him.

"Well, leave well alone tonight. I prefer to know what he is about, and intend to follow him. See that my horse is ready too, but keep it out of sight. I don't want him seeing it and realizing he's been rumbled."

"Right, sir." Gwilym was about to turn away, but then hesitated. "You must beware, sir. Prince Valentin comes from the spotted dog."

"I know, Gwilym."

The youth nodded. "It will not be resolved until St. Petersburg, but you will know happiness before then."

"I trust that is as much a promise as a prediction?"

"You will be happy before this coming dawn." Gwilym smiled, then melted away as silently as he had come.

It was pitch dark as Valentin rode out of the castle and followed the narrow lane down toward the humpbacked bridge over the brook at the bottom of the valley. He knew which way to go, having memorized everything while being driven to the castle earlier in the day. He reined in once, thinking he heard hooves behind him, but when he listened, all was quiet. So he rode on, over the bridge where the brook was swollen from the mountains, then left at the fork with the track that led up to the church he'd noticed high on the side of the mountain. The lane led through trees, and he heard a vixen scream and owls hooting. Overhead the moon and stars were hidden by clouds that scudded swiftly, and now and then he felt the touch of raindrops on his face.

At last the trees ended, and he saw Nantgarth House and

the china works ahead. He rode slowly to the gate, not wanting to make more sound than necessary; then he dismounted and tethered the horse to the holly tree. The gate opened silently, and his spurs jingled faintly as he walked along the path. The door opened at his approach, John having been looking out of the parlor window. Putting a finger to his lips, he beckoned Valentin inside, then along the entrance passage to the kitchens, where he took a lighted candle from the mantel and led his unwanted visitor down the steep spiral steps to the cellars. He paused at the door of the workroom.

"It is not my habit to reveal my work before it is finally complete."

"I don't care about your habits, sir. I just need to see the tureen."

With great reluctance, John unlocked the door and led Valentin inside.

Out in the alley, Athan dismounted and left his horse well out of sight of Valentin's. He had seen John admit the Russian to the house, and the fact that no light appeared at the parlor window seemed to indicate they had adjourned either to the kitchen or the cellar. Both of these could be observed from the wharf, so he made his way quickly down toward the canal. He was outside the double doors to the cellar when John's candle shone briefly beneath it, and then the workroom door closed before the muffled sound of voices ensued.

Athan was about to test the cellar doors, to see if by any stroke of luck they had been left unbolted, when to his astonishment he heard someone pulling the bolt across. Then one of the doors opened softly, and he saw Ellie's pale face in the darkness. Like her uncle before her, she put a finger to her lips and beckoned him inside. They went to the workroom door and pressed their ears to the wood to listen.

John was speaking to Valentin. "You are your uncle's nephew, sir, a veritable cut from the same damnable cloth," he said in French, a language he hadn't employed since fleeing from St. Petersburg.

"I shall take that as a compliment, sir," Valentin responded, leaning back against one of the trestles and then glancing around with a twist of contempt on his lips. "So this is where Britain's finest ceramic ware is made? How very primitive and modest, to be sure."

"One does not need more."

"I will take your word for it, but can see why Britain will never emulate France in such matters. Porcelain of Sèvres quality cannot possibly come out of this hovel. Surely you will admit that, Mr. Billersley?" Valentin was careful to use John's real name, as a reminder of the hold he had over him.

"Enough of this engrossing chitter chatter, sir," John said dryly. "What exactly is required of me?"

"You have the tureen?"

"I have three tureens," John replied.

"Three? My, how industrious you are, to be sure."

"Select whichever pleases you," John invited, indicating the magnificently decorated and gilded tureens on the trestle farthest from the wharf.

Valentin stared at them, for items of such rare beauty were the last thing he'd really expected to find. He had never seen such delicate white-and-gold *pâte tendre,* or such lavish yet exquisite gilding and applied beading. As for the extravagantly painted decoration of flowers and fruit, it was so true to life that he felt he could pluck one of the peaches and eat it. The brushwork was almost diaphanous, the colors as soft as in nature, and the technical skill so great that Valentin had to concede that it was probably unequaled even at Sèvres—not that he would have admitted it to John, of course.

"I do not care which one it is," he said, pretending not to be impressed. "All I care is that you can conceal this in the lid or the base, wherever it is best." He produced the diamond, and held it up so that it flashed bloodred in the light from the candle.

John stared at it. "Great God above, it's the diamond from the Tower of London!"

"That's right, my dear sir, and all you have to do is make it safe from discovery so that it can be taken to Russia, where it belongs."

John gave an incredulous laugh. "Make it safe from discovery? In a soup tureen? You're quite mad. And anyway, the tureens are complete."

"Are they?" Valentin crossed to pick one up, glancing

first in the lid, and then picking up the base and looking underneath. "There are places where you can conceal the stone. A little unfired clay, a little paint, and voilà."

John gazed at him. "You're serious, aren't you?"

"Of course. You don't imagine I have gone to all this trouble simply to pass the time? The czar wants a soup tureen that will rank with the British porcelain purchased by his beloved grandmother, Catherine the Great. He also wants the diamond, which he believes will look fetching in his private cabinet alongside its twin. So here I am, eager to kill the two birds with but one stone." Valentin laughed at his own wit.

"And I am to go back to St. Petersburg in order to face your uncle's revenge. Is that right?"

"I imagine there is something like that, but I do not know my uncle's purpose. He has kept it to himself, except to say that it is a matter of the heart, and that I should bear in mind the old saying that there is no one as jealous as a Dalmatian." Valentin eyed John. "You are like him, aren't you? Another old queen. You girls fell out over something . . . or was it someone?"

John's face went a dull red. "That is none of your business."

"Nor do I wish it to be, believe me. I despise your kind." Valentin tossed the diamond into the air and then caught it again. "So perform the miracle, John Billersley. Hide this little bauble in the wretched tureen, and then I will be able to go back to the castle and . . . relax a little."

John took the diamond from him. "It will take a little time," he warned.

"Don't think to fob me off or trick me, because if you do, it will be the worse for you. And for the relatives of someone I am told you once loved," he added. "I do not know who they are, except there are four brothers, two sisters, and a mother, all my uncle's serfs."

Nikolai and the entire Trepov family had been Paul Dalmatsky's serfs. John turned away, unable to even look at Valentin.

"Do everything that is required, and their blood will not be on your conscience," Valentin said softly.

"Do you even understand what conscience is?" John inquired, the lightness of his tone belying the utter loathing and disgust he felt for this man and his absent, although omnipresent, uncle.

"I do not need to." Valentin took out his pistol, and smiled. "So get on with it, and don't take long, because my patience is thin. And remember, when I have gone but the diamond is still here, you will have seven deaths to your credit if you do anything foolish."

With a heavy heart John set about mixing the tiny amount of clay he would need for the task. He decided to conceal the diamond in the lid, where an indentation beneath the knob seemed an obvious place. When he finished, it would be impossible for the average eye to tell the ceramic finish had been tampered with, and there would certainly be no way of knowing that the notorious red diamond was hidden inside it.

At the door, Ellie looked anxiously at Athan. "You were right about Prince Paul killing two birds with one stone, for this concerns Nikolai Trepov as well! We must do something, Athan!" she breathed.

He drew her outside to the wharf, where he removed his coat to place it around her shoulders. "I agree that something must be done, but what?" he said, keeping his voice very low so that no sound should penetrate the workroom.

She spoke softly too. "Uncle John's newspaper was full of the diamond's theft this morning! And now it's here, within a few feet of us. . . ." She put shaking hands to her cheeks, trying to think clearly, but her mind was racing too much. Her thoughts flew back to her meeting with Gwilym by St. Dwynwen's well. *I can see that you will cross seas, and . . . that you will hold a diamond in your hand, a diamond as red as blood.*

Athan pulled her into his arms, and held her tightly.

She hid her face against his chest. "Poor Uncle John; this is so cruel! If this should be discovered, he will go to jail and never be allowed out again." An even more dreadful thought struck her, and she looked up at him again. "The diamond is part of the Crown Jewels! Does that mean this crime is one of high treason?"

Athan smiled and shook his head as he continued to embrace her. "I think that is very doubtful." His mind was racing too, but not entirely without the glimmer of a plan. As a possibility began to form, he suddenly held her away and tilted her face so that he could kiss her tenderly on the lips. "Leave it all to me, my love. I will do whatever is necessary."

"What do you have in mind?"

He kissed the tip of her nose. "That is for me to know, and you not to concern yourself about. Just don't say anything to your uncle about what we've heard and seen here tonight. Nothing at all, do you understand?"

"Nothing? But he will need my comfort and support."

"No, Ellie, he needs to behave exactly as Valentin expects him to behave, and he can only do that really well if he is unaware of our involvement. Well, my involvement anyway, because I am determined that you are to be protected at all times. That means no St. Petersburg for you."

She bridled a little. "You cannot make me stay behind."

"No, that's true, but I will beg you to do as I wish in this. Trust me, my darling, because it's for the best."

"And you won't tell me what you have in mind?" She didn't argue any more about St. Petersburg, because nothing, *nothing,* was going to make her stay behind.

"No, because I've barely thought it through myself. All I want you to do now is return to your bed and try to sleep."

"I can't possibly do that, not while all this is happening."

"Do as you are told, Miss Rutherford," he said gently, and smoothed her hair back from her face. He was so sentient of everything about her that it was almost as if they breathed as one. The rhythm of their heartbeats was a single sound, the stirring of their desire the manifestation of complete union. He touched her face again. "Would that I too could ascend those stairs and slip beneath the coverlet with you," he whispered. "Would that I could make love to you over and over until my strength was drained and my passion sated for a while."

She was oblivious to the cold as she pressed to him again. Memories returned of the wedding night she had seen because of the tea leaves, memories that even now, when danger was only a few feet away, had the power to kindle desire through her. She raised her lips to be kissed, and he was not slow to obey such tender bidding. He was aroused by the soft warmth of her body, which was so willing and needful beneath her nightclothes. His masculinity came readily to life, so eager for her that his hands slid down to her buttocks, pulling her onto him so there was nothing she could not feel. He heard her sigh, and felt the tremor of excitement that shivered through her, oh, such excitement. She awakened to him, her body answering his, and as he pressed her even harder onto his ardent virility, he knew that she was experiencing the deep, delicious joy of physical pleasure. Maybe it was not the ecstasy of complete consummation, but it made her heart beat wildly in her breast and brought a flush to her entire body.

He found her lips again, so longing to press her to the wall, free the monstrous erection that pounded at his loins, and sink into her warmth, that he felt close to the very edge of restraint. He was a man of the world, far from celibate, but he had never experienced feelings as strong as these, never known the incredible power of absolute love. To send her from him now would require tremendous strength of will, but somehow he managed to draw back from her. "Go," he whispered.

"Athan—"

He stopped her words with a last kiss so sensuous with pent-up desire that he had to push her toward the cellar door. "Go," he breathed again, "before I forget I am a gentleman and surrender to a need that right now consumes me like the basest lust. If you would keep your chastity, Ellie Rutherford, leave me while I am yet in control and worthy of your love."

Slowly she slipped his coat from her shoulders and returned it to him, then she caught up her skirts to hurry softly into the cellar, past the workroom door, and up through the house to her bed. There she curled up, her flesh still warm with the joy he'd given her. Wild sensations tingled over her skin, wonderful sensations that seemed to ease her soul. She felt in her heart that everything was going to be all right. Neither of the Russian princes would achieve his aim, Uncle John would be free to live his life as he wished and would enjoy the recognition and reward his talent deserved, and she and Athan would indeed share the wedding night shown to her through a supernatural fantasy.

Athan remained on the wharf, his tumult of emotion gradually subsiding now she was no longer with him. He drew a long breath and clenched his fists tightly to bring back some semblance of composure. Then he glanced at the cellar door. The plan that had begun to take shape was not impossible. He would have to think carefully, but he was sure it would work.

Leaving John still closeted in the workroom with Valentin, he made his way up the alley to the road, and then rode back to Castle Griffin.

Twenty-four

John had very little to say the next morning. He looked tired and drawn, would not have any breakfast, and closeted himself alone in his workroom. Ellie longed to break her promise to Athan, but did not. If he thought it was best for poor Uncle John *not* to know anything, then she would go along with his wish—for the time being, at least, because she had a little more faith in her uncle's ability to conceal their involvement from Valentin. It should not be forgotten that John Arbuthnot Billersley had been playing a part for years, and in many ways had already proved himself a consummate actor.

Ellie lingered over another cup of tea in the sunlit kitchen, and Mrs. Lewis watched her for some time before eventually coming to the point. "The gentleman in the fancy uniform came here late last night, didn't he, Miss Ellie?"

"Oh? I don't know. I was asleep." But Ellie couldn't meet the housekeeper's eyes.

"He has upset Mr. Bailey," Mrs. Lewis went on.

"My uncle is certainly not in a happy mood this morning."

"Gwilym came here not long after first light. He said that it would be of benefit if you and I were in the front garden this morning, at about noon."

Ellie looked at her at last. "In the garden? Why?"

Mrs. Lewis shrugged. "I don't know, Miss Ellie, but I think it's best we do as he says. We will do a little spring weeding, or some such thing to pass the time. That way we will not stand out."

From what? Ellie wondered.

"Shall we do that?" the housekeeper inquired.
"Yes, of course."

The amiable morning weather had lured Fleur and Valentin for a ride along the bank of the Taff. Athan ought to have been with them, but couldn't find the stomach for their company, so he'd taken refuge behind the amount of estate and stud affairs, local politics, and general county matters that had accumulated in his absence. Fleur's flirtatious conduct at the dinner table had aroused his suspicion that she would actually be so brazen as to commence a liaison with Valentin, but her manner had been more circumspect in the solar, and by the time she retired she'd been the very model of propriety. Athan wished it were otherwise, for to trap her in such a dalliance would give him all the reason in the world to send her and her mother packing—and Valentin too, for that matter.

Valentin's prolonged visit to Nantgarth House seemed to preclude any notion of visiting Fleur's apartment on his return, and at breakfast she had been the model of good behavior, displaying no particular interest in the Russian. As for Valentin, he was more interested in feeding like a horse at a trough, seeming able to devour enough for four. His morning conversation was nonexistent, and his charm as nonexistent as ever. Athan construed that the attraction that had been obvious at dinner had, for whatever reason, abruptly faded into nothing. He was even persuaded by Fleur's display of disappointment when he declined to join the suggested morning ride by the Taff.

Athan's calculations were, of course, entirely wrong, and as she and Valentin enjoyed the fine morning air along the riverbank, Fleur was in a sleek mood. Valentin was a lover such as none she had known before, and had not even come to her apartment in the conventional manner. No doors for him; instead he had climbed down the ivy on the outside wall, his rooms being providentially directly above hers. It had delighted Fleur to have her prince arrive in such a time-honored fairy-tale fashion, and she had subsequently relished his rough but vigorous notion of lovemaking. He may not have had finesse, or the ability to prolong a single act of pleasure, but he possessed the sort of rampancy that enabled him to provide his services over and over, thus satiating even a woman of her reckless promiscuity. Today she was exhausted, but that would not prevent her from repeating the exercise tonight; indeed, she could hardly bear the suspense of waiting.

She looked elegant and stylish, wearing a new yellow silk riding habit that had arrived only the day before from her Cardiff dressmaker. With it she put a brown satin jockey bonnet that trailed a floating white gauze scarf, and tight brown leather gloves that had required much finger-flexing to put on. It flattered her vanity to have Valentin at her side, because his eye-catching uniform turned every head they passed, and the fact that he was so darkly handsome and exuded such an air of almost primitive virility made it all the better. She didn't so much ride with him as parade with him, exulting in the stir that followed wherever they went.

They rode back to Castle Griffin through Nantgarth, toward the canal bridge and Nantgarth House, where Ellie and Mrs. Lewis were busying themselves with the promised weeding. The "gardeners" kneeled on a mat apiece, pretending to be intent upon things horticultural, when in fact they were constantly glancing all around, waiting for noon and wondering what to expect. Daffodils and hyacinths nodded in the breeze, the camellia was so bright with flowers that it was almost dazzling, and a robin sang in the holly bush. The kilns had been freshly fired, with curls of smoke rising high over the budding spring greenery of the nearby woods, and there was the sound of a fine tenor voice from the canal, where a barge was approaching the bridge from the direction of Cardiff. It was not alone in approaching the bridge, for Fleur and Valentin were too; indeed, they went over as the barge slid under.

The tenor voice broke off in midnote, and the man to whom it belonged exclaimed loudly in Welsh, raising his rather battered hat to wave it up at Fleur.

Fleur ignored him, but moved her horse on more quickly. Valentin turned in the saddle to look down at the barge, then looked at Fleur. "Is he addressing you?"

"No, I think not," she replied. Her cheeks were suddenly fiery, and she glanced back at the man on the canal as if she wished he would drown before her eyes.

The backward glance encouraged the boatman, who shouted

to her again, clearly under the impression of knowing her. Fleur's response was to spur her mount on so that it broke into a swift canter that soon placed distance between her and the canal. Valentin hesitated, then rode after her.

Ellie looked askance at Mrs. Lewis. "What's happened? What did the man say?"

"Come with me, and you will find out," the housekeeper answered, and scrambled hastily to her feet. Ellie followed her out of the garden and then down to the wharf, just as the barge slid by, drawn by a horse on the towpath.

Mrs. Lewis hailed the boatman in Welsh, and Ellie could tell she was asking him to stop so she could talk to him.

The man, a burly fellow whose barrel chest housed the lungs of an undiscovered opera singer, cupped his hands to shout ahead to the boy who accompanied the horse, then steered the barge to the canal bank just beyond the works. He jumped ashore and made the mooring rope fast to a bollard. He then removed his hat and grinned at Mrs. Lewis, but as he began to speak in Welsh again, the housekeeper interrupted in English.

"Not in Welsh unless you have no English. I wish this young lady to understand what we say."

"Do you indeed?" he replied. "Very well, English it is. Taliesin Rees is my name. How may I be of assistance, my lovely? Did you want me for my fine body or my lusty voice?" He winked at Mrs. Lewis.

"That's enough of that," the housekeeper replied a little crossly.

"Oh, so we don't have a sense of humor, eh?"

She put her hands on her hips. "I have too much of importance on my mind to waste time being foolish, Mr. Rees. I want to know why you called the lady rider by the name of Blodyn Evans."

Rees shrugged. "Because that's who she is. Oh, she's become too fancy a fowl to want to acknowledge the likes of me anymore, but I knew her right enough, and she knew me. I may have been away in Liverpool these past ten years, but I haven't changed much. She and her mother used to live in the same Merthyr street as my family. No one knew much of what became of them, but looking at her now, I'd say they've done well for themselves after all."

Ellie stared at him. "Are you saying that you know the lady rider as someone called Blodyn Evans?"

"But of course. Merthyr born and bred she is, and no better than she should be, just like her mother. Begging your pardon, miss." Rees nodded apologetically at Ellie, then continued. "There was a whisper that Flossie Evans, that's Blodyn's mother, got to be some gentleman's fancy piece down near Cowbridge. Or was it Bridgend? Somewhere in the Vale of Glamorgan anyway."

Mrs. Lewis drew a long breath, thinking that it had to be General Tudor of Ty Newydd, Bridgend. "And this gentleman isn't Blodyn's father?"

"*Duw*, no. Blodyn's father is a clergyman from Caerphilly, the youngest son of a baronet, or some such. He was married with ten children, but that didn't stop him fathering more all over the county. Begging your pardon again, miss. One thing though, he took some responsibility for Blodyn, and saw to it that she was educated. Not that she turned out more of a lady on account of it. Indeed, no." He chuckled. "Anyway, be that as it may, I couldn't believe my eyes when I saw her riding by like the queen of England herself."

Mrs. Lewis feared any room for doubt. "And there is no chance that you are wrong? That the rider merely *resembled* this Blodyn Evans?"

"I'd know Blodyn anywhere. She's not the sort a man could forget in a hurry." He folded his arms and looked at them both a little curiously. "Why all the interest?"

"That doesn't matter for the moment," Mrs. Lewis replied. "Would you be prepared to *swear* that the woman you just saw was Blodyn Evans?"

"Swear?" Rees became cautious, because his employer's business along the canal wasn't always legitimate.

"She is passing herself off as someone else and is now betrothed to an upright and generous man who knows nothing of her past," Mrs. Lewis replied.

His face changed. "Marry Blodyn Evans? One might as well invite every man in the neighborhood into the wedding bed." He had the grace to again look a little sheepishly at Ellie. "Begging your pardon yet again, miss, I should not have spoken so crudely." He returned his glance to Mrs. Lewis. "What's in it for me?" he inquired bluntly.

"Oh, you'll be amply rewarded, make no mistake of that. Can you wait here while I send word to the gentleman in question?"

"I'm behind time getting up to Ponty as it is, and can't afford to waste more time now, but I have to go down to Cardiff again tomorrow, about this time. I can hang around more then."

Mrs. Lewis eyed him. "I can trust you to do that?"

He bridled a little. "Taliesin Rees is a man of his word, especially if there is a reward in it. You can count on me being here at the same time tomorrow. I'll tell your gentleman friend whatever he needs to know. Right now, however, I have business to attend to." He turned, whistled to his boy, and then leapt back aboard the barge as the horse strained on the towrope again.

As the long narrow vessel slid away again through the shining water, Mrs. Lewis looked at Ellie. "There seems no mistake. Miss Tudor is actually someone called Blodyn Evans. *Blodyn* means flower, you know, as I believe Fleur does too. How much more *elegant* to be a Fleur than a Blod. Well, elegant or not, she was born out of wedlock and isn't General Tudor's daughter." The housekeeper chuckled a little. "And her mother is really a Flossie? Well, she's Hermione now, and no mistake."

"They've put their past well and truly behind them." Ellie was shaken. Everything seemed to have happened so suddenly—perhaps too suddenly.

"That's a fact." Mrs. Lewis smoothed her hands on her apron. "Well, now, if all this can be proved, do you see what it means? Those two harpies have tricked Lord Griffin. They have no claim upon General Tudor, no right to be at the castle, and his lordship certainly does not have to go ahead with the marriage."

Ellie hardly dared to hope. Could it really be true? Were the lies and pretense of Fleur and her mother about to provide Athan with a simple and *honorable* means to end his betrothal? It was too good to be true.

"We must see to it that a message is sent to Lord Griffin without delay," Mrs. Lewis declared, but Ellie put a hand on her arm.

"No, not so quickly. If Miss Tudor and the prince are on their way back to the castle, it may alert her if Athan is immediately requested to come down here. We have until tomorrow before Mr. Rees comes back this way, and I happen to know that Lord Griffin is going to Merthyr in the morning to keep some appointment or other. He won't be returning until the day after tomorrow, and has already told me he will stop at Nantgarth House on his way past in both directions. We can tell him then, and Miss Tudor will not detect any change of plan."

The housekeeper nodded. "You are right. Oh, if you only knew how much I *relish* this! It will be so good to witness the complete downfall of that wicked pair of conniving, deceitful witches. And you, Miss Ellie, will be Lady Griffin, just as I knew you would the moment I saw you. And as he himself wishes so much, is that not so?"

Ellie looked at her. "There does not seem to be much that you do not know, Mrs. Lewis."

"Gwilym is the one who always knows, Miss Ellie. Things come to him, knowledge and wisdom hidden from the rest of us. He does not see everything, just enough to make sure the path taken by the wicked is a stony one. All is going to be well, and nothing will prevent you from becoming mistress of Castle Griffin."

"The battle isn't quite won yet, Mrs. Lewis," Ellie warned.

Twenty-five

The early morning sun shone through a misty haze, and rooks called around the castle's southwest tower as Fleur accompanied Athan down the courtyard steps to the carriage that was to take him to Merthyr. She wore a white muslin gown sprinkled with cherry dots; there were cherry ribbons in her red hair, and her laughter drifted daintily around the grassy quadrangle. A fringed gray silk shawl trailed the steps behind her. Both arms linked through Athan's, she was the very picture of betrothed happiness, but she failed to cast a spell over the man she was to marry. He felt like disengaging his arm rather than suffering her touch, but something prevented him. Perhaps he was too aware of Valentin standing in the castle entrance behind them, of various servants going about their tasks, and of the coachman waiting by the carriage.

Fleur paused at the bottom of the steps. "You will not stay away longer than is truly necessary? Please say you will not."

"I will be back some time the day after tomorrow." He turned as if to enter the carriage, but she caught his arm again.

"You surely do not mean to part so coldly?"

"I'm not being cold," he replied, although everything about him said he was.

"Have you no kiss for me, my lord?" She smiled, a hint of tears in her eyes, a suggestion of a quiver about her soft lips. It was not difficult to summon tears, for she was becoming more and more aware of his withdrawal. It was Ellie Rutherford's fault; everything was Ellie's fault. . . .

"A kiss? In front of the servants? I think not," he murmured, but took her hand and raised it toward his lips. He did not kiss it, though, and within a heartbeat had released it again to get into the carriage.

Fleur's heart sank deeper as the coachman slammed the door and then moments later stirred the team into action. The sounds of hooves and wheels and the jingle of harness seemed to sound from wall to wall as the vehicle skirted the close-clipped lawn and then drove out beneath the great barbican. As it disappeared down the track toward the valley, Fleur turned slowly to make her way back into the castle. Her cheeks were touched with specks of red to match the ribbons in her hair, and she was aware of the servants' curious glances following her up the steps. Had Athan pushed her away he could not have been more obvious. Nothing she did seemed to heal the rift that Ellie Rutherford had caused between them, and the vulnerability of her position was becoming more and more clear. She had already realized that Valentin was using her, and that she stood no more chance of becoming his princess than she had his uncle's, but his almost animal virility was intoxicating to her. She would use him while she could, because he satisfied the hunger that was always with her.

He was no longer in the doorway, but just as she wondered where he had gone, her mother appeared instead, a warning look on her face. "Be sensible now, Fleur, and stay away from the Russian," she said in a low voice. "You've seen how Lord Griffin is with you, and who knows how many servants might be ready to betray you to him."

As always when her mother saw fit to lecture her, Fleur heaped scorn upon the warning. "You worry too much, Mama. I am still betrothed to him, and that is what matters."

"But for how long will your betrothal endure, my girl? You are behaving like a whore, and the risks you take are so foolish that I despair of—"

"Enough, Mama. I am not going to be a failure as you were. A wedding ring will grace my finger in fact, not just fiction, so have done with it. Your security is not in danger because of what I do. Rest easy, for Athan will never know how we've lied about everything."

Fleur swept on into the castle, leaving her mother in the

doorway, an anxious figure in blue lawn and a gaudy pink-and-gold Persian shawl. Fleur did not look back, for nothing, *nothing,* would permit such an admission of uncertainty. But then all thought of insecurity was banished as Valentin's hand reached from the embrasure of a tall oriel window. Catching her hand, he pulled her behind the heavy green velvet drapes, and into his arms. He was in need of instant gratification and showed no gentleness at all. He took her there and then against the embrasure wall, with just the drapes to hide them from the world, and had to put his hand over her mouth to stop her cries as waves of pleasure shook her body.

Athan called at Nantgarth House as promised, and was astounded by the news that awaited him there. He set aside all thought of his appointment in Merthyr in order to be at the wharf when Taliesin Rees returned.

The barge arrived at the wharf as expected, and Rees was a little alarmed to realize that the fine gentleman waiting with Ellie, Mrs. Lewis, and John Bailey was none other than Lord Griffin, the greatest landowner in the county. Blodyn Evans was hoping to make such a particularly grand match? Who would have thought it? On being reassured that the only matter of interest to Athan was Blodyn Evans, Rees proved as informative as he had the day before, providing Athan with the names and addresses of people who'd known Fleur and her mother at Merthyr. After being paid for his trouble, and being hopeful of further remuneration to come, he told Athan that he would be prepared to stand up in court and repeat what he knew.

As the barge slid on its way south toward Cardiff, Athan turned to Ellie. "I must go to Merthyr after all, and follow up these names and addresses. Ellie, if what Rees says really is true, then I am no longer bound to marry Fleur. Or perhaps I should refer to her as Blodyn from now on." He put a hand to Ellie's cheek, ignoring the glances of nearby china workers. "I have asked you before, but I ask you again now. If I become free, will you marry me?"

"Yes."

He embraced her in front of everyone, his lips meeting with hers in a way that should only have happened in private, but neither of them could help themselves. Happiness seemed in sight after all, and such a joyful prospect took precedence over discretion.

Then he put his hand to her chin, and tilted her face so that she looked at him. "One thing, my darling. You may not like it at all, but my damned sense of duty still ties me a little to Fleur and her mother. Oh, not in the way you think, but because they were part of General Tudor's life. He may not have made an honest woman of Fleur's mother, but he was fond enough of her. Bearing this in mind, I mean to purchase them somewhere else to live, somewhere modest, but sufficient, and I will provide them with enough to live on. It will be a far cry from Castle Griffin, and the funds will not stretch to London or every new fashion, but they will not starve. There my conscience will end. I will be satisfied I've done right by the general, and what they do and how they live their lives will be up to them. Will it upset you if I do these things?"

"They don't deserve it, but I am content with whatever you decide."

He kissed the tip of her nose. "I adore you, Ellie Rutherford," he whispered, then looked past her as he noticed that John had withdrawn in order to return to his workroom.

Ellie turned. "Uncle John?" As the door closed behind him, she knew it wasn't that he lacked happiness for Athan and her, rather that he was too burdened with responsibility about the diamond . . . and the fate of the innocent Trepov family in Russia.

Athan put a gentle hand on her arm. "I'll speak to him. I have things to say anyway, for I have my plan to explain."

"Am I not to know what it is too?" she protested.

"I will allow your uncle to tell you when I have taken myself off to Merthyr. In the meantime, I need to be alone with him. You and Mrs. Lewis go back inside now."

He ushered them before him, and as they disappeared upon the spiral stone steps to the kitchen, he knocked on the workroom door. "John, a word with you, if you please."

John admitted him, and tried to smile. "Have you come to tell me the ground rent is still overdue?" he inquired wryly, being too heavyhearted to really make light of anything.

"Right now I could not care less about the ground rent."

"What then?"

Athan looked intently at him. "I wish you to know that you have my support in the matter of the diamond."

John became very still. "Diamond?"

"There is no need to play the innocent, for Ellie and I were outside last night. We know what was said in here between you and Prince Valentin."

John's forced smile faded, and his face seemed suddenly old and quite gray. "I have to do as he says, Athan, so if you mean to persuade me to return the diamond, pray save your breath."

"Oh, the diamond will be returned to the Tower soon enough, but right now, I want you to consider this." Athan put a hand in his pocket and took out a walnut, which he placed on the nearest trestle.

"A walnut? But—"

"It is the same size as the diamond, I think. Well, more or less."

"Yes, it is, but I fail to see the significance."

Athan waved a hand to encompass the three tureens. "One of them contains the diamond, but I could only tell you which if I took each lid and looked inside. What if a second lid were tampered with in the same way, and it was this second lid that was taken to St. Petersburg?"

John looked at the tureens, then at him. "The decoration of each lid, as of each tureen and stand, is slightly different. The prince would know immediately that it wasn't the same lid."

"You think so? Come now, Prince Valentin Andreyov is many things, but a connoisseur of porcelain decoration he is not. Besides, they are similar enough to fool me, so I am certain the finer points will pass him by too."

John nodded. "Maybe," he conceded, "but even so, you are suggesting that I take a *walnut* to Czar Alexander? I cannot imagine that he will be greatly amused."

"I'd stake my life that Alexander isn't party to this. He might want to possess both diamonds, but not if the second one has been stolen from the country with which he's desperate to sign a treaty against France. I believe that Dalmatsky has badly miscalculated. His judgment is clouded by his thirst for revenge upon you. His nephew, of course, has no judgment, and is simply his uncle's pawn."

John continued to gaze at him. "You may be right," he said after a while, and plumped wearily on his high stool. "I have been so intimidated by the threat to Nikolai's family, that I haven't been able to see clearly."

"Well, I cannot claim to be seeing all that clearly, but common sense leads me to my conclusions. That, and the fact that I have met Alexander, of course, and know that right now he's more interested in an alliance than he is in uniting the diamonds. It stands to reason that the sudden appearance of the second stone in St. Petersburg is going to cause a monumental rift with Britain. It may please Prince Valentin, who reveres Bonaparte to the point of worship, and maybe Dalmatsky is for the French as well, but Alexander *isn't* for the French. He wants Britain, and that is the key. So let Dalmatsky and his nephew find nothing more than a nice Welsh walnut when they look in the lid." Athan grinned. "What do you say? Is it worth trying?"

John was about to smile too, but then remembered. "Nikolai's family . . ."

"I have considered that too. They may be Dalmatsky's serfs, but Alexander is Dalmatsky's emperor. I am promised another audience when I return to St. Petersburg, and if I use the opportunity to *give* the horses to the imperial stud as a gift, Alexander will ask me what he may do in return, as a token of his appreciation. Don't forget how keen he is for a treaty with Britain against the French, which I believe will render him well disposed toward a request about protecting the Trepovs. Dalmatsky will not dare harm them after that." Athan drew a long breath. "I know it's all tenuous, and that it might not succeed, but I'm prepared to match myself against Dalmatsky, and if I know you at all, John Arbuthnot Billersley, then I think that you are too. Let us prove that the British can outwit any impertinent Russian bastards who think they can ride roughshod over everyone and everything. And if at the same time we can honor Nikolai's memory by securing the freedom of his family, then so much the better. Come now, what do you say?"

John straightened from the stool and took Athan's hand to pump it wildly. "Yes, I say yes!" he cried, suddenly more enheartened than he would have dreamed was possible.

"Good man! And in the meantime, can you extricate the diamond from the lid without harming the latter?"

"I can do my damnedest."

"Well, if the lid is lost, it is lost. There is nothing that can be done, but the diamond can be returned to the Tower. Secretly, of course, for it won't do for the Russians to find out. Oh, and one more thing . . ."

"Yes?"

"When this Blodyn Evans business is dealt with, may I have your niece's hand in marriage?"

"I'll think about it." John pretended to be serious, but then gave a broad grin. "I've thought. Yes, of course you can!"

Twenty-six

Athan's visit to the town of Merthyr, at the head of the Taff valley, proved to be very rewarding in the matter of ending his betrothal to Fleur. Everything that Taliesin Rees had said was the truth, and before nightfall Athan knew that he had been lied to with a vengeance. Fleur and her mother were no more General Tudor's family than they were saints, although they had indeed lived with him. They were about to receive a very salutary shock about their future.

He lodged overnight at the Star Inn, where Lord Nelson and the Hamiltons had stayed during their tour of 1802, and early the next morning drove back down the Taff valley to the busy market town of Pontypridd. There he sought an immediate meeting with his local lawyer, Mr. Iwan Vaughan, whose premises overlooked the world-renowned single-span stone bridge that gave the town its other name, Newbridge. Vaughan, who was known for his utmost discretion, owned a number of properties in the county that he rented or leased, and it was in this connection that Athan wished to see him.

The lawyer's smile and warm greeting concerning Athan's betrothal died away in shock when he learned for whom a leased house was being sought. He was even more shocked when he learned why. He showed Athan a list of available properties, from small cottages to modest estates, and it was not long before the latter decided upon one that was perfect for his unwanted lady guests. It was a small house in a village on the far western boundary of the county, well away from Castle Griffin, and from society in general. Athan swiftly arranged the lease, and for a sum of money that would ensure that Fleur and her mother did not starve; then he left again, the keys in his pocket.

He was just about to shake hands with the lawyer and leave again, when Mr. Vaughan said something that made him pause.

"Lord Griffin, are you acquainted with an English gentleman whom I would describe as being your age, with dark blond hair that he quite clearly curls of a night. He has very pale blue eyes, and reminds me of a lizard, although a very well dressed one, to be sure. I believe that in the best circles he would be termed a Corinthian."

Freddie Forrester-Phipps, Athan thought. "I think I may be. Why do you ask?"

"Such a man has been staying at the Newbridge alehouse, down by the river, and has been asking questions about Miss Tudor. Not that anyone around here could help him, beyond confirming what we believed to be true—that she was General Tudor's heiress daughter, and betrothed to you. I would not have mentioned it, but now that you have come here like this today. . . ."

"Thank you, Mr. Vaughan. I am grateful to you. Is the fellow still at the Newbridge?"

"Yes. Is there anything you wish me to do about him?"

Athan smiled. "You have friends in low places, I take it?"

"I have friends everywhere, my lord."

"That I can well believe. No, I don't wish you to do anything, except perhaps have a quiet word with the landlord of the Newbridge, to warn him that his guest is a slippery fellow who is likely to flit in the middle of the night without paying his bill. Mind you, such information did not come from me, is that clear? I don't want the gentleman in question to know that I am aware of his presence."

"As you wish, my lord."

Athan emerged from the lawyer's doorway to walk to his carriage, which had been obliged to wait a little way up the street, but as he walked the few yards he suddenly heard Gwilym call him.

"My lord? Look this way, if you please."

"Gwilym?" Athan turned in surprise, wondering why the horse charmer was in Pontypridd. The youth was standing there behind him, but did not seem to be really there at all, because Athan could see right through him.

Gwilym swept an arm to encompass the busy street, then pointed at a horseman who was about to emerge from a lane that ran down to the riverbank. It was Freddie, spurs gleaming, top hat at rakish angle, Corinthian attire making him the very picture of high fashion. He wouldn't have been observed if Gwilym hadn't drawn attention to him, but as Athan thought about calling out in order to confront Freddie, Gwilym wagged a reproving finger to silence him. Then, becoming less distant with each step until he'd disappeared altogether, the horse charmer crossed the street. But he was still there, as Athan soon realized from what happened next.

There was a large stone horse trough on the corner where Freddie emerged. Quite suddenly there was a wild splashing from it, and something silver leapt into the air and then plunged down again. Freddie's horse was frightened and reared up with such force that he was caught completely off guard. Losing his stirrups, Freddie fell heavily to the ground, where he lay winded. No one else around seemed to have seen the eel in the horse trough, but everyone saw Freddie take a tumble.

Gwilym spoke softly in Athan's ear, just his voice, for there was no sign of the youth himself. "You will see this Englishman fall again before the year is out, my lord."

Athan continued to watch the scene on the corner, where there was much amusement among the bystanders at the sight of such a starched and stylish gentleman lying flat on his back, but several men went to assist him. He wasn't particularly gracious, snatching his riding crop from a helpful hand, and then doing the same with his top hat. He glowered at the watching townsfolk, who quickly went on about their business; then he went to examine the horse trough. The water was still again and did not seem murky enough for anything to be hiding at the bottom. Nevertheless, he jabbed around with his riding crop. There was nothing. Yet he had distinctly seen an eel. Hadn't he? He glanced at the trough again, then tugged his top hat angrily over his forehead. Damn this place to hell; the sooner he secured the Tudor fortune, the better, so he could return to London . . . and civilization!

Athan's carriage followed Freddie as he left Pontypridd

behind and rode south along the turnpike in the direction of Nantgarth. After about a mile he struck to the left up an old packhorse track that crossed the canal and then led up over the mountain toward Caerphilly. It was the same mountain that three miles ahead would end above Nantgarth House.

As the carriage continued along the turnpike down in the valley, Athan twisted to watch until the contours of the mountain hid the no-longer-quite-so-elegant horseman from view. Was Freddie making for St. Dwynwen's in the hope of finding another message from Fleur? Perhaps he was hoping to meet the lady herself. Athan sat back again and gazed at the rich upholstery of the opposite seat, aware that the incident outside the lawyer's premises had been very supernatural indeed. Yet he, Athan, Lord Griffin, a supposedly educated man, had observed almost without raising an eyebrow. Such was his acceptance of Gwilym Lewis.

He sighed, and looked out of the carriage window again, his thoughts turning instead to the problem of Fleur. Somehow he still thought of her by that name, because she really did not seem like a Blodyn. He wondered just what her game really was. She had secured a very fine match, yet did not seem capable of devoting herself to just one man. Was Freddie her lover? And if so, why? Was she hedging her bets? Keeping a second lover in the background in case things went wrong with the first? Maybe, but Freddie had been disinherited, which was hardly likely to make him appealing to a woman like Fleur. Athan could understand a passing fancy during her Season in London, when there hadn't been a betrothal anyway, but not that it would continue now. Could it be true love? Athan doubted it, for Freddie was incapable of such an emotion, and so, he suspected, was Fleur. But what if neither of them was aware of the other's true situation? Might Freddie be hoping to get his disinherited hands on General Tudor's fictitious fortune, and Fleur be keeping Freddie dangling because she believed he had his banker father's estate? Freddie would take second place in her estimation compared with the Griffin title and vast fortune, but he was far better than nothing at all, should her betrothal end—and it was about to, in no uncertain fashion!

The carriage drove on, and after calling at Nantgarth House to tell Ellie and her uncle what he'd found out, Athan continued to the castle, intent upon ejecting Fleur and her mother that very day. The very last thing he expected to happen upon was Fleur in flagrante, not with Freddie, but with Prince Valentin Andreyov! The early return from Merthyr caught everyone by surprise. He intercepted Mrs. Tudor—or rather, Flossie Evans—going through the papers in his desk, and before she could recover from the horror of realizing the game was up, he'd gone to Fleur's apartment and discovered Valentin fleeing from her bed as if the hounds of hell were upon him.

The Russian darted out through the window and clambered up the ivy, his escape assisted by Fleur's hysterical sobs as she flung herself upon Athan's mercy. Naked and still warm from her lover's attentions, she sank to her knees and grasped Athan's thigh, thus inadvertently preventing him from lunging after Valentin. It wasn't her intention to aid Valentin's flight, but that was what she achieved. Athan decided against dealing with Valentin there and then. Let him go. His downfall would be much greater to effect at the undoing of the plans he and his uncle had hatched. In the meantime the fellow could report to Dalmatsky that the diamond was in place in the tureen.

These thoughts flew through Athan's mind as Fleur, weeping distractedly, begged him to believe that she had been forced to surrender because Valentin had vowed to harm Athan himself if she did not become his lover.

Athan looked contemptuously down at her. "Come now, Blodyn, my dear, you don't really expect me to believe that, do you?"

She was a consummate actress, recoiling in puzzlement, her fiery hair cascading magnificently over her shoulders, her upturned breasts revealed to full advantage as she raised her big green eyes to his face. "I . . . I don't understand. . . ."

"Oh, yes, you do." He wrenched himself from her grasp, and stepped back several feet to look at her. "You are the illegitimate offspring of Flossie Evans of Merthyr and an incontinent Caerphilly clergyman, and you and your mother have been masquerading as General Tudor's dependents. Well, you've been rumbled, and I want you both out of here within the hour." He tossed the keys on the floor in front of her. "You have a new home now, and a small income, but only because of the respect I had for the general. The coachman knows the address. I warn you, it's not a castle."

Fleur stared at the keys as if they were about to turn into a poisonous viper. This wasn't happening, it couldn't happen, not to her. . . .

"Get dressed," Athan snapped, "for I meant it when I said I wanted you out of here within the hour."

She tried to collect her wits. "There is a mistake, Athan," she said, her voice gathering momentum as she regained a little control. "I really do not know what you are talking about. I'm not called Evans, and Mama certainly was married to the general, whose daughter I swear that I am." She crossed trembling arms over her breasts, and bowed her head so that her hair fell forward. Oh, she could play the martyr.

"Don't waste your breath, or my time. I know about you, and about Freddie Forrester-Phipps. I confess I hadn't thought you'd go quite so far as to bed Andreyov too, but it seems you will stoop to anything."

The mention of Freddie convinced her that the game was indeed up, and as she struggled to her feet, her lovely face became twisted with loathing. "Well, it took you long enough, Athan. How amusing it would have been had you remained in ignorance until *after* the nuptials."

He turned from her in disgust. "I advise you to get on with your packing."

"How did you find out?" she demanded. "Was it Taliesin Rees?"

"Yes."

"He couldn't have told you about Freddie," she observed suspiciously, "so how . . . ?"

"My lawyer in Pontypridd," he replied, for it was true enough, in a manner of speaking. "Freddie has attracted attention by making inquiries about you. I would hazard he's trying to discover how much you are worth. Oh, that vast Tudor fortune must be a great carrot to him." Athan laughed when he saw the flush that stained her cheeks. "A word to the wise, Fleur. Freddie is penniless too. His late father disowned him, so don't imagine you can fall back on him. You won't see his elegant heels for dust when he discovers exactly how destitute you really are."

"I don't believe you," she breathed. "This is just your petty spite."

He shrugged. "View it how you please; it makes no difference to me. I am going to marry the woman I love, and you cannot even *begin* to know how good that is."

Her face became ugly with loathing. "The potter's niece? Well, I suppose one adventuress is as good as another. She isn't the angel you think, you know. Somehow she found out about her likeness to Caroline and—"

"There was never a Caroline, Fleur. I lied to be free of marriage-seekers. The portrait is of Ellie, and I bought it before I ever saw her. I also fell in love with her before I ever saw her. Sweet serendipity brought her here to me. You have never meant anything to me, any more than I have meant anything to you, beyond being your provider, of course."

"Serendipity? Well, how very cozy."

"Don't make matters worse by venting your spleen on Ellie. You and your mother have only yourselves to blame for your present predicament. If you had been honest with me when the general died, I would have been generous enough. I'd have thought you both meant something to him, and I'd have recompensed you accordingly. As things are, you may count yourselves fortunate that I am fool enough to give you a roof of any kind over your heads, as well as enough money to buy your bread. Beyond that, I owe you nothing."

"You think you and Ellie Rutherford are going to emerge from this unscathed? When society sees Mama and me reduced to lowly circumstances while you take a new wife, you will be ostracized for—"

"Oh, no, Fleur, for if you imagine I will let you say what you please and hold my own tongue, you could not be more wrong. If you speak out of turn about Ellie, or even hint that she is the reason for the ending of our betrothal, I will tell the world about your lies, and about how I found you in bed with Andreyov. Your silence will mean my silence. Do you understand?"

"Perfectly. Well, it seems Mama and I are at your

mercy," she replied, hating him with everything she had. "You will regret not marrying me, Athan."

"I think not." He inclined his head, then walked from the room.

She gazed after him. "Oh, yes, you will," she breathed as the door closed.

An hour later she and her weeping mother were driven out of the castle. Valentin had already departed, having cravenly left many of his belongings behind rather than risk coming face-to-face with Athan. He stole a horse from the stables and put as much distance as possible between himself and Castle Griffin. His destination was Lowestoft, where the *Troitskoe* waited to take him back to St. Petersburg. He wasn't afraid to leave the diamond, being certain that no matter what, in due course it would follow him to Russia.

That evening, at a very small dinner party at Nantgarth House, Athan and Ellie became engaged. That evening too, John was sadly unsuccessful in his efforts to save the tureen lid when he removed the diamond, but the diamond itself was utterly perfect. He placed it on the table before them all, its many facets flashing red, crimson, scarlet, and even gold in the shifting light of a candle.

Athan put it in Ellie's hand. "There," he murmured, "you are holding a jewel so rare and flawless that an emperor dreams of possessing it."

She gazed at the magnificent stone, then smiled at him. "I prefer to dream of being your bride," she said softly as she handed it back to him.

John breathed out slowly. "And I prefer to dream of Athan and I being safely back here from St. Petersburg."

Ellie looked at him, then at Athan. "And where does my name figure in this?"

"You are to stay here," Athan replied.

Her eyes flashed. "Remain behind while you and Uncle John are embroiled in heaven knows what dangers? Never!"

"Ellie—" they both began together, but she would have none of it.

"I am coming with you. The only way you will stop me

is by locking me up, and if either of you contemplates doing something like *that*, I will never speak to him again!"

John looked at her, saw the steely shades of her late mother, and raised his hands in submission. Athan looked crossly at him. "John, we cannot possibly allow Ellie to—"

Ellie interrupted. "Oh, yes we can, sir. I'm accompanying you to St. Petersburg, and that is positively the last word."

Athan gazed at her. "You are a very stubborn woman, Ellie Rutherford."

"Mulish is the word you actually wished to use," she replied with a smile.

"Possibly."

"Definitely."

John glanced at them both and drew the conversation back to the business of the diamond. "*Mes enfants*, it occurs to me that there is something rather odd about this business of hiding the diamond in the lid of the tureen. My softpaste porcelain is so very delicate that if even I could not retrieve the diamond without breaking the lid, then it is certain that no one else will be able to either."

"Meaning?" Athan looked inquiringly at him.

"Meaning that it will be impossible for Czar Alexander to have both the diamond *and* the complete tureen. Now, from what you say, Athan, the czar is definitely expecting the tureen."

"Yes."

"Then Dalmatsky is going to find himself with a dilemma. He will have to hope that the czar will find the acquisition of the diamond sufficient compensation for the ruining of the tureen."

Fleur did not dally in her desire to get even with Ellie and chose to hurt her through John. She knew from Valentin that Ellie's uncle was living under a false name and was still being sought by duns, and she knew where those duns were to be found. Using money she could ill afford in her severely reduced circumstances, she went to London to lay evidence against him and see if there was a reward. She was disappointed on both counts, for Athan had already settled all John's debts, and there had never been a reward anyway.

So Fleur, bitter and defeated, returned to the simple

abode she now shared with her mother, who these days was seldom to be found without a handkerchief into which to sob. Fleur's only recourse now was to encourage Freddie Forrester-Phipps, through whom she was sure she would be able to secure a comfortable future.

She could not and would not believe Athan's warning about Freddie being disinherited. Arranging to meet the banker's son at Cardiff's most splendid inn, she dressed in her finest clothes and made herself look every inch the Tudor heiress. She wasn't to know that when she saw him coming toward her in *his* finest clothes, he was pulling as much wool over her eyes as she was over his.

Twenty-seven

Ellie and Athan chose May Day for their wedding. The bride was about to leave the house to enter the garlanded landau waiting at the gate. The weather was glorious, the hedgerows foamed white with hawthorn blossom, and the gardens of Nantgarth were bright with lilacs and laburnum. Roses would soon come fully into their own, but for the moment wallflowers were sweet and velvety against the houses, and tulips and forget-me-nots bordered the paths. On the mountains the bracken was tall and green, and there were foxgloves in the hollows. No bride could have asked for a more delightful day . . . or for so much joy after the misery of the previous year.

Everyone for miles around had come to see the simple ceremony at St. Dwynwen's Church, for this was not a grand occasion. Neither bride nor groom had wanted that. Those many members of Glamorgan society whom Athan regarded as friends had all been invited, and Castle Griffin was filled to overflowing with guests. Numerous fine carriages were visible up on the mountain by the church, as well as traps, gigs, and other lesser vehicles belonging to more ordinary folk. People lined the route to the church, and there was a small crowd outside Nantgarth House, waiting for a first glimpse of Ellie.

The stir caused by Fleur's departure had been a fleeting storm in a teacup. Now that she and her mother were out of the way at the other end of the county, the rumors that had been circulating in Cardiff about her conduct in London became much stronger and more widespread. As a result, few people thought ill of Athan for marrying Ellie instead.

The diamond had been returned to the Tower of London, where the authorities had consented to keep the matter secret until the perpetrators could be dealt with. Major Carver, of course, went through the tortures of the damned when the diamond came back to the Tower. He feared imminent arrest, but he need not have worried.

Freddie Forrester-Phipps had never returned to the Newbridge alehouse after Athan saw him, and had disappeared without paying, as predicted. No one knew where he was now, but he had left before news got out of Fleur's downfall, so whether or not he was aware of it was anyone's guess.

The moment had come to leave the house. Ellie shook her skirts out nervously and then adjusted her veil for what must have been the hundredth time. She wore a gown made of the finest lavender silk, because in Wales lavender was considered a very lucky color for brides. It was stitched with tiny beads that sparkled like frost as the train brushed behind her. Her ivory silk bonnet had a lavender lace veil, and she carried a dainty posy of pink rosebuds, lilies of the valley, and a sprig of myrtle that had been presented to her by her eight-year-old bridesmaid, Margred, who was the daughter of one of the china workers and also Mrs. Lewis's grandniece.

The little girl waited downstairs now in a frilled pink dress with a lavender velvet sash, a wreath of lilies of the valley in her curly red hair. Ellie would return the myrtle to her after the wedding so that Margred could plant it in the garden of her home in Nantgarth, and one day be able to carry a sprig of it at her own wedding.

"Are you sure I look all I should, Mrs. Lewis?" Ellie asked the patient housekeeper, who had been fussing around her for an hour or more.

"You look beautiful, Miss Ellie."

"Do you promise?"

Mrs. Lewis smiled. "I promise." Then she turned as John tapped at the door. "Ellie, my dear? It's time."

The housekeeper took Ellie's hand and squeezed it warmly. "This is the perfect outcome to it all, Miss Ellie. Now all that has to be done is see that your uncle's past can never hurt him again. Gwilym will see to it, you mark my words." With that she raised the edge of Ellie's veil to kiss her cheek, then hastened out past John, who came in a little hesitantly.

"Is it all right for a mere male to enter this sanctuary?" he inquired, smiling proudly at his niece. He was wearing his very best clothes and was ready to carry out the duty that Ellie's father would have undertaken, had he still been alive. He had presented the bridal couple with one of the remaining tureens, there being only one surviving lid. The wedding gift had been finished to the same exactingly high standard as that which would be given to the czar, and differed only in that there were forget-me-nots among the delicately painted roses and fruit.

"You know it is, Uncle," Ellie replied.

"You look lovely, my dear. Athan is a very fortunate man."

She pulled a wry face. "I rather think that by any yardstick *I* am the fortunate one to be making such a good match." She blinked back tears that had been close all day. "I wish Mother and Father were here," she whispered.

"I am sure they will be watching, my dear."

"I hope so."

He took her by the arms and looked intently at her through her veil. "I feel certain that today just marks the beginning of all the good news. Your father's name is going to be cleared, and I am not only going to give the czar the finest tureen the world has ever seen, but be finally rid of Prince Paul Dalmatsky too. And you and Athan will—"

"—live happily ever after?" she supplied.

He nodded. "Yes, just that. And make me a granduncle many times over, I trust. Now then, I want you to let me fix this to your sleeve. There." He pinned something to her gown, and she looked down to see just that . . . a pin.

"What is it for, Uncle?"

"When you leave the house, you are to throw it over your shoulder for good luck," he explained. "It is a Welsh custom, like wearing lavender and giving back a sprig of myrtle. One must observe all these things, or risk incurring bad luck instead."

"What a superstitious soul you are," she teased.

He raised an eyebrow. "In Nantgarth, with the likes of Gwilym around, it is very difficult to be anything else."

"But I notice you didn't kidnap me last night. Isn't that

what the bride's family is supposed to do? So the bridegroom can rescue her?"

"Well, I was afraid Athan might change his mind and not give chase," he replied with a straight face, then he grinned again. "Speaking of superstition, let me warn you that you will find it in abundance in Russia."

They were to leave for St. Petersburg in two weeks, and Athan's plan to involve the czar had received a considerable fillip when a government courier arrived at Castle Griffin, requesting Athan to carry a personal letter to the czar from the prime minister, Mr. Pitt. The letter contained friendly overtures and an olive branch designed to remove any lingering ill feeling caused by the theft of the red diamond. Athan believed the contents of the letter would ensure Alexander's willingness to intervene in the matter of the Trepov family.

Ellie felt a thrill of excitement at the prospect of going to Russia, but also a tingle of unease that the enigmatic and dangerous Prince Paul Dalmatsky might yet emerge triumphant. Athan had done his best to dissuade her from making the journey, but she would have none of it. The thought of remaining back here, pacing, wringing her hands, worrying herself silly, and generally going through agonies of suspense was simply too much to bear. She had wondered if Athan would resort to male tactics and *forbid* her to come—after all, she would be his wife when the time came—but he had eventually accepted how strongly she felt. There was no longer any suggestion of her remaining behind.

John drew her hand through his arm. "Come then, it's your wedding day, so let us face them all."

There were cheers and cries of delight as Ellie and he emerged into the sunshine, followed by little Margred. The path to the gate was strewn with rushes and herbs, and flowers were thrown as Ellie was helped into the landau. As Margred was lifted up too, Ellie removed the pin from the wedding gown sleeve and tossed it over her shoulder, much to the approval of the gathering.

Progress to the church was slow because so many people had turned out to watch. The way was often blocked, and the coachman had to halt the horses until it was clear again. So many flowers were tossed into the landau that Ellie's feet quite disappeared beneath them, and her bonnet became a veritable bouquet.

The mountain air had a wild scent of its own, of heather, blueberries, and thyme, and Ellie felt almost exhilarated as the landau halted at last by the churchyard gate. St. Dwynwen's well shone in the sunshine, and Ellie noticed that countless new cloths had been tied to the thorn trees. Perhaps it was good luck at a wedding, she thought as her uncle alighted and then reached up to assist her down too. She was aware of all the carriages drawn up wherever a place was afforded, of the coachmen and postilions watching her, of the crowds of people. Was this really happening to her? Had Ellie Rutherford's luck changed so much that she really was about to make her vows with Athan?

Everything seemed to suddenly be viewed through a haze. She felt she was in a dream as she and John went up the churchyard path to the garlanded porch. Then they were inside, where everything smelled of flowers. She heard the shuffle of feet, coughs, and a general stir as people turned to look at her. And she remembered a moment when she had been here before, and heard Athan's voice uttering the marriage vows: "... *to be my lawful wedded wife, to have and to hold from this day forward, for better for worse, for richer for poorer, in sickness and in health, to love and to cherish, till death us do part* ..."

She had taken it for granted that he had been speaking to Fleur, but he had not. He'd been making his vows to her, to Ellie Rutherford. . . .

John escorted her down the aisle. Athan was there, tall, handsome, and dashing in his bridegroom's royal blue coat with the round flat silver buttons. She felt the touch of his hand, basked in the adoring warmth of his eyes, and heard his voice as if the dream continued. She must have made her vows too, although she did not know it. His ring was on her finger, his lips against her palm. She heard the sighs of approval in the congregation and knew that she was his wife. She really was his wife. His wife. Athan's wife . . .

Salt pricked her eyes as he turned back her veil. "I worship you, Ellie," he whispered, then kissed her there before the altar, with everyone looking on.

They left the church arm in arm, and the moment they stepped from the porch they were pelted with flowers; as they reached the churchyard gate, they were confronted by all the children from the vicinity. They were dressed in animal costumes, as they had been when Ellie had seen the Mari Llwyd, and they chanted loudly.

"Throw out! Throw out! Throw out!"

Ellie looked curiously at Athan. "What do they want?"

"This!" he answered, and stood to toss a handful of coins. The children squealed with delight, and soon were chanting for more. Three times they chanted, and three times he threw them coins; then the children ran in front of the landau, leaping and dancing like wild creatures.

The landau's way was barred with floral ropes as it returned down the mountain, and at each rope the coachman had to pay a toll, or the bridal couple would not be permitted to pass. One by one all the other carriages were charged, so that when the last vehicle had passed by, there was more than enough money for the people to have as excellent a feast as the guests at the castle.

That night, after a magnificent wedding banquet and dancing in the great hall, Athan and his new bride retired at last to private apartments that had been solely his, but were now hers as well. There she at last saw the portrait that had been just in shadow when she'd seen this night in the tea leaves. It had been familiar then because it was a portrait of her, and now she blushed to think that Thomas Lawrence had presumed to portray her in such a way. She saw other remembered things in the rooms too, beautiful furniture, gilded plasterwork, the bowl of roses at the bedside, the tureen on the mantel. What she had seen in the tea leaves hadn't been wishful thinking after all, but the truth, because this was indeed her wedding night, and she was about to give herself to Athan, who would show her what it really was to love and be loved.

She lay naked in the bed, waiting for him. The room was in shadow, and then came the glimmer of candlelight as he came toward the bed in the maroon silk dressing gown she knew from before. She also remembered what she had said on that occasion, about it being unlucky to light candles in daylight. But it wasn't day, it was night, and by the glow of such flames she could see his beloved face as he smiled down at her.

"I have yearned for this moment, Ellie," he whispered,

and placed the candlestick next to the bowl of roses on the little table at the side of the bed. Then he untied his dressing gown and let it fall. He was naked . . . and so excitingly perfect. She was conscious of sharp pangs of desire in the most intimate parts of her body, eager waves of yearning that she no longer needed to control. Not now, for she was in the marriage bed, and he was her husband. Her nipples were hard with arousal as she gazed upon his maleness. How splendid he was, how vigorous and ready to take her. *Oh, Athan, my love, my love . . .*

"You are my bride and I love you, Ellie," he whispered.

"Do you? Do you really?" She was suddenly insecure. This was all too good, too wonderful. . . .

"My ring is on your finger, my darling, so how can you doubt? You are my life from now on, Ellie."

"Do you swear it?" she whispered.

"Upon my very soul," he breathed. "I am going to make sweet love to you, Ellie. Before dawn I will have proved my adoration over and over, and will have shown you ecstasies and delights that you have not dreamed existed."

"Are there truly such delights?" she asked.

He smiled and slipped into the bed with her. The candle flames swayed seductively, sending warm shadows over her skin. He leaned over, kissed her on the lips, and drew her down from the pillows so their bodies touched.

The delicious sensation of his skin against hers sent her pulse racing. Her entire being yearned for all of him, wanted to rush toward satisfaction, but she was afraid her utter innocence would disappoint him. "I may fail you, Athan. I'm so green, so ignorant of—"

"I will teach you." He kissed her mouth again, and her lips softened and parted. Oh, such a kiss, slow, luxurious, enticing, and filled with such promise that she thought she would die of anticipation. Kiss followed kiss, and caress followed caress as they explored each other for the first time. Her need for him made her feel as if she would ignite, but at last he was inside her and they were one. Her virginity was stormed and then vanquished. "Look at me, Ellie," he whispered. "Look at me for this one moment."

She obeyed, her eyes dark with such fierce desire that she would have done anything he wished of her. He smiled, and began to move inside her. "This is love, Ellie. This is true love."

She gazed into his eyes, loving him so much that she thought she would die of ecstasy. Joy tumbled wildly through her veins, and her soul seemed to melt into such a wild storm of gratification that she felt she would drown in its fiery waves. It was too much, too much. . . . Her eyes closed, and she floated away on a sea of pleasure that seemed to stretch to every horizon. This truly was love, the most beautiful love, and it was theirs to share forever, *forever, forever.* . . .

Oh, how far away now the green girl kissed by a stranger at the Crown Inn, Hounslow.

Twenty-eight

Two weeks later, on a misty mid-May dawn that heralded yet another fine day, Ellie, Athan, and Mrs. Lewis joined John in his workroom to look a final time on the tureen before it was packed in a crate of sawdust for the long journey to St. Petersburg. The czar's horses had already been taken on one of the two barges that were moored at the wharf in readiness to take the travelers on the first stage to Cardiff. There, a coastal vessel waited to take them around the Cornish peninsula to London, from where an ocean-going merchantman would sail for the Baltic. For the moment the horses were quiet and composed with Gwilym looking after them, and did not even twitch when something startled a moorhen into flapping noisily over the surface of the glassy water.

Mrs. Lewis had brought a tray of tea to the workroom, to send the travelers off properly, as she said. Now the cups and saucers had been set aside, and all eyes were upon the tureen. Candles illuminated the dawn gloom as John looked proudly at his craftsmanship. "Do you think it will do?" he asked, not seeking praise, but genuinely needing reassurance.

Athan, elegant but practical in a sage green coat and pale gray breeches, slapped him on the shoulder. "Do? My dear fellow, it's simply the most magnificent tureen there has ever been. Well, the second most magnificent, for I think the laurels must go to the one you so kindly gave to Ellie and me."

Ellie lowered her eyes, for she had a little secret about her uncle's wedding gift. Truth to tell, it no longer occupied the mantel in Castle Griffin, but had been wrapped in a woolen shawl and hidden in one of the hatboxes she was taking to St. Petersburg. She didn't know why she was taking it with them, just that it seemed a wise precaution.

Athan continued speaking. "And to think that such things came out of this little works. Wedgwood, Royal Worcester, Crown Derby, Sèvres, Chantilly—name them all. They can look to their laurels after this."

"I pray so," John answered, "although to be sure I do not wish Worcester and Derby to ever learn who I really am."

"The formula is yours, not theirs," Athan reminded him, "and you have worked so much upon it since you were employed by them that I doubt if it could be identified as the same mixture anyway."

"I know, but even so, they are forces to be reckoned with. The world of British ceramic ware is a small one."

"We will cross bridges as and when we come to them," Athan said.

John looked at him, an eyebrow quirked. "We?"

"Well, we are one family now, are we not?"

John smiled. "Yes, I suppose we are," he replied, looking fondly at Ellie, who had blossomed in the two weeks since the wedding. There was a glow on her cheeks, a lovely light in her eyes, and even the sheen of her hair seemed more becoming. Marriage suited her, or at least, marriage to Athan suited her. Today she wore a gown and matching pelisse of worked strawberry silk, and a wide-brimmed straw hat with an ostrich plume curled around the crown.

Athan took out his watch. "I think it's time to leave," he advised.

John nodded, and with infinite care lifted the precious tureen into the crate. When it was safely embedded in the sawdust, more of which was tipped over and around it, the lid of the crate was secured in place, and two china workers carried it carefully out to the second barge, upon which all the luggage was loaded.

Athan was about to usher Ellie outside too when she remembered something. "Athan, we haven't told Uncle John about what we've heard of the bank!"

"Damn, I've been so preoccupied with the journey that I quite forgot," he replied, and turned apologetically to John. "Forgive me, John, for a letter arrived this morning that may be of interest to you. As you may recall, I left someone at the Unicorn Bank to secretly find out all he could about the embezzling of Josiah Rutherford's fortune. It seems that he and Toby Richardson, an old friend of mine who happens to be a barrister, have dug to the bottom of the problem. The late Albert Forrester-Phipps, father of the ignoble Freddie, was indeed responsible for stealing Ellie's father's fortune. Why he did it remains a mystery, because he was always a very honest man, and was certainly not in personal financial difficulty. His only crime appears to have been in connection with the Rutherford fortune, and with bringing your name into it as well, of course."

John exhaled slowly. "There will be a connection with Dalmatsky. You may rely upon it."

"If there is, Toby has yet to find it, and believe me, he's searched. To return to Forrester-Phipps, it has to be said that his family knew nothing of his interference in Josiah's affairs. The first they knew of something being wrong was when he threw himself from the cliff in Kent. It is his widow's contention that he was so guilt-ridden by what he'd done that he could no longer live with himself, and knowing what I now do of the man's character, I have to agree. Of course, he was also gravely disappointed in his son and heir, Freddie, whom he regarded as unfit to inherit."

Ellie was less charitable toward Freddie's father. "I don't think the late Mr. Forrester-Phipps could have been such a paragon, Athan. If he were, he wouldn't have done what he did to my father. I shall never make allowances, no matter what you may say of him now."

"Nor would I expect you to, my love. His actions drove your father to take his own life, and for that I cannot forgive him either. I'm just pointing out that there remains a mystery. *Why* did Albert Forrester-Phipps do it? Why weren't there other embezzlements too? Why just your father? I fear we may never know."

John pursed his lips. "It will still come back to Dalmatsky," he said again.

"Maybe. Anyway, John, I want you to know that the whole matter has been settled. Albert Forrester-Phipps's heir has made full restitution of Josiah's fortune, and all mention of your name has been removed from the records. There have been great upheavals at the bank, where people loyal to Forrester-Phipps detected his hand in the matter and made every effort to conceal his involvement."

John raised an eyebrow. "Which is, I think, exactly what you are now doing for me."

Athan smiled, not quite sheepishly. "It may be viewed in that light, I suppose, except that you weren't involved in anything. You had nothing whatsoever to do with the bank, beyond being the brother-in-law of one of its customers, so I see no comparison between making certain you are kept out of it and covering up Forrester-Phipps's known wrongdoing. Anyway, be that as it may, it has been made clear that from now on there is never *ever* to be a hint of skullduggery at the bank, no matter how slight. There is to be a fresh start for everyone, from the partners down to the lowliest clerk. Of course, it will be several months yet before the matter is entirely settled, which means that we will know nothing more until our return from St. Petersburg, but at least you can rest easy about your name having been implicated."

John nodded. "Thank you, Athan. It's a weight off my mind. I confess I was afraid that maybe you and Ellie would think there could not be so much smoke without a little fire, and that I had to be involved in some way."

"Never!" she cried, and hugged him tightly.

Athan ushered them both to the door. "Come on, now, or we will miss the Cardiff tide, and that won't do at all. It doesn't matter when we arrive in St. Petersburg, provided it's before July tenth, but if it should be one day *past* Saints Peter and Paul, the czar will not be pleased."

Mrs. Lewis stood on the wharf as the barges moved away into the tendrils of mist that floated above the water. Seagulls flew inland overhead, and somewhere a robin was singing its heart out. Some folk from Nantgarth had gathered on the bridge to see the famous tureen on its way, and they cheered as the barges slid beneath them.

The housekeeper gazed anxiously along the navigation until she couldn't see the barges any more. Let them come home again soon, she prayed as she went back into the workroom to collect the tray of cups and saucers. But as she touched the cup Ellie had used, a strange sensation passed from the porcelain into her fingers, a tingle like far-off lightning. What did it mean? Mrs. Lewis looked into the cup, at the final drop of tea and all the tea leaves, and wondered if she would be able to see something if she upended it in the saucer. She had never been able to read other people's cups before, just enable them to see things for themselves, but somehow this morning she felt it would be different.

Taking a quick breath, she swirled the cup and turned it over in the saucer. Nothing seemed to happen, but just as the housekeeper began to shake her head at her own foolishness, she heard a baby cry. A tiny baby, maybe only weeks old. Then she saw the font at St. Dwynwen's Church. It was May Day next year, and a christening group was gathered around: among them Ellie, in the contented glow of motherhood; Athan, the proudest father in the land; and the babe in Ellie's arms, a boy, small and helpless in a delicate knitted white shawl. They had just named him John.

Mrs. Lewis smiled through tears, but then her smile faded. Where was the child's namesake? Where was Mr. Bailey? She could not see his face among those around the font. What did it mean? Would he fail to return from St. Petersburg?

The vision faded, and the housekeeper looked anxiously around the workroom, a place so personal to him that she could almost hear his voice. "Please return safely, Mr. Bailey," she whispered, and with shaking hands picked up the tray to hurry out of the room.

On reaching London a week later, Ellie, Athan, and John learned it would be several days before the merchantman, the *Good Intent,* sailed for the Baltic, so they took rooms at a comfortable inn. London held sad memories for Ellie, but a visit to the Unicorn Bank reassured her that all stains on the Rutherford name had definitely been erased forever. John was similarly reassured about his own name, which, of course, was now once more without blemish. Not only had his debts been settled, but he had also learned that his old employers, Royal Worcester and Crown Derby, were no longer interested in preventing him from using his formula.

Another snippet of information elicited at the Unicorn Bank, where the name Forrester-Phipps continued to be of intense interest, was that Fleur and Freddie had married secretly, each under the impression that the other had an income that was at least comfortable. This grave error of judgment was soon borne in on them both, and their parting had been so acrimonious as to be likened in some quarters to a caterwaul.

The discovery that Fleur Tudor was really Blodyn Evans had rubbed salt into Freddie's self-pity. Feeling that she had not only cheated him, but made a fool of him too, he bewailed his plight loud and long throughout London. This resulted in contempt for himself and ridicule for Fleur, who with her mother in tow had prudently left the country and was now said to be running a small lodging house somewhere in the far southwest of Ireland.

Freddie languished in jail for having brawled with the cousin who'd inherited the Forrester-Phipps fortune. A mere brawl might not have resulted in arrest, but the theft and subsequent selling of the cousin's fob watch was another matter.

Twenty-nine

Ellie saw St. Petersburg at last on the morning before the feast of Saints Peter and Paul. The vessel *Good Intent* had not made good time from London, but just as the party from Nantgarth began to fear they would be too late for the all important day, a sea breeze picked up and carried the merchantman swiftly for the final few leagues.

The *Good Intent* carried too deep a draft for the shallow water and sandbanks at the mouth of the Neva, so had to be left before the fortifications of Kronstadt Island, which guarded the approaches to the capital. The weary travelers, including the czar's horses, were transferred to one of the many flat-bottomed lighters that flocked to carry goods and passengers the remaining distance.

From the deck of the lighter Ellie could see that the shingled shore to the south was forested, especially with birch, and there were palaces and estates where fountains played in wonderful gardens. There were also numerous small islands, where it appeared to be the thing to enjoy picnics, especially at this time of year, when these northern climes experienced the phenomenon of the White Nights. For weeks on end the sun did not dip low enough beyond the horizon for there to be true darkness, which was a very strange thing indeed for visitors accustomed to each day being duly followed by a proper night. Ellie had been on the *Good Intent*'s deck at midnight and not been able to see a single star in the clear ivory-colored sky, but since leaving Denmark behind, she had seen a double rainbow, and once, briefly, the aurora borealis. And could it really be that on midsummer night, she and Athan had noticed the exceedingly out-of-season fragrance of snowdrops in their cabin . . . ?

St. Petersburg, the world's most northern city, lay low upon the horizon, a thin line of green, blue, and gold turrets, domes, and spires caught between the sea and the wide northern sky. The closer the lighter sailed, the more the city's ramparts seemed to rear to its defense, not from attack, but from winter flooding, which was an all too frequent danger to a capital that was built upon a river delta only a few feet above sea level.

The wide Neva, thronged with the smaller vessels that could negotiate the bar, was blue and crystal clear as Ellie, Athan, and John were rowed ashore at midday toward the steps at English Quay, just as the traditional noon cannon was fired farther upstream at the Peter and Paul fortress, opposite the Winter Palace. A second rowing boat followed them, bringing their luggage, including the hatbox containing the second tureen, the presence of which was still Ellie's secret. She gazed around, taking in the splendid waterfronts, busy quays, and the spacious streets of colorful stucco buildings with lavish embellishment. English Quay itself seemed almost pearl and gold in the peculiarly brilliant sunshine. It was hard to imagine this place trapped in ice so thick that carriages could be driven from island to island.

John had been very quiet since first glimpsing the city spires on the horizon, and now that he was on the Neva he was positively withdrawn. Ellie and Athan did not try to lighten his mood, for they knew he was remembering that Nikolai had drowned in these waters, hounded to his death by Prince Paul Dalmatsky. John's mood also served as a reminder to them that their business here was not entirely without danger to themselves. Athan remained confident in his plan to enlist the czar's protection, but if it should go wrong, anything might happen.

Gwilym and the horses remained on the lighter until the czar's requirements could be established. The Imperial Stables were situated on the Moika Canal, and Athan would go there as soon as possible. The milk white mare and colt had already aroused a great deal of attention, and Gwilym was unable to resist making them do things at his silent behest, from rearing prettily like circus horses, to nipping the posterior of a particularly officious Russian who had shared the lighter.

These amusing antics attracted attention from passengers on a ferry that was also crossing toward English Quay, among them a pretty young woman of about seventeen, in traditional Russian dress, with a ribboned *kokoshnik* on her honey-colored hair. She wasn't upper class by any means, more probably a maid or seamstress, but her shy smile captured Gwilym's attention. He abandoned the tricks with the horses in order to stand at the rail of the lighter to watch the ferry. The young woman turned to gaze back at him, and to his delight made so bold as to give a little wave. Hesitantly he waved back. There was a movement in the Neva below where he stood, then a flash of silver as an eel leapt briefly into view before plunging down into the depths again.

Gwilym knew St. Dwynwen was watching over him, and in his mind's eye could suddenly see the young woman's face as clearly as if she were on the lighter beside him. Her name was Tatiana Demidova, and he realized not only that she was a maid at the Brasier residence, but that she would have much bearing on the outcome of this visit to St. Petersburg—much bearing too on his own future and happiness.

Athan helped Ellie and John out of the boat when they reached the steps, where a cluster of small boats rocked at their moorings, among them two belonging to Athan's brother-in-law, Charles Brasier. For a minute or so the trio were too unsteady to climb the steps. Everything seemed to sway after their being so long at sea, but at last they felt able to ascend to the quay, at a place almost directly opposite the house occupied by Athan's sister Louise and her husband, Charles. But between the steps and the house there was a roadway that was under considerable repair, as was most of St. Petersburg in the summer after the great damage done by the Russian winter. A small army of bearded workmen labored with the dislodged and very uneven cobbles. They wore loose trousers and coarse shirts that were tied at the waist with sashes, and had open, good-humored countenances, but did not seem to bother about the cleanliness of their clothes.

There was constant traffic, all of it apparently determined

to be somewhere as quickly as possible. A hooded two-wheeled vehicle drawn by four horses abreast approached at such speed that it seemed it *must* capsize at the repairs, but somehow it skimmed through, only to halt by the steps in a cloud of dust. The driver, a shadowy figure beneath the hood, seemed to find it amusing as the horses pranced and capered to such an extent that Athan had to pull Ellie back for fear she would be trampled. Looking angrily at the driver, Athan was startled to gaze into Valentin's shining dark eyes.

Paul's nephew, as splendid as ever in his uniform, his hair boasting side-plaits, accorded him a cool nod. "Lord Griffin."

"Andreyov." Athan did not return the nod.

Valentin smiled, and addressed him in French. "It is pleasant to see you again, my lord." His dark, shining glance encompassed Ellie for a moment. "Lady Griffin, I presume?" he murmured. "My congratulations upon your marriage, my lady."

As Ellie wondered how he knew about the marriage, since he'd left Britain before it had even been planned, let alone taken place, Athan stepped protectively in front of her. "State your piece, Andreyov," he said shortly.

"My piece? Why, my lord, I rather thought you would be thanking me for my assistance."

"Assistance?" The word was uttered coldly.

"If it were not for my services, you might by now have been married to that Tudor trollop."

Athan looked at him with loathing. "You are a dishonorable man, Andreyov, and one lacking the backbone to face me when you were caught without your breeches."

"Have a care, sir, for you are in *my* land now, and if you provoke me to a duel, be assured that all the petty little rules so cherished by the British do not apply here."

"And you, sir, can be assured that I would not bring those rules with me!" Athan snapped.

Ellie caught his arm uneasily. "Ignore him, Athan."

Valentin looked at her again. "I wondered what your potter's niece would be like, my lord, and confess I am a little disappointed. She is charming enough, I suppose, but hardly in the same class as Miss Tudor."

"And what would you know of class?" Athan inquired lightly.

Valentin's mocking smile was extinguished. "I have rank, and that is all that matters." His dark eyes swung to John. "See that the tureen is sent without delay to me at the Dalmatsky Palace." He waited, obviously hoping to see a dismayed reaction on hearing the name Dalmatsky.

But John merely nodded. "As you wish."

"You do not seem surprised to be reminded of my uncle."

"I am not so much a fool that I have not long since sniffed his stench," John replied.

"And still you have come here? You are either very brave, or a fool, and since I now understand you were once rash enough to dabble with Nikolai Trepov, I think you are the latter."

John held his eyes. "And what of you, Prince Valentin? How foolish are you to allow yourself to be dragged into your uncle's affairs? I don't know what carrot he held before you, but you may be sure that the moment you took a nibble of it, you became a donkey."

Valentin scowled. "Just see the tureen is sent without delay!" he snapped.

"What then?" John inquired. "I take it I will not be permitted to leave St. Petersburg without first confronting your uncle?"

"You will await his pleasure," Valentin replied, then flicked his whip and flung the four horses forward again. The vehicle leapt away from a standstill, scattering stones and dust as it disappeared in the direction of the Winter Palace.

Ellie shivered. "What a horrible man," she said with considerable understatement.

Athan nodded. "But he will soon learn the error of his ways."

"I hope so." She glanced up at him. "How does he know you and I are married? Surely he had left Britain before we were even betrothed?"

"Russia may be a vast land, but it has a network of spies that is second to none," Athan replied. "If someone of interest sneezes in Siberia, it is soon known in St. Petersburg. Dalmatsky has his creatures everywhere, and the *Good Intent* called at Riga, where he keeps his yacht. Spies make it their business to inquire about passengers on all foreign vessels, so the presence of a Lord and Lady Griffin would have been relayed to the Dalmatsky Palace. And the presence of a Mr. John Bailey," he added.

John gazed after the vanishing vehicle. "I do hope Andreyov and Dalmatsky enjoy the walnut when they share it," he murmured dryly, but although he gave the others a brave grin, inside he was very nervous indeed. This was Dalmatsky's territory, where only the very unwise trod without infinite care. "And in the meantime I simply wait to hear from Dalmatsky," he added heavily.

Athan drew Ellie's hand over his arm and they proceeded across the street toward the house with the blue door and bronze lion knocker. A huge Russian manservant with a black beard and white gloves, wearing a blue smock with a fringed red sash, admitted them to a spacious entrance hall with an inlaid wooden floor, blue and cream silk on the walls, a lofty golden ceiling, and handsome chandeliers. There were vases of flowers everywhere, both hothouse and garden, and a number of mirrors that gave the illusion of even more space.

Hardly had the weary trio stepped over the threshold, than Athan's sister Louise came hurtling down the elegant curved staircase at the far end of the hall. She was small and dainty, her long dark hair worn *à la Russe* in a braid that was twisted on top of her head, but her red-and-gold gown was all that was western and stylish. That she was Athan's sister could not be doubted, for she had the same eyes and coloring, and even the same way of laughing. Her face was alight with joy, and she flung herself into her brother's arms with such forceful delight that he was hard put to keep his balance.

"Steady on, sweeting, for I still have sea legs," he laughed, and kissed her warmly on the forehead.

She stood back and inspected his face sternly, and then smiled again. "You are looking much better than when I last saw you. Marriage clearly suits you." Her eyes moved to Ellie, warmly yet speculatively, clearly hoping to like her new sister-in-law.

Athan hastened to effect the introduction. "Louise, this is my bride, Ellie. Ellie, my sister Louise."

Ellie didn't quite know whether to incline her head, dip a curtsy, or extend her hand, but the decision was made for her by Louise's welcoming hug. "I'm delighted to meet you, Ellie, and I know you and I will get on famously because you have wrought such a welcome change in my bear of a brother."

"I'm not a bear," Athan protested.

"Yes, you are. It's long since time you had a wife." Louise smiled at John. "And you, sir, must be Ellie's uncle, Mr. Bailey."

"Mrs. Brasier." John bowed gallantly over her little hand.

"I cannot wait to see the famous tureen, and I am so *proud* to think I am now related to such a gifted gentleman."

John blushed. "You flatter me, I think," he murmured diffidently, but Ellie knew he was pleased.

"You must all forgive my husband, Charles," Louise said, "for I fear he has been called away to Moscow on urgent business and will not return until next week. You will all have to put up with just me . . . and"—she paused for dramatic effect—"your unborn niece or nephew."

Athan was delighted for her. "A child? After all this time? Louise, I couldn't be happier for you and Charles! When is the baby due?"

"At Christmas, so you will be home at Castle Griffin again, I fear."

"You're looking very well," he said, studying her again.

"I feel well." Louise turned, suddenly remembering something. "Ellie, those flowers there are for you."

"For me?" Surprised, Ellie followed Louise's pointing finger to a particularly lavish arrangement of yellow and white lilies.

"They were delivered about an hour ago, and are to congratulate upon your marriage, although I confess I would prefer there to have been an odd number of flowers. In Russia even numbers are usually only given at funerals or in commemoration. Yellow and white are not good colors either. I was almost of a mind to have them sent back."

"Odd, even, yellow, white, it was nevertheless a very kind thought. Thank you," Ellie replied, naturally assuming they were from Louise and her husband.

"Oh, do not thank me, for they are from our landlord, and one does not lightly offend Prince Paul Dalmatsky."

Ellie was dismayed. "I don't want his flowers," she said firmly.

Athan put a calming hand on her arm. "No doubt it amused him to send them, so let him have his laugh, for it will be the last he enjoys in a long time." He turned to Louise. "Sis, the crate containing the tureen is to be sent to Dalmatsky Island without delay. Can you see to it? Care must be taken, for it is very fragile."

"Yes, of course." She beckoned the manservant, whose name was Vladimir, said something to him in Russian, and he hurried away.

Athan looked at Louise again. "Is the czar in St. Petersburg?"

"He and the court arrived yesterday from Tsarskoe Selo in readiness for the grand supper at the Dalmatsky Palace."

"Good, for I need an audience with him."

Louise's jaw dropped. "And you think that is easily achieved? Athan, you may as well bay at the moon!"

"He and I hit it off when last we met, and I think his interest in both the horses and the increasingly likely British treaty will make him gracious. I also have a letter from Mr. Pitt which is sure to please him."

"Maybe, maybe not. He was very angry when the British press accused Russia of involvement in the theft of that diamond," Louise warned.

"I want a message to be sent to the Imperial Stables, not only advising them of the horses' arrival, but also requesting them to see that the czar is informed. When I was fortunate enough to meet him before, he expressed a desire to accept the horses from me in person. I can only pray he remembers what he said."

Athan exchanged glances with Ellie and John, for the success of their entire plan hinged upon Alexander. Suddenly it was no longer easy to be brave and positive as they had been in Britain, because now the moment was actually upon them, their entire stratagem seemed uncomfortably flimsy.

Thirty

The baroque green-and-white splendor of the Prince Paul's palace rose like a diadem from the gardens that covered Dalmatsky Island, on the northern edge of the Neva delta. Like most Russian palaces, it had once been a single-story wooden dacha, or traditional country cottage. In the kitchens and cellars these more humble origins were still very evident, but outwardly it was now a palace in every sense of the word. At first glance it presented a gracious and tranquil countenance to the world, yet there was something brooding and dangerous about it—something unpleasant that would always be inextricably bound to the name Dalmatsky.

The palace, gardens, and outbuildings covered every inch of the island. English grottoes nestled amid shady leaves; Chinese pavilions graced areas of lawn that were clipped so close they might have been green baize; and marble fountains of Dalmatian dogs with water spouting from their mouths were to be found on all the terraces. Jetties and boathouses dotted the shore, where the tideless Neva lapped gently during these balmy summer months, and where elegant pleasure boats were always in readiness. Beyond the island lay the bleak marshes from which St. Petersburg had been wrested in the time of Peter the Great.

Tucked away on the northern shore were greenhouses, kennels, an aviary, kitchen gardens, and the large laundry that was necessary because Paul expected every sheet and towel in the palace to be changed daily, regardless of it having been used or not. At night it was quite usual to hear the sound of wheeled laundry baskets being trundled along the curving garden paths lined by Italian statues. Also tucked away on the northern shore of the island was a fine marble-fronted *banya,* or bathhouse. Bathhouses were essential to all Russians, and Paul had a special liking for them because they afforded him privacy in which to indulge his taste for handsome young men.

When Valentin returned to the island to tell his uncle of his encounter with the British party, he was told that Paul was in the bathhouse and was expecting him. Valentin made his way there with great reluctance, for he had no stomach at all for his kinsman's sexual preference. The path to the steps was flanked by pink, white, and crimson peonies, heavy blooms that seemed as sweet-scented and wanton as Paul Dalmatsky himself.

Inside, the bathhouse resembled a Roman bath, with naked male statues in alcoves, and carved animals made of jade, amethyst, chalcedony, and topaz. A large bowl of pineapples and peaches stood upon a low table, together with a slender-necked gold jug containing Paul's favorite Hungarian wine. There were three golden goblets beside it. In a corner, silent now but usually loud and raucous, was a bright green macaw on a silver perch. It had crafty eyes and a vicious curved beak that had left a scar on Valentin's hand. He thought it was a detestable bird.

Paul was lying naked and facedown on a marble bench, being ministered to by two rouged young men who wore the flimsiest white silk robes imaginable. They were rubbing lavender oil into his skin, and scowled jealously at each other. *Like whores in a brothel,* Valentin thought, at the same time noting that all his uncle's catamites were slender, brown-eyed and olive-skinned, with long black curls that reached down their shoulders. Valentin had now learned that the first to possess these particular looks had been Nikolai Trepov, of whom he had learned much since his return from Britain, enough to begin to suspect that being avenged for the young man's death had become Paul's obsession. This suspicion rekindled the unease Valentin first felt, but ignored, when Paul had taken him to see the red diamond at the Winter Palace. *Have you never heard the saying "as jealous as a Dalmatian"?*

Hearing his nephew's unmistakably military tread ring on the floor, Paul turned over and leaned back on his elbows to look at him. "Well?"

"The British travelers have arrived."

Paul nodded, then smiled up at the taller of the two young men. "Come to me in an hour, Bruno."

The young man beamed, while his companion looked close to tears. Paul reached out to caress the second man's loins. "Another time, little one," he said softly.

Valentin looked away in disgust, only looking back again when the young men had gone.

Paul smiled thinly. "You make your sanctimonious disapproval so obvious, my boy, yet you have never sampled what you condemn. An hour with Bruno would soon change your mind."

"I doubt it very much."

Paul reached for a towel, then rose from the marble to wrap it around his waist. "So the second diamond is in St. Petersburg at last, eh?"

"And will soon be here on the island. I instructed Bailey to send it without delay."

Paul nodded. "And how is my good friend John? In good health, I trust?"

"He knows you are involved."

"Does he indeed?" Paul smiled at his reflection in a floor-standing glass. "Is that because you told him, my boy?"

"I told him nothing. Tell me, Uncle, does my return to favor actually have any place in your stratagem? Or is it really just about Nikolai Trepov?"

Paul turned sharply. "Do not utter that name!"

"Very well, I won't utter his precious name, but I ask you this, Uncle: Are your schemes likely to endanger my neck?"

Paul met his gaze. "My boy, you are going to present Alexander with the second red diamond. How can that possibly endanger your pretty neck?"

"I am not as sure as you that the czar's desire to possess both diamonds outweighs his desire for a coalition with the British."

Paul raised an eyebrow. "Oh, how little faith you have in your dear old uncle. Has it not occurred to you that I have the czar's ear in almost everything? I know that no matter what he may say in public about a British treaty,

ial dream of uniting the
behind every word there lurks his dream of uniting the
diamonds here in St. Petersburg. Trust me, my boy."

Valentin regarded him. Uncle or not, could he trust such a man?

Paul came closer and put a loving hand to Valentin's cheek. "Tomorrow night, in front of the entire court here on this island, you will present Alexander with the soup tureen that John Bailey has so lovingly created. You will tell His Imperial Highness that the second diamond is hidden in the tureen's lid. Alexander will not believe you, so you will offer to prove it by breaking through the repairs and extracting the diamond in front of everyone. Your welcome back into the fold will be guaranteed."

Valentin gazed at him. "Have you *any* idea how delicate Bailey's porcelain is?"

"Porcelain is porcelain, my boy," Paul replied dismissively, and returned to admiring himself in the mirror.

"No, Uncle, Bailey's porcelain is like the most delicate glass. I've seen it, I know."

Paul became irritated. "Confound it, boy, you are to do as I say. I have done all the work for you, and have seen to it that Alexander will be here on the island. My part in the acquisition of the diamond is at an end, because I am now more concerned with other things. All you have to do is give Alexander the damned tureen, grovel in your best fashion, and pray he is pleased with you. Don't look to me for support if he isn't, because I will save my own skin before I save yours. If anything goes wrong, believe me, I will point the finger at you, Valentin."

Valentin recoiled a little. "What are these 'other things' that concern you?"

"Nothing I intend to confide."

A cold finger prodded Valentin's spine. "It's John Bailey, isn't it? *He* is the reason for your decision to involve yourself in my disgrace! You want to punish him for Nikolai Trepov, and you've used me to get him here!"

"I used you because I wish you to be restored to imperial favor. I could as easily have done it all without you, but I thought of your future and the restoration of your fortune and inheritance. If the czar learns of the great lengths to which you went in order to bring him the diamond, he will think more highly of you than he ever did before, and will once again welcome you into his coterie of close friends. Valentin, nephew, my plan may have been a little involved, but not because I wished to make things difficult for you. On the contrary, it pleased me to be obtuse for entirely different reasons." Paul turned sideways to see himself in the glass. "I have kept my figure, have I not? Mm?"

Valentin watched, and for the first time began to wonder if Nikolai Trepov's death had turned Paul Dalmatsky's mind.

To Athan's relief, the czar not only wished to accept the horses in person, but also without delay, and indicated that he would visit the Imperial Stables that very evening for Athan to present them. Thus a prompt private word with him was assured.

Word of the rare white mare and colt from Wales had spread through the capital like wildfire, as had the fact that their lanky, redheaded groom seemed to be a horse magician. A vein of superstition ran deep through every Russian, and people gathered to watch as Gwilym escorted the horses brought ashore by the Imperial Stables on the Moika Canal.

As fate would have it, the watching crowds were treated to an unforeseeable display of Gwilym's powers. A large, black, and very restive stallion was just being ridden back to the stables by a groom whose attention was more on a pair of pretty young women than what he was supposed to be doing. The stallion swerved and brushed against a stack of wooden buckets that fell with a clatter that frightened the creature. It reared and whinnied, threatening to not only harm itself but unsettle the Griffin horses as well.

Gwilym stepped swiftly forward and faced the stallion, speaking softly to it in Welsh, which, of course, sounded like a magical intonation to the watching Russians. The stallion became a little calmer, but still wouldn't obey its rider's commands. It was too close to the edge of the canal for comfort, and capered and tossed its head alarmingly. The groom cried out for help, but Gwilym silenced him with a single gesture, then went closer to the stallion, speaking quietly all the while. There was no one else within yards, just the motionless but compelling figure of the young Welshman. The stallion continued to caper, but its ears twitched forward, and Gwilym knew he had its attention. He took another step forward, still whispering gently, and slowly the capering died away until the stallion was standing right at the very edge of the canal. If it should move backward even a single step, it would fall into the waiting water below.

A hush had descended over the crowd, during which the arrival of the czar's carriage was clearly heard. Gwilym stepped closer, speaking to the horse as if to a lover. At last he was close enough to reach out and touch the trembling black coat. The stallion tossed its head and rolled its eyes, drawing some gasps from the onlookers, but Gwilym took no notice. He smiled and murmured gently, going closer still until he was able to breathe into the horse's nostrils.

The stallion still shook visibly with fear, but gradually the quivering stopped, and suddenly it nudged Gwilym gently, as if he were someone it had known and loved all its life. More gasps of wonder spread through the crowd, and the groom seized his moment to alight from the saddle, looking on in awe as Gwilym led the Griffin horses into the stables and the stallion followed behind like a tame dog.

Athan knew nothing of events outside the stable entrance, for he had been preparing for the czar to receive him. He wore court dress because even in a stable it was necessary to show full formality in Alexander's presence. Ellie had not been able to accompany him because protocol demanded she had to be presented to the czarina before she could be presented to the czar, so she stayed behind at English Quay with Louise and John.

Athan's audience with Alexander was cordial, although blighted here and there by the czar's deafness, which required a raised voice to be properly understood. But nothing could have been more genuine than the pleasure with which Mr. Pitt's letter and the Griffin mare and colt were received. Gwilym had groomed them to perfection, and it was doubtful if any other horses in the world could have appeared to better advantage.

Alexander, blond and stately, if a little chubby, in the

tight-fitting blue uniform of the Semeonovsky Regiment, was delighted with his new acquisitions, although at first it was of John and the commemorative tureen that he spoke.

"I am informed, Lord Griffin, that you are now married to a lady whose uncle, John Bailey, has made a most wonderful item of ceramic ware for me?" he inquired in French.

Athan bowed. "I have that honor, Your Imperial Majesty," he answered loudly.

"You must see that she is presented to the czarina, so that she may in turn be presented to me."

"You are most kind." Athan bowed again.

"I am intrigued about the tureen, which I believe has come from a very small enterprise."

"Very small indeed, sir, but I think you will soon see that it can produce the finest soft-paste porcelain in the world." And the most fragile, Athan thought, remembering what John had said about any attempt to remove what was hidden in the lid.

"Such praise intrigues me more and more. I look forward to seeing it. I believe it is to be presented to me at Prince Paul Dalmatsky's grand supper tomorrow night?"

"I believe so too, sir."

"I also believe that should I wish to extend my appreciation to Mr. Bailey, he is here in St. Petersburg?"

"Yes, sir."

Alexander nodded in that faintly absentminded way of his. "And where is the tureen now?" he inquired.

"It has already been sent to the Dalmatsky Palace, sir, and I believe Prince Valentin Andreyov will actually perform the presentation."

Alexander's good mood evaporated. "That had better not be so, Lord Griffin, for Prince Valentin gravely offended me some time ago, and remains in disfavor to this day."

"Then clearly I am in error," Athan said quickly, not wanting to irritate the czar in any way. It was the first he had heard of Valentin being in disgrace.

At last Alexander came to the matter of the horses. "I was not misinformed about the quality and beauty of your stud, Lord Griffin," he said in French.

"I am flattered by your praise, sir, and I wish to give them to you, as a mark of my respect." Athan glanced around, suddenly realizing that Gwilym was no longer there.

"A gift?" The czar's unexpectedly gentle blue eyes were thoughtful. "It may not be the thing to query such a generous gesture, but I cannot think you do not have something to ask of me in return."

"I would be dishonest if I pretended otherwise," Athan replied frankly.

Alexander appreciated the sincerity. "You are a man after my own heart, sir, as indeed is your entire nation, with which I am happy to say Mr. Pitt's letter clarifies the final points in the treaty we have been negotiating for so long. It was unfortunate that progress was held up by the regrettable theft of the diamond from the Tower of London, but I am now assured that my country is no longer suspected of involvement."

The last thing Athan had expected was for the czar to actually mention the diamond, and for a moment his composure was rattled. Should he tell Alexander the truth? Was this the perfect moment to have done with everything?

But Alexander had already turned away as a senior courtier approached to whisper in his ear. He nodded, and then looked apologetically at Athan. "Others await an audience, Lord Griffin, so I fear I must go. I can give you one minute more in which to ask your favor."

"I humbly request your gracious intervention to gain the freedom of a family that is presently in serfdom."

"They are my serfs?" Alexander inquired.

"I fear not, sir. Their name is Trepov, and they are the property of Prince Paul Dalmatsky."

Alexander drew a heavy breath. "It is not the thing, even for a czar, to meddle in matters concerning a nobleman's serfs, least of all a man of Prince Paul's standing. What are these Trepovs to you?"

"They are the family of a man for whom John Bailey, my wife's uncle and the maker of the tureen, had the greatest affection and respect. Mr. Bailey wishes to honor his dead friend's memory by winning freedom—and your protection—for the remaining relatives." Athan hoped he had chosen his words with sufficient care, for he wished to flatter Alexander into agreement, but not arouse his suspicions about the nature of John's past friendship.

"Mr. Bailey is here in St. Petersburg, I understand?"

"Indeed so, sir."

"Then might it not be better if Mr. Bailey had made this request to me himself?" Alexander waved the increasingly agitated courtier away. "Well, Lord Griffin? Do not tell me that Mr. Bailey could not have been with you here this evening."

Athan had to think quickly. "Indeed he could, sir, but he is a humble man, and would not presume to place himself in your presence without invitation. So I, who love and respect him, and regard him as virtually my father-in-law, have approached you instead. I trust my boldness has not caused offense."

"Offense?" Alexander beamed suddenly. "Why no, Lord Griffin, for I think you—and Mr. Bailey—have shown great delicacy and consideration. I will make an exception and intercede with Prince Paul on your behalf tomorrow night at the grand supper. Better than that, I will mediate between Mr. Bailey and the prince. See that Mr. Bailey attends at Dalmatsky Island tomorrow evening, and you as well, of course. My aide-de-camp will see that you receive passes." The czar gestured vaguely toward a rosy-faced young officer who hovered nearby, then nodded a last time at Athan and left the stables.

Thirty-one

While Athan was at the Imperial Stables, Ellie, John, and Louise were seated in the conservatory at the rear of the house on English Quay, enjoying pleasant conversation and one another's company. Outside, the sky remained pale and clear and the streets in no need of lighting, even though the hour was advanced. Fashionable ladies and gentlemen strolled along the quay, where musicians played tambourines and zithers beneath the trees.

There were many pleasure boats out on the Neva, and from several came the gentle notes of balalaikas. The Russian winter was long and unbelievably harsh, so the short summers, especially the enchanted period of the White Nights, were enjoyed to the full. One pleasure boat came to the foot of the steps where earlier the trio from the *Good Intent* had stepped ashore. Prince Paul Dalmatsky, hat low over his forehead, ascended to the quay and then crossed to the Brasier residence. He slipped around to a secluded side door, where trees and shrubs overhung the path.

Tatiana Demidova was waiting. Terrified, she flung herself to her knees before him, for she was not only his serf, but related to the Trepovs, and thus in fear of bringing his wrath upon her own family if she displeased him.

He looked contemptuously down at her, as he always had upon every serf, with the singular exception of Nikolai Trepov. "You have the information I require?" he demanded in halting Russian.

"Yes, Highness. As you instructed, Mr. Bailey has that room up there." She pointed up to closed French windows on a balcony above the door. The balcony was shaded by so many branches and leaves that it was impossible to see except from directly below.

"I trust the French windows are unlocked?"

"No, Highness. He has turned the key and now keeps it in his pocket, and he is most insistent that on no account are the bolts to be left open."

"One might almost think he feared abduction," Paul murmured wryly to himself in French. Well, it would take more than a bolt and a key to save John Arbuthnot Billersley from his fate. "There are spare keys," he continued in Russian. "See that you get one. As for the bolts, make sure they are not pushed across. Is that clear?"

"But—"

"How you do it is up to you, Tatiana Demidova, but if you wish to protect your relatives, I suggest you put your pretty mind to the problem."

"Highness." She was close to tears.

"Is there anything I should know?" he asked.

"Lord Griffin is with the czar at this moment," she offered, hoping to please him.

"The czar?" Paul stiffened. "Where? How?"

She explained about the meeting at the Imperial Stables. "I do not know much, Highness, but I overheard Lord Griffin say he intends to enlist the czar's assistance."

"Concerning what?"

"I do not know, Highness, but the Trepovs were mentioned."

Paul was silent, his sixth sense stirring uncomfortably. Had he underestimated his opponents?

"What am I to do next, Highness?" Tatiana asked.

"Just see that the laundry basket is down here where we are now, and that the French windows are unlocked and unbolted when Bailey sleeps tonight. Then all you have to do is admit my men to the house."

"But I cannot go into Mr. Bailey's room when he is there, Highness!" she protested.

"You'll do whatever is necessary!" he breathed, almost bending forward to strike her but thinking better of it.

"Forgive me, Highness!" she cried, pressing her forehead on the ground to indicate complete servility. "I wish only to please you, Master," she whimpered, hating herself, but hating him more.

"You will have pleased me only when I have Bailey on the island."

Tears filled her eyes. "I beg of you, Highness, do as you will with me, but do not punish my family."

"Do not presume to advise me, for I do not grant favors to serfs," he replied, and with the toe of a polished shoe pushed her until she sprawled on the ground.

She lay like a mouse, not daring to move, and did not know she'd been holding her breath until she heard his soft tread as he walked away. Still terrified, she sat up on her heels. She did not want to help him. She liked her English mistress, and had been treated kindly, but like all serfs she went in dread of the nobility, especially men like Prince Paul. Tears rolled down her cheeks, and she hid her face in her hands.

"Don't cry, Tatiana, *cariad*," a young male voice said kindly.

With a gasp she took her hands away and looked up to see Gwilym standing where the prince had been only moments before. Their eyes met again, as they had done on the Neva earlier in the day, and when he smiled, she smiled too. She spoke enough English for them to understand each other, but when he held out his hand to her, there was no need for words.

Love was a new experience for Gwilym, and it dulled the edges of his perception. Something had drawn him to the house, a feeling so strong that he had run all the way. He had felt her fear and had come to seek her out, but he had not seen Paul, nor did he realize why she was crying. All he knew was that Tatiana Demidova needed him, and he had adored her at first sight.

Much later that night, when Gwilym had returned to the Imperial Stables to watch over his equine charges, Ellie and Athan slept naked in each other's arms on the green quilt of their bed. It was warm, the sky outside was ivory in color, and the bed canopy above them was made of silver silk embroidered with a stag-hunting scene, with spotted hounds that could only have belonged to one master. Even the bed itself was carved with a hunting scene, reminding them that the house was Prince Paul Dalmatsky's property.

In another room across the landing, John lay fully dressed and sleepless. He hadn't been able to bring himself to wear a nightshirt, because he felt safer in his clothes. The bolts were fully across at the French windows, with their double glass panes and terracotta pots containing the luxuriant plants that were to be found in all homes in the Russian capital. He was satisfied the windows were secure, but still he feared the unnatural pallor of the summer night. He was in his old foe's city, and for one of them retribution was imminent. But for which one?

He tried to sleep, if only to be sure his wits were sharp the next day, but the restlessness would not relinquish him. He turned over, gazing at the French windows, where leafy shadows moved in the night breeze off the Neva. He heard a man singing in the street, a deep bass voice that defied the night, but he didn't hear the soft sound of the bedroom door opening as Tatiana admitted two of Paul's henchmen to take him. He knew nothing of the intruders until an explosion of pain and light occurred as someone struck him ferociously on the head.

Tatiana, struggling not to sob aloud, unlocked the French windows and then pulled back the bolts John had been so very careful to close. She leaned over the balcony and saw two more men waiting with the large wicker laundry basket that had been brought from the Dalmatsky Palace. The two men in the bedroom lowered John's unconscious body over the balcony, and their companions below eased him gently into the basket, where he was covered with crumpled sheets. One of the basket's little wheels squeaked slightly as it was pushed along the path toward the street.

No one paid any attention as it was taken across to the steps, then carried down to a waiting boat from which fluttered Paul's pennant. Soon John was on his way to his fate on Dalmatsky Island.

The bathhouse was silent and deserted as the laundry basket was rolled toward it through the ghostly paleness of the Russian night. John stirred among the sheets. By now his wrists and ankles were tied, and a cloth had been forced into his mouth. He knew where he was, however, for he recognized the noise of the hungry, maltreated Dalmatians in the kennels, and the croaking call of a macaw. Nikolai had loved that bird, and had often fed it with his own hand. The basket jolted as it was dragged up the bathhouse steps, and then the wheels echoed on the marble floor, before suddenly John found himself being tumbled out, sheets and all, to sprawl at Paul's feet. The macaw was disturbed, and shuffled noisily up and down its perch until Paul reached for a golden goblet of wine and hurled it. As the clatter of the goblet died away and the macaw fell wisely silent, Paul looked down at his prisoner.

"So, here you are at last, Englishman. How sad that you should have to be *tricked* into facing me after all this time." Paul nodded at the men who'd brought the basket, and one of them bent to remove the cloth from John's mouth.

Still trussed like a roasting goose, John tried to speak, but at first his mouth was too dry. He could smell the lavender oil that had been rubbed into Paul's body. It was an oil he remembered of old, because Nikolai had used it too. At last he managed to find his voice. "And how sad, Paul, that you are still unable to accept responsibility for Nikolai's death."

Paul's lips were thin. "Oh, no, I was innocent. *You* were the canker that destroyed him."

"Innocent? Paul, you set your damned dogs on him! How could you have done such a callous and cruel thing? To Nikolai, that sweet boy . . ."

"Hold your tongue!" Paul stepped forward and bent to strike John bitterly across the face. "He would be alive now if you had not interfered!"

John gazed up at him with loathing. "I wondered if you were mad when last we met; now I see that you definitely are. Is revenge *all* you have thought of these past years? Have you punished and tortured me so many times in your head that I have excluded everything else?"

Paul's eyes were bright. "You must pay for what you did."

"Kill me then."

"Oh, not just yet. First I will toy with you."

"Nothing you do to me now can be worse than the grief I felt on losing Nikolai."

"He was not yours to lose, Englishman," Paul breathed, "and if you really think you have suffered all you can, then you know nothing." Again he nodded at the two men who'd brought the basket; then he strode out of the bathhouse and left them to carry out his orders.

They dragged John to the rear of the bathhouse, where a narrow doorway gave into an area to which only a very few had ever been admitted. Here was to be found a torture chamber of chains, whips, knives, and other implements for the infliction of pain. There was a deep plunge bath with chains and manacles set into the marble around it. Water dripped steadily into it—no, not merely steadily, but *relentlessly*. . . . For a moment John thought the two men were going to commence his punishment, but he thought again almost immediately. Paul wasn't present, and there was no doubt that he would be there to watch every agonizing blow, twist, or stab of John Arbuthnot Billersley's atonement for the past.

The men hauled John to a cupboard and bundled him roughly inside. Then the cupboard was locked, as was the door of the chamber itself, and he heard the men leave the building. Silence ensued, except for the subtle dripping of water into the plunge bath, and the muffled noises of the macaw beyond the locked doors.

At the Imperial Stables, in the meantime, Gwilym was asleep in the stall with the Griffin mare and colt. He stirred suddenly as it seemed he was drowning, and then with a frightened cry he sat up. He wasn't in water after all, but lying on warm dry straw with the horses. His heart was beating swiftly, and he could smell lavender oil. Danger. There was danger. *Beware the spotted dog, beware the spotted dog.* . . .

At English Quay Ellie also awakened with a start. She gazed up at the hunting scene on the bed canopy, wondering what had disturbed her. The moments passed, and all was quiet. She could hear a balalaika on the Neva, and the clatter of a carriage driving slowly past along the quay, but there wasn't a sound in the house.

With a sigh she snuggled closer to Athan, slipping her arms around his warmth, and putting her lips to his bare shoulder. He turned and pulled her into his arms, pressing her body to his. They found each other's lips in a long sleepy kiss that sent rich feelings through them both, such rich, wonderful feelings. . . .

It was the following morning, the feast of Saints Peter and Paul, before John's disappearance was finally discovered. The capital awakened to the sound of bells as the city celebrated its saints' day, and the Neva was crowded with fishing boats, Saints Peter and Paul being patrons of fishermen as well. But no matter what the excitement outside, John did not come down to breakfast, and Ellie, Athan, and Louise believed that in spite of the noise of the bells, he was sleeping in after so many restless nights at sea. It was a natural enough assumption, and the last thing they thought was that something might have befallen him under their very roof.

The smell of rich dark coffee was in the warm air, and a dish of exotic fruit stood in the center of the damask tablecloth: melons from Astrakhan, grapes from the Crimea, apples from Georgia. Ellie tried not to think of what might happen to Athan and her uncle at the grand supper that night, especially her uncle, for whom Prince Paul had formed a very particular hatred. She had made an effort to appear relaxed and unconcerned, and to this end had chosen a yellow-and-white striped muslin gown that was particularly light and cheerful, but her stomach churned with nerves, and her hand trembled so her cup rattled softly when she replaced it in the saucer.

Athan wasn't exactly unconcerned about the coming night, but gave no sign of unease. His cup did not rattle, nor did he appear to be anything but his usual self as he entertained Louise with amusing anecdotes about mutual acquaintances back in Britain. He wore a maroon coat and cream cord breeches, and his dark hair shone in the brilliant sunlight streaming through the conservatory panes.

Suddenly Gwilym burst in unannounced, bringing a sobbing Tatiana with him.

Athan rose from his chair in astonishment. "What is the meaning of this, Gwilym?"

"My lord, Mr. Bailey has been taken!"

Ellie's cup clattered. "Taken? What do you mean, Gwilym?"

"He has been kidnapped, Miss Ellie!" Try as he would, Gwilym found it impossible to address her by her new title.

Tatiana's sobs became more distraught. Guilt had driven her to tell Gwilym everything, and now she was terrified that Prince Paul would learn of her betrayal.

Athan left the table to go to Gwilym. "Kidnapped? How? When?" he demanded, and Louise fled from the conservatory calling for Vladimir to go to John's room immediately.

Ellie was conscious of her racing heartbeats as they waited for the manservant to return. When he did, it was plain from his face that what Gwilym said was true. Tears welled from Ellie's eyes, although she did her best to prevent them. Where was her uncle now? Was he still alive?

"What happened, Gwilym?" Athan demanded.

"It was last night, when you were asleep, my lord. The spotted dog sent his men, and Tatiana was forced to help." Gwilym explained what the maid had told him. "It wasn't her fault, my lord," he finished urgently, "for she is a serf and her family was threatened."

Athan nodded. "Cravenly issuing threats to his victims' families seems to be one of Dalmatsky's favorite ploys."

Louise was trying to comfort Ellie, and looked stoutly at her brother. "We must do something, Athan. I don't care *how* important Prince Paul is here in St. Petersburg; he can't be allowed to simply abduct an Englishman because he feels like it!"

Athan gave a rueful smile. "Right now it rather seems a fait accompli, sis." He went to embrace Ellie. "Don't fret, my darling, for we'll rescue him."

"But we don't even know if he's still alive!" she cried, clinging to his lapels and wetting his neckcloth with her tears.

Gwilym spoke in the ensuing silence. "Mr. Bailey is alive, Miss Ellie, and still will be tonight when Lord Griffin goes to the grand supper."

They all looked at the lanky youth, and he gave a shy little smile. "He'll be rescued, have no fear of that," he said simply. "I know it as surely as I know that Tatiana will come home to Wales with me and become my wife."

Thirty-two

*D*ressed in his most formal clothes, a black corded silk coat, white satin waistcoat, white silk pantaloons, lace-trimmed shirt, and a three-cornered hat tucked beneath his arm, Athan took his leave of Ellie in the entrance hall at English Quay. It was time to go to the grand supper, and neither he nor Ellie knew what the evening ahead held, although both had complete faith in Gwilym's promise that John was still alive and would be rescued. Ellie didn't want to remain behind; indeed, she'd pleaded with Athan to take her with him, but this time he was adamant that she would stay with Louise, where it was safe.

Vladimir was to row him to Dalmatsky Island. Ellie watched from the doorway as the immense Russian led the way across the quay to the river steps, at the bottom of which were kept two rowboats belonging to Louise's absent husband, Charles. The Neva was still thronged with fishing vessels of all shapes and sizes, and the city bells had commenced their evening clamor. The strange light of the White Nights was beginning to settle across the sky, robbing the sun and withholding from the moon. There were no stars in the off-white sky, and St. Petersburg seemed to be tinted with silver.

It was all so unearthly, Ellie thought as she stood unhappily in the doorway, watching Athan and Vladimir go down the steps and out of sight. She was a forlorn figure in a blue taffeta gown and pink-and-silver cashmere shawl, and her eyes, already red from weeping for her uncle, stung again as fresh tears had their way. She felt as if she were asleep and in a nightmare, except that she knew it was all only too real. Louise came to put a gentle arm around her shoulder and drew her back inside. "Come, Ellie, for there is nothing more you can do, nothing either of us can do, come to that."

Ellie looked ruefully at her. "Forgive me for being so selfish, Louise."

"Selfish?"

"Well, he's your brother as well as my husband."

"And you have your uncle to worry over as well. As for Athan, well, I've known him for longer than you. He'll be all right, truly he will. He's unconquerable, and don't forget that the czar is his friend."

"I pray so, oh, how I pray so," Ellie whispered.

"You must simply be a good wife and do as you are told." Louise gave her a brave smile. "Mind you, that is not what I usually advocate, for I believe a wife should show her spirit, but on this occasion, I think Athan is right to make you stay here with me."

But Louise was about to change her mind on that particular point, for Gwilym and Tatiana accosted the two ladies in the entrance hall.

Gwilym was agitated and apologetic. "Begging your pardon, Miss Ellie . . . I—I mean, my lady—but I've seen where Mr. Bailey is being held."

"Seen?" Ellie looked urgently at him. "In your head, you mean?"

"Yes, Miss Ellie."

"Where is he, Gwilym?"

"In a cupboard in a bathhouse on Dalmatsky Island. I described it to Tatiana, and she knows exactly where I mean."

"Has he been harmed?"

"No, Miss Ellie, not yet, but we need to free him. There is not much time. Prince Paul means to end him tonight."

"End him?" she repeated faintly.

"He is to be drowned in the Neva, at the very place where someone called Nikolai died."

Ellie stared at him in horror, then looked at Louise. "I have to stop Athan from actually attending the supper. If we can find him, rescue my uncle, and simply come back here . . . ? Maybe we could all flee St. Petersburg and get back to Britain somehow . . . ?" She was babbling, hardly knowing what she was saying, but then Gwilym made so bold as to put a calming hand on her arm.

"All will be well, Miss Ellie. I will go to the island, and Tatiana will accompany me. She knows the way there, and where everything is on the island."

Ellie looked swiftly at him. "I'm coming too," she said flatly.

"But, Lord Griffin said—"

"I don't care what he said, Gwilym. I'm coming with you."

"Yes, Miss Ellie."

Louise didn't interfere. In Ellie's place she would have done the same, and the only reason she did not insist on going as well was that she was mindful of her unborn baby.

Ellie did not dither after that, for her decision had been made, and now she was quite clear about what had to be done. With Gwilym and Tatiana she hurried across the street and down the river steps to Charles Brasier's remaining rowboat.

Gwilym may have been long and lanky, but he was very strong, hauling surely upon the oars as the rowboat made its way through the crowded waters. There were laughter and merrymaking on the pleasure boats, and, as always, the sound of balalaika music. From time to time an opening through the clutter of vessels permitted them a glimpse of Athan and Vladimir in the other boat. Vladimir's size and strength should have made him more than a match for Gwilym, but the young Welshman seemed almost superhuman as he dragged rhythmically on the oars, making the rowboat skim over the water. Tatiana sat at the stern with the tiller, maneuvering the boat between the numerous other craft. Ellie sat in the prow, her pink-and-silver shawl tightly clutched around her shoulders, her face pale and determined. Nothing would be permitted to harm the two men she loved most in the world. Nothing!

Athan watched the lights of Dalmatsky Island draw closer. Every window of the palace was brightly illuminated, and the gardens were ablaze with colored lanterns. Sumptuous private barges, including several royal barges, rocked at the island jetties as what seemed like most of St.

Petersburg's highest society flocked to Prince Paul's grand supper. He did not quite know what to do once he arrived, for he had no idea where John might be. All he could think of was an approach to Alexander. But just as Vladimir was shipping the oars for the boat to glide the final yards to the nearest jetty, the huge Russian looked back toward St. Petersburg and saw the other boat. More than that, he recognized the occupants.

He pointed, and spoke urgently to Athan, who turned to look back. For a moment he too saw the second boat, and his brow darkened. Damn it all, hadn't he made himself perfectly clear? What was Ellie thinking? The last thing he needed tonight was for her to be placed in danger as well!

Vladimir made the boat fast, then clambered up onto the jetty and held out a huge white-gloved hand to help Athan up as well. The sound of orchestral music drifted faintly from the palace's open windows, and there were ladies and gentlemen everywhere, gentlemen in formal black, numerous officers in gaudy uniforms, and ladies in rich gowns and flashing jewels, with plumes wafting in their hair. Russia's grandest of the grand had turned out to be seen at the grandest of the grand suppers.

Athan and Vladimir left the jetty and stepped onto the lawns to wait for the second boat to arrive. Athan's brow darkened more and more as it came toward the island. He could see how frightened Ellie was, and was both fearful for her and angry. He would not be defied in such a matter as this, and she was about to be summarily turned back to English Quay! But as the other boat at last nudged the jetty, and Athan and Vladimir strode up to prevent it from making fast, Ellie looked up imploringly at him.

"Please don't be angry, Athan. I *had* to come because Gwilym knows where my uncle is imprisoned! Tatiana can take us to him!"

Tatiana nodded up at Athan. "Yes, I can," she said.

Athan hesitated, still of half a mind to send Ellie back, but then she begged him again.

"We don't have much time. Prince Paul means to drown my uncle in the same place that Nikolai drowned."

Gwilym stood in the rowboat and pointed out into the channel of the Neva that lay between Dalmatsky Island

and the next island to the south. "That is where the ice broke and the man drowned," he said quietly, and for a split second Athan saw the frozen river and Nikolai's fleeing figure, the furious pack of hounds in pursuit. The vision was over almost before it began, but the image remained clear. Without another word he bent to hold a hand out to Ellie, whose fingers closed gladly around his. He almost lifted her out of the boat, then assisted Gwilym and Tatiana as well.

Tatiana led them quickly away from the jetty and over lawns that were bathed in ghostly White Night pallor. They followed winding paths where statues cast dark shadows, and a grotto where variegated lanterns illuminated spilling water. At last, Tatiana stopped and pointed toward the bathhouse on the island's northern shore.

"Mr. Bailey," she said.

They approached the silent building cautiously, but there did not seem to be anyone around. The outer door opened easily, and then their steps echoed as they entered. Nikolai's macaw greeted them with loud cries that seemed to split the night, but was soon quieted when Tatiana went to stroke it.

Athan looked inquiringly at Gwilym, who closed his eyes and concentrated hard, before suddenly pointing to the door at the rear of the building. "Through there, my lord!"

But the door was locked, and the key had been taken. Athan would have kicked it down, but Gwilym halted him with a gentle hand. "I need no force, my lord," he said mildly, and stood in front of the door, his gaze fixed upon the lock. Vladimir crossed himself superstitiously, knowing that he was about to witness something magical.

Seconds passed, and Ellie felt a strange tingle pass down her spine; then she heard the sound of an invisible key turning. Just as always happened at Nantgarth House, the door opened of its own accord, allowing Gwilym to pass through into the room beyond. He halted on seeing what sort of room it was, and turned to put up a hand and shake his head so that Athan prevented the two women from following.

"Stay here, Ellie," he ordered, and nodded at Vladimir to see they did as they were told.

Tatiana immediately bowed her head meekly, but for a moment Ellie remained defiant. Then she saw the look in his eyes, and she too nodded meekly.

Leaving Vladimir to see the women were safe, Athan followed Gwilym into the other room, where a single uttering of John's first name brought forth a frantic shuffling and banging from a locked cupboard. Once again Gwilym employed his invisible key, and as the cupboard opened, poor John tumbled out onto the floor. Within moments he had been freed and helped to his feet. He was very unsteady, stiff, and sore, but otherwise unharmed, and when Athan and Gwilym helped him out to where Ellie was waiting, he was able to smile and hold out his arms to her.

She ran to him and hugged him tightly. "Uncle John! Oh, Uncle John!" she whispered, and burst into tears of relief.

Athan pulled her away. "There's no time now. The sooner we're off this damned island, the better. Come on."

They all hurried out of the bathhouse, but as they slipped along the path between the peonies, two men suddenly hailed them angrily in Russian. The fugitives hesitated, but only John knew the men were those who'd locked him in the cupboard.

"The game's up, Athan," he breathed in dismay as the men began to run toward them, shouting all the time to alert Paul's other servants in the vicinity. The alarm aroused the Dalmatians in the kennels, which set up an unholy racket of savage barking and snapping.

Tatiana suddenly caught Gwilym's arm and beckoned to the others. "Come! Quickly!" she cried, and began to run toward the palace.

Toward the palace? Ellie, Athan, and John held back, but Gwilym called to them. "It's safe! Come with us!"

Seeing Paul's men closing the distance, they didn't hesitate long, and with Vladimir bringing up the rear, followed Tatiana and Gwilym toward the palace kitchens, which lay beneath the green-and-white splendor of the modern building, in the old wooden world of the original dacha. Down here fires raged day and night, summer and winter, and a small army of serfs labored to see that those in the palace above them were served nothing but the finest French food. It had to be French, even though Alexander now favored the British politically, because when it came to food, only the French were deemed stylish enough to emulate.

As they fled through the kitchens, Ellie saw sparkling crystal, exquisite china, and numerous serving platters piled high with a tempting display of suckling pig, chicken cutlets, salads, and mounds of savory rice, all waiting to be taken up after the first course of turtle soup. Startled waiters, dark-skinned, wearing yellow jackets and turbans, stepped hastily out of the way as the fleeing party ran past. Then several gilt-domed dishes went flying as Paul's men followed in hot pursuit, shoving and elbowing their way past in their efforts to catch their quarry.

Tatiana knew the palace well and led the way through a little anteroom where there were Tatars whose sole duty was to prepare coffee. From there she made for a dark narrow staircase that led up toward the main palace. Athan was loath to go farther and caught her arm to hold her back.

"I thought you'd take us out to the grounds again. We need to be outside, not in the palace itself!" he breathed, glancing uneasily back down the staircase as he heard their pursuers shouting to the bemused Tatars.

Tatiana shook her head. "You speak to the czar," she said, and pulled her arm free to continue up the steps.

Athan looked at Ellie and John. "We have no choice, I fear," he said, then gave a resigned smile. "Well, I suppose that if Alexander has to publicly choose between Prince Paul and us, it's one way to discover just how genuinely well disposed toward the British he really is," he said as he followed Tatiana up the steps.

Thirty-three

The door at the top of the staircase was concealed in a mirror, and opened into the brilliant world of the new Russia. Mirrors reflected dazzling chandeliers, there were flowers everywhere, and the sweetest of music carried from the orchestra of eight men with flutes and violins in the main reception rooms on the second floor.

Tatiana and Vladimir would go no farther, but the maid indicated the archway that gave way to the crowded central staircase hall. There, a double flight of pink-and-gray marble steps, edged with wrought iron railings, led up to the next floor. Then she and Vladimir hastened away, for it was literally more than their lives were worth to be apprehended.

Gwilym did not accompany his new sweetheart, but remained with Ellie, Athan, and John as they made their way toward the parade staircase. Their odd appearance caused a great stir among some late-arriving guests: the tall gangling horse charmer, Athan in his very formal British attire, Ellie in a blue taffeta gown that really was not by any means grand enough for such an occasion, and John in his crumpled day clothes, looking, as he would later ruefully admit, like something the cat had dragged in.

Several of Paul's turbaned, yellow-jacketed servants made to apprehend them, but drew back respectfully when Athan showed the pass the czar had seen he was provided with. Something was clearly taking place on the floor above, for the orchestra suddenly died away on a jangle of notes, and instead of the babble of conversation that had hitherto issued over the staircase hall, there was something akin to a stunned silence. Ellie, Athan, and John had no idea what was happening, and were anyway only concerned with getting themselves into Alexander's presence before their pursuers could apprehend them. Gwilym was intent upon remaining with his countrymen.

As Paul's men burst from the hidden staircase, still in hot pursuit, the servants who had permitted the fugitives to pass had cause to regret their decision. But it was already too late, because Athan, moving swiftly ahead of the others, had reached the top of the staircase, where the guests had already formed a line to pass through an anteroom into the exquisitely decorated dining room. The guests, buzzing with startled interest in something taking place in the anteroom, were craning their necks to see what was going on in front of the czar, czarina, and Paul.

As Athan's good luck would have it, everyone parted just as Alexander happened to glance back at the landing. Seeing Athan, but not, at first, his two less reputable companions, the czar smiled graciously and bowed his head. Paul's men immediately drew back and quickly returned to the hidden staircase, for it was one thing to watch out for their master's interests, quite another to do so in the face of the czar's clear approval of the British lord.

But Alexander's attention had already returned to the startling scene directly in front of him, wherein lay the cause of the orchestra's shambolic halt and the guests' less than discreet show of interest. Valentin, resplendent in dress uniform, not a button undone or a ribbon out of place, was on his knees before the czar, holding the soup tureen up as if in supplication. He was in the very act of begging his emperor's mercy, imploring him to accept the tureen, which he promised was much more than a mere tureen.

It was at this point that the bemused guests, sandwiched between their host's discredited nephew and the tureen to the front, and three very odd British persons to the rear, began to discuss what on earth could be going on. Valentin, aware that someone else was stealing his thunder, glanced toward Paul, whose ashen-faced attention was on the landing. Following his uncle's gaze, Valentin stared too, and the tureen slipped from his suddenly numb fingers. It fell with a crash that brought several screams from nervous ladies, and all eyes swung to the floor, where the incongruous sight of a walnut lay amid the fragments of what had been one of the most exquisite pieces of soft-paste porcelain the world had ever seen.

Valentin tore his eyes from the landing, and in the hope of extricating himself from disaster, scrambled frantically amid the debris in search of the diamond. But there was only the walnut.

"The diamond! Where is the diamond?" he cried, falling onto all fours and redoubling his futile efforts to find what was obviously not there.

Alexander was angry about the tureen's destruction and alarmed by what seemed to be a display of lunacy. Gesturing for Valentin to be seized and hauled away, he then put a protective arm around the czarina's shoulders and ushered her through into the dining room, from where another staircase led down to the gardens. Like the tail of a donkey, the great line of guests followed. There would be no grand supper that night, but something much more tranquil and digestible at the Winter Palace.

Of Paul there was suddenly no sign. In those few seconds he had slipped away unnoticed, leaving his hapless nephew to his fate by passing through a concealed door into an adjacent, almost deserted room. From there he went out onto the landing, stepped silently up behind Ellie, and grabbed her. She would have screamed, but felt a knife against her throat as he hissed in her ear.

"Be quiet now, Lady Griffin, or I will not hesitate to put an end to you."

Terrified, she did not struggle as he began to back away, but then a lady guest saw what was happening and cried out. Athan and John whirled about, and Paul gave John a thin smile. "Well, just when you thought I was defeated, I snatch victory after all. Now you will do as I say, or your dear niece will breathe her last."

Athan stepped forward. "Let her go, Dalmatsky, or so help me I'll—!"

"You'll what, my lord?" Paul gave a mirthless chuckle. "I have the upper hand, Englishman, and I intend to go through with this until the very bitter end."

John looked at him and realized just how unhinged he had become. "You're mad, Paul. Nikolai feared it, but I didn't believe him. I do now, though, because only a madman would resort to all this."

"If it is madness to seek retribution for the loss of the only person I have ever loved, then I am glad to be mad," Paul breathed, then he jerked his head at Athan. "Back away, my lord, or your wife will regret it." His gaze moved to the other guests still on the landing. "The same applies to all of you. Back away now. Leave the staircase clear!"

They obeyed, and he forced Ellie toward the staircase. "Step pretty now, Lady Griffin, for I am not a man of endless patience, nor am I particularly understanding when it comes to the frailties of the fair sex." He glanced back at John. "You follow," he ordered, "for you are the one I really want."

"Then take me!" John cried.

"I can be more certain of your compliance if I have your niece," Paul replied frankly, and thrust Ellie down the first steps.

She tried not to stumble or do anything to anger him, for she knew he would not hesitate to kill her. As they descended, Paul ordered his amazed servants away from the staircase, and when some of the czar's bodyguards approached, he made them retreat again by threatening her.

Athan turned desperately to Gwilym. "Help her," he begged, although he did not know what he thought could be done.

Gwilym shook his head. "Not on the staircase, my lord, for she may fall."

Athan gazed at him and then at Ellie, so helpless in Paul's murderous grip. If anything should happen to her ...

At the foot of the staircase, Paul continued to force Ellie to do as he wished. He made her walk toward the mirror door that led down to the kitchens, and if anyone showed a sign of approaching him, he repeated his threat to her life. With John following as instructed, they entered the staircase and began the dark descent to the kitchens.

Athan would have followed, but Gwilym beckoned him another way. "Outside I may be able to help," he cried, making toward the palace's great main entrance. Athan needed no second bidding, but ran after him.

Ellie stumbled on the staircase, and choked back a cry of fear as Paul's knife pressed harder against her throat.

"Don't be clumsy, my dear. Don't they teach you deportment in England?"

John called out anxiously from behind. "Leave her alone, Paul! Can't you see she's terrified enough already?"

"Terror always amuses me," Paul answered.

"Let her go, and just take me. I'm the one you hate, the one who took Nikolai from you."

"I'm not so easily diverted now, John," Paul answered. "I know the game is up for me, but I intend to drag you down with me."

There was a stunned silence in the kitchens as Paul forced his way through, the knife glinting against Ellie's throat. Out into the night they went, where the St. Petersburg bells continued to ring, and the pale otherworldly light of the Russian summer seemed suddenly more eerie than ever.

Paul halted, casting around for one of his servants. It wasn't a servant whose eyes he found, but Bruno's. The young man flinched as Paul ordered him to see that a boat was ready at the nearest jetty. When Bruno didn't obey quickly enough to suit, Paul's voice rose unevenly. "Do it!" he shrieked, "Do it this instant, or I'll have you skinned alive!"

Bruno's eyes widened, and he ran off as if Paul had set fire to his heels.

Paul made Ellie move along the same path, and John followed wretchedly, wishing there was something he could do to save his niece, and wondering too what had happened to Athan and Gwilym, who were nowhere to be seen.

The kenneled Dalmatians, already disturbed by the earlier shouts of alarm, now sensed the tense atmosphere that pervaded the palace gardens. Their savage barking turned to bloodcurdling howls that overwhelmed the St. Petersburg bells. The closer Paul and Ellie drew to the jetty where Bruno had the boat waiting, the more Paul began to increase their pace. He had seen the guests beginning to assemble on the other jetties, and the czar assembling his bodyguards and many of the gentlemen guests, clearly with the intention of overcoming the obviously deranged master of Dalmatsky Island. Paul's eyes were diamond-bright. No one, not even the czar, was going to rob him of his final act of revenge!

Reaching the beginning of the jetty, Paul pulled Ellie aside and then told John to get into the boat.

"What are you going to do to my niece?" John demanded, not moving a step until he was satisfied Ellie would be safe.

"If you wish to guarantee her safety, you will do as I say," Paul replied; then his voice became shrill again. "Do it! Or I will slit her throat here and now!"

Athan stepped out of the shadows by some shrubs. "Do as he says, John," he said quietly.

Paul turned warily, still holding Ellie. "So here we have the adoring husband? How very homely, to be sure," he breathed.

"Release my wife, Dalmatsky."

"Back away, Englishman, for I am in no mood to humor you." Paul looked toward Bruno. "Release the dogs," he said in Russian, and the young man darted away in the direction of the kennels.

Athan didn't understand what had been said, but guessed it quickly enough. "Have you no wits left, Dalmatsky? If you let those creatures loose, they'll savage us all!"

"Correction, my lord, they'll savage everyone except me and this dear lady's uncle, for we will be out on the water." Paul began to edge along the jetty, still forcing Ellie with him. He glanced back at John, who was seated in the boat. "Undo the mooring rope, and get ready to row."

John obeyed, being far too fearful for Ellie to think of defiance at this critical point.

Paul and Ellie were now only inches from the end of the jetty. Suddenly he gave her a ferocious push that sent her screaming into the dark water, and as Athan rushed to help her, Paul leapt into the boat and pushed it away from the jetty. He sat down and tossed the knife into the water, then drew a pistol from inside his coat and leveled it at John's heart.

Ellie floundered in the Neva. She couldn't swim, and the train of her gown was trapping her legs. Athan flung himself onto his stomach and stretched down to her, somehow managing to grab her fingers. After a few moments he was able to haul her to safety. He gathered her into his arms. "You're safe now, my darling," he breathed, his lips moving against her wet hair.

Coughing and spluttering, she clung to him, but then remembered her uncle and pulled away again to look anxiously at the boat, which was now almost midchannel between Dalmatsky Island and the next island to the south. But there was no time to wonder about John, for Bruno had released the dogs, which were racing, barking and howling toward the jetty.

Just as it seemed they were bound to fall upon Ellie and Athan and tear them to shreds, Gwilym stepped calmly in front of them. He made no move, but just stood there making soft sounds. The frenzied creatures halted, some growling savagely, others whining more uncertainly. Gwilym smiled and spoke to them in Welsh. One or two tails began to wag, and then suddenly they all decided he was a friend. They milled around him, licking and whining as gently as if they were a child's pets.

Athan breathed out with relief. "Thank God for Mrs. Lewis's little boy," he said with feeling.

"I wish we were all back at Nantgarth now," Ellie whispered, half an eye still on the Dalmatians, for fear they would suddenly cease to be spellbound.

Out on the water, Paul commanded John to ship the oars. The Neva's current was sluggish, and the boat drifted very slowly downstream toward the Gulf of Finland.

"This is where Nikolai died," Paul said, glancing toward the shore of the other island, "and it is where you and I will die too. Is that not fitting?"

"You clearly think so." John searched his face in the pale night. "Will you at least answer some questions before consigning us to our watery grave?"

"What do you wish to know?"

"How did you find me? When I returned to Britain, I made damned sure I changed my name and covered my tracks, yet somehow you traced me to Nantgarth. How?"

"You did not cover your tracks as completely as you thought. My agents managed to follow you to an inn on the Pennines, where they learned you had talked much with Lord Griffin. So I ordered them to find out all they could about Griffin. Thus I discovered the new china works, and was then able to confirm your presence there by the simple expedient of questioning that foolish doxy, Miss Tudor. Her description of Mr. John Bailey tallied exactly with the John Arbuthnot Billersley I was seeking."

"It was really that simple?"

"Yes."

John drew a long breath. "And were you behind my brother-in-law's ruin?"

"Your brother-in-law?" For a moment Paul's face was blank, but then he remembered. "Ah, you mean Mr. Rutherford? Yes, of course I was. It amused me to implicate you in such goings-on. It was an idle whim on my part."

"An idle whim that cost him his life."

"I am not responsible for his weakness."

John looked at him with loathing. "Damn it all, I wasn't aware you even knew I had a brother-in-law."

Paul found that amusing. "My dear John, when you came to St. Petersburg before, and you and I were friends at first. You really were unguarded in the things you told me. So I knew you had a sister who married a man named Rutherford, and who resided on the Isle of Wight. From there it was easy enough to coerce the hitherto estimable Mr. Forrester-Phipps of the Unicorn Bank into doing as I wished. Most men will do as they are asked if they think their family is at risk."

"And you went through all this simply to get me here again?"

Paul nodded. "Yes, John, and I would do it again. You took Nikolai, and you made me hunt him down. It is all your fault, and now the time has come for you to make the supreme sacrifice."

The Neva was calm, and Paul did not think twice about getting to his feet in the rowboat. He took careful aim at John, meaning to shoot him in the forehead, but he reckoned with Gwilym and Athan.

Athan had removed his coat and wrapped it around Ellie as she sat shivering on the jetty. He had scrambled to his feet, a pistol of his own drawn and cocked, and was waiting with Gwilym for an opportune moment to pluck Paul from the rowboat. The moment their prey stood to take aim at John, Gwilym exerted all his strength to make the little craft rock from side to side.

"What the—?" Paul staggered and almost lost his balance. What was happening? The river was as smooth as a millpond! He braced himself, and took aim again. As he began to squeeze the trigger, the boat rocked more violently, and the pistol shot went wide, zinging past John's head and striking the water ahead of the boat.

The moment that single shot was fired, Athan knew John was safe, and took careful aim. With Paul well and truly in his sights, he fired.

Paul grunted and his eyes widened with shock as the bullet entered his heart. "No!" he breathed, and still found the strength to lunge forward to try to grab John by the throat. But John jerked aside, and Paul pitched past him into the waiting water. He floundered there for a moment, but Athan's aim had been true. The last thing the dying man uttered, before disappearing beneath the Neva forever, was Nikolai Trepov's name.

Athan knelt on the jetty to cradle Ellie in his arms again. "It's over, sweeting, it's over," he said gently.

"My uncle . . . ?"

"Is safe, and I can see him rowing back to us right now."

Within moments the boat bumped against the jetty, and Athan caught the rope John tossed to him. John grinned. "That was damned fine shooting, Athan."

"It needed to be," Athan replied frankly. "The angle was tight, and an inch or two to the wrong side and I'd have shot you instead."

John clambered out of the boat, and glanced past him at the people hurrying across the lawns, drawn by the shots. "Well, I came here to give the czar a tureen, but Prince Valentin's butterfingers put a stop to that."

Ellie began to laugh, and they both looked at her in astonishment. She smiled at them. "The czar will still have his tureen, for I brought the other complete one with me in a hatbox," she explained.

It was May Day the following year, and a christening party was gathered around the font at St. Dwynwen's Church. Ellie, dressed in lemon silk and fine ivory lace, had her baby boy, John, in her arms, wrapped in a shawl that Mrs. Lewis had crocheted for him. Athan, in a gray coat and cream cord pantaloons, was the proudest man in the world, and so happy he felt he would burst with joy. He had Ellie and a new son, and the future was full of promise.

The church was crowded with Castle Griffin servants and

the people of Nantgarth, as Athan gazed lovingly at his wife and child. He whispered, "I love you, Lady Griffin."

"And I love you, Lord Griffin," she whispered back, and smiled as the baby made a little cooing noise.

The church door opened, and John strode in. He hurried to the font, his expression filled with apology. "I'm so sorry I'm late, but a fellow from London called just as I was leaving, and has given me the biggest order I have ever received. The fact that the czar has one of my tureens has certainly done wonders for business! And do you know, he just happened to have visited the Tower of London last week, and saw the new Sword of Concord. He says the red diamond looks very handsome, very handsome indeed."

Mrs. Lewis smiled to herself. Well, at least she now knew why Mr. Bailey had not been by the font when she looked in the tea leaves. Nothing sinister at all, just a fine fat order for his wonderful porcelain.

Outside, the mountain was cloaked in the vivid greens of late spring, and the sky was a matchless blue. Gwilym watched as Tatiana tied a little handkerchief in the thorn tree. She turned, their eyes met, and they smiled adoringly at each other. They were to be married at midsummer. Tatiana still found it hard to believe that the czar himself had granted her freedom, as he had her entire family, including the Trepovs. They had learned of their liberty only a few weeks after Prince Paul's ill-fated grand supper, on the day that the czar ratified the long-awaited treaty between Britain and Russia. St. Petersburg seemed a million miles away, and Tatiana was glad. This was her home now, and Gwilym was her world. She went to kiss him, and as their lips met, there was a swirl of water in the well, and a flash of silver.

Tatiana laughed and clasped both his hands. "I shall call you Merlin," she said. "That is the name, yes? Merlin?"

SIGNET

Regency Romances From
SANDRA HEATH

"Ms. Heath delivers a most pleasing mixture of wit [and] romance...for Regency connoisseurs." —Romantic Times

Now Available:

Winter Dreams
0-451-21236-3

Regency 2-in-1
My Lady Domino and A Commercial Enterprise
0-451-21371-8

Available wherever books are sold or at
www.penguin.com